The History of Rasselas, Prince of Abyssinia

By

Samuel Johnson

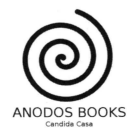

ANODOS BOOKS
Candida Casa

Samuel Johnson (1709-1784)
Originally published in 1759
Editing, cover, and internal design by Alisdair MacNoravaich for Anodos Books.
Copyright © 2017 Anodos Books. All rights reserved.

Anodos Books
1c Kings Road
Whithorn
Newton Stewart
Dumfries & Galloway
DG8 8PP

Contents

I. Description of a Palace in a Valley

Ye who listen with credulity to the whispers of fancy, and pursue with eagerness the phantoms of hope; who expect that age will perform the promises of youth, and that the deficiencies of the present day will be supplied by the morrow, attend to the history of Rasselas, Prince of Abyssinia.

Rasselas was the fourth son of the mighty Emperor in whose dominions the father of waters begins his course—whose bounty pours down the streams of plenty, and scatters over the world the harvests of Egypt.

According to the custom which has descended from age to age among the monarchs of the torrid zone, Rasselas was confined in a private palace, with the other sons and daughters of Abyssinian royalty, till the order of succession should call him to the throne.

The place which the wisdom or policy of antiquity had destined for the residence of the Abyssinian princes was a spacious valley in the kingdom of Amhara, surrounded on every side by mountains, of which the summits overhang the middle part. The only passage by which it could be entered was a cavern that passed under a rock, of which it had long been disputed whether it was the work of nature or of human industry. The outlet of the cavern was concealed by a thick wood, and the mouth which opened into the valley was closed with gates of iron, forged by the artificers of ancient days, so massive that no man, without the help of engines, could open or shut them.

From the mountains on every side rivulets descended that filled all the valley with verdure and fertility, and formed a lake in the middle, inhabited by fish of every species, and frequented by every fowl whom nature has taught to dip the wing in water. This lake discharged its superfluities by a stream, which entered a dark cleft of the mountain on the northern side, and fell with dreadful noise from precipice to precipice till it was heard no more.

The sides of the mountains were covered with trees, the banks of the brooks were diversified with flowers; every blast shook spices from the rocks, and every month dropped fruits upon the ground. All animals that bite the grass or browse the shrubs, whether wild or tame, wandered in this extensive circuit, secured from beasts of prey by the mountains which confined them. On one part were flocks and herds feeding in the pastures, on another all the beasts of chase frisking in the lawns, the sprightly kid was bounding on the rocks, the subtle monkey frolicking in the trees, and the solemn elephant reposing in the shade. All the diversities of the world were brought together, the blessings of nature were collected, and its evils extracted and excluded.

The valley, wide and fruitful, supplied its inhabitants with all the necessaries of life, and all delights and superfluities were added at the annual visit which the Emperor paid his children, when the iron gate was opened to the sound of music, and during eight days every one that resided in the valley was required to propose whatever might contribute to make seclusion pleasant, to fill up the vacancies of attention, and lessen the tediousness of time. Every desire was immediately granted. All the artificers of pleasure were called to gladden the festivity; the musicians exerted the power of harmony, and the dancers showed their activity before the princes, in hopes that they should pass their lives in blissful captivity, to which those only were admitted whose performance was thought able to add novelty to luxury. Such was the appearance of security and delight which this retirement afforded, that they to whom it was new always desired that it might be perpetual; and as those on whom the iron gate had once closed were never suffered to return, the effect of longer experience could not be known. Thus every year produced new scenes of delight, and new competitors for imprisonment.

The palace stood on an eminence, raised about thirty paces above the surface of the lake. It was divided into many squares or courts, built with greater or less magnificence according to the rank of those for whom they were designed. The roofs were turned into arches of massive stone, joined by a cement that grew harder by time, and the building stood from century to century, deriding the solstitial rains and equinoctial hurricanes, without need of reparation.

This house, which was so large as to be fully known to none but some ancient officers, who successively inherited the secrets of the place, was built as if Suspicion herself had dictated the plan. To every room there was an open and secret passage; every square had a communication with the rest, either from the upper storeys by private galleries, or by subterraneous passages from the lower apartments. Many of the columns had unsuspected cavities, in which a long race of monarchs had deposited their treasures. They then closed up the opening with marble, which was never to be removed but in the utmost exigences of the kingdom, and recorded their accumulations in a book, which was itself concealed in a tower, not entered but by the Emperor, attended by the prince who stood next in succession.

II. The Discontent of Rasselas in the Happy Valley

Here the sons and daughters of Abyssinia lived only to know the soft vicissitudes of pleasure and repose, attended by all that were skilful to delight, and gratified with whatever the senses can enjoy. They wandered in gardens of fragrance, and slept in the fortresses of security. Every art was practised to make them pleased with their own condition. The sages who instructed them told them of nothing but the miseries of public life, and described all beyond the mountains as regions of calamity, where discord was always racing, and where man preyed upon man. To heighten their opinion of their own felicity, they were daily entertained with songs, the subject of which was the Happy Valley. Their appetites were excited by frequent enumerations of different enjoyments, and revelry and merriment were the business of every hour, from the dawn of morning to the close of the evening.

These methods were generally successful; few of the princes had ever wished to enlarge their bounds, but passed their lives in full conviction that they had all within their reach that art or nature could bestow, and pitied those whom nature had excluded from this seat of tranquillity as the sport of chance and the slaves of misery.

Thus they rose in the morning and lay down at night, pleased with each other and with themselves, all but Rasselas, who, in the twenty-sixth year of his age, began to withdraw himself from the pastimes and assemblies, and to delight in solitary walks and silent meditation. He often sat before tables covered with luxury, and forgot to taste the dainties that were placed before him; he rose abruptly in the midst of the song, and hastily retired beyond the sound of music. His attendants observed the change, and endeavoured to renew his love of pleasure. He neglected their officiousness, repulsed their invitations, and spent day after day on the banks of rivulets sheltered with trees, where he sometimes listened to the birds in the branches, sometimes observed the fish playing in the streams, and anon cast his eyes upon the pastures and mountains filled with animals, of which some were biting the herbage, and some sleeping among the bushes. The singularity of his humour made him much observed. One of the sages, in whose conversation he had formerly delighted, followed him secretly, in hope of discovering the cause of his disquiet. Rasselas, who knew not that any one was near him, having for some time fixed his eyes upon the goats that were browsing among the rocks, began to compare their condition with his own.

"What," said he, "makes the difference between man and all the rest of the animal creation? Every beast that strays beside me has the same corporal necessities with myself: he is hungry, and crops the grass; he is thirsty, and drinks the stream; his thirst and hunger are appeased; he is satisfied, and sleeps; he rises again, and is hungry; he is again fed, and is at rest. I am hungry and thirsty, like him, but when thirst and hunger cease, I am not at rest. I am, like him, pained with want, but am not, like him, satisfied with fulness. The intermediate hours are tedious and gloomy; I long again to be hungry that I may again quicken the attention. The birds peck the berries or the corn, and fly away to the groves, where they sit in seeming happiness on the branches, and waste their lives in tuning one unvaried series of sounds. I likewise can call the lutist and the singer; but the sounds that pleased me yesterday weary me to-day, and will grow yet more wearisome to- morrow. I can discover in me no power of perception which is not glutted with its proper pleasure, yet I do not feel myself delighted. Man surely has some latent sense for which this place affords no gratification; or he has some desire distinct from sense, which must be satisfied before he can be happy."

After this he lifted up his head, and seeing the moon rising, walked towards the palace. As he passed through the fields, and saw the animals around him, "Ye," said he, "are happy, and need not envy me that walk thus among you, burdened with myself; nor do I, ye gentle beings, envy your felicity; for it is not the felicity of man. I have many distresses from which you are free; I fear pain when I do not feel it; I sometimes shrink at evils recollected, and sometimes start at evils anticipated: surely the equity of Providence has balanced peculiar sufferings with peculiar enjoyments."

With observations like these the Prince amused himself as he returned, uttering them with a plaintive voice, yet with a look that discovered him to feel some complacence in his own perspicacity, and to receive some solace of the miseries of life from consciousness of the delicacy with which he felt and the eloquence with which he bewailed them. He mingled cheerfully in the diversions of the evening, and all rejoiced to find that his heart was lightened.

III. The Wants of Him that Wants Nothing

On the next day, his old instructor, imagining that he had now made himself acquainted with his disease of mind, was in hope of curing it by counsel, and officiously sought an opportunity of conference, which the Prince, having long considered him as one whose intellects were exhausted, was not very willing to afford. "Why," said he, "does this man thus intrude upon me? Shall I never be suffered to forget these lectures, which pleased only while they were new, and to become new again must be forgotten?" He then walked into the wood, and composed himself to his usual meditations; when, before his thoughts had taken any settled form, he perceived his pursuer at his side, and was at first prompted by his impatience to go hastily away; but being

4

unwilling to offend a man whom he had once reverenced and still loved, he invited him to sit down with him on the bank.

The old man, thus encouraged, began to lament the change which had been lately observed in the Prince, and to inquire why he so often retired from the pleasures of the palace to loneliness and silence. "I fly from pleasure," said the Prince, "because pleasure has ceased to please: I am lonely because I am miserable, and am unwilling to cloud with my presence the happiness of others." "You, sir," said the sage, "are the first who has complained of misery in the Happy Valley. I hope to convince you that your complaints have no real cause. You are here in full possession of all the Emperor of Abyssinia can bestow; here is neither labour to be endured nor danger to be dreaded, yet here is all that labour or danger can procure or purchase. Look round and tell me which of your wants is without supply: if you want nothing, how are you unhappy?"

"That I want nothing," said the Prince, "or that I know not what I want, is the cause of my complaint: if I had any known want, I should have a certain wish; that wish would excite endeavour, and I should not then repine to see the sun move so slowly towards the western mountains, or to lament when the day breaks, and sleep will no longer hide me from myself. When I see the kids and the lambs chasing one another, I fancy that I should be happy if I had something to pursue. But, possessing all that I can want, I find one day and one hour exactly like another, except that the latter is still more tedious than the former. Let your experience inform me how the day may now seem as short as in my childhood, while nature was yet fresh, and every moment showed me what I never had observed before. I have already enjoyed too much: give me something to desire." The old man was surprised at this new species of affliction, and knew not what to reply, yet was unwilling to be silent. "Sir," said he, "if you had seen the miseries of the world, you would know how to value your present state." "Now," said the Prince, "you have given me something to desire. I shall long to see the miseries of the world, since the sight of them is necessary to happiness."

IV. The Prince Continues to Grieve and Muse

At this time the sound of music proclaimed the hour of repast, and the conversation was concluded. The old man went away sufficiently discontented to find that his reasonings had produced the only conclusion which they were intended to prevent. But in the decline of life, shame and grief are of short duration: whether it be that we bear easily what we have borne long; or that, finding ourselves in age less regarded, we less regard others; or that we look with slight regard upon afflictions to which we know that the hand of death is about to put an end.

The Prince, whose views were extended to a wider space, could not speedily quiet his emotions. He had been before terrified at the length of life which nature promised him, because he considered that in a long time much must be endured: he now rejoiced in his youth, because in many years much might be done. The first beam of hope that had been ever darted into his mind rekindled youth in his cheeks, and doubled the lustre of his eyes. He was fired with the desire of doing something, though he knew not yet, with distinctness, either end or means. He was now no longer gloomy and unsocial; but considering himself as master of a secret stock of happiness, which he could only enjoy by concealing it, he affected to be busy in all the schemes of diversion, and endeavoured to make others pleased with the state of which he himself was weary. But pleasures can never be so multiplied or continued as not to leave much of life unemployed; there were many hours, both of the night and day, which he could spend without suspicion in solitary thought. The load of life was much lightened; he went eagerly into the assemblies, because he supposed the frequency of his presence necessary to the success of his purposes; he retired gladly to privacy, because he had now a subject of thought. His chief amusement was to picture to himself that world which he had never seen, to place himself in various conditions, to be entangled in imaginary difficulties, and to be engaged in wild adventures; but, his benevolence always terminated his projects in the relief of distress, the detection of fraud, the defeat of oppression, and the diffusion of happiness.

Thus passed twenty months of the life of Rasselas. He busied himself so intensely in visionary bustle that he forgot his real solitude; and amidst hourly preparations for the various incidents of human affairs, neglected to consider by what means he should mingle with mankind.

One day, as he was sitting on a bank, he feigned to himself an orphan virgin robbed of her little portion by a treacherous lover, and crying after him for restitution. So strongly was the image impressed upon his mind that he started up in the maid's defence, and ran forward to seize the plunderer with all the eagerness of real pursuit. Fear naturally quickens the flight of guilt. Rasselas could not catch the fugitive with his utmost efforts; but, resolving to weary by perseverance him whom he could not surpass in speed, he pressed on till the foot of the mountain stopped his course.

Here he recollected himself, and smiled at his own useless impetuosity. Then raising his eyes to the mountain, "This," said he, "is the fatal obstacle that hinders at once the enjoyment of pleasure and the exercise of virtue. How long is it that my hopes and wishes have flown beyond this boundary of my life, which yet I never have attempted to surmount?"

Struck with this reflection, he sat down to muse, and remembered that since he first resolved to escape from his confinement, the sun had passed twice over him in his annual course. He now felt a degree of regret with which he had never been before acquainted. He considered how much might have been done in the time which had passed, and left nothing real behind it. He compared twenty months with the life of man. "In life," said he, "is not to be counted the ignorance of infancy or imbecility of age. We are long before we are able to think, and we soon cease from the power of acting. The true period of human existence may be reasonably estimated at forty years, of which I have mused away the four-and-twentieth part. What I have lost was certain, for I have certainly possessed it; but of twenty months to come, who can assure me?"

The consciousness of his own folly pierced him deeply, and he was long before he could be reconciled to himself. "The rest of my time," said he, "has been lost by the crime or folly of my ancestors, and the absurd institutions of my country; I remember it with disgust, yet without remorse: but the months that have passed since new light darted into my soul, since I formed a scheme of reasonable felicity, have been squandered by my own fault. I have lost that which can never be restored; I have seen the sun rise and set for twenty months, an idle gazer on the light of heaven; in this time the birds have left the nest of their mother, and committed themselves to the woods and to the skies; the kid has forsaken the teat, and learned by degrees to climb the rocks in quest of independent sustenance. I only have made no advances, but am still helpless and ignorant. The moon, by more than twenty changes, admonished me of the flux of life; the stream that rolled before my feet upbraided my inactivity. I sat feasting on intellectual luxury, regardless alike of the examples of the earth and the instructions of the planets. Twenty months are passed: who shall restore them?"

These sorrowful meditations fastened upon his mind; he passed four months in resolving to lose no more time in idle resolves, and was awakened to more vigorous exertion by hearing a maid, who had broken a porcelain cup, remark that what cannot be repaired is not to be regretted.

This was obvious; and Rasselas reproached himself that he had not discovered it—having not known, or not considered, how many useful hints are obtained by chance, and how often the mind, hurried by her own ardour to distant views, neglects the truths that lie open before her.

He for a few hours regretted his regret, and from that time bent his whole mind upon the means of escaping from the Valley of Happiness.

V. The Prince Meditates His Escape

He now found that it would be very difficult to effect that which it was very easy to suppose effected. When he looked round about him, he saw himself confined by the bars of nature, which had never yet been broken, and by the gate through which none that had once passed it were ever able to return. He was now impatient as an eagle in a grate. He passed week after week in clambering the mountains to see if there was any aperture which the bushes might conceal, but found all the summits inaccessible by their prominence. The iron gate he despaired to open for it was not only secured with all the power of art, but was always watched by successive sentinels, and was, by its position, exposed to the perpetual observation of all the inhabitants.

He then examined the cavern through which the waters of the lake were discharged; and, looking down at a time when the sun shone strongly upon its mouth, he discovered it to be full of broken rocks, which, though they permitted the stream to flow through many narrow passages, would stop any body of solid bulk. He returned discouraged and dejected; but having now known the blessing of hope, resolved never to despair.

In these fruitless researches he spent ten months. The time, however, passed cheerfully away—in the morning he rose with new hope; in the evening applauded his own diligence; and in the night slept soundly after his fatigue. He met a thousand amusements, which beguiled his labour and diversified his thoughts. He discerned the various instincts of animals and properties of plants, and found the place replete with wonders, of which he proposed to solace himself with the contemplation if he should never be able to accomplish his flight—rejoicing that his endeavours, though yet unsuccessful, had supplied him with a source of inexhaustible inquiry. But his original curiosity was not yet abated; he resolved to obtain some knowledge of the ways of men. His wish still continued, but his hope grew less. He ceased to survey any longer the walls of his prison, and spared to search by new toils for interstices which he knew could not be found, yet determined to keep his design always in view, and lay hold on any expedient that time should offer.

VI. A Dissertation on the Art of Flying

Among the artists that had been allured into the Happy Valley, to labour for the accommodation and pleasure of its inhabitants, was a man eminent for his knowledge of the mechanic powers, who had contrived many engines both of use and recreation. By a wheel which the stream turned he forced the water into a tower, whence it was distributed to all the apartments of the palace. He erected a pavilion in the garden, around which he kept the air always cool by artificial showers. One of the groves, appropriated to the ladies, was ventilated by fans, to which the rivulets that ran through it gave a constant motion; and instruments of soft music were played at proper distances, of which some played by the impulse of the wind, and some by the power of the stream.

This artist was sometimes visited by Rasselas who was pleased with every kind of knowledge, imagining that the time would come when all his acquisitions should be of use to him in the open world. He came one day to amuse himself in his usual manner, and found the master busy in building a sailing chariot. He saw that the design was practicable upon a level surface, and with expressions of great esteem solicited its completion. The workman was pleased to find himself so much regarded by the Prince, and resolved to gain yet higher honours. "Sir," said he, "you have seen but a small part of what the mechanic sciences can perform. I have been long of opinion that, instead of the tardy conveyance of ships and chariots, man might use the swifter migration of wings, that the fields of air are open to knowledge, and that only ignorance and idleness need crawl upon the ground."

This hint rekindled the Prince's desire of passing the mountains. Having seen what the mechanist had already performed, he was willing to fancy that he could do more, yet resolved to inquire further before he suffered hope to afflict him by disappointment. "I am afraid," said he to the artist, "that your imagination prevails over your skill, and that you now tell me rather what you wish than what you know. Every animal has his element assigned him; the birds have the air, and man and beasts the earth." "So," replied the mechanist, "fishes have the water, in which yet beasts can swim by nature and man by art. He that can swim needs not despair to fly; to swim is to fly in a grosser fluid, and to fly is to swim in a subtler. We are only to proportion our power of resistance to the different density of matter through which we are to pass. You will be necessarily up-borne by the air if you can renew any impulse upon it faster than the air can recede from the pressure."

"But the exercise of swimming," said the Prince, "is very laborious; the strongest limbs are soon wearied. I am afraid the act of flying will be yet more violent; and wings will be of no great use unless we can fly further than we can swim."

"The labour of rising from the ground," said the artist, "will be great, as we see it in the heavier domestic fowls; but as we mount higher the earth's attraction and the body's gravity will be gradually diminished, till we shall arrive at a region where the man shall float in the air without any tendency to fall; no care will then be necessary but to move forward, which the gentlest impulse will effect. You, sir, whose curiosity is so extensive, will easily conceive with what pleasure a philosopher, furnished with wings and hovering in the sky, would see the earth and all its inhabitants rolling beneath him, and presenting to him successively, by its diurnal motion, all the countries within the same parallel. How must it amuse the pendent spectator to see the moving scene of land and ocean, cities and deserts; to survey with equal security the marts of trade and the fields of battle; mountains infested by barbarians, and fruitful regions gladdened by plenty and lulled by peace. How easily shall we then trace the Nile through all his passages, pass over to distant regions, and examine the face of nature from one extremity of the earth to the other."

"All this," said the Prince, "is much to be desired, but I am afraid that no man will be able to breathe in these regions of speculation and tranquillity. I have been told that respiration is difficult upon lofty mountains, yet from these precipices, though so high as to produce great tenuity of air, it is very easy to fall; therefore I suspect that from any height where life can be supported, there may be danger of too quick descent."

"Nothing," replied the artist, "will ever be attempted if all possible objections must be first overcome. If you will favour my project, I will try the first flight at my own hazard. I have considered the structure of all volant animals, and find the folding continuity of the bat's wings most easily accommodated to the human form. Upon this model I shall begin my task to-morrow, and in a year expect to tower into the air beyond the malice and pursuit of man. But I will work only on this condition, that the art shall not be divulged, and that you shall not require me to make wings for any but ourselves."

"Why," said Rasselas, "should you envy others so great an advantage? All skill ought to be exerted for universal good; every man has owed much to others, and ought to repay the kindness that he has received."

"If men were all virtuous," returned the artist, "I should with great alacrity teach them to fly. But what would be the security of the good if the bad could at pleasure invade them from the sky? Against an army sailing through the clouds neither walls, mountains, nor seas could afford security. A flight of northern savages might hover in the wind and light with irresistible violence upon the capital of a fruitful reason. Even this valley, the retreat of princes, the abode of happiness, might be violated by the sudden descent of some of the naked nations that swarm on the coast of the southern sea!"

The Prince promised secrecy, and waited for the performance, not wholly hopeless of success. He visited the work from time to time, observed its progress, and remarked many ingenious contrivances to facilitate motion and unite levity with strength. The artist was every day more certain that he should leave vultures and eagles behind him, and the contagion of his confidence seized upon the Prince. In a year the wings were finished; and on a morning appointed the maker appeared, furnished for flight, on a little promontory; he waved his pinions awhile to gather air, then leaped from his stand, and in an instant dropped into the lake. His wings, which were of no use in the air, sustained him in the water; and the Prince drew him to land half dead with terror and vexation.

VII. The Prince Finds a Man of Learning

The Prince was not much afflicted by this disaster, having suffered himself to hope for a happier event only because he had no other means of escape in view. He still persisted in his design to leave the Happy Valley by the first opportunity.

His imagination was now at a stand; he had no prospect of entering into the world, and, notwithstanding all his endeavours to support himself, discontent by degrees preyed upon him, and he began again to lose his thoughts in sadness when the rainy season, which in these countries is periodical, made it inconvenient to wander in the woods.

The rain continued longer and with more violence than had ever been known; the clouds broke on the surrounding mountains, and the torrents streamed into the plain on every side, till the cavern was too narrow to discharge the water. The lake overflowed its banks, and all the level of the valley was covered with the inundation. The eminence on which the palace was built, and some other spots of rising ground, were all that the eye could now discover. The herds and flocks left the pasture, and both the wild beasts and the tame retreated to the mountains.

This inundation confined all the princes to domestic amusements, and the attention of Rasselas was particularly seized by a poem (which Imlac rehearsed) upon the various conditions of humanity. He commanded the poet to attend him in his apartment, and recite his verses a second time; then entering into familiar talk, he thought himself happy in having found a man who knew the world so well, and could so skilfully paint the scenes of life. He asked a thousand questions about things to which, though common to all other mortals, his confinement from childhood had kept him a stranger. The poet pitied his ignorance, and loved his curiosity, and entertained him from day to day with novelty and instruction so that the Prince regretted the necessity of sleep, and longed till the morning should renew his pleasure.

As they were sitting together, the Prince commanded Imlac to relate his history, and to tell by what accident he was forced, or by what motive induced, to close his life in the Happy Valley. As he was going to begin his narrative, Rasselas was called to a concert, and obliged to restrain his curiosity till the evening.

VIII. The History of Imlac

The close of the day is, in the regions of the torrid zone, the only season of diversion and entertainment, and it was therefore midnight before the music ceased and the princesses retired. Rasselas then called for his companion, and required him to begin the story of his life.

"Sir," said Imlac, "my history will not be long: the life that is devoted to knowledge passes silently away, and is very little diversified by events. To talk in public, to think in solitude, to read and to hear, to inquire and answer inquiries, is the business of a scholar. He wanders about the world without pomp or terror, and is neither known nor valued but by men like himself.

"I was born in the kingdom of Goiama, at no great distance from the fountain of the Nile. My father was a wealthy merchant, who traded between the inland countries of Africa and the ports of the Red Sea. He was honest, frugal, and diligent, but of mean sentiments and narrow comprehension; he desired only to be rich, and to conceal his riches, lest he should be spoiled by the governors of the province."

"Surely," said the Prince, "my father must be negligent of his charge if any man in his dominions dares take that which belongs to another. Does he not know that kings are accountable for injustice permitted as well as done? If I were Emperor, not the meanest of my subjects should he oppressed with impunity. My blood boils when I am told that a merchant durst not enjoy his honest gains for fear of losing them by the rapacity of power. Name the governor who robbed the people that I may declare his crimes to the Emperor!"

"Sir," said Imlac, "your ardour is the natural effect of virtue animated by youth. The time will come when you will acquit your father, and perhaps hear with less impatience of the governor. Oppression is, in the Abyssinian dominions, neither frequent nor tolerated; but no form of government has been yet discovered by which cruelty can be wholly prevented. Subordination supposes power on one part and subjection on the other; and if power be in the hands of men it will sometimes be abused. The vigilance of the supreme magistrate may do much, but much will still remain undone. He can never know all the crimes that are committed, and can seldom punish all that he knows."

"This," said the Prince, "I do not understand; but I had rather hear thee than dispute. Continue thy narration."

"My father," proceeded Imlac, "originally intended that I should have no other education than such as might qualify me for commerce; and discovering in me great strength of memory and quickness of apprehension, often declared his hope that I should be some time the richest man in Abyssinia."

"Why," said the Prince, "did thy father desire the increase of his wealth when it was already greater than he durst discover or enjoy? I am unwilling to doubt thy veracity, yet inconsistencies cannot both be true."

"Inconsistencies," answered Imlac, "cannot both be right; but, imputed to man, they may both be true. Yet diversity is not inconsistency. My father might expect a time of greater security. However, some desire is necessary to keep life in motion; and he whose real wants are supplied must admit those of fancy."

"This," said the Prince, "I can in some measure conceive. I repent that I interrupted thee."

"With this hope," proceeded Imlac, "he sent me to school. But when I had once found the delight of knowledge, and felt the pleasure of intelligence and the pride of invention, I began silently to despise riches, and determined to disappoint the purposes of my father, whose grossness of conception raised my pity. I was twenty years old before his tenderness would expose me to the fatigue of travel; in which time I had been instructed, by successive masters, in all the literature of my native country. As every hour taught me something new, I lived in a continual course of gratification; but as I advanced towards manhood, I lost much of the reverence with which I had been used to look on my instructors; because when the lessons were ended I did not find them wiser or better than common men.

"At length my father resolved to initiate me in commerce; and, opening one of his subterranean treasuries, counted out ten thousand pieces of gold. 'This, young man,' said he, 'is the stock with which you must negotiate. I began with less than a fifth part, and you see how diligence and parsimony have increased it. This is your own, to waste or improve. If you squander it by negligence or caprice, you must wait for my death before you will be rich; if in four years you double your stock, we will thenceforward let subordination cease, and live together as friends and partners, for he shall be always equal with me who is equally skilled in the art of growing rich.'

"We laid out our money upon camels, concealed in bales of cheap goods, and travelled to the shore of the Red Sea. When I cast my eye on the expanse of waters, my heart bounded like that of a prisoner escaped. I felt an inextinguishable curiosity kindle in my mind, and resolved to snatch this opportunity of seeing the manners of other nations, and of learning sciences unknown in Abyssinia.

"I remembered that my father had obliged me to the improvement of my stock, not by a promise, which I ought not to violate, but by a penalty, which I was at liberty to incur; and therefore determined to gratify my predominant desire, and, by drinking at the fountain of knowledge, to quench the thirst of curiosity.

"As I was supposed to trade without connection with my father, it was easy for me to become acquainted with the master of a ship, and procure a passage to some other country. I had no motives of choice to regulate my voyage. It was sufficient for me that, wherever I wandered, I should see a country which I had not seen before. I therefore entered a ship bound for Surat, having left a letter for my father declaring my intention."

IX. The History of Imlac (continued)

"When I first entered upon the world of waters, and lost sight of land, I looked round about me in pleasing terror, and thinking my soul enlarged by the boundless prospect, imagined that I could gaze around me for ever without satiety; but in a short time I grew weary of looking on barren uniformity, where I could only see again what I had already seen. I then descended into the ship, and doubted for awhile whether all my future pleasures would not end, like this, in disgust and disappointment. 'Yet surely,' said I, 'the ocean and the land are very different. The only variety of water is rest and motion. But the earth has mountains and valleys, deserts and cities; it is inhabited by men of different customs and contrary opinions; and I may hope to find variety in life, though I should miss it in nature.'

"With this thought I quieted my mind, and amused myself during the voyage, sometimes by learning from the sailors the art of navigation, which I have never practised, and sometimes by forming schemes for my conduct in different situations, in not one of which I have been ever placed.

"I was almost weary of my naval amusements when we safely landed at Surat. I secured my money and, purchasing some commodities for show, joined myself to a caravan that was passing into the inland country. My companions, for some reason or other, conjecturing that I was rich, and, by my inquiries and admiration, finding that I was ignorant, considered me as a novice whom they had a right to cheat, and who was to learn, at the usual expense, the art of fraud. They exposed me to the theft of servants and the exaction of officers, and saw me plundered upon false pretences, without any advantage to themselves but that of rejoicing in the superiority of their own knowledge."

"Stop a moment," said the Prince; "is there such depravity in man as that he should injure another without benefit to himself? I can easily conceive that all are pleased with superiority; but your ignorance was merely accidental, which, being neither your crime nor your folly, could afford them no reason to applaud themselves; and the knowledge which they had, and which you wanted, they might as effectually have shown by warning as betraying you."

"Pride," said Imlac, "is seldom delicate; it will please itself with very mean advantages, and envy feels not its own happiness but when it may be compared with the misery of others. They were my enemies because they grieved to think me rich, and my oppressors because they delighted to find me weak."

"Proceed," said the Prince; "I doubt not of the facts which you relate, but imagine that you impute them to mistaken motives."

"In this company," said Imlac, "I arrived at Agra, the capital of Hindostan, the city in which the Great Mogul commonly resides. I applied myself to the language of the country, and in a few months was able to converse with the learned men; some of whom I found morose and reserved, and others easy and communicative; some were unwilling to teach another what they had with difficulty learned themselves; and some showed that the end of their studies was to gain the dignity of instructing.

"To the tutor of the young princes I recommended myself so much that I was presented to the Emperor as a man of uncommon knowledge.

The Emperor asked me many questions concerning my country and my travels, and though I cannot now recollect anything that he uttered above the power of a common man, he dismissed me astonished at his wisdom and enamoured of his goodness.

"My credit was now so high that the merchants with whom I had travelled applied to me for recommendations to the ladies of the Court. I was surprised at their confidence of solicitation and greatly reproached them with their practices on the road. They heard me with cold indifference, and showed no tokens of shame or sorrow.

"They then urged their request with the offer of a bribe, but what I would not do for kindness I would not do for money, and refused them, not because they had injured me, but because I would not enable them to injure others; for I knew they would have made use of my credit to cheat those who should buy their wares.

"Having resided at Agra till there was no more to be learned, I travelled into Persia, where I saw many remains of ancient magnificence and observed many new accommodations of life. The Persians are a nation eminently social, and their assemblies afforded me daily opportunities of remarking characters and manners, and of tracing human nature through all its variations.

"From Persia I passed into Arabia, where I saw a nation pastoral and warlike, who lived without any settled habitation, whose wealth is their flocks and herds, and who have carried on through ages an hereditary war with mankind, though they neither covet nor envy their possessions."

X. Imlac's History (continued)—A Dissertation upon Poetry

"Wherever I went I found that poetry was considered as the highest learning, and regarded with a veneration somewhat approaching to that which man would pay to angelic nature. And yet it fills me with wonder that in almost all countries the most ancient poets are considered as the best; whether it be that every other kind of knowledge is an acquisition greatly attained, and poetry is a gift conferred at once; or that the first poetry of every nation surprised them as a novelty, and retained the credit by consent which it received by accident at first; or whether, as the province of poetry is to describe nature and passion, which are always the same, the first writers took possession of the most striking objects for description and the most probable occurrences for fiction, and left nothing to those that followed them but transcription of the same events and new combinations of the same images. Whatever be the reason, it is commonly observed that the early writers are in possession of nature, and their followers of art; that the first excel in strength and invention, and the latter in elegance and refinement.

"I was desirous to add my name to this illustrious fraternity. I read all the poets of Persia and Arabia, and was able to repeat by memory the volumes that are suspended in the mosque of Mecca. But I soon found that no man was ever great by imitations. My desire of excellence impelled me to transfer my attention to nature and to life. Nature was to be my subject, and men to be my auditors. I could never describe what I had not seen. I could not hope to move those with delight or terror whose interests and opinions I did not understand.

Being now resolved to be a poet, I saw everything with a new purpose; my sphere of attention was suddenly magnified; no kind of knowledge was to be overlooked. I ranged mountains and deserts for images and resemblances, and pictured upon my mind every tree of the forest and flower of the valley. I observed with equal care the crags of the rock and the pinnacles of the palace. Sometimes I wandered along the mazes of the rivulet, and sometimes watched the changes of the summer clouds. To a poet nothing can be useless. Whatever is beautiful and whatever is dreadful must be familiar to his imagination; he must be conversant with all that is awfully vast or elegantly little. The plants of the garden, the animals of the wood, the minerals of the earth, and meteors of the sky, must all concur to store his mind with inexhaustible variety; for every idea is useful for the enforcement or decoration of moral or religious truth, and he who knows most will have most power of diversifying his scenes and of gratifying his reader with remote allusions and unexpected instruction.

"All the appearances of nature I was therefore careful to study, and every country which I have surveyed has contributed something to my poetical powers."

"In so wide a survey," said the Prince, "you must surely have left much unobserved. I have lived till now within the circuit of the mountains, and yet cannot walk abroad without the sight of something which I had never beheld before, or never heeded."

"This business of a poet," said Imlac, "is to examine, not the individual, but the species; to remark general properties and large appearances. He does not number the streaks of the tulip, or describe the different shades of the verdure of the forest. He is to exhibit in his portraits of nature such prominent and striking features as recall the original to every mind, and must neglect the minuter discriminations, which one may have remarked and another have neglected, for those characteristics which are alike obvious to vigilance and carelessness.

"But the knowledge of nature is only half the task of a poet; he must be acquainted likewise with all the modes of life. His character requires that he estimate the happiness and misery of every condition, observe the power of all the passions in all their combinations, and trace the changes of the human mind, as they are modified by various institutions and accidental influences of climate or custom, from the sprightliness of infancy to the despondence of decrepitude. He must divest himself of the prejudices of his age and country; he must consider right and wrong in their abstracted and invariable state; he must disregard present laws and opinions, and rise to general and transcendental truths, which will always be the same. He must, therefore, content himself with the slow progress of his name, contemn the praise of his own time, and commit his claims to the justice of posterity. He must write as the interpreter of nature and the legislator of mankind, and consider himself as presiding over the thoughts and manners of future generations, as a being superior to time and place.

"His labour is not yet at an end. He must know many languages and many sciences, and, that his style may be worthy of his thoughts, must by incessant practice familiarise to himself every delicacy of speech and grace of harmony."

XI. Imlac's Narrative (continued)—A Hint of Pilgrimage

Imlac now felt the enthusiastic fit, and was proceeding to aggrandise his own profession, when then Prince cried out: "Enough! thou hast convinced me that no human being can ever be a poet. Proceed with thy narration."

"To be a poet," said Imlac, "is indeed very difficult."

"So difficult," returned the Prince, "that I will at present hear no more of his labours. Tell me whither you went when you had seen Persia."

"From Persia," said the poet, "I travelled through Syria, and for three years resided in Palestine, where I conversed with great numbers of the northern and western nations of Europe, the nations which are now in possession of all power and all knowledge, whose armies are irresistible, and whose fleets command the remotest parts of the globe. When I compared these men with the natives of our own kingdom and those that surround us, they appeared almost another order of beings. In their countries it is difficult to wish for anything that may not be obtained; a thousand arts, of which we never heard, are continually labouring for their convenience and pleasure, and whatever their own climate has denied them is supplied by their commerce."

"By what means," said the Prince, "are the Europeans thus powerful? or why, since they can so easily visit Asia and Africa for trade or conquest, cannot the Asiatics and Africans invade their coast, plant colonies in their ports, and give laws to their natural princes? The same wind that carries them back would bring us thither."

"They are more powerful, sir, than we," answered Imlac, "because they are wiser; knowledge will always predominate over ignorance, as man governs the other animals. But why their knowledge is more than ours I know not what reason can be given but the unsearchable will of the Supreme Being."

"When," said the Prince with a sigh, "shall I be able to visit Palestine, and mingle with this mighty confluence of nations? Till that happy moment shall arrive, let me fill up the time with such representations as thou canst give me. I am not ignorant of the motive that assembles such numbers in that place, and cannot but consider it as the centre of wisdom and piety, to which the best and wisest men of every land must be continually resorting."

"There are some nations," said Imlac, "that send few visitants to Palestine; for many numerous and learned sects in Europe concur to censure pilgrimage as superstitious, or deride it as ridiculous."

"You know," said the Prince, "how little my life has made me acquainted with diversity of opinions; it will be too long to hear the arguments on both sides; you, that have considered them, tell me the result."

"Pilgrimage," said Imlac, "like many other acts of piety, may be reasonable or superstitious, according to the principles upon which it is performed. Long journeys in search of truth are not commanded. Truth, such as is necessary to the regulation of life, is always found where it is honestly sought. Change of place is no natural cause of the increase of piety, for it inevitably produces dissipation of mind. Yet, since men go every day to view the fields where great actions have been performed, and return with stronger impressions of the event, curiosity of the same kind may naturally dispose us to view that country whence our religion had its beginning, and I believe no man surveys those awful scenes without some confirmation of holy resolutions. That the Supreme Being may be more easily propitiated in one place than in another is the dream of idle superstition, but that some places may operate upon our own minds in an uncommon manner is an opinion which hourly experience will justify. He who supposes that his vices may be more successfully combated in Palestine, will perhaps find himself mistaken; yet he may go thither without folly; he who thinks they will be more freely pardoned, dishonours at once his reason and religion."

"These," said the Prince, "are European distinctions. I will consider them another time. What have you found to be the effect of knowledge? Are those nations happier than we?"

"There is so much infelicity," said the poet, "in the world, that scarce any man has leisure from his own distresses to estimate the comparative happiness of others. Knowledge is certainly one of the means of pleasure, as is confessed by the natural desire which every mind feels of increasing its ideas. Ignorance is mere privation, by which nothing can be produced; it is a vacuity in which the soul sits motionless and torpid for want of attraction, and, without knowing why, we always rejoice when we learn, and grieve when we forget. I am therefore inclined to conclude that if nothing counteracts the natural consequence of learning, we grow more happy as out minds take a wider range.

"In enumerating the particular comforts of life, we shall find many advantages on the side of the Europeans. They cure wounds and diseases with which we languish and perish. We suffer inclemencies of weather which they can obviate. They have engines for the despatch of many laborious works, which we must perform by manual industry. There is such communication between distant places that one friend can hardly be said to be absent from another. Their policy removes all public inconveniences; they have roads cut through the mountains, and bridges laid over their rivers. And, if we descend to the privacies of life, their habitations are more commodious and their possessions are more secure."

"They are surely happy," said the Prince, "who have all these conveniences, of which I envy none so much as the facility with which separated friends interchange their thoughts."

"The Europeans," answered Imlac, "are less unhappy than we, but they are not happy. Human life is everywhere a state in which much is to be endured and little to be enjoyed."

XII. The Story of Imlac (continued)

"I am not willing," said the Prince, "to suppose that happiness is so parsimoniously distributed to mortals, nor can I believe but that, if I had the choice of life, I should be able to fill every day with pleasure. I would injure no man, and should provoke no resentments; I would relieve every distress, and should enjoy the benedictions of gratitude. I would choose my friends among the wise and my wife among the virtuous, and therefore should be in no danger from treachery or unkindness. My children should by my care be learned and pious, and would repay to my age what their childhood had received. What would dare to molest him who might call on every side to thousands enriched by his bounty or assisted by his power? And why should not life glide away in the soft reciprocation of protection and reverence? All this may be done without the help of European refinements, which appear by their effects to be rather specious than useful. Let us leave them and pursue our journey."

"From Palestine," said Imlac, "I passed through many regions of Asia; in the more civilised kingdoms as a trader, and among the barbarians of the mountains as a pilgrim. At last I began to long for my native country, that I might repose after my travels and fatigues in the places where I had spent my earliest years, and gladden my old companions with the recital of my adventures. Often did I figure to myself those with whom I had sported away the gay hours of dawning life, sitting round me in its evening, wondering at my tales and listening to my counsels.

"When this thought had taken possession of my mind, I considered every moment as wasted which did not bring me nearer to Abyssinia. I hastened into Egypt, and, notwithstanding my impatience, was detained ten months in the contemplation of its ancient magnificence and in inquiries after the remains of its ancient learning. I found in Cairo a mixture of all nations: some brought thither by the love of knowledge, some by the hope of gain; many by the desire of living after their own manner without observation, and of lying hid in the obscurity of multitudes; for in a city populous as Cairo it is possible to obtain at the same time the gratifications of society and the secrecy of solitude.

"From Cairo I travelled to Suez, and embarked on the Red Sea, passing along the coast till I arrived at the port from which I had departed twenty years before. Here I joined myself to a caravan, and re-entered my native country.

"I now expected the caresses of my kinsmen and the congratulations of my friends, and was not without hope that my father, whatever value he had set upon riches, would own with gladness and pride a son who was able to add to the felicity and honour of the nation. But I was soon convinced that my thoughts were vain. My father had been dead fourteen years, having divided his wealth among my brothers, who were removed to some other provinces. Of my companions, the greater part was in the grave; of the rest, some could with difficulty remember me, and some considered me as one corrupted by foreign manners.

"A man used to vicissitudes is not easily dejected. I forgot, after a time, my disappointment, and endeavoured to recommend myself to the nobles of the kingdom; they admitted me to their tables, heard my story, and dismissed me. I opened a school, and was prohibited to teach. I then resolved to sit down in the quiet of domestic life, and addressed a lady that was fond of my conversation, but rejected my suit because my father was a merchant.

"Wearied at last with solicitation and repulses, I resolved to hide myself for ever from the world, and depend no longer on the opinion or caprice of others. I waited for the time when the gate of the Happy Valley should open, that I might bid farewell to hope and fear; the day came, my performance was distinguished with favour, and I resigned myself with joy to perpetual confinement."

"Hast thou here found happiness at last?" said Rasselas. "Tell me, without reserve, art thou content with thy condition, or dost thou wish to be again wandering and inquiring? All the inhabitants of this valley celebrate their lot, and at the annual visit of the Emperor invite others to partake of their felicity."

"Great Prince," said Imlac, "I shall speak the truth. I know not one of all your attendants who does not lament the hour when he entered this retreat. I am less unhappy than the rest, because I have a mind replete with images, which I can vary and combine at pleasure. I can amuse my solitude by the renovation of the knowledge which begins to fade from my memory, and by recollection of the accidents of my past life. Yet all this ends in the sorrowful consideration that my acquirements are now useless, and that none of my pleasures can be again enjoyed. The rest, whose minds have no impression but of the present moment, are either corroded by malignant passions or sit stupid in the gloom of perpetual vacancy."

"What passions can infest those," said the Prince, "who have no rivals? We are in a place where impotence precludes malice, and where all envy is repressed by community of enjoyments."

"There may be community," said Imlac, "of material possessions, but there can never be community of love or of esteem. It must happen that one will please more than another; he that knows himself despised will always be envious, and still more envious and malevolent if he is condemned to live in the presence of those who despise him. The invitations by which they allure others to a state which they feel to be wretched, proceed from the natural malignity of hopeless misery. They are weary of themselves and of each other, and expect to find relief in new companions. They envy the liberty which their folly has forfeited, and would gladly see all mankind imprisoned like themselves.

"From this crime, however, I am wholly free. No man can say that he is wretched by my persuasion. I look with pity on the crowds who are annually soliciting admission to captivity, and wish that it were lawful for me to warn them of their danger."

"My dear Imlac," said the Prince, "I will open to thee my whole heart. I have long meditated an escape from the Happy Valley. I have examined the mountain on every side, but find myself insuperably barred—teach me the way to break my prison; thou shalt be the companion of my flight, the guide of my rambles, the partner of my fortune, and my sole director in the CHOICE OF LIFE.

"Sir," answered the poet, "your escape will be difficult, and perhaps you may soon repent your curiosity. The world, which you figure to yourself smooth and quiet as the lake in the valley, you will find a sea foaming with tempests and boiling with whirlpools; you will be sometimes overwhelmed by the waves of violence, and sometimes dashed against the rocks of treachery. Amidst wrongs and frauds, competitions and anxieties, you will wish a thousand times for these seats of quiet, and willingly quit hope to be free from fear."

"Do not seek to deter me from my purpose," said the Prince. "I am impatient to see what thou hast seen; and since thou art thyself weary of the valley, it is evident that thy former state was better than this. Whatever be the consequence of my experiment, I am resolved to judge with mine own eyes of the various conditions of men, and then to make deliberately my CHOICE OF LIFE."

"I am afraid," said Imlac, "you are hindered by stronger restraints than my persuasions; yet, if your determination is fixed, I do not counsel you to despair. Few things are impossible to diligence and skill."

XIII. Rasselas Discovers the Means of Escape

The Prince now dismissed his favourite to rest; but the narrative of wonders and novelties filled his mind with perturbation. He revolved all that he had heard, and prepared innumerable questions for the morning.

Much of his uneasiness was now removed. He had a friend to whom he could impart his thoughts, and whose experience could assist him in his designs. His heart was no longer condemned to swell with silent vexation. He thought that even the Happy Valley might be endured with such a companion, and that if they could range the world together he should have nothing further to desire.

In a few days the water was discharged, and the ground dried. The Prince and Imlac then walked out together, to converse without the notice of the rest. The Prince, whose thoughts were always on the wing, as he passed by the gate said, with a countenance of sorrow, "Why art thou so strong, and why is man so weak?"

"Man is not weak," answered his companion; "knowledge is more than equivalent to force. The master of mechanics laughs at strength. I can burst the gate, but cannot do it secretly. Some other expedient must be tried."

As they were walking on the side of the mountain they observed that the coneys, which the rain had driven from their burrows, had taken shelter among the bushes, and formed holes behind them tending upwards in an oblique line. "It has been the opinion of antiquity," said Imlac, "that human reason borrowed many arts from the instinct of animals; let us, therefore, not think ourselves degraded by learning from the coney. We may escape by piercing the mountain in the same direction. We will begin where the summit hangs over the middle part, and labour upward till we shall issue out beyond the prominence."

The eyes of the Prince, when he heard this proposal, sparkled with joy. The execution was easy and the success certain.

No time was now lost. They hastened early in the morning to choose a place proper for their mine. They clambered with great fatigue among crags and brambles, and returned without having discovered any part that favoured their design. The second and the third day were spent in the same manner, and with the same frustration; but on the fourth day they found a small cavern concealed by a thicket, where they resolved to make their experiment.

Imlac procured instruments proper to hew stone and remove earth, and they fell to their work on the next day with more eagerness than vigour. They were presently exhausted by their efforts, and sat down to pant upon the grass. The Prince for a moment appeared to be discouraged. "Sir," said his companion, "practice will enable us to continue our labour for a longer time. Mark, however, how far we have advanced, and ye will find that our toil will some time have an end. Great works are performed not by strength, but perseverance; yonder palace was raised by single stones, yet you see its height and spaciousness. He that shall walk with vigour three hours a day, will pass in seven years a space equal to the circumference of the globe."

They returned to their work day after day, and in a short time found a fissure in the rock, which enabled them to pass far with very little obstruction. This Rasselas considered as a good omen. "Do not disturb your mind," said Imlac, "with other hopes or fears than reason may suggest; if you are pleased with the prognostics of good, you will be terrified likewise with tokens of evil, and your whole life will be a prey to superstition. Whatever facilitates our work is more than an omen; it is a cause of success. This is one of those pleasing surprises which often happen to active resolution. Many things difficult to design prove easy to performance."

XIV. Rasselas and Imlac Receive an Unexpected Visit

They had now wrought their way to the middle, and solaced their toil with the approach of liberty, when the Prince, coming down to refresh himself with air, found his sister Nekayah standing at the mouth of the cavity. He started, and stood confused, afraid to tell his design, and yet hopeless to conceal it. A few moments determined him to repose on her fidelity, and secure her secrecy by a declaration without reserve.

"Do not imagine," said the Princess, "that I came hither as a spy. I had long observed from my window that you and Imlac directed your walk every day towards the same point, but I did not suppose you had any better reason for the preference than a cooler shade or more fragrant bank, nor followed you with any other design than to partake of your conversation. Since, then, not suspicion, but fondness, has detected you, let me not lose the advantage of my discovery. I am equally weary of confinement with yourself, and not less desirous of knowing what is done or suffered in the world. Permit me to fly with you from this tasteless tranquillity, which will yet grow more loathsome when you have left me. You may deny me to accompany you, but cannot hinder me from following."

The Prince, who loved Nekayah above his other sisters, had no inclination to refuse her request, and grieved that he had lost an opportunity of showing his confidence by a voluntary communication. It was, therefore, agreed that she should leave the valley with them; and that in the meantime she should watch, lest any other straggler should, by chance or curiosity, follow them to the mountain.

At length their labour was at an end. They saw light beyond the prominence, and, issuing to the top of the mountain, beheld the Nile, yet a narrow current, wandering beneath them.

The Prince looked round with rapture, anticipated all the pleasures of travel, and in thought was already transported beyond his father's dominions. Imlac, though very joyful at his escape, had less expectation of pleasure in the world, which he had before tried and of which he had been weary.

Rasselas was so much delighted with a wider horizon, that he could not soon be persuaded to return into the valley. He informed his sister that the way was now open, and that nothing now remained but to prepare for their departure.

XV. The Prince and Princess Leave the Valley, and See Many Wonders

The Prince and Princess had jewels sufficient to make them rich whenever they came into a place of commerce, which, by Imlac's direction, they hid in their clothes, and on the night of the next full moon all left the valley. The Princess was followed only by a single favourite, who did not know whither she was going.

They clambered through the cavity, and began to go down on the other side. The Princess and her maid turned their eyes toward every part, and seeing nothing to bound their prospect, considered themselves in danger of being lost in a dreary vacuity. They stopped and trembled. "I am almost afraid," said the Princess, "to begin a journey of which I cannot perceive an end, and to venture into this immense plain where I may be approached on every side by men whom I never saw." The Prince felt nearly the same emotions, though he thought it more manly to conceal them.

Imlac smiled at their terrors, and encouraged them to proceed. But the Princess continued irresolute till she had been imperceptibly drawn forward too far to return.

In the morning they found some shepherds in the field, who set some milk and fruits before them. The Princess wondered that she did not see a palace ready for her reception and a table spread with delicacies; but being faint and hungry, she drank the milk and ate the fruits, and thought them of a higher flavour than the products of the valley.

They travelled forward by easy journeys, being all unaccustomed to toil and difficulty, and knowing that, though they might be missed, they could not be pursued. In a few days they came into a more populous region, where Imlac was diverted with the admiration which his companions expressed at the diversity of manners, stations, and employments. Their dress was such as might not bring upon them the suspicion of having anything to conceal; yet the Prince, wherever he came, expected to be obeyed, and the Princess was frighted because those who came into her presence did not prostrate themselves. Imlac was forced to observe them with great vigilance, lest they should betray their rank by their unusual behaviour, and detained them several weeks in the first village to accustom them to the sight of common mortals.

By degrees the royal wanderers were taught to understand that they had for a time laid aside their dignity, and were to expect only such regard as liberality and courtesy could procure. And Imlac having by many admonitions prepared them to endure the tumults of a port and the ruggedness of the commercial race, brought them down to the sea-coast.

The Prince and his sister, to whom everything was new, were gratified equally at all places, and therefore remained for some months at the port without any inclination to pass further. Imlac was content with their stay, because he did not think it safe to expose them, unpractised in the world, to the hazards of a foreign country.

At last he began to fear lest they should be discovered, and proposed to fix a day for their departure. They had no pretensions to judge for themselves, and referred the whole scheme to his direction. He therefore took passage in a ship to Suez, and, when the time came, with great difficulty prevailed on the Princess to enter the vessel.

They had a quick and prosperous voyage, and from Suez travelled by land to Cairo.

XVI. They Enter Cairo, and Find Every Man Happy

As they approached the city, which filled the strangers with astonishment, "This," said Imlac to the Prince, "is the place where travellers and merchants assemble from all corners of the earth. You will here find men of every character and every occupation. Commerce is here honourable. I will act as a merchant, and you shall live as strangers who have no other end of travel than curiosity; it will soon be observed that we are rich. Our reputation will procure us access to all whom we shall desire to know; you shall see all the conditions of humanity, and enable yourselves at leisure to make your CHOICE OF LIFE."

They now entered the town, stunned by the noise and offended by the crowds. Instruction had not yet so prevailed over habit but that they wondered to see themselves pass undistinguished along the streets, and met by the lowest of the people without reverence or notice. The Princess could not at first bear the thought of being levelled with the vulgar, and for some time continued in her chamber, where she was served by her favourite Pekuah, as in the palace of the valley.

Imlac, who understood traffic, sold part of the jewels the next day, and hired a house, which he adorned with such magnificence that he was immediately considered as a merchant of great wealth. His politeness attracted many acquaintances, and his generosity made him courted by many dependants. His companions, not being able to mix in the conversation, could make no discovery of their ignorance or surprise, and were gradually initiated in the world as they gained knowledge of the language.

The Prince had by frequent lectures been taught the use and nature of money; but the ladies could not for a long time comprehend what the merchants did with small pieces of gold and silver, or why things of so little use should be received as an equivalent to the necessaries of life.

They studied the language two years, while Imlac was preparing to set before them the various ranks and conditions of mankind. He grew acquainted with all who had anything uncommon in their fortune or conduct. He frequented the voluptuous and the frugal, the idle and the busy, the merchants and the men of learning.

The Prince now being able to converse with fluency, and having learned the caution necessary to be observed in his intercourse with strangers, began to accompany Imlac to places of resort, and to enter into all assemblies, that he might make his CHOICE OF LIFE.

For some time he thought choice needless, because all appeared to him really happy. Wherever he went he met gaiety and kindness, and heard the song of joy or the laugh of carelessness. He began to believe that the world overflowed with universal plenty, and that nothing was withheld either from want or merit; that every hand showered liberality and every heart melted with benevolence: "And who then," says he, "will be suffered to be wretched?"

Imlac permitted the pleasing delusion, and was unwilling to crush the hope of inexperience: till one day, having sat awhile silent, "I know not," said the Prince, "what can be the reason that I am more unhappy than any of our friends. I see them perpetually and unalterably cheerful, but feel my own mind restless and uneasy. I am unsatisfied with those pleasures which I seem most to court. I live in the crowds of jollity, not so much to enjoy company as to shun myself, and am only loud and merry to conceal my sadness."

"Every man," said Imlac, "may by examining his own mind guess what passes in the minds of others. When you feel that your own gaiety is counterfeit, it may justly lead you to suspect that of your companions not to be sincere. Envy is commonly reciprocal. We are long before we are convinced that happiness is never to be found, and each believes it possessed by others, to keep alive the hope of obtaining it for himself. In the assembly where you passed the last night there appeared such sprightliness of air and volatility of fancy as might have suited beings of a higher order, formed to inhabit serener regions, inaccessible to care or sorrow; yet, believe me, Prince, was there not one who did not dread the moment when solitude should deliver him to the tyranny of reflection."

"This," said the Prince, "may be true of others since it is true of me; yet, whatever be the general infelicity of man, one condition is more happy than another, and wisdom surely directs us to take the least evil in the CHOICE OF LIFE."

"The causes of good and evil," answered Imlac, "are so various and uncertain, so often entangled with each other, so diversified by various relations, and so much subject to accidents which cannot be foreseen, that he who would fix his condition upon incontestable reasons of preference must live and die inquiring and deliberating."

"But, surely," said Rasselas, "the wise men, to whom we listen with reverence and wonder, chose that mode of life for themselves which they thought most likely to make them happy."

"Very few," said the poet, "live by choice. Every man is placed in the present condition by causes which acted without his foresight, and with which he did not always willingly co-operate, and therefore you will rarely meet one who does not think the lot of his neighbour better than his own."

"I am pleased to think," said the Prince, "that my birth has given me at least one advantage over others by enabling me to determine for myself. I have here the world before me. I will review it at leisure: surely happiness is somewhere to be found."

XVII. The Prince Associates with Young Men of Spirit and Gaiety

Rasselas rose next day, and resolved to begin his experiments upon life. "Youth," cried he, "is the time of gladness: I will join myself to the young men whose only business is to gratify their desires, and whose time is all spent in a succession of enjoyments."

To such societies he was readily admitted, but a few days brought him back weary and disgusted. Their mirth was without images, their laughter without motive; their pleasures were gross and sensual, in which the mind had no part; their conduct was at once wild and mean —they laughed at order and at law, but the frown of power dejected and the eye of wisdom abashed them.

The Prince soon concluded that he should never be happy in a course of life of which he was ashamed. He thought it unsuitable to a reasonable being to act without a plan, and to be sad or cheerful only by chance. "Happiness," said he, "must be something solid and permanent, without fear and without uncertainty."

But his young companions had gained so much of his regard by their frankness and courtesy that he could not leave them without warning and remonstrance. "My friends," said he, "I have seriously considered our manners and our prospects, and find that we have mistaken our own interest. The first years of man must make provision for the last. He that never thinks, never can be wise. Perpetual levity must end in ignorance; and intemperance, though it may fire the spirits for an hour, will make life short or miserable. Let us consider that youth is of no long duration, and that in mature age, when the enchantments of fancy shall cease, and phantoms of delight dance no more about us, we shall have no comforts but the esteem of wise men and the means of doing good. Let us therefore stop while to stop is in our power: let us live as men who are some time to grow old, and to whom it will be the most dreadful of all evils to count their past years by follies, and to be reminded of their former luxuriance of health only by the maladies which riot has produced."

They stared awhile in silence one upon another, and at last drove him away by a general chorus of continued laughter.

The consciousness that his sentiments were just and his intention kind was scarcely sufficient to support him against the horror of derision. But he recovered his tranquillity and pursued his search.

XVIII. The Prince Finds a Wise and Happy Man

As he was one day walking in the street he saw a spacious building which all were by the open doors invited to enter. He followed the stream of people, and found it a hall or school of declamation, in which professors read lectures to their auditory. He fixed his eye upon a sage raised above the rest, who discoursed with great energy on the government of the passions. His look was venerable, his action graceful, his pronunciation clear, and his diction elegant. He showed with great strength of sentiment and variety of illustration that human nature is degraded and debased when the lower faculties predominate over the higher; that when fancy, the parent of passion, usurps the dominion of the mind, nothing ensues but the natural effect of unlawful government, perturbation, and confusion; that she betrays the fortresses of the intellect to rebels, and excites her children to sedition against their lawful sovereign. He compared reason to the sun, of which the light is constant, uniform, and lasting; and fancy to a meteor, of bright but transitory lustre, irregular in its motion and delusive in its direction.

He then communicated the various precepts given from time to time for the conquest of passion, and displayed the happiness of those who had obtained the important victory, after which man is no longer the slave of fear nor the fool of hope; is no more emaciated by envy, inflamed by anger, emasculated by tenderness, or depressed by grief; but walks on calmly through the tumults or privacies of life, as the sun pursues alike his course through the calm or the stormy sky.

He enumerated many examples of heroes immovable by pain or pleasure, who looked with indifference on those modes or accidents to which the vulgar give the names of good and evil. He exhorted his hearers to lay aside their prejudices, and arm themselves against the shafts of malice or misfortune, by invulnerable patience: concluding that this state only was happiness, and that this happiness was in every one's power.

Rasselas listened to him with the veneration due to the instructions of a superior being, and waiting for him at the door, humbly implored the liberty of visiting so great a master of true wisdom. The lecturer hesitated a moment, when Rasselas put a purse of gold into his hand, which he received with a mixture of joy and wonder.

"I have found," said the Prince at his return to Imlac, "a man who can teach all that is necessary to be known; who, from the unshaken throne of rational fortitude, looks down on the scenes of life changing beneath him. He speaks, and attention watches his lips. He reasons, and conviction closes his periods. This man shall be my future guide: I will learn his doctrines and imitate his life."

"Be not too hasty," said Imlac, "to trust or to admire the teachers of morality: they discourse like angels, but they live like men."

Rasselas, who could not conceive how any man could reason so forcibly without feeling the cogency of his own arguments, paid his visit in a few days, and was denied admission. He had now learned the power of money, and made his way by a piece of gold to the inner apartment, where he found the philosopher in a room half darkened, with his eyes misty and his face pale. "Sir," said he, "you are come at a time when all human friendship is useless; what I suffer cannot be remedied: what I have lost cannot be supplied. My daughter, my only daughter, from whose tenderness I expected all the comforts of my age, died last night of a fever. My views, my purposes, my hopes, are at an end: I am now a lonely being, disunited from society."

"Sir," said the Prince, "mortality is an event by which a wise man can never be surprised: we know that death is always near, and it should therefore always be expected." "Young man," answered the philosopher, "you speak like one that has never felt the pangs of separation." "Have you then forgot the precepts," said Rasselas, "which you so powerfully enforced? Has wisdom no strength to arm the heart against calamity? Consider that external things are naturally variable, but truth and reason are always the same." "What comfort," said the mourner, "can truth and reason afford me? Of what effect are they now, but to tell me that my daughter will not be restored?"

The Prince, whose humanity would not suffer him to insult misery with reproof, went away, convinced of the emptiness of rhetorical sounds, and the inefficacy of polished periods and studied sentences.

XIX. A Glimpse of Pastoral Life

He was still eager upon the same inquiry; and having heard of a hermit that lived near the lowest cataract of the Nile, and filled the whole country with the fame of his sanctity, resolved to visit his retreat, and inquire whether that felicity which public life could not afford was to be found in solitude, and whether a man whose age and virtue made him venerable could teach any peculiar art of shunning evils or enduring them.

Imlac and the Princess agreed to accompany him, and after the necessary preparations, they began their journey. Their way lay through the fields, where shepherds tended their flocks and the lambs were playing upon the pasture. "This," said the poet, "is the life which has been often celebrated for its innocence and quiet; let us pass the heat of the day among the shepherds' tents, and know whether all our searches are not to terminate in pastoral simplicity."

The proposal pleased them; and they induced the shepherds, by small presents and familiar questions, to tell the opinion of their own state. They were so rude and ignorant, so little able to compare the good with the evil of the occupation, and so indistinct in their narratives and descriptions, that very little could be learned from them. But it was evident that their hearts were cankered with discontent; that they considered themselves as condemned to labour for the luxury of the rich, and looked up with stupid malevolence towards those that were placed above them.

The Princess pronounced with vehemence that she would never suffer these envious savages to be her companions, and that she should not soon be desirous of seeing any more specimens of rustic happiness; but could not believe that all the accounts of primeval pleasures were fabulous, and was in doubt whether life had anything that could be justly preferred to the placid gratification of fields and woods. She hoped that the time would come when, with a few virtuous and elegant companions, she should gather flowers planted by her own hands, fondle the lambs of her own ewe, and listen without care, among brooks and breezes, to one of her maidens reading in the shade.

XX. The Danger of Prosperity

On the next day they continued their journey till the heat compelled them to look round for shelter. At a small distance they saw a thick wood, which they no sooner entered than they perceived that they were approaching the habitations of men. The shrubs were diligently cut away to open walks where the shades ware darkest; the boughs of opposite trees were artificially interwoven; seats of flowery turf were raised in vacant spaces; and a rivulet that wantoned along the side of a winding path had its banks sometimes opened into small basins, and its stream sometimes obstructed by little mounds of stone heaped together to increase its murmurs.

They passed slowly through the wood, delighted with such unexpected accommodations, and entertained each other with conjecturing what or who he could be that in those rude and unfrequented regions had leisure and art for such harmless luxury.

As they advanced they heard the sound of music, and saw youths and virgins dancing in the grove; and going still farther beheld a stately palace built upon a hill surrounded by woods. The laws of Eastern hospitality allowed them to enter, and the master welcomed them like a man liberal and wealthy.

He was skilful enough in appearances soon to discern that they were no common guests, and spread his table with magnificence. The eloquence of Imlac caught his attention, and the lofty courtesy of the Princess excited his respect. When they offered to depart, he entreated their stay, and was the next day more unwilling to dismiss them than before. They were easily persuaded to stop, and civility grew up in time to freedom and confidence.

The Prince now saw all the domestics cheerful and all the face of nature smiling round the place, and could not forbear to hope that he should find here what he was seeking; but when he was congratulating the master upon his possessions he answered with a sigh, "My condition has indeed the appearance of happiness, but appearances are delusive. My prosperity puts my life in danger; the Bassa of Egypt is my enemy, incensed only by my wealth and popularity. I have been hitherto protected against him by the princes of the country; but as the favour of the great is uncertain I know not how soon my defenders may be persuaded to share the plunder with the Bassa. I have sent my treasures into a distant country, and upon the first alarm am prepared to follow them. Then will my enemies riot in my mansion, and enjoy the gardens which I have planted."

They all joined in lamenting his danger and deprecating his exile; and the Princess was so much disturbed with the tumult of grief and indignation that she retired to her apartment. They continued with their kind inviter a few days longer, and then went to find the hermit.

XXI. The Happiness of Solitude—The Hermit's History

They came on the third day, by the direction of the peasants, to the hermit's cell. It was a cavern in the side of a mountain, overshadowed with palm trees, at such a distance from the cataract that nothing more was heard than a gentle uniform murmur, such as composes the mind to pensive meditation, especially when it was assisted by the wind whistling among the branches. The first rude essay of Nature had been so much improved by human labour that the cave contained several apartments appropriated to different uses, and often afforded lodging to travellers whom darkness or tempests happened to overtake.

The hermit sat on a bench at the door, to enjoy the coolness of the evening. On one side lay a book with pens and paper; on the other mechanical instruments of various kinds. As they approached him unregarded, the Princess observed that he had not the countenance of a man that had found or could teach the way to happiness.

They saluted him with great respect, which he repaid like a man not unaccustomed to the forms of Courts. "My children," said he, "if you have lost your way, you shall be willingly supplied with such conveniences for the night as this cavern will afford. I have all that Nature requires, and you will not expect delicacies in a hermit's cell."

They thanked him; and, entering, were pleased with the neatness and regularity of the place. The hermit set flesh and wine before them, though he fed only upon fruits and water. His discourse was cheerful without levity, and pious without enthusiasm. He soon gained the esteem of his guests, and the Princess repented her hasty censure.

At last Imlac began thus: "I do not now wonder that your reputation is so far extended: we have heard at Cairo of your wisdom, and came hither to implore your direction for this young man and maiden in the CHOICE OF LIFE."

"To him that lives well," answered the hermit, "every form of life is good; nor can I give any other rule for choice than to remove all apparent evil."

"He will most certainly remove from evil," said the Prince, "who shall devote himself to that solitude which you have recommended by your example."

"I have indeed lived fifteen years in solitude," said the hermit, "but have no desire that my example should gain any imitators. In my youth I professed arms, and was raised by degrees to the highest military rank. I have traversed wide countries at the head of my troops, and seen many battles and sieges. At last, being disgusted by the preferments of a younger officer, and feeling that my vigour was beginning to decay, I resolved to close my life in peace, having found the world full of snares, discord, and misery. I had once escaped from the pursuit of the enemy by the shelter of this cavern, and therefore chose it for my final residence. I employed artificers to form it into chambers, and stored it with all that I was likely to want.

"For some time after my retreat I rejoiced like a tempest-beaten sailor at his entrance into the harbour, being delighted with the sudden change of the noise and hurry of war to stillness and repose. When the pleasure of novelty went away, I employed my hours in examining the plants which grow in the valley, and the minerals which I collected from the rocks. But that inquiry is now grown tasteless and irksome. I have been for some time unsettled and distracted: my mind is disturbed with a thousand perplexities of doubt and vanities of imagination, which hourly prevail upon me, because I have no opportunities of relaxation or diversion. I am sometimes ashamed to think that I could not secure myself from vice but by retiring from the exercise of virtue, and begin to suspect that I was rather impelled by resentment than led by devotion into solitude. My fancy riots in scenes of folly, and I lament that I have lost so much, and have gained so little. In solitude, if I escape the example of bad men, I want likewise the counsel and conversation of the good. I have been long comparing the evils with the advantages of society, and resolve to return into the world to-morrow. The life of a solitary man will be certainly miserable, but not certainly devout."

They heard his resolution with surprise, but after a short pause offered to conduct him to Cairo. He dug up a considerable treasure which he had hid among the rocks, and accompanied them to the city, on which, as he approached it, he gazed with rapture.

XXII. The Happiness of a Life Led According to Nature

Rasselas went often to an assembly of learned men, who met at stated times to unbend their minds and compare their opinions. Their manners were somewhat coarse, but their conversation was instructive, and their disputations acute, though sometimes too violent, and often continued till neither controvertist remembered upon what question he began. Some faults were almost general among them: every one was pleased to hear the genius or knowledge of another depreciated.

In this assembly Rasselas was relating his interview with the hermit, and the wonder with which he heard him censure a course of life which he had so deliberately chosen and so laudably followed. The sentiments of the hearers were various. Some were of opinion that the folly of his choice had been justly punished by condemnation to perpetual perseverance. One of the youngest among them, with great vehemence, pronounced him a hypocrite. Some talked of the right of society to the labour of individuals, and considered retirement as a desertion of duty. Others readily allowed that there was a time when the claims of the public were satisfied, and when a man might properly sequester himself, to review his life and purify his heart.

One who appeared more affected with the narrative than the rest thought it likely that the hermit would in a few years go back to his retreat, and perhaps, if shame did not restrain or death intercept him, return once more from his retreat into the world. "For the hope of happiness," said he, "is so strongly impressed that the longest experience is not able to efface it. Of the present state, whatever it be, we feel and are forced to confess the misery; yet when the same state is again at a distance, imagination paints it as desirable. But the time will surely come when desire will no longer be our torment and no man shall be wretched but by his own fault.

"This," said a philosopher who had heard him with tokens of great impatience, "is the present condition of a wise man. The time is already come when none are wretched but by their own fault. Nothing is more idle than to inquire after happiness which Nature has kindly placed within our reach. The way to be happy is to live according to Nature, in obedience to that universal and unalterable law with which every heart is originally impressed; which is not written on it by precept, but engraven by destiny; not instilled by education, but infused at our nativity. He that lives according to Nature will suffer nothing from the delusions of hope or importunities of desire; he will receive and reject with equability of temper; and act or suffer as the reason of things shall alternately prescribe. Other men may amuse themselves with subtle definitions or intricate ratiocination. Let them learn to be wise by easier means: let them observe the hind of the forest and the linnet of the grove: let them consider the life of animals, whose motions are regulated by instinct; they obey their guide, and are happy. Let us therefore at length cease to dispute, and learn to live: throw away the encumbrance of precepts, which they who utter them with so much pride and pomp do not understand, and carry with us this simple and intelligible maxim: that deviation from Nature is deviation from happiness.

When he had spoken he looked round him with a placid air, and enjoyed the consciousness of his own beneficence.

"Sir," said the Prince with great modesty, "as I, like all the rest of mankind, am desirous of felicity, my closest attention has been fixed upon your discourse: I doubt not the truth of a position which a man so learned has so confidently advanced. Let me only know what it is to live according to Nature."

"When I find young men so humble and so docile," said the philosopher, "I can deny them no information which my studies have enabled me to afford. To live according to Nature is to act always with due regard to the fitness arising from the relations and qualities of causes and effects; to concur with the great and unchangeable scheme of universal felicity; to co-operate with the general disposition and tendency of the present system of things."

The Prince soon found that this was one of the sages whom he should understand less as he heard him longer. He therefore bowed and was silent; and the philosopher, supposing him satisfied and the rest

37

vanquished, rose up and departed with the air of a man that had co-operated with the present system.

XXIII. The Prince and His Sister Divide between Them the Work of Observation

Rasselas returned home full of reflections, doubting how to direct his future steps. Of the way to happiness he found the learned and simple equally ignorant; but as he was yet young, he flattered himself that he had time remaining for more experiments and further inquiries. He communicated to Imlac his observations and his doubts, but was answered by him with new doubts and remarks that gave him no comfort. He therefore discoursed more frequently and freely with his sister, who had yet the same hope with himself, and always assisted him to give some reason why, though he had been hitherto frustrated, he might succeed at last.

"We have hitherto," said she, "known but little of the world; we have never yet been either great or mean. In our own country, though we had royalty, we had no power; and in this we have not yet seen the private recesses of domestic peace. Imlac favours not our search, lest we should in time find him mistaken. We will divide the task between us; you shall try what is to be found in the splendour of Courts, and I will range the shades of humbler life. Perhaps command and authority may be the supreme blessings, as they afford the most opportunities of doing good; or perhaps what this world can give may be found in the modest habitations of middle fortune—too low for great designs, and too high for penury and distress."

XXIV. The Prince Examines the Happiness of High Stations

Rasselas applauded the design, and appeared next day with a splendid retinue at the Court of the Bassa. He was soon distinguished for his magnificence, and admitted, as a Prince whose curiosity had brought him from distant countries, to an intimacy with the great officers and frequent conversation with the Bassa himself.

He was at first inclined to believe that the man must be pleased with his own condition whom all approached with reverence and heard with obedience, and who had the power to extend his edicts to a whole kingdom. "There can be no pleasure," said he, "equal to that of feeling at once the joy of thousands all made happy by wise administration. Yet, since by the law of subordination this sublime delight can be in one nation but the lot of one, it is surely reasonable to think that there is some satisfaction more popular and accessible, and that millions can hardly be subjected to the will of a single man, only to fill his particular breast with incommunicable content."

These thoughts were often in his mind, and he found no solution of the difficulty. But as presents and civilities gained him more familiarity, he found that almost every man who stood high in his employment hated all the rest and was hated by them, and that their lives were a continual succession of plots and detections, stratagems and escapes, faction and treachery. Many of those who surrounded the Bassa were sent only to watch and report his conduct: every tongue was muttering censure, and every eye was searching for a fault.

At last the letters of revocation arrived: the Bassa was carried in chains to Constantinople, and his name was mentioned no more.

"What are we now to think of the prerogatives of power?" said Rasselas to his sister: "is it without efficacy to good, or is the subordinate degree only dangerous, and the supreme safe and glorious? Is the Sultan the only happy man in his dominions, or is the Sultan himself subject to the torments of suspicion and the dread of enemies?"

In a short time the second Bassa was deposed. The Sultan that had advanced him was murdered by the Janissaries, and his successor had other views or different favourites.

XXV. The Princess Pursues Her Inquiry with More Diligence than Success

The Princess in the meantime insinuated herself into many families; for there are few doors through which liberality, joined with good humour, cannot find its way. The daughters of many houses were airy and cheerful; but Nekayah had been too long accustomed to the conversation of Imlac and her brother to be much pleased with childish levity and prattle which had no meaning. She found their thoughts narrow, their wishes low, and their merriment often artificial. Their pleasures, poor as they were, could not be preserved pure, but were embittered by petty competitions and worthless emulation. They were always jealous of the beauty of each other, of a quality to which solicitude can add nothing, and from which detraction can take nothing away. Many were in love with triflers like themselves, and many fancied that they were in love when in truth they were only idle. Their affection was not fixed on sense or virtue, and therefore seldom ended but in vexation. Their grief, however, like their joy, was transient; everything floated in their mind unconnected with the past or future, so that one desire easily gave way to another, as a second stone, cast into the water, effaces and confounds the circles of the first.

With these girls she played as with inoffensive animals, and found them proud of her countenance and weary of her company.

But her purpose was to examine more deeply, and her affability easily persuaded the hearts that were swelling with sorrow to discharge their secrets in her ear, and those whom hope flattered or prosperity delighted often courted her to partake their pleasure.

The Princess and her brother commonly met in the evening in a private summerhouse on the banks of the Nile, and related to each other the occurrences of the day. As they were sitting together the Princess cast her eyes upon the river that flowed before her. "Answer," said she, "great father of waters, thou that rollest thy goods through eighty nations, to the invocations of the daughter of thy native king. Tell me if thou waterest through all thy course a single habitation from which thou dost not hear the murmurs of complaint."

"You are then," said Rasselas, "not more successful in private houses than I have been in Courts." "I have, since the last partition of our provinces," said the Princess, "enabled myself to enter familiarly into many families, where there was the fairest show of prosperity and peace, and know not one house that is not haunted by some fury that destroys their quiet.

"I did not seek ease among the poor, because I concluded that there it could not be found. But I saw many poor whom I had supposed to live in affluence. Poverty has in large cities very different appearances. It is often concealed in splendour and often in extravagance. It is the care of a very great part of mankind to conceal their indigence from the rest. They support themselves by temporary expedients, and every day is lost in contriving for the morrow.

"This, however, was an evil which, though frequent, I saw with less pain, because I could relieve it. Yet some have refused my bounties; more offended with my quickness to detect their wants than pleased with my readiness to succour them; and others, whose exigencies compelled them to admit my kindness, have never been able to forgive their benefactress. Many, however, have been sincerely grateful without the ostentation of gratitude or the hope of other favours."

XXVI. The Princess Continues Her Remarks upon Private Life

Nekayah, perceiving her brother's attention fixed, proceeded in her narrative.

"In families where there is or is not poverty there is commonly discord. If a kingdom be, as Imlac tells us, a great family, a family likewise is a little kingdom, torn with factions and exposed to revolutions. An unpractised observer expects the love of parents and children to be constant and equal. But this kindness seldom continues beyond the years of infancy; in a short time the children become rivals to their parents. Benefits are allowed by reproaches, and gratitude debased by envy.

"Parents and children seldom act in concert; each child endeavours to appropriate the esteem or the fondness of the parents; and the parents, with yet less temptation, betray each other to their children. Thus, some place their confidence in the father and some in the mother, and by degrees the house is filled with artifices and feuds.

"The opinions of children and parents, of the young and the old, are naturally opposite, by the contrary effects of hope and despondency, of expectation and experience, without crime or folly on either side. The colours of life in youth and age appear different, as the face of Nature in spring and winter. And how can children credit the assertions of parents which their own eyes show them to be false?

"Few parents act in such a manner as much to enforce their maxims by the credit of their lives. The old man trusts wholly to slow contrivance and gradual progression; the youth expects to force his way by genius, vigour, and precipitance. The old man pays regard to riches, and the youth reverences virtue. The old man deifies prudence; the youth commits himself to magnanimity and chance. The young man, who intends no ill, believes that none is intended, and therefore acts with openness and candour; but his father; having suffered the injuries of fraud, is impelled to suspect and too often allured to practise it. Age looks with anger on the temerity of youth, and youth with contempt on the scrupulosity of age. Thus parents and children for the greatest part live on to love less and less; and if those whom Nature has thus closely united are the torments of each other, where shall we look for tenderness and consolations?"

"Surely," said the Prince, "you must have been unfortunate in your choice of acquaintance. I am unwilling to believe that the most tender of all relations is thus impeded in its effects by natural necessity."

"Domestic discord," answered she, "is not inevitably and fatally necessary, but yet it is not easily avoided. We seldom see that a whole family is virtuous; the good and the evil cannot well agree, and the evil can yet less agree with one another. Even the virtuous fall sometimes to variance, when their virtues are of different kinds and tending to extremes. In general, those parents have most reverence who most deserve it, for he that lives well cannot be despised.

"Many other evils infest private life. Some are the slaves of servants whom they have trusted with their affairs. Some are kept in continual anxiety by the caprice of rich relations, whom they cannot please and dare not offend. Some husbands are imperious and some wives perverse, and, as it is always more easy to do evil than good, though the wisdom or virtue of one can very rarely make many happy, the folly or vice of one makes many miserable."

"If such be the general effect of marriage," said the Prince, "I shall for the future think it dangerous to connect my interest with that of another, lest I should be unhappy by my partner's fault."

"I have met," said the Princess, "with many who live single for that reason, but I never found that their prudence ought to raise envy. They dream away their time without friendship, without fondness, and are driven to rid themselves of the day, for which they have no use, by childish amusements or vicious delights. They act as beings under the constant sense of some known inferiority that fills their minds with rancour and their tongues with censure. They are peevish at home and malevolent abroad, and, as the outlaws of human nature, make it their business and their pleasure to disturb that society which debars them from its privileges. To live without feeling or exciting sympathy, to be fortunate without adding to the felicity of others, or afflicted without tasting the balm of pity, is a state more gloomy than solitude; it is not retreat but exclusion from mankind. Marriage has many pains, but celibacy has no pleasures."

"What then is to be done?" said Rasselas. "The more we inquire the less we can resolve. Surely he is most likely to please himself that has no other inclination to regard."

XXVII. Disquisition upon Greatness

The conversation had a short pause. The Prince, having considered his sister's observation, told her that she had surveyed life with prejudice and supposed misery where she did not find it. "Your narrative," says he, "throws yet a darker gloom upon the prospects of futurity. The predictions of Imlac were but faint sketches of the evils painted by Nekayah. I have been lately convinced that quiet is not the daughter of grandeur or of power; that her presence is not to be bought by wealth nor enforced by conquest. It is evident that as any man acts in a wider compass he must be more exposed to opposition from enmity or miscarriage from chance. Whoever has many to please or to govern must use the ministry of many agents, some of whom will be wicked and some ignorant, by some he will be misled and by others betrayed. If he gratifies one he will offend another; those that are not favoured will think themselves injured, and since favours can be conferred but upon few the greater number will be always discontented."

"The discontent," said the Princess, "which is thus unreasonable, I hope that I shall always have spirit to despise and you power to repress."

"Discontent," answered Rasselas, "will not always be without reason under the most just and vigilant administration of public affairs. None, however attentive, can always discover that merit which indigence or faction may happen to obscure, and none, however powerful, can always reward it. Yet he that sees inferior desert advanced above him will naturally impute that preference to partiality or caprice, and indeed it can scarcely be hoped that any man, however magnanimous by Nature or exalted by condition, will be able to persist for ever in fixed and inexorable justice of distribution; he will sometimes indulge his own affections and sometimes those of his favourites; he will permit some to please him who can never serve him; he will discover in those whom he loves qualities which in reality they do not possess, and to those from whom he receives pleasure he will in his turn endeavour to give it. Thus will recommendations sometimes prevail which were purchased by money or by the more destructive bribery of flattery and servility.

"He that hath much to do will do something wrong, and of that wrong must suffer the consequences, and if it were possible that he should always act rightly, yet, when such numbers are to judge of his conduct, the bad will censure and obstruct him by malevolence and the good sometimes by mistake.

"The highest stations cannot therefore hope to be the abodes of happiness, which I would willingly believe to have fled from thrones and palaces to seats of humble privacy and placid obscurity. For what can hinder the satisfaction or intercept the expectations of him whose abilities are adequate to his employments, who sees with his own eyes the whole circuit of his influence, who chooses by his own knowledge all whom he trusts, and whom none are tempted to deceive by hope or fear? Surely he has nothing to do but to love and to be loved; to be virtuous and to be happy."

"Whether perfect happiness would be procured by perfect goodness," said Nekayah, "this world will never afford an opportunity of deciding. But this, at least, may be maintained, that we do not always find visible happiness in proportion to visible virtue. All natural and almost all political evils are incident alike to the bad and good; they are confounded in the misery of a famine, and not much distinguished in the fury of a faction; they sink together in a tempest and are driven together from their country by invaders. All that virtue can afford is quietness of conscience, a steady prospect of a happier state; this may enable us to endure calamity with patience; but remember that patience must suppose pain."

XXVIII. Rasselas and Nekayah Continue Their Conversation

"Dear Princess," said Rasselas, "you fall into the common errors of exaggeratory declamation, by producing in a familiar disquisition examples of national calamities and scenes of extensive misery which are found in books rather than in the world, and which, as they are horrid, are ordained to be rare. Let us not imagine evils which we do not feel, nor injure life by misrepresentations. I cannot bear that querulous eloquence which threatens every city with a siege like that of Jerusalem, that makes famine attend on every flight of locust, and suspends pestilence on the wing of every blast that issues from the south.

"On necessary and inevitable evils which overwhelm kingdoms at once all disputation is vain; when they happen they must be endured. But it is evident that these bursts of universal distress are more dreaded than felt; thousands and tens of thousands flourish in youth and wither in age, without the knowledge of any other than domestic evils, and share the same pleasures and vexations, whether their kings are mild or cruel, whether the armies of their country pursue their enemies or retreat before them. While Courts are disturbed with intestine competitions and ambassadors are negotiating in foreign countries, the smith still plies his anvil and the husbandman drives his plough forward; the necessaries of life are required and obtained, and the successive business of the season continues to make its wonted revolutions.

"Let us cease to consider what perhaps may never happen, and what, when it shall happen, will laugh at human speculation. We will not endeavour to modify the motions of the elements or to fix the destiny of kingdoms. It is our business to consider what beings like us may perform, each labouring for his own happiness by promoting within his circle, however narrow, the happiness of others.

"Marriage is evidently the dictate of Nature; men and women were made to be the companions of each other, and therefore I cannot be persuaded but that marriage is one of the means of happiness."

"I know not," said the Princess, "whether marriage be more than one of the innumerable modes of human misery. When I see and reckon the various forms of connubial infelicity, the unexpected causes of lasting discord, the diversities of temper, the oppositions of opinion, the rude collisions of contrary desire where both are urged by violent impulses, the obstinate contest of disagreeing virtues where both are supported by consciousness of good intention, I am sometimes disposed to think, with the severer casuists of most nations, that marriage is rather permitted than approved, and that none, but by the instigation of a passion too much indulged, entangle themselves with indissoluble compact."

"You seem to forget," replied Rasselas, "that you have, even now represented celibacy as less happy than marriage. Both conditions may be bad, but they cannot both be worse. Thus it happens, when wrong opinions are entertained, that they mutually destroy each other and leave the mind open to truth."

"I did not expect," answered, the Princess, "to hear that imputed to falsehood which is the consequence only of frailty. To the mind, as to the eye, it is difficult to compare with exactness objects vast in their extent and various in their parts. When we see or conceive the whole at once, we readily note the discriminations and decide the preference, but of two systems, of which neither can be surveyed by any human being in its full compass of magnitude and multiplicity of complication, where is the wonder that, judging of the whole by parts, I am alternately affected by one and the other as either presses on my memory or fancy? We differ from ourselves just as we differ from each other when we see only part of the question, as in the multifarious relations of politics and morality, but when we perceive the whole at once, as in numerical computations, all agree in one judgment, and none ever varies in his opinion."

"Let us not add," said the Prince, "to the other evils of life the bitterness of controversy, nor endeavour to vie with each other in subtilties of argument. We are employed in a search of which both are equally to enjoy the success or suffer by the miscarriage; it is therefore fit that we assist each other. You surely conclude too hastily from the infelicity of marriage against its institution; will not the misery of life prove equally that life cannot be the gift of Heaven? The world must be peopled by marriage or peopled without it."

"How the world is to be peopled," returned Nekayah, "is not my care and need not be yours. I see no danger that the present generation should omit to leave successors behind them; we are not now inquiring for the world, but for ourselves."

XXIX. The Debate on Marriage (continued)

"The good of the whole," says Rasselas, "is the same with the good of all its parts. If marriage be best for mankind, it must be evidently best for individuals; or a permanent and necessary duty must be the cause of evil, and some must be inevitably sacrificed to the convenience of others. In the estimate which you have made of the two states, it appears that the incommodities of a single life are in a great measure necessary and certain, but those of the conjugal state accidental and avoidable. I cannot forbear to flatter myself that prudence and benevolence will make marriage happy. The general folly of mankind is the cause of general complaint. What can be expected but disappointment and repentance from a choice made in the immaturity of youth, in the ardour of desire, without judgment, without foresight, without inquiry after conformity of opinions, similarity of manners, rectitude of judgment, or purity of sentiment?

"Such is the common process of marriage. A youth and maiden, meeting by chance or brought together by artifice, exchange glances, reciprocate civilities, go home and dream of one another. Having little to divert attention or diversify thought, they find themselves uneasy when they are apart, and therefore conclude that they shall be happy together. They marry, and discover what nothing but voluntary blindness before had concealed; they wear out life in altercations, and charge Nature with cruelty.

"From those early marriages proceeds likewise the rivalry of parents and children: the son is eager to enjoy the world before the father is willing to forsake it, and there is hardly room at once for two generations. The daughter begins to bloom before the mother can be content to fade, and neither can forbear to wish for the absence of the other.

"Surely all these evils may be avoided by that deliberation and delay which prudence prescribes to irrevocable choice. In the variety and jollity of youthful pleasures, life may be well enough supported without the help of a partner. Longer time will increase experience, and wider views will allow better opportunities of inquiry and selection; one advantage at least will be certain, the parents will be visibly older than their children."

"What reason cannot collect," and Nekayah, "and what experiment has not yet taught, can be known only from the report of others. I have been told that late marriages are not eminently happy. This is a question too important to be neglected; and I have often proposed it to those whose accuracy of remark and comprehensiveness of knowledge made their suffrages worthy of regard. They have generally determined that it is dangerous for a man and woman to suspend their fate upon each other at a time when opinions are fixed and habits are established, when friendships have been contracted on both sides, when life has been planned into method, and the mind has long enjoyed the contemplation of its own prospects.

"It is scarcely possible that two travelling through the world under the conduct of chance should have been both directed to the same path, and it will not often happen that either will quit the track which custom has made pleasing. When the desultory levity of youth has settled into regularity, it is soon succeeded by pride ashamed to yield, or obstinacy delighting to contend. And even though mutual esteem produces mutual desire to please, time itself, as it modifies unchangeably the external mien, determines likewise the direction of the passions, and gives an inflexible rigidity to the manners. Long customs are not easily broken; he that attempts to change the course of his own life very often labours in vain, and how shall we do that for others which we are seldom able to do for ourselves?"

"But surely," interposed the Prince, "you suppose the chief motive of choice forgotten or neglected. Whenever I shall seek a wife, it shall be my first question whether she be willing to be led by reason."

"Thus it is," said Nekayah, "that philosophers are deceived. There are a thousand familiar disputes which reason never can decide; questions that elude investigation, and make logic ridiculous; cases where something must be done, and where little can be said. Consider the state of mankind, and inquire how few can be supposed to act upon any occasions, whether small or great, with all the reasons of action present to their minds. Wretched would be the pair, above all names of wretchedness, who should be doomed to adjust by reason every morning all the minute details of a domestic day.

"Those who marry at an advanced age will probably escape the encroachments of their children, but in the diminution of this advantage they will be likely to leave them, ignorant and helpless, to a guardian's mercy; or if that should not happen, they must at least go out of the world before they see those whom they love best either wise or great.

"From their children, if they have less to fear, they have less also to hope; and they lose without equivalent the joys of early love, and the convenience of uniting with manners pliant and minds susceptible of new impressions, which might wear away their dissimilitudes by long cohabitation, as soft bodies by continual attrition conform their surfaces to each other.

"I believe it will be found that those who marry late are best pleased with their children, and those who marry early with their partners."

"The union of these two affections," said Rasselas, "would produce all that could be wished. Perhaps there is a time when marriage might unite them—a time neither too early for the father nor too late for the husband."

"Every hour," answered the Princess, "confirms my prejudice in favour of the position so often uttered by the mouth of Imlac, that 'Nature sets her gifts on the right hand and on the left.' Those conditions which flatter hope and attract desire are so constituted that as we approach one we recede from another. There are goods so opposed that we cannot seize both, but by too much prudence may pass between them at too great a distance to reach either. This is often the fate of long consideration; he does nothing who endeavours to do more than is allowed to humanity. Flatter not yourself with contrarieties of pleasure. Of the blessings set before you make your choice, and be content. No man can taste the fruits of autumn while he is delighting his scent with the flowers of the spring; no man can at the same time fill his cup from the source and from the mouth of the Nile."

XXX. Imlac Enters, and Changes the Conversation

Here Imlac entered, and interrupted them. "Imlac," said Rasselas, "I have been taking from the Princess the dismal history of private life, and am almost discouraged from further search."

"It seems to me," said Imlac, "that while you are making the choice of life you neglect to live. You wander about a single city, which, however large and diversified, can now afford few novelties, and forget that you are in a country famous among the earliest monarchies for the power and wisdom of its inhabitants—a country where the sciences first dawned that illuminate the world, and beyond which the arts cannot be traced of civil society or domestic life.

"The old Egyptians have left behind them monuments of industry and power before which all European magnificence is confessed to fade away. The ruins of their architecture are the schools of modern builders; and from the wonders which time has spared we may conjecture, though uncertainly, what it has destroyed."

"My curiosity," said Rasselas, "does not very strongly lead me to survey piles of stone or mounds of earth. My business is with man. I came hither not to measure fragments of temples or trace choked aqueducts, but to look upon the various scenes of the present world."

"The things that are now before us," said the Princess, "require attention, and deserve it. What have I to do with the heroes or the monuments of ancient times—with times which can never return, and heroes whose form of life was different from all that the present condition of mankind requires or allows?"

"To know anything," returned the poet, "we must know its effects; to see men, we must see their works, that we may learn what reason has dictated or passion has excited, and find what are the most powerful motives of action. To judge rightly of the present, we must oppose it to the past; for all judgment is comparative, and of the future nothing can be known. The truth is that no mind is much employed upon the present; recollection and anticipation fill up almost all our moments. Our passions are joy and grief, love and hatred, hope and fear. Of joy and grief, the past is the object, and the future of hope and fear; even love and hatred respect the past, for the cause must have been before the effect.

"The present state of things is the consequence of the former; and it is natural to inquire what were the sources of the good that we enjoy, or the evils that we suffer. If we act only for ourselves, to neglect the study of history is not prudent. If we are entrusted with the care of others, it is not just. Ignorance, when it is voluntary, is criminal; and he may properly be charged with evil who refused to learn how he might prevent it.

"There is no part of history so generally useful as that which relates to the progress of the human mind, the gradual improvement of reason, the successive advances of science, the vicissitudes of learning and ignorance (which are the light and darkness of thinking beings), the extinction and resuscitation of arts, and the revolutions of the intellectual world. If accounts of battles and invasions are peculiarly the business of princes, the useful or elegant arts are not to be neglected; those who have kingdoms to govern have understandings to cultivate.

"Example is always more efficacious than precept. A soldier is formed in war, and a painter must copy pictures. In this, contemplative life has the advantage. Great actions are seldom seen, but the labours of art are always at hand for those who desire to know what art has been able to perform.

"When the eye or the imagination is struck with any uncommon work, the next transition of an active mind is to the means by which it was performed. Here begins the true use of such contemplation. We enlarge our comprehension by new ideas, and perhaps recover some art lost to mankind, or learn what is less perfectly known in our own country. At least we compare our own with former times, and either rejoice at our improvements, or, what is the first motion towards good, discover our defects."

"I am willing," said the Prince, "to see all that can deserve my search."

"And I," said the Princess, "shall rejoice to learn something of the manners of antiquity."

"The most pompous monument of Egyptian greatness, and one of the most bulky works of manual industry," said Imlac, "are the Pyramids: fabrics raised before the time of history, and of which the earliest narratives afford us only uncertain traditions. Of these the greatest is still standing, very little injured by time."

"Let us visit them to-morrow," said Nekayah. "I have often heard of the Pyramids, and shall not rest till I have seen them, within and without, with my own eyes."

XXXI. They Visit the Pyramids

The resolution being thus taken, they set out the next day. They laid tents upon their camels, being resolved to stay among the Pyramids till their curiosity was fully satisfied. They travelled gently, turned aside to everything remarkable, stopped from time to time and conversed with the inhabitants, and observed the various appearances of towns ruined and inhabited, of wild and cultivated nature.

When they came to the Great Pyramid they were astonished at the extent of the base and the height of the top. Imlac explained to them the principles upon which the pyramidal form was chosen for a fabric intended to co-extend its duration with that of the world: he showed that its gradual diminution gave it such stability as defeated all the common attacks of the elements, and could scarcely be overthrown by earthquakes themselves, the least resistible of natural violence. A concussion that should shatter the pyramid would threaten the dissolution of the continent.

They measured all its dimensions, and pitched their tents at its foot. Next day they prepared to enter its interior apartments, and having hired the common guides, climbed up to the first passage; when the favourite of the Princess, looking into the cavity, stepped back and trembled. "Pekuah," said the Princess, "of what art thou afraid?"

"Of the narrow entrance," answered the lady, "and of the dreadful gloom. I dare not enter a place which must surely be inhabited by unquiet souls. The original possessors of these dreadful vaults will start up before us, and perhaps shut us in for ever." She spoke, and threw her arms round the neck of her mistress.

"If all your fear be of apparitions," said the Prince, "I will promise you safety. There is no danger from the dead: he that is once buried will be seen no more."

"That the dead are seen no more," said Imlac, "I will not undertake to maintain against the concurrent and unvaried testimony of all ages and of all nations. There is no people, rude or learned, among whom apparitions of the dead are not related and believed. This opinion, which perhaps prevails as far as human nature is diffused, could become universal only by its truth: those that never heard of one another would not have agreed in a tale which nothing but experience can make credible. That it is doubted by single cavillers can very little weaken the general evidence, and some who deny it with their tongues confess it by their fears.

"Yet I do not mean to add new terrors to those which have already seized upon Pekuah. There can be no reason why spectres should haunt the Pyramid more than other places, or why they should have power or will to hurt innocence and purity. Our entrance is no violation of their privileges: we can take nothing from them; how, then, can we offend them?"

"My dear Pekuah," said the Princess, "I will always go before you, and Imlac shall follow you. Remember that you are the companion of the Princess of Abyssinia."

"If the Princess is pleased that her servant should die," returned the lady, "let her command some death less dreadful than enclosure in this horrid cavern. You know I dare not disobey you—I must go if you command me; but if I once enter, I never shall come back."

The Princess saw that her fear was too strong for expostulation or reproof, and, embracing her, told her that she should stay in the tent till their return. Pekuah was not yet satisfied, but entreated the Princess not to pursue so dreadful a purpose as that of entering the recesses of the Pyramids. "Though I cannot teach courage," said Nekayah, "I must not learn cowardice, nor leave at last undone what I came hither only to do."

XXXII. They Enter the Pyramid

Pekuah descended to the tents, and the rest entered the Pyramid. They passed through the galleries, surveyed the vaults of marble, and examined the chest in which the body of the founder is supposed to have been deposited. They then sat down in one of the most spacious chambers to rest awhile before they attempted to return.

"We have now," said Imlac, "gratified our minds with an exact view of the greatest work of man, except the wall of China.

"Of the wall it is very easy to assign the motive. It secured a wealthy and timorous nation from the incursions of barbarians, whose unskilfulness in the arts made it easier for them to supply their wants by rapine than by industry, and who from time to time poured in upon the inhabitants of peaceful commerce as vultures descend upon domestic fowl. Their celerity and fierceness made the wall necessary, and their ignorance made it efficacious.

"But for the Pyramids, no reason has ever been given adequate to the cost and labour of the work. The narrowness of the chambers proves that it could afford no retreat from enemies, and treasures might have been reposited at far less expense with equal security. It seems to have been erected only in compliance with that hunger of imagination which preys incessantly upon life, and must be always appeased by some employment. Those who have already all that they can enjoy must enlarge their desires. He that has built for use till use is supplied must begin to build for vanity, and extend his plan to the utmost power of human performance that he may not be soon reduced to form another wish.

"I consider this mighty structure as a monument of the insufficiency of human enjoyments. A king whose power is unlimited, and whose treasures surmount all real and imaginary wants, is compelled to solace, by the erection of a pyramid, the satiety of dominion and tastelessness of pleasures, and to amuse the tediousness of declining life by seeing thousands labouring without end, and one stone, for no purpose, laid upon another. Whoever thou art that, not content with a moderate condition, imaginest happiness in royal magnificence, and dreamest that command or riches can feed the appetite of novelty with perpetual gratifications, survey the Pyramids, and confess thy folly!"

XXXIII. The Princess Meets with an Unexpected Misfortune

They rose up, and returned through the cavity at which they had entered; and the Princess prepared for her favourite a long narrative of dark labyrinths and costly rooms, and of the different impressions which the varieties of the way had made upon her. But when they came to their train, they found every one silent and dejected: the men discovered shame and fear in their countenances, and the women were weeping in their tents.

What had happened they did not try to conjecture, but immediately inquired. "You had scarcely entered into the Pyramid," said one of the attendants, "when a troop of Arabs rushed upon us: we were too few to resist them, and too slow to escape. They were about to search the tents, set us on our camels, and drive us along before them, when the approach of some Turkish horsemen put them to flight: but they seized the Lady Pekuah with her two maids, and carried them away: the Turks are now pursuing them by our instigation, but I fear they will not be able to overtake them."

The Princess was overpowered with surprise and grief. Rasselas, in the first heat of his resentment, ordered his servants to follow him, and prepared to pursue the robbers with his sabre in his hand. "Sir," said Imlac, "what can you hope from violence or valour? The Arabs are mounted on horses trained to battle and retreat; we have only beasts of burden. By leaving our present station we may lose the Princess, but cannot hope to regain Pekuah."

In a short time the Turks returned, having not been able to reach the enemy. The Princess burst out into new lamentations, and Rasselas could scarcely forbear to reproach them with cowardice; but Imlac was of opinion that the escape of the Arabs was no addition to their misfortune, for perhaps they would have killed their captives rather than have resigned them.

XXXIV. They Return to Cairo without Pekuah

There was nothing to be hoped from longer stay. They returned to Cairo, repenting of their curiosity, censuring the negligence of the government, lamenting their own rashness, which had neglected to procure a guard, imagining many expedients by which the loss of Pekuah might have been prevented, and resolving to do something for her recovery, though none could find anything proper to be done.

Nekayah retired to her chamber, where her women attempted to comfort her by telling her that all had their troubles, and that Lady Pekuah had enjoyed much happiness in the world for a long time, and might reasonably expect a change of fortune. They hoped that some good would befall her wheresoever she was, and that their mistress would find another friend who might supply her place.

The Princess made them no answer; and they continued the form of condolence, not much grieved in their hearts that the favourite was lost.

Next day the Prince presented to the Bassa a memorial of the wrong which he had suffered, and a petition for redress. The Bassa threatened to punish the robbers, but did not attempt to catch them; nor indeed could any account or description be given by which he might direct the pursuit.

It soon appeared that nothing would be done by authority. Governors being accustomed to hear of more crimes than they can punish, and more wrongs than they can redress, set themselves at ease by indiscriminate negligence, and presently forget the request when they lose sight of the petitioner.

Imlac then endeavoured to gain some intelligence by private agents. He found many who pretended to an exact knowledge of all the haunts of the Arabs, and to regular correspondence with their chiefs, and who readily undertook the recovery of Pekuah. Of these, some were furnished with money for their journey, and came back no more; some were liberally paid for accounts which a few days discovered to be false. But the Princess would not suffer any means, however improbable, to be left untried. While she was doing something, she kept her hope alive. As one expedient failed, another was suggested; when one messenger returned unsuccessful, another was despatched to a different quarter.

Two months had now passed, and of Pekuah nothing had been heard; the hopes which they had endeavoured to raise in each other grew more languid; and the Princess, when she saw nothing more to be tried, sunk down inconsolable in hopeless dejection. A thousand times she reproached herself with the easy compliance by which she permitted her favourite to stay behind her. "Had not my fondness," said she, "lessened my authority, Pekuah had not dared to talk of her terrors. She ought to have feared me more than spectres. A severe look would have overpowered her; a peremptory command would have compelled obedience. Why did foolish indulgence prevail upon me? Why did I not speak, and refuse to hear?"

"Great Princess," said Imlac, "do not reproach yourself for your virtue, or consider that as blameable by which evil has accidentally been caused. Your tenderness for the timidity of Pekuah was generous and kind. When we act according to our duty, we commit the events to Him by whose laws our actions are governed, and who will suffer none to be finally punished for obedience. When, in prospect of some good, whether natural or moral, we break the rules prescribed us, we withdraw from the direction of superior wisdom, and take all consequences upon ourselves. Man cannot so far know the connection of causes and events as that he may venture to do wrong in order to do right. When we pursue our end by lawful means, we may always console our miscarriage by the hope of future recompense. When we consult only our own policy, and attempt to find a nearer way to good by over-leaping the settled boundaries of right and wrong, we cannot be happy even by success, because we cannot escape the consciousness of our fault; but if we miscarry, the disappointment is irremediably embittered. How comfortless is the sorrow of him who feels at once the pangs of guilt and the vexation of calamity which guilt has brought upon him!

"Consider, Princess, what would have been your condition if the Lady Pekuah had entreated to accompany you, and, being compelled to stay in the tents, had been carried away; or how would you have borne the thought if you had forced her into the Pyramid, and she had died before you in agonies of terror?"

"Had either happened," said Nekayah, "I could not have endured life till now; I should have been tortured to madness by the remembrance of such cruelty, or must have pined away in abhorrence of myself."

"This, at least," said Imlac, "is the present reward of virtuous conduct, that no unlucky consequence can oblige us to repent it."

XXXV. The Princess Languishes for Want of Pekuah

Nekayah, being thus reconciled to herself, found that no evil is insupportable but that which is accompanied with consciousness of wrong. She was from that time delivered from the violence of tempestuous sorrow, and sunk into silent pensiveness and gloomy tranquillity. She sat from morning to evening recollecting all that had been done or said by her Pekuah, treasured up with care every trifle on which Pekuah had set an accidental value, and which might recall to mind any little incident or careless conversation. The sentiments of her whom she now expected to see no more were treasured in her memory as rules of life, and she deliberated to no other end than to conjecture on any occasion what would have been the opinion and counsel of Pekuah.

The women by whom she was attended knew nothing of her real condition, and therefore she could not talk to them but with caution and reserve. She began to remit her curiosity, having no great desire to collect notions which she had no convenience of uttering. Rasselas endeavoured first to comfort and afterwards to divert her; he hired musicians, to whom she seemed to listen, but did not hear them; and procured masters to instruct her in various arts, whose lectures, when they visited her again, were again to be repeated. She had lost her taste of pleasure and her ambition of excellence; and her mind, though forced into short excursions, always recurred to the image of her friend.

Imlac was every morning earnestly enjoined to renew his inquiries, and was asked every night whether he had yet heard of Pekuah; till, not being able to return the Princess the answer that she desired, he was less and less willing to come into her presence. She observed his backwardness, and commanded him to attend her. "You are not," said she, "to confound impatience with resentment, or to suppose that I charge you with negligence because I repine at your unsuccessfulness. I do not much wonder at your absence. I know that the unhappy are never pleasing, and that all naturally avoid the contagion of misery. To hear complaints is wearisome alike to the wretched and the happy; for who would cloud by adventitious grief the short gleams of gaiety which life allows us, or who that is struggling under his own evils will add to them the miseries of another?

"The time is at hand when none shall be disturbed any longer by the sighs of Nekayah: my search after happiness is now at an end. I am resolved to retire from the world, with all its flatteries and deceits, and will hide myself in solitude, without any other care than to compose my thoughts and regulate my hours by a constant succession of innocent occupations, till, with a mind purified from earthly desires, I shall enter into that state to which all are hastening, and in which I hope again to enjoy the friendship of Pekuah."

"Do not entangle your mind," said Imlac, "by irrevocable determinations, nor increase the burden of life by a voluntary accumulation of misery. The weariness of retirement will continue to increase when the loss of Pekuah is forgot. That you have been deprived of one pleasure is no very good reason for rejection of the rest."

"Since Pekuah was taken from me," said the Princess, "I have no pleasure to reject or to retain. She that has no one to love or trust has little to hope. She wants the radical principle of happiness. We may perhaps allow that what satisfaction this world can afford must arise from the conjunction of wealth, knowledge, and goodness. Wealth is nothing but as it is bestowed, and knowledge nothing but as it is communicated. They must therefore be imparted to others, and to whom could I now delight to impart them? Goodness affords the only comfort which can be enjoyed without a partner, and goodness may be practised in retirement."

"How far solitude may admit goodness or advance it, I shall not," replied Imlac, "dispute at present. Remember the confession of the pious hermit. You will wish to return into the world when the image of your companion has left your thoughts."

"That time," said Nekayah, "will never come. The generous frankness, the modest obsequiousness, and the faithful secrecy of my dear Pekuah will always be more missed as I shall live longer to see vice and folly."

"The state of a mind oppressed with a sudden calamity," said Imlac, "is like that of the fabulous inhabitants of the new-created earth, who, when the first night came upon them, supposed that day would never return. When the clouds of sorrow gather over us, we see nothing beyond them, nor can imagine how they will be dispelled; yet a new day succeeded to the night, and sorrow is never long without a dawn of ease. But they who restrain themselves from receiving comfort do as the savages would have done had they put out their eyes when it was dark. Our minds, like our bodies, are in continual flux; something is hourly lost, and something acquired. To lose much at once is inconvenient to either, but while the vital power remains uninjured, nature will find the means of reparation. Distance has the same effect on the mind as on the eye; and while we glide along the stream of time, whatever we leave behind us is always lessening, and that which we approach increasing in magnitude. Do not suffer life to stagnate: it will grow muddy for want of motion; commit yourself again to the current of the world; Pekuah will vanish by degrees; you will meet in your way some other favourite, or learn to diffuse yourself in general conversation."

"At least," said the Prince, "do not despair before all remedies have been tried. The inquiry after the unfortunate lady is still continued, and shall be carried on with yet greater diligence, on condition that you will promise to wait a year for the event, without any unalterable resolution."

Nekayah thought this a reasonable demand, and made the promise to her brother, who had been obliged by Imlac to require it. Imlac had, indeed, no great hope of regaining Pekuah; but he supposed that if he could secure the interval of a year, the Princess would be then in no danger of a cloister.

XXXVI. Pekuah Is Still Remembered. The Progress of Sorrow

Nekayah, seeing that nothing was omitted for the recovery of her favourite, and having by her promise set her intention of retirement at a distance, began imperceptibly to return to common cares and common pleasures. She rejoiced without her own consent at the suspension of her sorrows, and sometimes caught herself with indignation in the act of turning away her mind from the remembrance of her whom yet she resolved never to forget.

She then appointed a certain hour of the day for meditation on the merits and fondness of Pekuah, and for some weeks retired constantly at the time fixed, and returned with her eyes swollen and her countenance clouded. By degrees she grew less scrupulous, and suffered any important and pressing avocation to delay the tribute of daily tears. She then yielded to less occasions, and sometimes forgot what she was indeed afraid to remember, and at last wholly released herself from the duty of periodical affliction.

Her real love of Pekuah was not yet diminished. A thousand occurrences brought her back to memory, and a thousand wants, which nothing but the confidence of friendship can supply, made her frequently regretted. She therefore solicited Imlac never to desist from inquiry, and to leave no art of intelligence untried, that at least she might have the comfort of knowing that she did not suffer by negligence or sluggishness. "Yet what," said she, "is to be expected from our pursuit of happiness, when we find the state of life to be such that happiness itself is the cause of misery? Why should we endeavour to attain that of which the possession cannot be secured? I shall henceforward fear to yield my heart to excellence, however bright, or to fondness, however tender, lest I should lose again what I have lost in Pekuah."

XXXVII. The Princess Hears News of Pekuah

In seven months one of the messengers who had been sent away upon the day when the promise was drawn from the Princess, returned, after many unsuccessful rambles, from the borders of Nubia, with an account that Pekuah was in the hands of an Arab chief, who possessed a castle or fortress on the extremity of Egypt. The Arab, whose revenue was plunder, was willing to restore her, with her two attendants, for two hundred ounces of gold.

The price was no subject of debate. The Princess was in ecstasies when she heard that her favourite was alive, and might so cheaply be ransomed. She could not think of delaying for a moment Pekuah's happiness or her own, but entreated her brother to send back the messenger with the sum required. Imlac, being consulted, was not very confident of the veracity of the relater, and was still more doubtful of the Arab's faith, who might, if he were too liberally trusted, detain at once the money and the captives. He thought it dangerous to put themselves in the power of the Arab by going into his district; and could not expect that the rover would so much expose himself as to come into the lower country, where he might be seized by the forces of the Bassa.

It is difficult to negotiate where neither will trust. But Imlac, after some deliberation, directed the messenger to propose that Pekuah should be conducted by ten horsemen to the monastery of St. Anthony, which is situated in the deserts of Upper Egypt, where she should be met by the same number, and her ransom should be paid.

That no time might be lost, as they expected that the proposal would not be refused, they immediately began their journey to the monastery; and when they arrived, Imlac went forward with the former messenger to the Arab's fortress. Rasselas was desirous to go with them; but neither his sister nor Imlac would consent. The Arab, according to the custom of his nation, observed the laws of hospitality with great exactness to those who put themselves into his power, and in a few days brought Pekuah, with her maids, by easy journeys, to the place appointed, where, receiving the stipulated price, he restored her, with great respect, to liberty and her friends, and undertook to conduct them back towards Cairo beyond all danger of robbery or violence.

The Princess and her favourite embraced each other with transport too violent to be expressed, and went out together to pour the tears of tenderness in secret, and exchange professions of kindness and gratitude. After a few hours they returned into the refectory of the convent, where, in the presence of the prior and his brethren, the Prince required of Pekuah the history of her adventures.

XXXVIII. The Adventures of Lady Pekuah

"At what time and in what manner I was forced away," said Pekuah, "your servants have told you. The suddenness of the event struck me with surprise, and I was at first rather stupefied than agitated with any passion of either fear or sorrow. My confusion was increased by the speed and tumult of our flight, while we were followed by the Turks, who, as it seemed, soon despaired to overtake us, or were afraid of those whom they made a show of menacing.

"When the Arabs saw themselves out of danger, they slackened their course; and as I was less harassed by external violence, I began to feel more uneasiness in my mind. After some time we stopped near a spring shaded with trees, in a pleasant meadow, where we were set upon the ground, and offered such refreshments as our masters were partaking. I was suffered to sit with my maids apart from the rest, and none attempted to comfort or insult us. Here I first began to feel the full weight of my misery. The girls sat weeping in silence, and from time to time looked on me for succour. I knew not to what condition we were doomed, nor could conjecture where would be the place of our captivity, or whence to draw any hope of deliverance. I was in the hands of robbers and savages, and had no reason to suppose that their pity was more than their justice, or that they would forbear the gratification of any ardour of desire or caprice of cruelty. I, however, kissed my maids, and endeavoured to pacify them by remarking that we were yet treated with decency, and that since we were now carried beyond pursuit, there was no danger of violence to our lives.

"When we were to be set again on horseback, my maids clung round me, and refused to be parted; but I commanded them not to irritate those who had us in their power. We travelled the remaining part of the day through an unfrequented and pathless country, and came by moonlight to the side of a hill, where the rest of the troop was stationed. Their tents were pitched and their fires kindled, and our chief was welcomed as a man much beloved by his dependents.

"We were received into a large tent, where we found women who had attended their husbands in the expedition. They set before us the supper which they had provided, and I ate it rather to encourage my maids than to comply with any appetite of my own. When the meat was taken away, they spread the carpets for repose. I was weary, and hoped to find in sleep that remission of distress which nature seldom denies. Ordering myself, therefore, to be undressed, I observed that the women looked very earnestly upon me, not expecting, I suppose, to see me so submissively attended. When my upper vest was taken off, they were apparently struck with the splendour of my clothes, and one of them timorously laid her hand upon the embroidery. She then went out, and in a short time came back with another woman, who seemed to be of higher rank and greater authority. She did, at her entrance, the usual act of reverence, and, taking me by the hand placed me in a smaller tent, spread with finer carpets, where I spent the night quietly with my maids.

"In the morning, as I was sitting on the grass, the chief of the troop came towards me. I rose up to receive him, and he bowed with great respect. 'Illustrious lady,' said he, 'my fortune is better than I had presumed to hope: I am told by my women that I have a princess in my camp.' 'Sir,' answered I, 'your women have deceived themselves and you; I am not a princess, but an unhappy stranger who intended soon to have left this country, in which I am now to be imprisoned for ever.' 'Whoever or whencesoever you are,' returned the Arab, 'your dress and that of your servants show your rank to be high and your wealth to be great. Why should you, who can so easily procure your ransom, think yourself in danger of perpetual captivity? The purpose of my incursions is to increase my riches, or, more property, to gather tribute. The sons of Ishmael are the natural and hereditary lords of this part of the continent, which is usurped by late invaders and low-born tyrants, from whom we are compelled to take by the sword what is denied to justice. The violence of war admits no distinction: the lance that is lifted at guilt and power will sometimes fall on innocence and gentleness.'

"'How little,' said I, 'did I expect that yesterday it should have fallen upon me!'

"'Misfortunes,' answered the Arab, 'should always be expected. If the eye of hostility could learn reverence or pity, excellence like yours had been exempt from injury. But the angels of affliction spread their toils alike for the virtuous and the wicked, for the mighty and the mean. Do not be disconsolate; I am not one of the lawless and cruel rovers of the desert; I know the rules of civil life; I will fix your ransom, give a passport to your messenger, and perform my stipulation with nice punctuality.'

"You will easily believe that I was pleased with his courtesy, and finding that his predominant passion was desire for money, I began now to think my danger less, for I knew that no sum would be thought too great for the release of Pekuah. I told him that he should have no reason to charge me with ingratitude if I was used with kindness, and that any ransom which could be expected for a maid of common rank would be paid, but that he must not persist to rate me as a princess. He said he would consider what he should demand, and then, smiling, bowed and retired.

"Soon after the women came about me, each contending to be more officious than the other, and my maids themselves were served with reverence. We travelled onward by short journeys. On the fourth day the chief told me that my ransom must be two hundred ounces of gold, which I not only promised him, but told him that I would add fifty more if I and my maids were honourably treated.

"I never knew the power of gold before. From that time I was the leader of the troop. The march of every day was longer or shorter as I commanded, and the tents were pitched where I chose to rest. We now had camels and other conveniences for travel; my own women were always at my side, and I amused myself with observing the manners of the vagrant nations, and with viewing remains of ancient edifices, with which these deserted countries appear to have been in some distant age lavishly embellished.

"The chief of the band was a man far from illiterate: he was able to travel by the stars or the compass, and had marked in his erratic expeditions such places as are most worthy the notice of a passenger. He observed to me that buildings are always best preserved in places little frequented and difficult of access; for when once a country declines from its primitive splendour, the more inhabitants are left, the quicker ruin will be made. Walls supply stones more easily than quarries; and palaces and temples will be demolished to make stables of granite and cottages of porphyry.'"

XXXIX. The Adventures of Pekuah (continued)

"We wandered about in this manner for some weeks, either, as our chief pretended, for my gratification, or, as I rather suspected, for some convenience of his own. I endeavoured to appear contented where sullenness and resentment would have been of no use, and that endeavour conduced much to the calmness of my mind; but my heart was always with Nekayah, and the troubles of the night much overbalanced the amusements of the day. My women, who threw all their cares upon their mistress, set their minds at ease from the time when they saw me treated with respect, and gave themselves up to the incidental alleviations of our fatigue without solicitude or sorrow. I was pleased with their pleasure, and animated with their confidence. My condition had lost much of its terror, since I found that the Arab ranged the country merely to get riches. Avarice is a uniform and tractable vice: other intellectual distempers are different in different constitutions of mind; that which soothes the pride of one will offend the pride of another; but to the favour of the covetous there is a ready way—bring money, and nothing is denied.

"At last we came to the dwelling of our chief; a strong and spacious house, built with stone in an island of the Nile, which lies, as I was told, under the tropic. 'Lady,' said the Arab, 'you shall rest after your journey a few weeks in this place, where you are to consider yourself as Sovereign. My occupation is war: I have therefore chosen this obscure residence, from which I can issue unexpected, and to which I can retire unpursued. You may now repose in security: here are few pleasures, but here is no danger.' He then led me into the inner apartments, and seating me on the richest couch, bowed to the ground.

"His women, who considered me as a rival, looked on me with malignity; but being soon informed that I was a great lady detained only for my ransom, they began to vie with each other in obsequiousness and reverence.

"Being again comforted with new assurances of speedy liberty, I was for some days diverted from impatience by the novelty of the place. The turrets overlooked the country to a great distance, and afforded a view of many windings of the stream. In the day I wandered from one place to another, as the course of the sun varied the splendour of the prospect, and saw many things which I had never seen before. The crocodiles and river-horses are common in this unpeopled region; and I often looked upon them with terror, though I knew they could not hurt me. For some time I expected to see mermaids and tritons, which, as Imlac has told me, the European travellers have stationed in the Nile; but no such beings ever appeared, and the Arab, when I inquired after them, laughed at my credulity.

"At night the Arab always attended me to a tower set apart for celestial observations, where he endeavoured to teach me the names and courses of the stars. I had no great inclination to this study; but an appearance of attention was necessary to please my instructor, who valued himself for his skill, and in a little while I found some employment requisite to beguile the tediousness of time, which was to be passed always amidst the same objects. I was weary of looking in the morning on things from which I had turned away weary in the evening: I therefore was at last willing to observe the stars rather than do nothing, but could not always compose my thoughts, and was very often thinking on Nekayah when others imagined me contemplating the sky. Soon after, the Arab went upon another expedition, and then my only pleasure was to talk with my maids about the accident by which we were carried away, and the happiness we should all enjoy at the end of our captivity."

"There were women in your Arab's fortress," said the Princess; "why did you not make them your companions, enjoy their conversation, and partake their diversions? In a place where they found business or amusement, why should you alone sit corroded with idle melancholy? or why could not you bear for a few months that condition to which they were condemned for life?"

"The diversions of the women," answered Pekuah, "were only childish play, by which the mind accustomed to stronger operations could not be kept busy. I could do all which they delighted in doing by powers merely sensitive, while my intellectual faculties were flown to Cairo. They ran from room to room, as a bird hops from wire to wire in his cage. They danced for the sake of motion, as lambs frisk in a meadow. One sometimes pretended to be hurt that the rest might be alarmed, or hid herself that another might seek her. Part of their time passed in watching the progress of light bodies that floated on the river, and part in marking the various forms into which clouds broke in the sky.

"Their business was only needlework, in which I and my maids sometimes helped them; but you know that the mind will easily straggle from the fingers, nor will you suspect that captivity and absence from Nekayah could receive solace from silken flowers.

"Nor was much satisfaction to be hoped from their conversation: for of what could they be expected to talk? They had seen nothing, for they had lived from early youth in that narrow spot: of what they had not seen they could have no knowledge, for they could not read. They had no idea but of the few things that were within their view, and had hardly names for anything but their clothes and their food. As I bore a superior character, I was often called to terminate their quarrels, which I decided as equitably as I could. If it could have amused me to hear the complaints of each against the rest, I might have been often detained by long stories; but the motives of their animosity were so small that I could not listen without interrupting the tale."

"How," said Rasselas, "can the Arab, whom you represented as a man of more than common accomplishments, take any pleasure in his seraglio, when it is filled only with women like these? Are they exquisitely beautiful?"

"They do not," said Pekuah, "want that unaffecting and ignoble beauty which may subsist without sprightliness or sublimity, without energy of thought or dignity of virtue. But to a man like the Arab such beauty was only a flower casually plucked and carelessly thrown away. Whatever pleasures he might find among them, they were not those of friendship or society. When they were playing about him he looked on them with inattentive superiority; when they vied for his regard he sometimes turned away disgusted. As they had no knowledge, their talk could take nothing from the tediousness of life; as they had no choice, their fondness, or appearance of fondness, excited in him neither pride nor gratitude. He was not exalted in his own esteem by the smiles of a woman who saw no other man, nor was much obliged by that regard of which he could never know the sincerity, and which he might often perceive to be exerted not so much to delight him as to pain a rival. That which he gave, and they received, as love, was only a careless distribution of superfluous time, such love as man can bestow upon that which he despises, such as has neither hope nor fear, neither joy nor sorrow."

"You have reason, lady, to think yourself happy," said Imlac, "that you have been thus easily dismissed. How could a mind, hungry for knowledge, be willing, in an intellectual famine, to lose such a banquet as Pekuah's conversation?"

"I am inclined to believe," answered Pekuah, "that he was for some time in suspense; for, notwithstanding his promise, whenever I proposed to despatch a messenger to Cairo he found some excuse for delay. While I was detained in his house he made many incursions into the neighbouring countries, and perhaps he would have refused to discharge me had his plunder been equal to his wishes. He returned always courteous, related his adventures, delighted to hear my observations, and endeavoured to advance my acquaintance with the stars. When I importuned him to send away my letters, he soothed me with professions of honour and sincerity; and when I could be no longer decently denied, put his troop again in motion, and left me to govern in his absence. I was much afflicted by this studied procrastination, and was sometimes afraid that I should be forgotten; that you would leave Cairo, and I must end my days in an island of the Nile.

"I grew at last hopeless and dejected, and cared so little to entertain him, that he for a while more frequently talked with my maids. That he should fall in love with them or with me, might have been equally fatal, and I was not much pleased with the growing friendship. My anxiety was not long, for, as I recovered some degree of cheerfulness, he returned to me, and I could not forbear to despise my former uneasiness.

"He still delayed to send for my ransom, and would perhaps never have determined had not your agent found his way to him. The gold, which he would not fetch, he could not reject when it was offered. He hastened to prepare for our journey hither, like a man delivered from the pain of an intestine conflict. I took leave of my companions in the house, who dismissed me with cold indifference."

Nekayah having heard her favourite's relation, rose and embraced her, and Rasselas gave her a hundred ounces of gold, which she presented to the Arab for the fifty that were promised.

XL. The History of a Man of Learning

They returned to Cairo, and were so well pleased at finding themselves together that none of them went much abroad. The Prince began to love learning, and one day declared to Imlac that he intended to devote himself to science and pass the rest of his days in literary solitude.

"Before you make your final choice," answered Imlac, "you ought to examine its hazards, and converse with some of those who are grown old in the company of themselves. I have just left the observatory of one of the most learned astronomers in the world, who has spent forty years in unwearied attention to the motion and appearances of the celestial bodies, and has drawn out his soul in endless calculations. He admits a few friends once a month to hear his deductions and enjoy his discoveries. I was introduced as a man of knowledge worthy of his notice. Men of various ideas and fluent conversation are commonly welcome to those whose thoughts have been long fixed upon a single point, and who find the images of other things stealing away. I delighted him with my remarks. He smiled at the narrative of my travels, and was glad to forget the constellations and descend for a moment into the lower world.

"On the next day of vacation I renewed my visit, and was so fortunate as to please him again. He relaxed from that time the severity of his rule, and permitted me to enter at my own choice. I found him always busy, and always glad to be relieved. As each knew much which the other was desirous of learning, we exchanged our notions with great delight. I perceived that I had every day more of his confidence, and always found new cause of admiration in the profundity of his mind. His comprehension is vast, his memory capacious and retentive, his discourse is methodical, and his expression clear.

"His integrity and benevolence are equal to his learning. His deepest researches and most favourite studies are willingly interrupted for any opportunity of doing good by his counsel or his riches. To his closest retreat, at his most busy moments, all are admitted that want his assistance; 'For though I exclude idleness and pleasure, I will never,' says he, 'bar my doors against charity. To man is permitted the contemplation of the skies, but the practice of virtue is commanded.'"

"Surely," said the Princess, "this man is happy."

"I visited him," said Imlac, "with more and more frequency, and was every time more enamoured of his conversation; he was sublime without haughtiness, courteous without formality, and communicative without ostentation. I was at first, great Princess, of your opinion, thought him the happiest of mankind, and often congratulated him on the blessing that he enjoyed. He seemed to hear nothing with indifference but the praises of his condition, to which he always returned a general answer, and diverted the conversation to some other topic.

"Amidst this willingness to be pleased and labour to please, I had quickly reason to imagine that some painful sentiment pressed upon his mind. He often looked up earnestly towards the sun, and let his voice fall in the midst of his discourse. He would sometimes, when we were alone, gaze upon me in silence with the air of a man who longed to speak what he was yet resolved to suppress. He would often send for me with vehement injunction of haste, though when I came to him he had nothing extraordinary to say; and sometimes, when I was leaving him, would call me back, pause a few moments, and then dismiss me."

XLI. The Astronomer Discovers the Cause of His Uneasiness

"At last the time came when the secret burst his reserve. We were sitting together last night in the turret of his house watching the immersion of a satellite of Jupiter. A sudden tempest clouded the sky and disappointed our observation. We sat awhile silent in the dark, and then he addressed himself to me in these words: 'Imlac, I have long considered thy friendship as the greatest blessing of my life. Integrity without knowledge is weak and useless, and knowledge without integrity is dangerous and dreadful. I have found in thee all the qualities requisite for trust—benevolence, experience, and fortitude. I have long discharged an office which I must soon quit at the call of Nature, and shall rejoice in the hour of imbecility and pain to devolve it upon thee.'

"I thought myself honoured by this testimony, and protested that whatever could conduce to his happiness would add likewise to mine.

"'Hear, Imlac, what thou wilt not without difficulty credit. I have possessed for five years the regulation of the weather and the distribution of the seasons. The sun has listened to my dictates, and passed from tropic to tropic by my direction; the clouds at my call have poured their waters, and the Nile has overflowed at my command. I have restrained the rage of the dog-star, and mitigated the fervours of the crab. The winds alone, of all the elemental powers, have hitherto refused my authority, and multitudes have perished by equinoctial tempests which I found myself unable to prohibit or restrain. I have administered this great office with exact justice, and made to the different nations of the earth an impartial dividend of rain and sunshine. What must have been the misery of half the globe if I had limited the clouds to particular regions, or confined the sun to either side of the equator?'"

XLII. The Opinion of the Astronomer Is Explained and Justified

"I suppose he discovered in me, through the obscurity of the room, some tokens of amazement and doubt, for after a short pause he proceeded thus:-

"'Not to be easily credited will neither surprise nor offend me, for I am probably the first of human beings to whom this trust has been imparted. Nor do I know whether to deem this distinction a reward or punishment. Since I have possessed it I have been far less happy than before, and nothing but the consciousness of good intention could have enabled me to support the weariness of unremitted vigilance.'

"'How long, sir,' said I, 'has this great office been in your hands?'

"'About ten years ago,' said he, 'my daily observations of the changes of the sky led me to consider whether, if I had the power of the seasons, I could confer greater plenty upon the inhabitants of the earth. This contemplation fastened on my mind, and I sat days and nights in imaginary dominion, pouring upon this country and that the showers of fertility, and seconding every fall of rain with a due proportion of sunshine. I had yet only the will to do good, and did not imagine that I should ever have the power.

"'One day as I was looking on the fields withering with heat, I felt in my mind a sudden wish that I could send rain on the southern mountains, and raise the Nile to an inundation. In the hurry of my imagination I commanded rain to fall; and by comparing the time of my command with that of the inundation, I found that the clouds had listened to my lips.'

"'Might not some other cause,' said I, 'produce this concurrence? The Nile does not always rise on the same day.'

"'Do not believe,' said he, with impatience, 'that such objections could escape me. I reasoned long against my own conviction, and laboured against truth with the utmost obstinacy. I sometimes suspected myself of madness, and should not have dared to impart this secret but to a man like you, capable of distinguishing the wonderful from the impossible, and the incredible from the false.'

"'Why, sir,' said I, 'do you call that incredible which you know, or think you know, to be true?'

"'Because,' said he, 'I cannot prove it by any external evidence; and I know too well the laws of demonstration to think that my conviction ought to influence another, who cannot, like me, be conscious of its force. I therefore shall not attempt to gain credit by disputation. It is sufficient that I feel this power that I have long possessed, and every day exerted it. But the life of man is short; the infirmities of age increase upon me, and the time will soon come when the regulator of the year must mingle with the dust. The care of appointing a successor has long disturbed me; the night and the day have been spent in comparisons of all the characters which have come to my knowledge, and I have yet found none so worthy as thyself.'"

XLIII. The Astronomer Leaves Imlac His Directions

"'Hear, therefore, what I shall impart with attention, such as the welfare of a world requires. If the task of a king be considered as difficult, who has the care only of a few millions, to whom he cannot do much good or harm, what must be the anxiety of him on whom depends the action of the elements and the great gifts of light and heat? Hear me, therefore, with attention.

"'I have diligently considered the position of the earth and sun, and formed innumerable schemes, in which I changed their situation. I have sometimes turned aside the axis of the earth, and sometimes varied the ecliptic of the sun, but I have found it impossible to make a disposition by which the world may be advantaged; what one region gains another loses by an imaginable alteration, even without considering the distant parts of the solar system with which we are acquainted. Do not, therefore, in thy administration of the year, indulge thy pride by innovation; do not please thyself with thinking that thou canst make thyself renowned to all future ages by disordering the seasons. The memory of mischief is no desirable fame. Much less will it become thee to let kindness or interest prevail. Never rob other countries of rain to pour it on thine own. For us the Nile is sufficient.'

"I promised that when I possessed the power I would use it with inflexible integrity; and he dismissed me, pressing my hand. 'My heart,' said he, 'will be now at rest, and my benevolence will no more destroy my quiet; I have found a man of wisdom and virtue, to whom I can cheerfully bequeath the inheritance of the sun.'"

The Prince heard this narration with very serious regard; but the Princess smiled, and Pekuah convulsed herself with laughter. "Ladies," said Imlac, "to mock the heaviest of human afflictions is neither charitable nor wise. Few can attain this man's knowledge and few practise his virtues, but all may suffer his calamity. Of the uncertainties of our present state, the most dreadful and alarming is the uncertain continuance of reason."

The Princess was recollected, and the favourite was abashed. Rasselas, more deeply affected, inquired of Imlac whether he thought such maladies of the mind frequent, and how they were contracted.

XLIV. The Dangerous Prevalence of Imagination

"Disorders of intellect," answered Imlac, "happen much more often than superficial observers will easily believe. Perhaps if we speak with rigorous exactness, no human mind is in its right state. There is no man whose imagination does not sometimes predominate over his reason, who can regulate his attention wholly by his will, and whose ideas will come and go at his command. No man will be found in whose mind airy notions do not sometimes tyrannise, and force him to hope or fear beyond the limits of sober probability. All power of fancy over reason is a degree of insanity, but while this power is such as we can control and repress it is not visible to others, nor considered as any deprivation of the mental faculties; it is not pronounced madness but when it becomes ungovernable, and apparently influences speech or action.

"To indulge the power of fiction and send imagination out upon the wing is often the sport of those who delight too much in silent speculation. When we are alone we are not always busy; the labour of excogitation is too violent to last long; the ardour of inquiry will sometimes give way to idleness or satiety. He who has nothing external that can divert him must find pleasure in his own thoughts, and must conceive himself what he is not; for who is pleased with what he is? He then expatiates in boundless futurity, and culls from all imaginable conditions that which for the present moment he should most desire, amuses his desires with impossible enjoyments, and confers upon his pride unattainable dominion. The mind dances from scene to scene, unites all pleasures in all combinations, and riots in delights which Nature and fortune, with all their bounty, cannot bestow.

"In time some particular train of ideas fixes the attention; all other intellectual gratifications are rejected; the mind, in weariness or leisure, recurs constantly to the favourite conception, and feasts on the luscious falsehood whenever she is offended with the bitterness of truth. By degrees the reign of fancy is confirmed; she grows first imperious and in time despotic. Then fictions begin to operate as realities, false opinions fasten upon the mind, and life passes in dreams of rapture or of anguish.

"This, sir, is one of the dangers of solitude, which the hermit has confessed not always to promote goodness, and the astronomer's misery has proved to be not always propitious to wisdom."

"I will no more," said the favourite, "imagine myself the Queen of Abyssinia. I have often spent the hours which the Princess gave to my own disposal in adjusting ceremonies and regulating the Court; I have repressed the pride of the powerful and granted the petitions of the poor; I have built new palaces in more happy situations, planted groves upon the tops of mountains, and have exulted in the beneficence of royalty, till, when the Princess entered, I had almost forgotten to bow down before her."

"And I," said the Princess, "will not allow myself any more to play the shepherdess in my waking dreams. I have often soothed my thoughts with the quiet and innocence of pastoral employments, till I have in my chamber heard the winds whistle and the sheep bleat; sometimes freed the lamb entangled in the thicket, and sometimes with my crook encountered the wolf. I have a dress like that of the village maids, which I put on to help my imagination, and a pipe on which I play softly, and suppose myself followed by my flocks."

"I will confess," said the Prince, "an indulgence of fantastic delight more dangerous than yours. I have frequently endeavoured to imagine the possibility of a perfect government, by which all wrong should be restrained, all vice reformed, and all the subjects preserved in tranquillity and innocence. This thought produced innumerable schemes of reformation, and dictated many useful regulations and salutary effects. This has been the sport and sometimes the labour of my solitude, and I start when I think with how little anguish I once supposed the death of my father and my brothers."

"Such," said Imlac, "are the effects of visionary schemes. When we first form them, we know them to be absurd, but familiarise them by degrees, and in time lose sight of their folly."

XLV. They Discourse with an Old Man

The evening was now far past, and they rose to return home. As they walked along the banks of the Nile, delighted with the beams of the moon quivering on the water, they saw at a small distance an old man whom the Prince had often heard in the assembly of the sages.

"Yonder," said he, "is one whose years have calmed his passions, but not clouded his reason. Let us close the disquisitions of the night by inquiring what are his sentiments of his own state, that we may know whether youth alone is to struggle with vexation, and whether any better hope remains for the latter part of life."

Here the sage approached and saluted them. They invited him to join their walk, and prattled awhile as acquaintance that had unexpectedly met one another. The old man was cheerful and talkative, and the way seemed short in his company. He was pleased to find himself not disregarded, accompanied them to their house, and, at the Prince's request, entered with them. They placed him in the seat of honour, and set wine and conserves before him.

"Sir," said the Princess, "an evening walk must give to a man of learning like you pleasures which ignorance and youth can hardly conceive. You know the qualities and the causes of all that you behold—the laws by which the river flows, the periods in which the planets perform their revolutions. Everything must supply you with contemplation, and renew the consciousness of your own dignity."

"Lady," answered he, "let the gay and the vigorous expect pleasure in their excursions: it is enough that age can attain ease. To me the world has lost its novelty. I look round, and see what I remember to have seen in happier days. I rest against a tree, and consider that in the same shade I once disputed upon the annual overflow of the Nile with a friend who is now silent in the grave. I cast my eyes upwards, fix them on the changing moon, and think with pain on the vicissitudes of life. I have ceased to take much delight in physical truth; for what have I to do with those things which I am soon to leave?"

"You may at least recreate yourself," said Imlac, "with the recollection of an honourable and useful life, and enjoy the praise which all agree to give you."

"Praise," said the sage with a sigh, "is to an old man an empty sound. I have neither mother to be delighted with the reputation of her son, nor wife to partake the honours of her husband. I have outlived my friends and my rivals. Nothing is now of much importance; for I cannot extend my interest beyond myself. Youth is delighted with applause, because it is considered as the earnest of some future good, and because the prospect of life is far extended; but to me, who am now declining to decrepitude, there is little to be feared from the malevolence of men, and yet less to be hoped from their affection or esteem. Something they may yet take away, but they can give me nothing. Riches would now be useless, and high employment would be pain. My retrospect of life recalls to my view many opportunities of good neglected, much time squandered upon trifles, and more lost in idleness and vacancy. I leave many great designs unattempted, and many great attempts unfinished. My mind is burdened with no heavy crime, and therefore I compose myself to tranquillity; endeavour to abstract my thoughts from hopes and cares which, though reason knows them to be vain, still try to keep their old possession of the heart; expect, with serene humility, that hour which nature cannot long delay, and hope to possess in a better state that happiness which here I could not find, and that virtue which here I have not attained."

He arose and went away, leaving his audience not much elated with the hope of long life. The Prince consoled himself with remarking that it was not reasonable to be disappointed by this account; for age had never been considered as the season of felicity, and if it was possible to be easy in decline and weakness, it was likely that the days of vigour and alacrity might be happy; that the noon of life might be bright, if the evening could be calm.

The Princess suspected that age was querulous and malignant, and delighted to repress the expectations of those who had newly entered the world. She had seen the possessors of estates look with envy on their heirs, and known many who enjoyed pleasures no longer than they could confine it to themselves.

Pekuah conjectured that the man was older than he appeared, and was willing to impute his complaints to delirious dejection; or else supposed that he had been unfortunate, and was therefore discontented. "For nothing," said she, "is more common than to call our own condition the condition of life."

Imlac, who had no desire to see them depressed, smiled at the comforts which they could so readily procure to themselves; and remembered that at the same age he was equally confident of unmingled prosperity, and equally fertile of consolatory expedients. He forbore to force upon them unwelcome knowledge, which time itself would too soon impress. The Princess and her lady retired; the madness of the astronomer hung upon their minds; and they desired Imlac to enter upon his office, and delay next morning the rising of the sun.

XLVI. The Princess and Pekuah Visit the Astronomer

The Princess and Pekuah, having talked in private of Imlac's astronomer, thought his character at once so amiable and so strange that they could not be satisfied without a nearer knowledge, and Imlac was requested to find the means of bringing them together.

This was somewhat difficult. The philosopher had never received any visits from women, though he lived in a city that had in it many Europeans, who followed the manners of their own countries, and many from other parts of the world, that lived there with European liberty. The ladies would not be refused, and several schemes were proposed for the accomplishment of their design. It was proposed to introduce them as strangers in distress, to whom the sage was always accessible; but after some deliberation it appeared that by this artifice no acquaintance could be formed, for their conversation would be short, and they could not decently importune him often. "This," said Rasselas, "is true; but I have yet a stronger objection against the misrepresentation of your state. I have always considered it as treason against the great republic of human nature to make any man's virtues the means of deceiving him, whether on great or little occasions. All imposture weakens confidence and chills benevolence. When the sage finds that you are not what you seemed, he will feel the resentment natural to a man who, conscious of great abilities, discovers that he has been tricked by understandings meaner than his own, and perhaps the distrust which he can never afterwards wholly lay aside may stop the voice of counsel and close the hand of charity; and where will you find the power of restoring his benefactions to mankind, or his peace to himself?"

To this no reply was attempted, and Imlac began to hope that their curiosity would subside; but next day Pekuah told him she had now found an honest pretence for a visit to the astronomer, for she would solicit permission to continue under him the studies in which she had been initiated by the Arab, and the Princess might go with her, either as a fellow-student, or because a woman could not decently come alone. "I am afraid," said Imlac, "that he will soon be weary of your company. Men advanced far in knowledge do not love to repeat the elements of their art, and I am not certain that even of the elements, as he will deliver them, connected with inferences and mingled with reflections, you are a very capable auditress." "That," said Pekuah, "must be my care. I ask of you only to take me thither. My knowledge is perhaps more than you imagine it, and by concurring always with his opinions I shall make him think it greater than it is."

The astronomer, in pursuance of this resolution, was told that a foreign lady, travelling in search of knowledge, had heard of his reputation, and was desirous to become his scholar. The uncommonness of the proposal raised at once his surprise and curiosity, and when after a short deliberation he consented to admit her, he could not stay without impatience till the next day.

The ladies dressed themselves magnificently, and were attended by Imlac to the astronomer, who was pleased to see himself approached with respect by persons of so splendid an appearance. In the exchange of the first civilities he was timorous and bashful; but when the talk became regular, he recollected his powers, and justified the character which Imlac had given. Inquiring of Pekuah what could have turned her inclination towards astronomy, he received from her a history of her adventure at the Pyramid, and of the time passed in the Arab's island. She told her tale with ease and elegance, and her conversation took possession of his heart. The discourse was then turned to astronomy. Pekuah displayed what she knew. He looked upon her as a prodigy of genius, and entreated her not to desist from a study which she had so happily begun.

They came again and again, and were every time more welcome than before. The sage endeavoured to amuse them, that they might prolong their visits, for he found his thoughts grow brighter in their company; the clouds of solitude vanished by degrees as he forced himself to entertain them, and he grieved when he was left, at their departure, to his old employment of regulating the seasons.

The Princess and her favourite had now watched his lips for several months, and could not catch a single word from which they could judge whether he continued or not in the opinion of his preternatural commission. They often contrived to bring him to an open declaration; but he easily eluded all their attacks, and, on which side soever they pressed him, escaped from them to some other topic.

As their familiarity increased, they invited him often to the house of Imlac, where they distinguished him by extraordinary respect. He began gradually to delight in sublunary pleasures. He came early and departed late; laboured to recommend himself by assiduity and compliance; excited their curiosity after new arts, that they might still want his assistance; and when they made any excursion of pleasure or inquiry, entreated to attend them.

By long experience of his integrity and wisdom, the Prince and his sister were convinced that he might be trusted without danger; and lest he should draw any false hopes from the civilities which he received, discovered to him their condition, with the motives of their journey, and required his opinion on the choice of life.

"Of the various conditions which the world spreads before you which you shall prefer," said the sage, "I am not able to instruct you. I can only tell that I have chosen wrong. I have passed my time in study without experience—in the attainment of sciences which can for the most part be but remotely useful to mankind. I have purchased knowledge at the expense of all the common comforts of life; I have missed the endearing elegance of female friendship, and the happy commerce of domestic tenderness. If I have obtained any prerogatives above other students, they have been accompanied with fear, disquiet, and scrupulosity; but even of these prerogatives, whatever they were, I have, since my thoughts have been diversified by more intercourse with the world, begun to question the reality. When I have been for a few days lost in pleasing dissipation, I am always tempted to think that my inquiries have ended in error, and that I have suffered much, and suffered it in vain."

Imlac was delighted to find that the sage's understanding was breaking through its mists, and resolved to detain him from the planets till he should forget his task of ruling them, and reason should recover its original influence.

From this time the astronomer was received into familiar friendship, and partook of all their projects and pleasures; his respect kept him attentive, and the activity of Rasselas did not leave much time unengaged. Something was always to be done; the day was spent in making observations, which furnished talk for the evening, and the evening was closed with a scheme for the morrow.

The sage confessed to Imlac that since he had mingled in the gay tumults of life, and divided his hours by a succession of amusements, he found the conviction of his authority over the skies fade gradually from his mind, and began to trust less to an opinion which he never could prove to others, and which he now found subject to variation, from causes in which reason had no part. "If I am accidentally left alone for a few hours," said he, "my inveterate persuasion rushes upon my soul, and my thoughts are chained down by some irresistible violence; but they are soon disentangled by the Prince's conversation, and instantaneously released at the entrance of Pekuah. I am like a man habitually afraid of spectres, who is set at ease by a lamp, and wonders at the dread which harassed him in the dark; yet, if his lamp be extinguished, feels again the terrors which he knows that when it is light he shall feel no more. But I am sometimes afraid, lest I indulge my quiet by criminal negligence, and voluntarily forget the great charge with which I am entrusted. If I favour myself in a known error, or am determined by my own ease in a doubtful question of this importance, how dreadful is my crime!"

"No disease of the imagination," answered Imlac, "is so difficult of cure as that which is complicated with the dread of guilt; fancy and conscience then act interchangeably upon us, and so often shift their places, that the illusions of one are not distinguished from the dictates of the other. If fancy presents images not moral or religious, the mind drives them away when they give it pain; but when melancholy notions take the form of duty, they lay hold on the faculties without opposition, because we are afraid to exclude or banish them. For this reason the superstitious are often melancholy, and the melancholy almost always superstitious.

"But do not let the suggestions of timidity overpower your better reason; the danger of neglect can be but as the probability of the obligation, which, when you consider it with freedom, you find very little, and that little growing every day less. Open your heart to the influence of the light, which from time to time breaks in upon you; when scruples importune you, which you in your lucid moments know to be vain, do not stand to parley, but fly to business or to Pekuah; and keep this thought always prevalent, that you are only one atom of the mass of humanity, and have neither such virtue nor vice as that you should be singled out for supernatural favours or afflictions."

XLVII. The Prince Enters, and Brings a New Topic

"All this," said the astronomer, "I have often thought; but my reason has been so long subjugated by an uncontrollable and overwhelming idea, that it durst not confide in its own decisions. I now see how fatally I betrayed my quiet, by suffering chimeras to prey upon me in secret; but melancholy shrinks from communication, and I never found a man before to whom I could impart my troubles, though I had been certain of relief. I rejoice to find my own sentiments confirmed by yours, who are not easily deceived, and can have no motive or purpose to deceive. I hope that time and variety will dissipate the gloom that has so long surrounded me, and the latter part of my days will be spent in peace."

"Your learning and virtue," said Imlac, "may justly give you hopes."

Rasselas then entered, with the Princess and Pekuah, and inquired whether they had contrived any new diversion for the next day. "Such," said Nekayah, "is the state of life, that none are happy but by the anticipation of change; the change itself is nothing; when we have made it the next wish is to change again. The world is not yet exhausted: let me see something to-morrow which I never saw before."

"Variety," said Rasselas, "is so necessary to content, that even the Happy Valley disgusted me by the recurrence of its luxuries; yet I could not forbear to reproach myself with impatience when I saw the monks of St. Anthony support, without complaint, a life, not of uniform delight, but uniform hardship."

"Those men," answered Imlac, "are less wretched in their silent convent than the Abyssinian princes in their prison of pleasure. Whatever is done by the monks is incited by an adequate and reasonable motive. Their labour supplies them with necessaries; it therefore cannot be omitted, and is certainly rewarded. Their devotion prepares them for another state, and reminds them of its approach while it fits them for it. Their time is regularly distributed; one duty succeeds another, so that they are not left open to the distraction of unguided choice, nor lost in the shades of listless inactivity. There is a certain task to be performed at an appropriated hour, and their toils are cheerful, because they consider them as acts of piety by which they are always advancing towards endless felicity."

"Do you think," said Nekayah, "that the monastic rule is a more holy and less imperfect state than any other? May not he equally hope for future happiness who converses openly with mankind, who succours the distressed by his charity, instructs the ignorant by his learning, and contributes by his industry to the general system of life, even though he should omit some of the mortifications which are practised in the cloister, and allow himself such harmless delights as his condition may place within his reach?"

"This," said Imlac, "is a question which has long divided the wise and perplexed the good. I am afraid to decide on either part. He that lives well in the world is better than he that lives well in a monastery. But perhaps everyone is not able to stem the temptations of public life, and if he cannot conquer he may properly retreat. Some have little power to do good, and have likewise little strength to resist evil. Many are weary of the conflicts with adversity, and are willing to eject those passions which have long busied them in vain. And many are dismissed by age and diseases from the more laborious duties of society. In monasteries the weak and timorous may be happily sheltered, the weary may repose, and the penitent may meditate. Those retreats of prayer and contemplation have something so congenial to the mind of man, that perhaps there is scarcely one that does not purpose to close his life in pious abstraction, with a few associates serious as himself."

"Such," said Pekuah, "has often been my wish, and I have heard the Princess declare that she should not willingly die in a crowd."

"The liberty of using harmless pleasures," proceeded Imlac, "will not be disputed, but it is still to be examined what pleasures are harmless. The evil of any pleasure that Nekayah can image is not in the act itself but in its consequences. Pleasure in itself harmless may become mischievous by endearing to us a state which we know to be transient and probatory, and withdrawing our thoughts from that of which every hour brings us nearer to the beginning, and of which no length of time will bring us to the end. Mortification is not virtuous in itself, nor has any other use but that it disengages us from the allurements of sense. In the state of future perfection to which we all aspire there will be pleasure without danger and security without restraint."

The Princess was silent, and Rasselas, turning to the astronomer, asked him whether he could not delay her retreat by showing her something which she had not seen before.

"Your curiosity," said the sage, "has been so general, and your pursuit of knowledge so vigorous, that novelties are not now very easily to be found; but what you can no longer procure from the living may be given by the dead. Among the wonders of this country are the catacombs, or the ancient repositories in which the bodies of the earliest generations were lodged, and where, by the virtue of the gums which embalmed them, they yet remain without corruption."

"I know not," said Rasselas, "what pleasure the sight of the catacombs can afford; but, since nothing else is offered, I am resolved to view them, and shall place this with my other things which I have done because I would do something."

They hired a guard of horsemen, and the next day visited the catacombs. When they were about to descend into the sepulchral caves, "Pekuah," said the Princess, "we are now again invading the habitations of the dead; I know that you will stay behind. Let me find you safe when I return." "No, I will not be left," answered Pekuah, "I will go down between you and the Prince."

They then all descended, and roved with wonder through the labyrinth of subterraneous passages, where the bodies were laid in rows on either side.

XLVIII. Imlac Discourses on the Nature of the Soul

"What reason," said the Prince, "can be given why the Egyptians should thus expensively preserve those carcases which some nations consume with fire, others lay to mingle with the earth, and all agree to remove from their sight as soon as decent rites can be performed?"

"The original of ancient customs," said Imlac, "is commonly unknown, for the practice often continues when the cause has ceased; and concerning superstitious ceremonies it is vain to conjecture; for what reason did not dictate, reason cannot explain. I have long believed that the practice of embalming arose only from tenderness to the remains of relations or friends; and to this opinion I am more inclined because it seems impossible that this care should have been general; had all the dead been embalmed, their repositories must in time have been more spacious than the dwellings of the living. I suppose only the rich or honourable were secured from corruption, and the rest left to the course of nature.

"But it is commonly supposed that the Egyptians believed the soul to live as long as the body continued undissolved, and therefore tried this method of eluding death."

"Could the wise Egyptians," said Nekayah, "think so grossly of the soul? If the soul could once survive its separation, what could it afterwards receive or suffer from the body?"

"The Egyptians would doubtless think erroneously," said the astronomer, "in the darkness of heathenism and the first dawn of philosophy. The nature of the soul is still disputed amidst all our opportunities of clearer knowledge; some yet say that it may be material, who, nevertheless, believe it to be immortal."

"Some," answered Imlac, "have indeed said that the soul is material, but I can scarcely believe that any man has thought it who knew how to think; for all the conclusions of reason enforce the immateriality of mind, and all the notices of sense and investigations of science concur to prove the unconsciousness of matter.

"It was never supposed that cogitation is inherent in matter, or that every particle is a thinking being. Yet if any part of matter be devoid of thought, what part can we suppose to think? Matter can differ from matter only in form, density, bulk, motion, and direction of motion. To which of these, however varied or combined, can consciousness be annexed? To be round or square, to be solid or fluid, to be great or little, to be moved slowly or swiftly, one way or another, are modes of material existence all equally alien from the nature of cogitation. If matter be once without thought, it can only be made to think by some new modification; but all the modifications which it can admit are equally unconnected with cogitative powers."

"But the materialists," said the astronomer, "urge that matter may have qualities with which we are unacquainted."

"He who will determine," returned Imlac, "against that which he knows because there may be something which he knows not; he that can set hypothetical possibility against acknowledged certainty, is not to be admitted among reasonable beings. All that we know of matter is, that matter is inert, senseless, and lifeless; and if this conviction cannot he opposed but by referring us to something that we know not, we have all the evidence that human intellect can admit. If that which is known may be overruled by that which is unknown, no being, not omniscient, can arrive at certainty."

"Yet let us not," said the astronomer, "too arrogantly limit the Creator's power."

"It is no limitation of Omnipotence," replied the poet, "to suppose that one thing is not consistent with another, that the same proposition cannot be at once true and false, that the same number cannot be even and odd, that cogitation cannot be conferred on that which is created incapable of cogitation."

"I know not," said Nekayah, "any great use of this question. Does that immateriality, which in my opinion you have sufficiently proved, necessarily include eternal duration?"

"Of immateriality," said Imlac, "our ideas are negative, and therefore obscure. Immateriality seems to imply a natural power of perpetual duration as a consequence of exemption from all causes of decay: whatever perishes is destroyed by the solution of its contexture and separation of its parts; nor can we conceive how that which has no parts, and therefore admits no solution, can be naturally corrupted or impaired."

"I know not," said Rasselas, "how to conceive anything without extension: what is extended must have parts, and you allow that whatever has parts may be destroyed."

"Consider your own conceptions," replied Imlac, "and the difficulty will be less. You will find substance without extension. An ideal form is no less real than material bulk; yet an ideal form has no extension. It is no less certain, when you think on a pyramid, that your mind possesses the idea of a pyramid, than that the pyramid itself is standing. What space does the idea of a pyramid occupy more than the idea of a grain of corn? or how can either idea suffer laceration? As is the effect, such is the cause; as thought, such is the power that thinks, a power impassive and indiscerptible."

"But the Being," said Nekayah, "whom I fear to name, the Being which made the soul, can destroy it."

"He surely can destroy it," answered Imlac, "since, however imperishable, it receives from a superior nature its power of duration. That it will not perish by any inherent cause of decay or principle of corruption, may be shown by philosophy; but philosophy can tell no more. That it will not be annihilated by Him that made it, we must humbly learn from higher authority."

The whole assembly stood awhile silent and collected. "Let us return," said Rasselas, "from this scene of mortality. How gloomy would be these mansions of the dead to him who did not know that he should never die; that what now acts shall continue its agency, and what now thinks shall think on for ever. Those that lie here stretched before us, the wise and the powerful of ancient times, warn us to remember the shortness of our present state; they were perhaps snatched away while they were busy, like us, in the CHOICE OF LIFE."

"To me," said the Princess, "the choice of life is become less important; I hope hereafter to think only on the choice of eternity."

They then hastened out of the caverns, and under the protection of their guard returned to Cairo.

XLIX. The Conclusion, in Which Nothing Is Concluded

It was now the time of the inundation of the Nile. A few days after their visit to the catacombs the river began to rise.

They were confined to their house. The whole region being under water, gave them no invitation to any excursions; and being well supplied with materials for talk, they diverted themselves with comparisons of the different forms of life which they had observed, and with various schemes of happiness which each of them had formed.

Pekuah was never so much charmed with any place as the Convent of St. Anthony, where the Arab restored her to the Princess, and wished only to fill it with pious maidens and to be made prioress of the order. She was weary of expectation and disgust, and would gladly be fixed in some unvariable state.

The Princess thought that, of all sublunary things, knowledge was the best. She desired first to learn all sciences, and then proposed to found a college of learned women, in which she would preside, that, by conversing with the old and educating the young, she might divide her time between the acquisition and communication of wisdom, and raise up for the next age models of prudence and patterns of piety.

The Prince desired a little kingdom in which he might administer justice in his own person and see all the parts of government with his own eyes; but he could never fix the limits of his dominion, and was always adding to the number of his subjects.

Imlac and the astronomer were contented to be driven along the stream of life without directing their course to any particular port.

Of those wishes that they had formed they well knew that none could be obtained. They deliberated awhile what was to be done, and resolved, when the inundation should cease, to return to Abyssinia.

FINIS

Valthea
I READ PEOPLE

The Daughters, Book One

C.K. MALLICK

Valthea
I READ PEOPLE

The Daughters, Book One

C.K. Mallick

Canterbury House Publishing

www. canterburyhousepublishing. com
Sarasota, Florida

Canterbury House Publishing
www. canterburyhousepublishing. com

Copyright © 2016 C. K. Mallick
All rights reserved under International and Pan-American Copyright Conventions.
Book Design by Tracy Arendt

Library of Congress Cataloging-in-Publication Data

Names: Mallick, C. K.
Title: Valthea : I read people / C.K. Mallick.
Description: First edition. | Sarasota, Florida : Canterbury House Publishing,
Ltd., 2016. | Series: The daughters ; book 1 | Summary: "Exuberant and gifted
teen, Valthea Sarosi, reads people's past and excels at gymnastics. The determination to find her birth parents, headline a circus, and experience true love,
lead her to perform at festivals throughout Romania with a Gypsy troupe and
an East European, Cirque du Soleil-style circus"-- Provided by publisher.
Identifiers: LCCN 2015048887 (print) | LCCN 2016005296 (ebook) | ISBN
9780990841661 (trade pbk. : alk. paper) | ISBN 9780990841678 (E-Pub) Sub-
jects: | CYAC: Psychic ability--Fiction. | Supernatural--Fiction. | Birthparents-
-Fiction. | Love--Fiction. | Circus--Fiction. Classification: LCC PZ7.1.M347 Val
2016 (print) | LCC PZ7.1.M347 (ebook) | DDC [Fic]--dc23
LC record available at http://lccn.loc.gov/2015048887

First Edition: March 2016

For information about permission to reproduce selections from this book write to:
Permissions
Canterbury House Publishing, Ltd.
4535 Ottawa Trail
Sarasota, FL 34233-1946

Dear Readers,
Your acts of compassion
have great affects.

Circus Tour Countries

PART I

VALTHEA

ONE

"**H**urry, Valthea. The Gypsies are onstage."

My friend, Lyla and I made our way through the crowd at the Bucharest Spring Festival, down paths infused with cinnamon donuts, roasting garlic, and cotton candy. We passed elderly women in babushkas and long skirts, teen boys in black *Puma* sneakers, and nouveau riche couples in designer jeans and gold jewelry. Strolling festival-goers consumed gyro wraps, Italian ice, and Romanian beer. I scanned the faces of anyone over thirty-five with light brown hair and amber eyes. The woman at the ticket gate said the annual festival drew over two-thousand people on weekends. I hoped my mother and father, whoever they were, would be among them.

We hustled past rows of tents selling everything from dried herbs and bronze genie bottles to mobile phone and tablet cases. We positioned ourselves about twenty-feet from the front of the outdoor stage where the *Roma*, or "Gypsies" as they're commonly called, performed. The Gypsy troupe's musicians stood at the back playing violins, mandolins, and accordions. Three women in corseted blouses and colorful skirts danced in the center. On the right, a man with a ponytail juggled neon-orange Frisbees while riding a unicycle. On the left, a forty-something-year-old man pressed into a one-handed arm balance on top of a chair. Watching them perform fed my desire to fulfill my dream of joining a circus.

On the corner nearest us, an attractive guy about seventeen dipped the ends of three juggling clubs into a bucket. He looked about six-foot, and more Viking than Roma, with his blond hair and broad shoulders. He surveyed the audience with a big grin, nodding as he lit the clubs one-by-one. His eyes met mine. My pulse quickened. I didn't look away, but smiled. He dropped one of the torches. The audience gasped. He quickly grabbed it and then continued his act, tossing the clubs in the air.

My guardian, who I called Aunt Sylvie, told me that when I saw "the one", I'd know it right away. I thought the notion silly, yet I couldn't take my eyes off the golden-haired Gypsy.

Lyla nudged me. "The fire-juggler's primo, isn't he?"

Gorgeous was more like it. "He's all right."

"Are you crazy? He's *more* than all right."

Who was this blond Gypsy? What was he like? I slowed my breathing, softened my gaze and relaxed and waited. Seconds later, a vision came.

A toddler with white-blond hair stood alone, next to a pastry tent at a crowded festival. A girl, wearing a shawl tied over a long skirt, knelt down and offered him a crescent cookie. He smiled and took the cookie. She didn't look at him, but at the people walking by. She stood, scooped the toddler up on her hip, and trotted off. He cried. She quickly covered his mouth with one hand and ducked behind a neighboring tent.

Who was the girl? Was it his older sister? They didn't look anything alike. But if they were siblings, why'd he cry? Maybe he was her spoiled little brother. Or maybe she was a stranger. I wished the recent past of the primo guy had come to me instead of his childhood. I could *almost* always read the people I wanted to, but I could never control the timeframe of the visions that came through. I watched as the cute juggler continued to maneuver his flaming clubs in the air. What was this guy like? Was he nice or a jerk? Did he have a girlfriend? Did he want one? I never saw the future. Glancing into people's past was my gift, or curse, depending on what I saw. I didn't know why certain scenes appeared, but I knew not to misuse the insight. *Be careful*, Aunt Sylvie warned me. *You reap what you sow.*

Lyla and I clapped along with the festival-goers when the troupe finished their act.

"Your auntie would've loved this, Val. Why didn't she come? Miss Helga invited her."

"I don't know, she was going to but changed her mind when I showed her the flyer. Why didn't your parents come?"

"Out of town, as usual." Lyla shrugged.

The hand-balancing man ran to the front of the stage carrying a microphone. "*Mulţumesc!* Thank you," His voice sounded from the park's loud speakers. "Welcome my fellow Romanians and all visiting on this fine spring day. I am Cosmo Dobra. My family and I have traveled from Brasov to perform for you this weekend. We are—*The Gypsy Royales!*"

We moved forward, weaving through the crowd, until we were about twelve-feet from the stage.

The Gypsy leader moved across the front of the stage, stealth as a panther, and then stopped.

The crowd quieted.

The man's salt and pepper goatee framed his grin. "So ... " He spoke with command into the mike. "Who has a talent and would like to join us onstage in our next number?"

People shouted, "*Eu fac!* I do, I do!"

"Pick me!" I yelled, waving my arms overhead.

"Valthea—what are you doing?" Lyla pulled my arms down. "This isn't one of your staunch gymnastics competitions. This is a mob of people in a park, and some of them drunk. If you don't *wow* them, they'll boo you off stage."

"I know, Lyla. Thanks, but he has to pick me."

"It's not a good idea." She stepped in front of me, blocking my view of the stage. "The fire-juggler will think you're showing off."

"I don't care. This festival happens once a year. There's supposed to be over a thousand people here today, which could include my parents. I have to go up there so that they can see me.

"Yeah ... I forgot about that." Lyla shook her head and stepped aside. "You just don't give up, do you? You're always looking for them. But Val, how do you know they'll recognize you? You're fifteen. Miss Sylvie adopted you when you were under a year old. It's kind of hard to—"

"They'll recognize me. And I'm almost sixteen. I have to look like one, or both, of them by now. But for them to recognize me, they've got to see me."

"Volunteers, raise your hands." The Gypsy leader, Cosmo Dobra scanned the eclectic mix of park visitors like a panther scoping his potential prey. "Who will my sister, Apollonia, choose?"

The prettiest of the dancers, and the only one wearing a headscarf, glided down from the stage and into the first part of the crowd.

"I dance as good as any Gypsy!" said the hefty woman in a medieval-style dress, standing in front of me.

"I can sing!" a man hollered from the back, swinging a bottle of ale over his head.

"I volunteer!" I shouted, shooting my arms up overhead in a V.

Lyla jumped up and down, pointing at me, and yelled, "She's a gymnast. She can do aerials!"

"I doubt it," said the woman in the medieval-dress. "She's pretty scrawny."

"Prove it," someone yelled from behind us. "Show us!"

Lyla whipped around. "My friend will show you all right." She started clapping and chanting, "Choose Valthea! Choose Valthea!"

She tucked and wove in and through the crowd encouraging people to clap and chant along. Within thirty-seconds, a quarter of the crowd had joined in.

I'd met Lyla in first grade, riding bikes on the trail of the woods connecting our worlds. Although she went to a private girl's academy, and I went to public school, we had remained best friends. But I never told Lyla I could read people. Only Aunt Sylvie knew of my God-given gift.

Apollonia made her way through the crowd swishing her deep-purple Gypsy skirt and smiling. Her red, tightly-cinched corset, worn over a white, puff-sleeved blouse, accentuated her womanly figure. She shooed the crowd back, causing the area to clear around us. "You volunteered?" Her pomegranate-red lip gloss shined, and her eyes, dark and lined like Cleopatra's, held mine.

My heart pounded. "Yes."

She gripped my wrist with her hand and lifted my arm in the air. "I choose this girl!" She whispered, "What's your name?"

I stared at her headscarf, which covered Apollonia's forehead and crown. Did she wear the scarf, Gypsy-girl-style, as part of her costume, or to hide something … like a birthmark? Although the half-inch, pink V birthmark on my forehead looked more like a small scar than a birthmark, it was still distinct. Were birthmarks inherited? Could this woman be—? I brushed my bangs to the side.

Apollonia glanced up at my forehead, but said nothing.

I smoothed down my bangs. Even if Apollonia was twenty-nine, she was probably too young to be my mother.

"Hey." Apollonia jerked my arm. "I *said*, what's your name?"

Surprised at her roughness, I leaned away from her. "Valthea. Valthea Sarosi."

She smiled at Cosmo onstage, while digging her fingernails into the skin of my wrist. "Our guest performer is—Valthea!" She released her grip and dropped my arm. "Follow me."

I couldn't read Apollonia. Some people are hard to read, like those with multiple personalities or highly manipulative people who believe their own lies. I figured I couldn't read her because my thoughts were on giving a great performance on stage and praying that my parents were in the audience.

"Show them what you've got!" Lyla yelled.

Through applause and whistles, I followed Apollonia up the stage steps.

Cosmo Dobra put an arm around me and pointed to the front of the stage. "All right, Valthea. This is your area. Do only what you're comfortable doing." He lifted a brow. "No accidents. Just relax. Do your thing. Got it?"

"Got it."

"And remember," he said walking backwards, grinning, "smile!"

The Gypsy musicians started to play a lively piece while the dancers spun and shook tambourines. Cosmo climbed onto a stack of chairs and pressed himself into a handstand while the blond Gypsy tossed his flaming hoops.

I took a deep breath, kicked into a handstand, and then walked on my hands across the stage. The crowd applauded. I did a walkover to come to my feet and then turned around and assessed the space in front of me. Time to blow away the audience and especially that fire-juggler. I ran full speed into a series of back handsprings, finishing with a super high layout. The festival goers' cheers shot me up with adrenaline. I loved performing live. The musicians finished their song, and the troupe members struck a pose. I stretched my arms overhead, arched my back, and smiled.

Cosmo hopped down from his chair pyramid, ran to the microphone stand, and unhooked the mic. "*Mulţumesc*, thank you!" He gestured toward us. "We are *The Gypsy Royales*. Allow me to introduce you. Our beautiful and passionate dancers are Gabi, Lumi, and Apollonia. Our ever enthusiastic unicyclist and juggler is the talented Silver. At the far corner, our torch tosser is Sorin."

Sorin. I heard nothing after hearing his name—

"And Valthea Sarosi!" Cosmo waved me over to join him center stage. "Let's hear it for our amazing guest!"

I smiled and waved. *Yes*. The approving hollers and cheers fed something starving within me.

Cosmo turned off the mic, took my hand in his, and we bowed together. Bent over, my eyes went to his bulging forearm veins, weaving like highways across his olive skin. I wanted veins just like his.

We straightened from our bow. "You should come with us." He smiled and waved at the audience. "Travel and perform."

Was he serious? Performing was my dream.

He released my hand, turned on the mic, and strode to the microphone stand. "Our troupe will now come down and meet you. We'll tell you your fortune and teach you to juggle. We will return onstage in thirty-minutes for another show. Thank you, and see you then."

"Valthea!" Lyla stood at the side of the stage.

I ran down the steps.

She slapped my hand in a high-five. "You were awesome, girl!"

"Thanks. Hope I looked okay."

"Are you kidding? You looked like you belonged. *Stea de circ!*"

A circus star. That's what I wanted. I'd do anything to make that dream come true.

TWO

"**V**althea!"

Who called me? I climbed up the stage steps and looked out. My Aunt Sylvie approached the stage. "Auntie!" I ran down the steps and met her with a hug. "You came after all. Did you see me up there?"

"Yes, dear, I did. You were remarkable. I'm sorry I didn't come with you initially."

"That's all right."

"Hi, Miss Sarosi." Lyla greeted my auntie with a kiss to each cheek.

"Hello, dear."

"Valthea was awesome, wasn't she?"

"Yes, she's a superb gymnast, but I'm afraid I'm taking her home now."

"Home? Why? We can't go now. I was just onstage. A thousand people heard my name blasting from the loudspeakers." I whispered, "One of my parents could be—"

"Girls!" Miss Helga, Lyla's governess walked up behind Aunt Sylvie. "You two shouldn't have run off like that. But oh, Valthea, you were wonderful."

My auntie turned around. "Hello, Miss Helga."

"Oh, Miss Sarosi, you're here. I thought you didn't want to come. We invited you to—"

"Yes, I know, and thank you, Miss Helga. I decided to come at the last minute. Anyway, I'll see Valthea home. I so appreciate you inviting her. Come along, Valthea. Good day, Miss Helga. We'll see you soon, Lyla." Auntie turned and headed into the crowd.

"Thank you for inviting me, Miss Helga. Bye, Lyla." I glanced up at the stage. The troupe had cleared. I spotted two of the dancers mingling with the crowd, and one of the musicians talking to a set of parents with a young son. Where'd Sorin go?

"Hey, Valthea—"

"Yeah, Lyla?"

"You were a superstar today!" She shot her arms in the air in a V. "Superstar!"

"Thanks." That's what I wanted to hear. "Call you later."

I headed down the festival's pathway, not in hurry to catch up to my overly spry auntie. I passed a wood carver's booth, a kiosk selling chocolate truffles, and a table where an exotic-looking woman applied *mehndi* to a girl's hand. No Sorin. An attractive couple—old enough to be my parents, walked toward me with their arms around each other.

Look at me, I thought. Look at my birthmark. I could be the daughter you wished you kept. They passed without a glance. A woman pushing a stroller headed my way. Her toddler squirmed in his seat.

I stepped off the festival's center pathway to re-clip my bangs off my forehead. "Cute baby," I said, smiling at the baby's mother.

"Thank you," she said, pleasant enough, continuing to push the stroller.

I continued down the path. What if my mother's life improved after she abandoned me? Maybe she had other children, a year or two after I was born. I'd run a million Internet searches looking for my parents. I found nothing. Maybe my search, my hope, was silly.

Aunt Sylvie had gained fifty-feet on me. I ran to catch up to her. "Leaving already?"

I stopped and turned. "Mr. Dobra?"

"So formal." He put a hand on my shoulder and drew me off the pathway. "Call me, Cosmo."

I looked ahead on the pathway. Where'd my auntie go? I trembled. Stereotyping, or not, I did not want to be kidnapped. "I need to go," I said.

Cosmo dropped his hand from my shoulder and opened his arms wide while stepping back. "But, of course."

His past came in a flicker.

Cosmo, six-years-old, stood on a sidewalk between bunches of string balloons secured by buckets of dirt. He wore a blue satin jumpsuit and an orange bow tie. A man, maybe his father, nudged him toward a small crowd. Behind them, a brown bear with purple and yellow ruffles around its neck paced its cage. Little Cosmo juggled three beanbags in the air. After a few moments, he threw them to the side and walked on his hands for about fifteen-feet on the sidewalk.

Another vision appeared.

An eighteen-year-old Cosmo sat at the base of a three-tier fountain. He held hands with a girl with milk-white skin and peach-colored hair. They kissed.

"Great job up there, young lady," a man said, strolling by with two young girls.

He startled me back to the present. "Thank you," I said.

"Tremendous, isn't she?" Cosmo grinned. "Stick around. The troupe will be back onstage shortly."

The little girls waved good-bye.

I waved. "Bye-bye."

"So." Cosmo walked backward toward a pair of oak trees, two of many throughout the park. "Are you here with Sylvanna Sarosi?"

"You know my auntie?"

"Auntie?" He raised his eyebrows. "Is that what she is?" He leaned against the oak with scores of lovers' names etched in its trunk.

"Not by blood." I smoothed a few flyaway bangs to the side, hoping to draw his attention to my birthmark. "She adopted me when I was a—"

"Dad!" Sorin, ran from behind me up to Cosmo.

I quickly removed my hair clip and finger-combed my bangs down.

"Dad, where is—oh." He grinned. "Never mind. Here she is. Hi, Valthea."

"Uh ... hi."

"Let me officially introduce you two." Cosmo stepped in between us. "Sorin, this is Valthea. Valthea, this is my son, Sorin."

"Nice to meet you," I managed to say. The father and son didn't look anything alike. Cosmo had dark hair, rough skin, and a compact, muscular body. Sorin stood nearly a half a foot taller with a head of gold. Maybe Sorin's mother was German or Hungarian, with his blue, no, *azure* eyes.

"And nice to officially meet you, Valthea."

I liked how Sorin stretched out the end of my name, emphasizing the "ah" sound.

He leaned into me, and we greeted each other European-style, kissing one cheek then the other. Afterward, he stepped back, but his eyes never left mine. "You're not only excellent, but you're a brave gymnast. It takes courage to jump up on stage in front of a bunch of people. Very impressive."

My palms started to sweat. I was surprised no visions of Sorin's past came to me. "Thanks. Great juggling acts."

"I've been waiting for you."

We all turned.

Aunt Sylvie had made her way back and stepped out of the crowd to join us by the tree.

"Auntie, I just stopped to thank Cosmo—"

"It's entirely my fault." Cosmo bowed his head and clicked his boot heels together. "Sylvie. How long has it been?" He took her hand and kissed it. "It's amazing and wonderful to see you."

"I wish I could say the same, finding you here with my Valthea."

"Ah, feisty as ever. You haven't aged in the last sixteen years."

Aunt Sylvie remained stoic. "And you haven't changed your charming ways."

Sorin glanced at her and then back at me.

My auntie and I didn't look alike either. I'd always compared us to a black forest cake and a biscotti wafer. My hearty seventy-two-year-old guardian wore her graying-black hair in a loose bun, and her cheeks stayed blush against her porcelain skin. I had a slim body, long wheat-colored hair, and amber eyes. Against Auntie's wishes, I rimmed my eyes with black eyeliner to make them look more cat-like, like a wild Lynx.

Auntie stiffened. "I'm Valthea's sole guardian and parent."

"I see. Wonderful." Cosmo drew Sorin in closer to them. "Sylvie, look. Recognize him? This is the young man you saved as a boy. Amazing, huh? He's so strong now and smart. Smarter than all of us."

"Dad, please." Sorin pulled away from him.

My auntie's eyes welled.

What? Aunt Sylvie saved Sorin?

She stared at him. "I ... I can't believe it. You're a handsome, strong young man now."

"Miss Sylvie, I just want to tell you how much I appreciate what you did for me when I was little. I never had the chance to tell you thank you."

She opened her arms. "Oh." They hugged, and she patted his back, tears running down her cheeks. "I need a tissue," she said, giggling as she stepped away. She pulled one out of her pocketbook.

"Ah, Valthea." Cosmo put one arm around me. "You see? There's no such thing as a coincidence. You came to the festival today, not yesterday or tomorrow, but today. My sister selected you out of a huge crowd at the biggest festival in all of Romania. And as it turns out, I met your auntie years ago. You see, when my son was small, she saved his life using herbs. Amazing how God works, isn't it?"

"Aunt Sylvie, you never told me you saved someone's life."

"He exaggerates, as usual. Cosmo, if you recall, I gave the child herbs, but I also told you to take him to a doctor for antibiotics. That helped make him better, not the herbs alone."

"Except," Cosmo folded his arms across his chest and shrugged. "I never took him to the doctor."

Auntie's face blanched. "You didn't?"

"It's history now, Sylvie. Let's talk about the future, Valthea's future." He took her hand and put it inside the crook of his elbow and led her back onto the thoroughfare.

Sorin and I followed.

"I can't believe my auntie saved your life."

"Yeah, and I can't believe she's your aunt."

"Actually, she adopted me when I was a baby. I call her aunt, but she's really my mom."

We continued following Aunt Sylvie and Cosmo.

"Our show could use a good gymnast," Cosmo said, leaning into Aunt Sylvie. "Tumbling gets an audience loosened up and applauding. I'd like her to join us."

Auntie yanked her arm from Cosmo's. "Out of the question."

I walked up behind them. "But I want to. It'd be great preparation for a circus audition."

"Son, gather the troupe for the next show. I'll be right there."

"Okay, Dad. Miss Sylvie, I hope to see you again soon." Sorin hugged her good-bye. "Hey, wait a minute—Dad, why don't the four of us go to dinner tonight?"

"Wonderful idea!" Cosmo clapped his hands. "We'll dine with Miss Sylvie and our new friend."

"Can we, Auntie? You haven't seen them in a while. We can talk about—"

"Lots of things." Cosmo raised one brow high.

"My dad's told me so much about you, Miss Sylvie. I feel like I know you. I'd like to know more of you *and* of Valthea."

"What a fine young man you've grown up to be." Aunt Sylvie looked up at Sorin. "Very well. Valthea and I will join you gentlemen for dinner."

Thank God.

"*Magnific!*" Cosmo put one arm around my auntie and one around me.

Sorin walked backward toward the stage and waved at me. "I look forward to it, Miss Sylvie. See you tonight, Valthea."

My mouth had dried in my nervousness. "Bye!" I hoped ten yards was far enough away for him not to see my upper lip stuck to my gums.

"We'll dine, Cosmo," Aunt Sylvie said. "But there's nothing for us to discuss. Valthea is a straight-A student and a world-class gymnast. She doesn't need to play around at festivals pretending to be a Gypsy."

"Ah, Sylvie." Cosmo lowered his voice. "It's not so different than an aristocrat joining the circus. You could've had a posh life, a husband, children, and by now, grandchildren."

"Wait, Auntie. You never told me you were an aristocrat."

She waved a hand. "He exaggerates, as usual. Listen, Cosmo, my past has nothing to do with Valthea's future. If anything, it's something to learn from."

"Tell me Sylvie," Cosmo whispered, "how did you come to be Valthea's guardian?"

Aunt Sylvie's cheeks brightened to cherry red. "Properly. So don't get any ideas. She's not for sale, kidnap, or—"

"Easy, Sylvie. Just asking. You're such a mother bear. One of the many qualities I love about you." He kissed her on the cheek. "But perhaps it's time you let her out of your protective cave? Let Valthea travel with us. I'll look after her for the summer."

A Romanian polka blared from the park's loudspeakers. Through a split in the crowd, we saw the Gypsy musicians playing and the rest of the troupe assembling on stage.

"How's seven o'clock at *The Freesia Café*? It's in Old Town, across from the telecom skyscraper, next to that old Communist apartment building."

Auntie nodded. "Yes, across from St. John's Church."

"Right." Cosmo took her hands in his. "Listen, Sylvie, I'm not asking to—just take Valthea away from you. She could join us on her school's spring and summer breaks, like Sorin does."

"I'd love that!"

"Of course you would, Valthea." Cosmo kissed Aunt Sylvie's hands before releasing them. "Remember, Sylvie." He grinned. "You can't stop destiny." He turned and made his way through the crowd toward the stage, stealthy as a panther.

THREE

S trings of citron bulbs lined the outdoor terrace of the *Freesia Café*, setting it aglow under the night's moonless sky. Flowered vines of white freesia sprawled from huge terracotta pots set throughout the terrace, and stems of the flowers poked out of the green sea-glass vases set atop each dinner table. I inhaled the floral perfume and imagined a romantic first date with—

"There's Sorin." Aunt Sylvie waved as he walked toward us from the back of the café. They hugged. "My goodness, you're handsome." She looked at me with raised brows and wide eyes.

Total embarrassment.

"Thank you, Miss Sylvie. Hi, Valthea."

"Hi." Our eyes locked for half a second before we kissed each other's cheek.

We joined Cosmo at the back table. After greetings, Sorin held out the chair next to him. I sat and scooted forward as he tucked me in. Cosmo did the same for Aunt Sylvie.

"Good evening." The waitress placed a basket of bread on the center of our table and gave us each a menu. "Here you are. One of *Freesia Café's* many specialties—fresh-baked, sourdough potato bread. I'll give you a few minutes to look over the menu. Tonight's specials are clipped to the front."

"Thank you." Cosmo gave her back the wine menu. "In the meantime, would you please bring us a bottle of your house Merlot?" He leaned into Aunt Sylvie. "You'll love it. You can taste the black cherries." He straightened. "Oh, and miss, we'd like it room temperature, please. That's how you like it, right Sylvie?"

Auntie's eyes lit up. "Yes."

"Very good, sir. Be back in a moment."

"You surprise me, Cosmo, remembering such details."

"Ah, Sylvie, I remember everything about those I hold dear."

Sorin passed her the bread basket. "Miss Sylvie, I'm glad we're finally seeing each other again."

"I am too, Sorin." She took a piece of bread and passed the basket to Cosmo. "This bread smells delicious."

"My dad never wanted to bother you. He didn't want to pressure you to visit us just because you two knew each other a long time ago."

"Which is fine, Sorin. That's the one thing your father and I have in common." Auntie tore the crust off her piece of bread and buttered the remaining soft center. "We let the past be the past. We give thanks for our experiences and go on with our lives, happily. Actually, he's theatrical. I'm happy."

"Can't I be happy *and* theatrical?" Cosmo pulled two pieces of bread from the basket, extracted their soft middle, and put them on Auntie's bread plate. "There you go."

She smiled, but then spoke in a serious tone. "Thank you." She placed her bread's crust on his plate.

Cosmo grinned.

"But Auntie, you don't let go of the past. You save everything." I shifted in my chair to face Sorin. "She also rescues animals. We have a cat she brought back to health and a crow she raised since it was a fledgling."

Sorin rotated his chair to face me. "Does the crow do tricks?"

The waitress walked up to our table with the bottle of wine. She filled Cosmo and Aunt Sylvie's wine glasses three-quarters of the way, set the bottle between them, and headed back to the kitchen.

"Kind of. Nawa knows a bunch of commands, and he comes when we call him." I didn't tell Sorin how Nawa helped Aunt Sylvie find me when I was a baby, crying in the woods. Would I ever? Maybe he'd be the first person I'd tell about my gift. I peeked at him studying his menu. No vision came. My crush on Sorin must have dampened my ability to read him.

"Valthea, what are you hungry for?" Cosmo said, looking over the menu.

"Um, I don't know. Same as you." I handed the waitress my menu. She gave me a peculiar look before walking away. "What's her problem?" I mumbled.

"Amazing!" Cosmo slapped the table. "Our little Valthea likes blood sausage."

"Blood sausage? No I don't."

Sorin laughed and handed me his menu. "Pick something less scary and I'll tell her."

"Okay ... I'll have a feta, tomato salad."

"Safe choice." Sorin stood. "Be right back."

"Sylvie. Let's talk." Cosmo drummed on the table for several counts and then folded his hands, placing them on the table. "We have a win-win situation here. Our troupe needs something fresh and exciting to raise our popularity this summer. Valthea wants preparation for her future career in the circus."

I loved that he assumed I'd have a circus career.

C.K. Mallick

"If Valthea traveled with us, she'd also see our beloved Romania. She'd see the countryside and cities, the historical architecture, and our churches. So, what do you think?" Cosmo sat back in his chair.

"I think Valthea is a serious gymnast who shouldn't give up her training and technique to play around at festivals for three months."

"But Auntie—"

"Valthea—Cosmo and I are talking."

"Yeah, about my life. Please, Auntie. To get into a circus, I *have* to be a great entertainer. Please let me do this." I didn't voice it, but the exposure throughout Romania also increased the chances of my finding one or both of my parents or of them finding me. Sorin's eyes met mine. Three months allowed plenty of time for Sorin and I to become friends. My insides tingled. I looked away and then back at him again. His eyes hadn't left me. I sipped water to cool down. I wanted Sorin, and not just as a friend.

Cosmo leaned forward again, resting his folded hands on the table. He spoke quietly. "Sylvie, you know Valthea can work drills and technique on the road. That's not a problem. But holding her back from achieving her potential will be. This young lady's an achiever."

"I know she's an achiever. I raised her."

Cosmo's eyes went wild, and he threw his hands in the air. "Then why, Sylvie? Why would you want her to possess only the dry technique of going for a point score? What about artistic expression and *joie de vivre*? What about tumbling and dancing in front of a live audience because it's your love, and your life depends on it? Tell me, Sylvie. Why would you hold her back?" He caught his breath and continued. "You, Sylvie, you were a joyous circus dancer. I saw the photos." Cosmo winked at me. "She was dazzling. And you deserve to be, too."

Aunt Sylvie gulped the last of her wine. "You do make a good point regarding the education of travel."

"Great point." I added with enthusiasm.

Our waitress and one other walked up to our table, balancing plates on their arms and palms.

"Blood sausage?" the second waitress asked.

"Here." Cosmo held up his hand.

"Grilled eggplant for you." Our waitress served Sorin and then faced me. "And you ended up with the feta, tomato salad, correct?"

"Yes, thank you." Sorin and I looked at each other and laughed.

"And for you ma'am, the *sarmale*." The second waitress served my auntie the cabbage roll dinner.

"Thank you."

The waitresses refilled Sorin and my water glasses and Cosmo and Auntie's wine glasses and then left our table.

Auntie raised her wine glass. "Here's to our reunion and this fine meal. Thank you for the invitation gentlemen."

We tapped glasses.

Cosmo kept his wine glass raised. "And no more talk of this summer during the meal."

"Good," Aunt Sylvie muttered.

"We'll conclude after the meal." Cosmo winked at me.

I liked Sorin's father. He saw me as a person and respected my dreams.

At the end of our meal, Auntie had drunk three full glasses of wine. "Valthea—"

"Yes, Auntie?"

"If I decide you can travel with Cosmo and his troupe, I'd want a two-page letter from each city you visit. You'd write about what you saw and what you learned while there."

"No problem. I'll write ten-page letters. Plus, I'll keep Nawa's cage clean, weed the entire herb garden, and varnish the stairs. And remember, I'm getting all A's in school again."

"Ah, such a good girl, our Valthea. A little angel."

"Our?" Aunt Sylvie planted her pocketbook on the table, causing it to rock once.

"Yeah, Dad." Sorin said, tracing the outline of my face and shoulders with his eyes. "With the lights glowing behind her, Valthea does look like an angel."

I felt my face flush. The lights also illuminated Sorin's silhouette. He looked like a knight astride a stallion returning home from battle, glowing in the morning's first light.

Cosmo looked from me to Sorin and smirked. "So, Sylvie, what do you say?" He pulled several bills out from his stuffed wallet and paid the waitress.

"Thank you kindly for dinner, Cosmo." She stood.

He quickly helped her with her chair. "You're welcome, but you know what I'm asking."

"Yeah, Auntie, you never said whether I could—"

"Goodnight, Sorin." She gestured for me to get up. "We need to go, Valthea. Mr. Karl is probably waiting outside to pick us up this very minute."

"Still don't drive, eh Sylvie?" Cosmo moved her chair out of her way. "We could've picked you up and took you home. Who's Mr. Karl, anyway?"

"A neighbor and friend."

I stayed planted in my chair. "Auntie, what about all that good stuff Cosmo said? My seeing our homeland ... architecture ... churches?"

Auntie held her pocketbook with both hands. "Sorin, I look forward to seeing you perform tomorrow. Valthea and I will be in the audience. We need to see how a Gypsy Royale show is run. I want Valthea to know what to expect while travelling with your troupe this summer."

I jumped from my chair and hugged her. "Yes Auntie—thank you! Thank you so much!"

"Ah, that's my Sylvie!" Cosmo maneuvered around Sorin and threw his arms around her. "I *knew* you'd do what was best for our Valthea." He rocked her in a dance.

"Oh, stop." She playfully hit him with her pocketbook. 'It's only for one summer."

"Or maybe two." Cosmo pulled me into him and Aunt Sylvie and then waved over Sorin. "Come. Time for our reunion hug."

Sorin put an arm around my auntie. "Get used to it, Valthea. My dad makes the troupe huddle and all hug before every show." He put an arm around my waist.

My knees went weak. The golden-haired fire-juggler thrilled me in ways I'd only read about. I didn't care that I couldn't breathe, or that we stood in a group hug in the middle of a busy restaurant. Sorin's touch captured me. Now I wanted only one thing—more.

PART II

THE GYPSY ROYALES

FOUR

I traveled from Bucharest to Brasov on June 2nd, anxious and ready for my summer adventure with *The Gypsy Royales*. For the next three months, I'd work, live, and travel with a group of eleven strangers. Well, two of them I sort of knew. Over the past six weeks, Sorin and I'd spoke on the phone several times a week, sent each other pictures, and text-messaged daily. My auntie spoke with Cosmo multiple times regarding the "particulars" of my traveling with them.

As soon as my bus pulled into the Brasov station, I spotted Cosmo pacing the sidewalk and talking on his phone. "Valthea!" he yelled, when I stepped off the bus. He greeted me with a big hug. "How was the ride? Are you hungry? Let me get your bags."

"Uh, good, no, and thank you." Cosmo's attention and enthusiasm made me laugh and put me at ease right away.

"The troupe's excited you're joining us this summer." He picked up my stuffed duffel bags. "Most of them anyway. My car's this way."

Most of them? I followed Cosmo through the parking lot. He pushed a button on his keychain, and the trunk of the black Maserati parked ahead of us popped open.

"I've never ridden in a Maserati before."

"Ha! You'll love it." He put my bags in the trunk and opened the passenger door for me. Once in, he handed me a brand new pair of aviators from the glove box. "For you. Now, fasten your seat belt."

Cosmo drove us out of the city and fast along winding roads up a hill. Thirty-minutes later, he turned down a street leading to an old three-story stone home. I rolled down my window. Grandfather oaks and fir pines bookended the place like huge towering guards. Second story balconies shot out from the west side, overlooking bushes thick with sweet-smelling lilacs and bright fuchsia azaleas. On the other side, beds of yellow poppies spotted the ground like tossed handfuls of lemon drops.

"This is where you live? I had no idea that—"

"That *Romas* could do so well?" Cosmo's white teeth contrasted his dark sunglasses. "Just like all cultures of people, we have a range of income, priorities, and inclinations. My family's never traveled with other Gypsies or partook in some of the stereotypical cons and schemes. *Roma* is our background, but we are first and foremost, entertainers and property owners. Here, we have almost ten acres. Eight of it is forest. "

I sat up. "I love the woods."

"Sylvie said you were a nature girl. There's a pond on the east side. Great spot for a picnic. Maybe Sorin and my niece, Lumi, can take you there."

Or just Sorin. I pictured myself alone with him, sitting on a blanket holding hands, kissing—

"Here we are, the Dobra House." Cosmo parked in the front of the hillside home. "It's your home while we rehearse for the next two weeks and any other time you'd like to visit. Now let's get you inside. My son can't wait to see you."

"Really? I mean, that's nice. I look forward to seeing him too." Look forward? *Dying* to see him was more like it.

Cosmo carried my bags and led me up the steps.

Vines of dead roses climbed across the front of the house and part of the wide wooden door. He held it open for me as I walked in. The spacious front room held no furniture other than a foyer table holding a half a dozen sets of keys. Light from two gauze-covered windows cast shadows on the tile entranceway floor. Cosmo set my bags at the base of the stairs in the center of the room. The house smelled of espresso and patchouli. Although it was a summer afternoon, it seemed more like an autumn evening inside the Dobra House.

"My sister Gabi and her husband Gheorghe, our violinist, went to the market. You'll meet them later." He led me to the left of the stairs. "The rest of the gang's probably in the TV room."

I walked behind him, running my hand across one of the six rough-textured columns in the entry and front room. The sound of a television blaring came from the room ahead of us.

"Hey, everyone look who's here—Valthea!"

Four people, two of whom I recognized from the festival, lounged on a black leather, L-shaped sectional couch facing a huge, flat screen TV. Sorin wasn't with them. Cups, ashtrays, and a few coffee-stained auto magazines covered the glass coffee table. In its center sat a ceramic bowl of dead garden roses and a stick of burning incense.

"*Alo.*" I raised my hand in a meek side-to-side wave. The group wore almost entirely black. Only the model-handsome guy's distressed light blue jeans and white t-shirt, and the full-bodied woman's mauve blouse broke up the dark mass.

"This is Valthea," Cosmo spoke over the TV. "She's the wonderful acrobat who joined us on stage this spring. Remember?"

I didn't recognize the woman in the mauve top or the beefy man next to her. At least they looked away from the television and smiled at me. Why didn't Apollonia, the beauty who'd picked me from the crowd at the festival, come over and greet me? Didn't she remember me? She could have at least looked up. Just like the first time I met her, no vision came.

I crossed my arms in front of my chest. I thought the troupe would welcome me in and be excited to see me, like I'd been to see them. Maybe the whole touring-with-the-Gypsies-thing was a mistake. I looked over my shoulder at the empty hallway. Where was Sorin? Hopefully, he really was looking forward to seeing me.

Cosmo pointed to the guy wearing light blue jeans.

The thirty-something-year old man had a square jaw line, big, honey-colored eyes, and defined arms. He sat next to Apollonia on the couch.

"Strum, kill the TV, please."

The man called Strum aimed the remote at the screen and shut it off.

Strum looked about five years younger than he did now. He ran down a soccer field. He swiped the ball away from another player, and then kicked it into the goal. The crowd in the stands leapt to their feet and cheered.

"Now, let's try this again, shall we?" Cosmo gestured to Apollonia texting on her phone. "You've already met my youngest sister, Apollonia."

She didn't look up. "What's your cell phone number, Valthea?"

I brightened. Maybe Apollonia was one of those people who were shy when not on the stage. I told her my number. A moment later, my phone vibrated. I pulled it out of my jean's pocket.

"You don't belong here. Go home."

Sucker punch. I felt sick. I didn't look at Apollonia, Cosmo, or anyone, but slid my phone back into my jeans. I had wanted to emulate the confident woman *and* be her friend. Now I just wanted to go home.

"Apollonia," Cosmo said through clenched teeth, "say hello."

"*Alo,*" she mumbled, snuggling up to Strum. She whispered in his ear and then burst out laughing.

Apollonia's beauty wilted and dried before my eyes. Okay, so, she wasn't the goddess I imagined her to be. Fine. But intimidation by her was not an option. I had too much to gain in the summer ahead. I planted my feet on the floor.

Cosmo pointed to Strum. "Valthea, this is Strum, my sister's fiancé."

Apollonia pulled a cigarette out of a tarnished silver case and held it to her lips.

"He's one of our three musicians."

Strum flipped open a polished, brushed-silver lighter and lit Apollonia's cigarette.

She took a drag and relaxed back on the couch.

Strum looked up at me. "Welcome to the troupe, Valthea." His kind tone surprised me.

Apollonia elbowed him.

"Hey—" He faced her. "What's your problem?"

"Must introductions be so difficult?" Cosmo took a breath. "Valthea, Strum plays mandolin, acoustic guitar, and electric guitar."

"I remember. You and the other musicians played great."

Strum flipped open his lighter, clicked on a one-inch flame, and held it up. "Thank you, Valthea."

Apollonia shoved him again.

Strum shut the lighter and put his face to hers. "Calm the hell down, woman." He set his lighter on the coffee table and picked up the mandolin leaning against the wall. He tuned its strings as Cosmo continued introducing me. The sound of the tuning added a surreal layer to the shadowy house and the ribbon of incense weaving through the room.

"This is Bruno." Cosmo said, extending his arm toward the hefty man sitting in the center of the couch. "He's from Italy."

"This note's for Bruno." Strum changed the string he tuned, sounding a deeper, heavier note.

Big-Bruno chuckled. "Good one, Strum." He started to push off the sectional to stand.

"It's okay, Bruno. Don't get up. It's nice to meet you."

"Welcome, Valthea," he said with a grunt, sitting back down and depressing the cushion under him. "It's nice to have you with us."

I exhaled. Maybe the weird vibe I felt earlier was coming from Apollonia, not the group.

"Thank you, I'm excited to join troupe."

Apollonia pointed her cigarette at me. "Are you really?"

"Don't start, sis." Cosmo turned back to Bruno. "Bruno's the troupe's fantastic auto mechanic. He keeps us running. Why else would I let an Italian in our troupe?"

"I'll tell you why, Valthea." Bruno chuckled. "I'm in love with his older sister—my lovely bride." He brought the hand of the woman in the mauve blouse to his lips. The plump woman had a face like a cherub. I didn't remember seeing her at the spring festival.

"I'm Rosa." Bruno's bride walked around the coffee table and gave me a big hug. "Welcome to the troupe and our family."

"Thank you." I liked her already.

"Rosa is our incredible costume mistress," Cosmo said. "She's also my sister. I know we don't look alike. We're sort of half-siblings."

Rosa walked to the open counter area connecting the TV room to a wet bar. She grabbed a bowl full of pistachios. "Sorin's with the others in the game room. He must not know you're here because he's *very* excited to see you."

My heart skipped a beat.

"That's where we're going now." Cosmo led me down a narrow hall to a turquoise door with cat scratches at the base. Cosmo pushed the door open wide. The sound of dragons warring on a video game blared at full volume. I stepped into a game room painted half orange and half turquoise. A worn sofa faced a flat screen TV and pool table. Behind it, laptops and car models covered three desks. Sorin sat at the corner desk with his back to us, facing a laptop and wearing earphones.

"This is Dino." Cosmo yelled over the gaming roar. He pointed to the bearded man in his thirties sitting on the sofa. "He and our violinist are cousins. Dino plays percussion, accordion, *and* video games."

The guy mumbled hello and curved his body like it would help him win the game.

"This is Silver," Cosmo continued. "He—"

"Rides unicycle and juggles." I said, remembering his ponytail and the silver-gray streak in his coal-black hair.

Cosmo nodded. "Good memory."

Silver quickly waved, but stayed focused on the game "*Alo-eee!*"

"*Alo,*" I said.

"Valthea!" Sorin yanked off his earphones and leapt from his chair. "You're finally here." He ran up and hugged me tight, just like I'd imagined every night before falling asleep for the past six weeks.

His heart pounded in my ear. We loosened our grip and stepped back.

"At last a decent welcome for our girl." Cosmo turned off the TV.

Dino jumped up, holding his controller over his head. "What the hell are you doing?"

Silver dropped his controls to the floor and hopped up. "Forget the game! Let's welcome Valthea with a round of *le fee vert*." He waved his index finger in the air. "Also known as the green fairy." He shoved Dino. "Grab your lighter."

"I'm sure Miss Sylvie doesn't approve of the intoxicating absinthe. But, Valthea, if you like, we can toast with wine or soda instead."

"Thanks, Sorin. Soda sounds good." I didn't want to drink wine and risk acting silly.

"You sure?" Silver took my hand, kissed it, and let it go. "No green fairy?"

"Not this time." A vision flashed in my mind's eye of the hyper unicyclist kicking and head-butting soccer balls with the bearded musician, Dino.

Silver popped Dino on the shoulder. "Hey—say hello to Valthea."

Being friendly seemed to drain Dino's energy. "*Alo*," he mumbled. "So, what else do you like to do beside walk on your hands?"

"Well, I ... " I had to get *some* of the troupe on my side. "I love watching soccer."

"You like soccer? Yahoo!" Silver hooked his arm through mine and swung me around folk-dance-style.

Dino almost looked alive. "The new girl likes *fotbol*? That's cool."

"What's cool?" The blonde teen I'd seen dance at the spring festival walked in the room. I didn't remember her two-inch-thick black roots.

"Lumi," Dino quickly stepped away from me. "Want to join us for absinthe?"

Cosmo faced the girl in need of a box of hair dye. "First, meet our new acrobat."

Silver grabbed Dino by the shoulders and led him out to the hallway. "Let's drink!"

"Valthea, this is my niece, Luminata. She's my sister, Gabi, and violinist, Gheorghe's, daughter. You'll share a room with her in their family's motor home once we hit the road."

"Hi, Luminata."

She gave me a snide look. "What are you, my mother? I go by Lumi." She left the room.

Sorin whispered, "Lumi's always moody. It's not you." He brushed my bangs to the side. "Interesting mark. I like it."

I brushed my bangs down. "Thanks."

C.K. Mallick

"Okay, time to meet Grandmamma." Cosmo waved me out of the game room. "Ma prefers the old Roma language, but her Romanian's all right. She knows what you're saying."

"*And* thinking." Sorin guided me with his hand on the small of my back, whispering, "I'll come with you. She can be a little grouchy."

The shiver his touch sent through my body made me more than willing to tolerate a few grouches over the summer.

Cosmo walked us down the hall to the other side of the house. "Ma's over seventy now. But don't let her fool you. She doesn't miss a thing. She's sharp. Gabi, my sister you haven't met yet, thinks it's because Ma birthed Apollonia in her forties." He shrugged. "Kids keep you young. Anyway, we all started calling her *Grandmamma* after Gabi had Lumi." Cosmo stopped at the end of the hall. He opened the door slowly.

Muskiness and dim light seeped out of the room before we stepped in. Grandmamma sat on a black velvet chair in the center. Behind her, burgundy drapes hung heavy over the room's only window. The old woman's head scarf framed her potato-shaped face and accentuated her sour expression. Her right hand gripped the round head of a wooden cane. She narrowed her eyes and looked at me with an expression of disgust.

"This is my mother, Romilda Dobra—Grandmamma."

Twenty years ago, Grandmamma stood next to a mail box at the end of a long driveway. She scowled at the letter-size pink envelope she held in her hand. She glanced behind her at the property's three-story home. It was the Dobra House. She ripped the envelope in half. In the next image, Grandmamma wore a different apron, but the same scowl. She pulled two pink envelopes from the mail box. Without hesitation, she ripped them in half and tucked them into her apron pocket.

"Ma, say *alo.*"

The old woman's glare bore through me.

Sorin touched my shoulder, making me jump. "Don't mind her," he whispered. "It's nothing personal."

I nodded, but it sure felt personal. I pulled my vibrating cell phone out of my pocket. Apollonia.

"Hey, Acro-rat, Next bus leaves at 5. Get on it!"

FIVE

The next morning I awoke to one thought—*what a witch!* No way would I let Apollonia make a fool of me. I'd show her. I got out of bed, dressed, brushed my teeth, and went up to the practice room on the third floor an hour before rehearsal time.

The room equaled almost the length of a basketball court. Painted in terracotta, the room welcomed me with more warmth than most members of *The Gypsy Royales*. Sherbet colors from the sunrise poured through the east windows, splashing the walls and vaulted ceiling. On the opposite side, full-length mirrors reflected forest pines and far away mountains. I put my towel, wrist tape, and phone on a chair, and then opened the sliding glass door leading to the balcony. Hanging chimes tinkled from the morning breeze.

I warmed up for twenty minutes and then practiced gymnastic drills. I ran through the center of the room, shooting out stag leaps, switch leaps, and side leaps, imagining myself dashing through an Impressionist painting. I practiced walkovers and handsprings. Working out felt great and renewed my positivity about the summer ahead.

Lumi's mother, Gabi arrived first, at eight-forty-five. "*Bună dimineața*, Valthea."

"Good morning, Gabi." I'd met the thirty-seven year old brunette the night before at dinner, along with her musician husband, Gheorghe.

She left her slippers at the door, untied her wrap sweater, and tossed it on a stack of mats in the corner of the room. "Good. You're not one of those chronically late people."

The rest of the troupe had assembled in the rehearsal room by nine-fifteen. The musicians, Gheorghe on violin, Dino on percussion and accordion, and Strum on guitar and mandolin, set up and tuned their instruments. The rest of us warmed up our bodies. I stretched out on the mats farthest from the door.

At nine-thirty sharp, Cosmo strut the length of the room, coffee tumbler in hand. "My dear family, we must remember, it's not enough to simply dance, juggle, or play a mandolin. We must deliver more. Why? Because—" He beat his chest once with his free hand. "We are *The Gypsy Royales!* It is our job to bedazzle and electrify. We blend the Old World with the new. We show an audience what's possible." He continued to pace. "We're not amateur street performers. *Nooo*. We are talented messengers of skill and thrill. It's vital that from the moment we walk on stage we capture the hearts and minds of our audience."

The bearded musician, Dino mumbled, "Too much, too early."

Not for me. I sat on the gym mats, enthralled. I never heard such passion from my gymnastics' coach's pep talks. Coach Muzsnay focused and encouraged us, but Cosmo's speech made me want to dazzle him and every person in every festival audience. I'd make them love me.

"Remember," Cosmo said, quieter now. "They want us to command their attention. They want us to control them."

We rehearsed under Cosmo's guidance for three-hours, and then broke for thirty minutes before meeting back upstairs. As the troupe trickled in, Sorin joined me on the mats for stretching out. Apollonia walked by her fiancé, Strum, taking the wallet from his back pocket. She tapped his shoulder and waved it overhead. He grabbed it out of her hand and kissed her. They laughed and went out to the balcony.

"Sorin, does Apollonia pick pockets at the festivals?"

"She better not. Dad caught her doing it last year. She's only supposed to paint faces."

"It's such a negative stereotype."

"We each do something between shows to bring in additional income, you know, tips." Sorin stood and did side-to-side bends. "Don't worry. My dad calls pick-pocketing what it is—stealing. He's totally against it."

I hopped up and mirrored Sorin's moves. "How do *you* bring in additional money?"

"I book our troupe for parties. I contact charities and party planners weeks before we arrive in scheduled cities. They check out our website, and then some call me or come to the show. One good booking per month equals more than what everyone brings in combined."

"Pretty ingenious."

"I started doing it a couple of years ago. I used to teach kids how to juggle."

Sorin pantomimed juggling and then pretended to miss one of his imaginary objects. He stumbled into me and, for several divine seconds, his body pressed against mine. I stepped back and laughed it off, hoping no one saw.

"Uh, is that what Bruno does?"

Big-Bruno and Dino arm wrestled at a fold-out table in the corner.

"Yeah, he arm-wrestles for bets. He beats pretty much everyone, except little kids. He lets them win. He doesn't earn that much because kids love him." Sorin pointed to Gabi and Grandmamma standing by the front door. "They read cards, of course. Too bad Lumi's already making and selling jewelry. You'd probably be good at that."

"And what about you?" Apollonia startled me from behind. "What are *you* going to do? You can't just sit around like a spoiled primadonna gymnast."

"I'm not spoiled and—"

"Cut the name-calling." Sorin stepped between us. "It's rude and juvenile."

"How dare you speak that way to me? *I* am family. I'm here to stay. *She's* just some girl to entertain you for the time being."

Refusing to believe Apollonia's words didn't keep my heart from sinking.

"Valthea's not just some girl from the crowd," Sorin said. "She's traveling with our show, and she's family of Miss Sylvie. Reason enough to show her respect."

"No, it's not. Respect's earned. She hasn't earned anything. Forget her. Where's your respect for me? I raised you, took care of you. I gave up my teen years for you."

"Come on, Apollonia. Let's not get into this."

"Why? You afraid your little friend will hear the truth?"

"The truth? The truth is that *Cosmo* was always there for me." Sorin stood between me and Apollonia. "He raised me. *You* babied me. And as I grew older, you sabotaged my friendships and told lies to every girl I liked so they'd stay clear of me. The truth is you don't respect me."

Cosmo walked into the room, talking on his phone. Sorin and Apollonia didn't see him.

"That's not true," Apollonia hissed. "I cared for you as if you were my son, not just a nephew. This thing. ... " She pointed at me. "She just came into your life minutes ago. She'll mean nothing to you come September."

A lump swelled in my throat.

Cosmo threw up his arms. "Enough!" He slipped off his shoes, put down his phone, and walked on the mats to the center of the room.

Apollonia planted her fists on her hips. "Well, how *is* she going to earn extra cash?"

C.K. Mallick

Cosmo faced me. "Valthea, do you have an idea of what you'd like to do?"

I glared at Apollonia. "Not steal."

"Of course not." Cosmo glanced at Apollonia. "I forbid such behavior."

"I have an idea for the girl, and it's a profitable one." Apollonia walked to her fiancé. Her sly smile warned me venom would follow.

"What's the idea?" Cosmo huffed.

"Several times a year high schools set up fairs to raise money for whatever. They have target games, dunking booths, and those cardboard cut-outs for stupid-looking photographs. Of all the stations, the most profitable is always the kissing booth. It's not really a booth, but a loveseat placed on a raised platform or stage, so people can see. A popular senior girl sits on the loveseat and kisses boys who pay the fee. Of course at our festivals, Valthea would kiss boys and men of all ages and walks of life. I'm sure your little pet can learn to kiss in a week. I could teach her." She grabbed Strum's shoulders, pulled him close, and kissed him on the lips.

Strum quickly wiped the lipstick from his mouth with the back of his hand. "Don't make me part of your little game." He pulled a cigarette from his shirt pocket and headed toward the balcony.

Apollonia laughed at him—or maybe at me. I couldn't tell. Either way, her cackling sounded like one of Disney's evil sorceresses.

Sorin and my eyes met.

Cosmo caught our exchange. "Watch yourself, sister. You sound like a jealous witch."

Good. Cosmo and I thought alike.

"Jealous? Of what? A mousey-haired tomboy? Please. Her own mother didn't want her."

With a single bite, Apollonia's fangs tore open my deepest wound. Her words flung me into a dark pit with no air. Suffocating inside, I didn't have the strength to chop the reptile into pieces. Apollonia slithered outside onto the balcony. Lucky snake.

"Hey—" Cosmo yelled after her. "I didn't call a break." He waved her off. "I'll deal with her later. Valthea, I have to ask the same of you as I do the others."

Sorin practically lunged at Cosmo. "I don't think a kissing booth is a good idea."

"Son, she's not going to kiss anyone." Cosmo held his stance on the squishy mats.

Apollonia stormed back into the rehearsal room. "If I can paint the faces of snotty-nosed kids, this acro-rat can kiss their perverted, idiot fathers."

"No, Apollonia. She's not going to kiss any men. It's not right. Sylvie would have my head, and I believe my son would, too."

The troupe whoo-whooed and someone sang, "*Love birds, love birds ...* "

I wanted to become invisible or better yet, sprout wings and fly off the balcony. I took a deep breath and spoke over everyone. "I'll tell fortunes."

The moment of silence didn't last.

"Really?" Cosmo raised an eyebrow. "Unless Sylvie's changed her viewpoint on divining in the last two decades, you didn't learn how to read cards from her."

Sorin looked perplexed.

Grandmamma scowled.

"You read cards?" Gabi asked. "I don't believe it."

"I believe her." Rosa sat by the door, stitching a ripped costume.

"She never told me she read cards." Lumi put the wristbands she'd been working on in a cigar box and closed the lid. "What do you do—shuffle the deck while walking on your hands?"

Sorin put his hand on my shoulder. "If Valthea says she can—"

"Enough!" Cosmo sliced the air with his hand, quieting everyone. "Valthea, do you or do you not, read cards?"

"Not cards. I read ... uh ... palms."

He drew his chin in. "Really?"

I nodded. I had to fib.

Sorin smirked. Did he like that I read palms?

"No!" Grandmamma heaved herself from her chair. "Mouse insult Dobra family. Pretends to read palm—ruin true fortune telling." She flicked her hand. "No good. Go home."

Cosmo walked toward her and Gabi. "Ma, Valthea works hard. She's a good gymnast. The crowd will love her on stage. She's perfect for our show. She's not going anywhere."

Apollonia folded her arms. "Ma, why don't we let her prove herself—right now?" She smiled her fakest smile.

"Good," Grandmamma grunted. "Cosmo pick two. I listen. Others eat *gogosi* donuts in kitchen."

Apollonia grabbed Strum's hand and, in exaggerated flamboyance, sashayed toward the hall. "Count us out."

Cosmo scanned the room. "All right, uh, Dino?"

"I'll volunteer, Dad." Sorin stepped forward.

"No!" Grandmamma pounded her cane on the wood floor. "Dino."

"I can't believe this family." Sorin stormed out of the room. "Fine. I've college applications to work on."

Dino stopped polishing his accordion and set it on its stand.

Silver, the unicyclist with the ponytail, stopped juggling tennis balls and tossed them into a wood crate near the door. "Love to stay and play, but caffeine and sugar call my name."

"I'll volunteer." Rosa laid the mended costume on the chair next to her and stood. "Valthea can read my palm."

Big Bruno kissed Rosa on the cheek on his way out of the room. "I'll save you a doughnut, my rose."

"Thank you, bear."

Cosmo rubbed his hands together. "All right, Valthea. Greet Dino like he was someone at a festival. Go ahead, Dino."

Dino walked across the mats in his black socks.

"Sir," I said in an upbeat tone, "would you like your palm read?"

"No." Dino kept walking.

"Val, don't ask a question that can be answered with a yes-or-no," Cosmo coached like he was a film director. "Try again. Okay, Dino, go."

"Sir, give me your hand," I said in a seductive way. "I'll read your palm and tell you your past based on the lines I see."

"No thanks." Dino walked by me again.

"Sheesh. This is harder than I thought."

"*Da*," Grandmamma said. "More hard when telling future."

I spun around. "I don't see the future, Mrs. Dobra. I see the past and what makes people who they are." She glared at me from underneath her hooded eyes, but I didn't care.

"Hey, Cosmo, am I done here?"

"No Dino, one more time."

Dino walked slower this time.

Dino sat a bar. A blond, with her back to him, flirted with a broad-shouldered man wearing a baseball cap. Dino stood and exchanged heated words with the man. In the next moment, they wrestled on the bar-room floor.

"Sir, give me your palm and I'll tell you why your right hand and wrist bother you." I offered my upturned hand.

Dino stopped this time and inched his right hand toward me. I took it and then held out my other hand. "Donation, please."

"That's my girl!" Cosmo gave me a thumbs-up. "Tell him the fee is ten *lei*."

"The fee is ten *lei*."

Dino mimed handing me money.

I didn't look at Dino's palm, but gazed past him, recalling the image I'd seen. "You fell on your hand during a fight. Your wrist is pretty much healed. But the reason for the fight gnaws at you."

"Come on, Dino," Cosmo said. "Play along. Ask Valthea something, like what caused the fight."

"A female, of course," I said. "The girl provoked the fight. You told her it was time to go. She said, no. She wasn't finished talking to her new friend. When you went to take her hand to leave, the big-shouldered guy told you to back off and respect the young ladies wishes. Again, you told her, 'let's go.' Again she refused, and the guy said, 'Hey, buddy, either you're not her man, or she's not a lady.' With your chest puffed out, you said, 'Watch what you say.' And then—*boom*—down you went to the floor from his push. You said nothing afterward, but her immature behavior wears on you."

"All guessing!" Grandmamma shouted. "Mouse knows nothing. Dino put ice on hand last night. Girls love Dino. The boyfriends don't. If this festival, he'd want money back."

I kept Dino's hand in mine. Aunt Sylvie taught me to never show off or abuse my ability, but this old woman needed to be put in her place. Traveling with the troupe offered me the chance to perform for thousands of people, possibly find my parents, and the chance to get to know Sorin.

"I'm sorry, Mrs. Dobra, but Dino wouldn't ask for his money back if I said the girl's *name*."

"Whoa, that's not necessary." Dino spoke clearly for the first time. "What you said was enough." He flipped me a fifty-*bani* coin. "Keep it," he said loud enough for Grandmamma to hear. He then slipped a few bills in my pocket while making eye contact and whispered, "Say no more." He passed Grandmamma on the way to the door. "She's good. Let her read palms."

Grandmamma pointed her cane at his back. "No, she—"

"Ma, its fine." Rosa joined me on the center mat. "Dino warmed her up. Now she's ready for me." She gave me her hand. "I'd like my palm read, please."

"Thanks," I whispered and then play acted. "I'd be happy to, ma'am." Two flashes of Rosa's recent past appeared.

Grandmamma shouted across the room. "Rosa easy. Simple girl." She waved her hand. "Not hard to read chubby goose."

Rosa cast her eyes to the floor.

"Rosa," I whispered, holding her hand with both of mine, "you are a lovely person. Grandmamma is lucky to have you as a daughter." If Grandmamma wanted to be rude to an outsider like me, fine. But Rosa was her eldest and most obedient daughter. It wasn't right.

The old woman stacked her palms atop her cane, leaned forward on her chair, and pursed her lips like a wolverine ready to spit.

I focused on Rosa. She reminded me of a fairy godmother, with her sparkling eyes, pink cheeks, and joyful disposition.

Rosa sat hunched over a sewing machine facing an open window. "Listen to you, Molly Mockingbird," she said to the bird heard singing outside. She giggled. "Your songs keep me working." In another scene, Rosa stood amongst festival-goers near the stage watching her family's troupe perform on stage. She cheered along with crowd. Afterward, she walked back to the troupe's caravan of motor homes, staring at the ground the whole way.

Was Rosa sad because she wasn't a performer, or did she simply long for appreciation? "Rosa," I whispered, "everyone knows you're an excellent seamstress and a kind person. What you do, you do with love. When you sew, you imagine Cosmo, Sorin, Silver, and the musicians looking handsome, and Gabi, Lumi, and Apollonia looking beautiful in their costumes. You see them in your mind juggling, singing, and dancing. Every stitch you sew and every mend you make enhances the troupe's performance. That love, *your* love, helps bind the troupe."

Rosa's lower lip quivered.

I placed a hand on her shoulder. "When an audience applauds, it's also for you. You probably don't get praise for your work, but it *is* appreciated. Most of the family knows you put your heart and soul into it. Bruno, Cosmo, and Sorin, they know. And—so does God."

Rosa threw her arms around me, sobbing. "Thank you."

Twice my size, she nearly smothered me, but I held her and hugged her back.

"*Prostie!* Silly." Grandmamma banged her cane on the floor. "Orphan mouse makes tears. What she whisper, we don't want."

"Hush, Ma!" Rosa let go of me, wiped her eyes, and faced the old woman. "Valthea's readings are sound. Leave her alone. She whispered out of respect. And by the way, my tears are not sad ones. They're happy ones." She faced me. Her voice softened. "What Valthea told me, I've wanted to hear for long a time." Rosa thrust her hand into her skirt pocket and drew out some crumpled Romanian bills equal to five American dollars. She stuffed them in my hand.

"No, Rosa." I tried giving them back, but she wouldn't take them.

"Valthea, if I was at a festival I'd give you five-times this for what you told me."

Cosmo stepped in closer to me and under his breath said, "Just take the money." He stepped behind me and Rosa and put an arm around each of us. "Then it's settled. Valthea will read palms. Now, let's join the others for espresso and *gogosi.*"

Grandmamma pounded her cane on the floor. "I head of family." Her face turned radish-red and shined with perspiration. "I must *hear* reading. Rosa weak. Too nice. Mouse no good."

"Why does she hate me?" I whispered to Cosmo.

"She doesn't hate you. She's just not fond of outsiders. Give me a second." He walked to the mirrored wall, grabbed two folding chairs, and carried them to the part of the floor without mats. "First of all, Ma, I'm the director of *The Gypsy Royales.*" He opened the chairs and set them facing each other. "And I say Valthea has talent for both on and off stage." He sat in one of the chairs. "Valthea, please come sit and read my palm out loud." He patted the seat of the empty chair.

As I walked toward Cosmo, Rosa whispered, "Ma's impossible." She lingered at the doorway.

I sat on the folding chair.

Cosmo leaned forward. "Say anything, and I'll agree. Let's just get this over with." He sat straight and gave me his hand, palm up.

But I couldn't just, 'say anything.' I had to say the truth. After a slow breath, images of Cosmo's past tumbled through my head. "You have a fierce presence, filled with exuberance."

"You're right. And I love flattery, especially when it's true."

"There's also sadness. A piece is missing from your heart."

Cosmo's normally animated face dropped. Lines and crinkles, like the ones on the corners of our acrobatic mats, appeared from nowhere at the corners of his eyes and around his mouth.

"This emptiness I see isn't new," I continued. "It's ten or fifteen years old." The vision of Cosmo's past started to dissipate. I spoke quicker, "The cause of this emptiness is a girl, an exquisite girl you once loved with all your heart." I looked him in the eyes. "She was in love with you, too." The picture of his past and the girl with the milk-white skin and peach-colored hair fragmentized into strange, tiny sparkles and floated away. "That's all I see."

Cosmo paled.

Did the memory hurt him? Did something bad happen between him and the girl he loved? What were those sparks at the end of the vision? I prayed to know what to say next. "My auntie says that true love can be had more than once. The second time may not be exactly like the first, but she says it can be deep and powerful."

"Don't need Sylvie!" Grandmamma pointed her cane at Cosmo. "Is mouse bad or *real* bad?"

"First of all, Ma, her name is Valthea. And she's *not* bad at all. She's good." Cosmo folded up our chairs and leaned them against the wall. He walked halfway to the sliding glass door and then stopped. "Like it or not, Ma, at least for the summer, Valthea is a member of this troupe." He nodded to Rosa. "Please tell the others we'll start back up after lunch. I need some air." He shoved open the sliding glass door.

Grandmamma struggled to stand, but then worked her cane like a pro. She paused at the doorway. "Valthea—" She kept her back to me. "Next time, *look* at palm."

I choked. "Yes, Mrs. Dobra."

I stood alone in the center of the empty rehearsal room for several moments. Like Cosmo, I had a piece of my heart missing. I knew emptiness.

Cosmo opened the sliding glass door a few inches. "Val, come join me."

"Okay." I grabbed my phone, towel, and two waters from the room's mini-fridge.

He pushed the door open further and took the waters from me. I stepped out onto the sixteen-foot long balcony and sat in the black wrought-iron chair next to him facing the view. He twisted off the bottle caps and handed me one of the waters. "Cheers."

We sat in silence for several minutes. I gazed out at the blue Christmas pines and milk-white birch trees filling his backyard and beyond. Fragrant lilac bushes hugged the overgrown lawn. The sun warmed my face and shoulders.

"You know, Valthea, inside the depths of that forest live wolves, lynx, and eagles."

"I've never seen a lynx."

"Tell me, where did you pick up your skill? It's more than feminine intuition."

"It's nothing. I listen and watch people." I wanted Cosmo to see me as an entertainer and a future circus star, not a clairvoyant.

He took a gulp of his water. "What you said in there was right, you know."

Here it comes. A psychic once told me that after people get a reading, they want to tell you their life story, confess all kinds of stuff, and ask for advice. She said it was because readings open the door to their emotions, and when that happens, the flood gates also open.

"Valthea, I trust you. I want to tell you the story of the woman you mentioned. She wasn't just any woman. She was the only woman who ever held my heart."

SIX

I sat back in the wrought-iron chair, honored that Cosmo wanted to confide in me. My cell phone vibrated on the iron table. A text from Apollonia lit up.

"I'm not thru with you—acro-rat. 12 wks is a long time."

"Is that Sylvie?" Cosmo asked. "She missing you already?"

"No." I forced a smile. "Everything's fine." I deleted Apollonia's text, wishing I'd deleted her from the planet. I laid my phone face down and pushed the witch out of my mind. "So, Cosmo, I can't believe you've loved only one woman your whole life. Aren't you like, forty years old?"

"I prefer forty-one years young." He clasped both hands around his water bottle. "And let me clarify, I've dated many women. In fact—"

A man and woman in bed. I couldn't see their faces, but the blankets covered their bodies. They moaned and gasped. A floor heater pointed toward the bed. A framed photo of Cosmo and a brunette woman with pointy eyebrows sat on the nightstand. It was Cosmo's bedroom. The door swung open. It was Cosmo. He stepped inside the room wearing a winter coat, gloves, and a hat, damp from snowfall. The woman in bed sat up, covering herself with the blankets. She was the girl in the photo.

"—last year, I almost settled with a woman I wasn't in love with."

"So then you're glad it didn't work out?"

"Correct." He rested his elbows on the table and folded his arms. "Valthea, you'll meet many boys and men in your lifetime, but you'll know it when you meet the one special one."

I already had. *Sorin.* "Tell me everything, Cosmo. I'd love to hear about your special girl.

"Okay, but keep in mind, I don't talk to my family about personal things."

"I understand. I'm private, too."

"Do you want to pick some herbs while I tell you the story?" He pointed to the half-a-dozen potted plants lining the balcony. "Gabi loves cooking with fresh herbs."

"Sure." Walking to the first pot, blooming with curly parsley, I glanced to the sliding glass door into the rehearsal room. I didn't want Apollonia bursting onto the balcony and ruining my special time with Cosmo.

"While you do that, I'll share the full drama of my love story."

"Drama?"

"*Da.* Yes." Cosmo lounged back and put his feet up on one of the chairs. "I'd performed in my father's troupe since I was five-years-old. To our audiences, I'm sure we appeared to be a band of carefree Gypsies. We weren't. My father kept our family from other travelers, wanting to set us apart and break from the stereotypical *Roma.* He insisted on excellence in our abilities and our character. A stubborn old wolf of a man, no one could tell him what to do. But he kept our family together. We performed to traditional Romanian music, wearing the old world costumes. The men wore white pants and tunics, black vests and knee boots, and felt caps. The women layered their white skirts and blouses with red vests and skirt overlays decorated with elaborate embroidery. Our troupes' dependability and skill set us apart from other local groups. The wealthy socialites and politicians often hired us for their parties."

"How exciting." I laid the bouquet of parsley I'd gathered on the center of the table.

"One summer, seventeen years ago, a wealthy family in Bucharest hired us to perform at their daughter's birthday party. We roamed the home and lawn, juggling, dancing, and tumbling."

"I'd love a birthday party like that."

"My cousin, Silver, who was just as hyper-active then, insisted we meet rich girls at the party. What could I say? We were in our mid-twenties, our prime."

I brushed my palms across the top of the basil plants. "I'm sure meeting girls wasn't a problem for either of you."

Cosmo wagged an index finger. "Ah, but aristocrat women are different than Roma women. For instance, Gypsy girls are passionate. They want to enrapture their men and then tame us. They expect us to shift from tiger to house cat on command." He raised an eyebrow. "Roma girls are very jealous. Actually, we're all extremely jealous."

"What about aristocratic girls?" I held a bouquet of rosemary toward Cosmo.

He put his feet down, leaned forward, and took a whiff. "Nice." He leaned back. "Aristocratic women don't want to tame Gypsy men. They want us to unleash the wild within them, but that's all they want. They capture us, play, and then release us back into the wild. When a cultured girl's ready to marry, she returns to the rigueur of properly courting affluent and often older men of their own class."

I picked only a few sprigs of dill. "So they used you, like you used them?"

"I suppose." Cosmo pulled a handkerchief out of his pocket, slid off the panther head ring he always wore, and began polishing it. "Valthea, my special girl was the reason for the party that night. She was the birthday girl."

"You fell for the *birthday* girl?" I laid the sprigs of lovage on the table next to the other herbs. "Give me your ring, I'll polish it. You concentrate on telling the story."

He handed me his ring and the kerchief. "I joined Silver for his smoke break. We watched guests peruse the terrace lit by ropes of lights and fire-torches. Silver pointed to a girl with her back to us chatting with an elderly couple. He challenged me to go down and talk to her."

"Did you? What did she look like?"

"I could only see her apricot hair and her white dress. She seemed lovely. The graceful way she moved her hands and the way she tilted her head mesmerized me. Her posture was like a ballerina's.

"She sounds pretty. Like a swan."

He grinned. "Yes, but a swan princess."

I wondered how Sorin saw me. Was I mesmerizing a swan, or something else?

"Although the birthday girl wasn't overtly sexy, she took my breath away. She was pretty … luminous … almost angelic with her wide eyes and heart-shaped lips. I fell for her instantly."

"My auntie says people know right away when they meet their soul mate."

Cosmo nodded. "Sylvie's wise. This girl was my soul mate. I wanted to spend the rest of my life with her."

"So romantic. Where is she now? What's her name?"

He sighed as if reliving a dream. "Not a name, Valthea. A song … *Gisella.*"

"The name suits her. Tell me more. What was her dress like?"

"White was the party's theme, so her gown was all white." He chuckled. "You would've loved it. It sparkled like a costume with beads and pearls and rhinestones. It was her seventeenth birthday, and she had the body of a woman, no—a Greek goddess. She looked amazing in her dress."

Part of me wished I'd a body of goddess, except weight and curves hinder gymnastics and weren't best for my circus future.

Cosmo picked up a handful of basil from the table and inhaled it. He pulled out one stem and tucked it behind his ear. "I overheard her burly father refer to his daughter as, *more angel than girl.* I understood why. Throughout the night, Gisella glided from guest to servant, treating all with equal kindness. She could've acted stuck up. She was pretty, rich, and the birthday girl. Several times throughout the night, we caught each other's eyes. One time, we, looked at each other and froze. I thought my heart might burst from my chest. The neckline of Gisella's gown didn't hide that her breath had quickened too." Cosmo's eyes lit up. "It excited me that she found me as exciting as I found her."

The silver panther ring shined in my hand under the sunlight. "Sounds like you didn't have to act stealth or try to captivate her, because she'd already captivated you."

"*Da!* Yes, she had captivated and enchanted me." Cosmo chuckled for a moment, but then his eyes quickly blazed with intensity. "That night, all my senses heightened. I noticed things I would've *never* paid attention to before. White outdoor lights wrapped around the estate's columns, trees, and fences in tight spirals. The band's Romanian and classical music pulsed through my veins. I could smell the roast hen with onions and the halibut with cabbage on the buffet table set up forty-feet away. I could *taste* the white chocolate and the Sambuca liqueur on Gisella's birthday cake." He sat back and lowered his voice, "Servants and entertainers aren't given the catered food. But falling for Gisella made the night delicious."

I wished I could've see visions of Cosmo's party—smelled the cake, seen the white dresses, and met the swan-princess. But no insights came. I had to listen and imagine like a normal person.

"There were four, three-foot-high ice sculptures anchoring the cake table." Cosmo used his hands as if sculpting each one. "There was a swan, a lynx, a dolphin, and a fox."

"What a party." I handed him his ring.

He slid it on over his knuckle. "*Magnific*, Valthea. It's shiny again. *Mulțumesc.* Thank you."

"You're welcome. So, who came to Gisella's party?"

"It was more like a society affair than a teen girl's birthday party. Bucharest's general mayor and his wife attended, along with several of his councilmen and their wives. The chief of police was there. Gentlemen smoked cigars and sipped brandy. While others argued politics and threw vodka down their throats. They all appeared very continental in their stiff, white dinner jackets."

"What about the women?"

"Thin to hefty, in stacks of diamonds or rows of pearls. The ladies floated about, sipping champagne and chatting."

"You remember so many details."

"I always will, Valthea. You don't understand—the stars twinkled double-time that night. I'm telling you, God winked at me." Cosmo stood and thumped his chest with his fist." He gave me a sign. I wasn't the only one who felt the specialness of the night. The guests did, too." Cosmo paced the narrow balcony. "All night, I heard, 'What a fabulous evening!' 'What a superb night!' I agreed. But not because of the food, the music, or the decorations."

"Because of the birthday girl, right?"

"*Da.* Yes. Finally Gisella stood alone by the backyard fountain. I introduced myself, and then held out my hand, offering her seven coins." Cosmo acted out his story. "*For you,* I said, *coins for birthday wishes.* I had to meet her. She took one coin at a time and threw it into the fountain. She faced me, our bodies no more than a couple feet apart. The goddess in her sent my blood racing. I desired every part of her. I moved in closer. Her green-tourmaline eyes danced mischievous, but she held out a clenched fist. She opened her hand, and in the center of her palm laid a single coin. She insisted I make a wish, too. I stared into her eyes, took the coin, and tossed it over my shoulder into the fountain."

"Pretty debonair. What'd you wish for?"

"Ha! What else? To be with her forever."

I hoped Sorin inherited his father's romantic genes.

"I agreed to meet Gisella behind the fountain late that night. She snuck out of her bedroom window on the second floor by climbing down a tree. She ran towards me, her shirt billowing at her sides like angel wings. The moon lit a path leading her directly to me. Mother Nature confirmed what I already knew—our meeting was destiny."

Cosmo sat. "I held Gisella's hand as soon as she sat next to me at the fountain. It took her several moments to catch her breath. She said her heart was a little weak. I told her I'd make it strong. We kissed each other's hands. It was an exciting, yet peaceful moment. The party, with all its lights and noise, had finished hours before. Now it was nature's turn. There were moon shadows, musical crickets and katydids, and the scent of jasmine and potted peppermint." He picked up the bunch of the mint sprigs I'd gathered. He inhaled it. "Ahh." He handed me the sprigs. "But the finest gift from nature was Gisella."

I closed my eyes and inhaled the mint.

"She was the real deal, Val. Pure class. Perhaps part angel."

48

I opened my eyes.

"I stayed at a friend's flat in town that night and met Gisella at a sidewalk café at noon the next day. The weather was gorgeous, but Gisella insisted we sit inside at a back table. I wanted to meet her parents and ask their permission to date her. No more climbing trees and hiding in corners. But she shut out the idea." Cosmo stood and shoved his chair out of his way. He walked to the balcony railing and leaned against it, half facing me. "Her father was prejudice. She wanted to ease him into the idea of her dating someone different than her."

"Different as in Roma or as an entertainer?"

"Both. I told her I wasn't afraid to meet her father. I was a hardworking, talented athlete from an honest family. Gisella begged me to be patient, insisting we meet secretly until she loosened up her father's thinking. I agreed, knowing better." Cosmo shook his head. "Prejudice takes more than a generation to overcome, never mind a couple of weeks."

"So what did you and Gisella do?" I pressed the bouquet of mint to my heart.

"We met in bistros, museums, parks. At night, we'd meet at the fountain behind her home. I felt like a second-class rebel sneaking around. But I'd fallen in love with her. I'd do anything to be near her. In two weeks, she and her family would leave for their vacation home on the coast for the entire month of August. I asked her not to go. She didn't have a choice." Cosmo paced the narrow balcony again, this time like caged panther.

"The night before she left, we met at the fountain. We laid on a blanket in each other's arms and whispered words of love. We kissed for hours. But that's all. I didn't want her to see me as a flakey entertainer or a here today, gone tomorrow Gypsy. I respected her, and I wanted her to respect me."

I set down the mint and fidgeted with the rest of the herbs, nervous how Cosmo's story may end.

He came back to the table and pulled his chair closer to me and sat. "Gisella and I talked for hours almost every night during her time away." His eyes twinkled. "Our connection was real. Our relationship didn't wane, but grew. When she returned to Bucharest with her family, we didn't waste any time." Cosmo's energy brightened. He spoke quicker. "We planned to meet on her first night back at the edge of the forest behind her home. I got there early, laid out a blanket, and unpacked a bottle of champagne, several barks of dark chocolate, and a bowl of strawberries. I trembled, glancing at my watch every five minutes. A half hour later, Gisella showed up. It didn't matter that she was late. We were together. She joined me on the blanket and I poured her a glass of champagne."

Cosmo chuckled. "Valthea let me tell you, she was the most adorable person I'd ever met. She dunked pieces of chocolate into her champagne and ate it. We fed each other strawberries. We laughed. We kissed. We hugged. It was like what you see in movies." He sighed and lounged back. "My swan-princess—so beautiful, so silly. My God—she was more than I could've ever wished for." Cosmo locked his eyes to mine. "Valthea, I didn't hold back my feelings. I told Gisella I loved her, and I gave her a ruby promise ring."

My affection and admiration for Cosmo grew with every scene of his romantic story.

"I slid the ruby on Gisella's ring finger, and promised to date only her until the time was right for me to propose marriage."

"Wow, how perfect. What'd she say?"

"She accepted my promise and then promised the same thing back to me, giving me this." He held up his hand with the panther ring. "Do you believe it?" He grinned and folded his arms across his chest. "We didn't plan it. We just both bought rings for each other. We were so in tune. It was the happiest moment of my life. In my heart, Gisella was already my bride."

I wanted adventure and love, too. I'd never been to fancy parties, snuck out of my house in the middle of the night, or been given a promise ring. My whole life I ate, drank, and slept gymnastics. My first real adventure would be traveling with the Gypsies over the summer. I wanted my first kiss to be with Sorin.

"The next morning, we met for breakfast. I couldn't sleep all night. My head was in the sky after our night of being together. We sat on the same side of the booth, ignoring our coffees, and just kissed and kissed. Suddenly, we heard her name called from the front of the restaurant. We looked up. I'd never seen her look so pale."

I gasped. "Her father?"

"Da, do you believe it? His frame blocked the entire doorway. He drilled holes right through me with his glare. He stormed over, snatched Gisella from the booth, and said that if I ever saw his daughter again, he'd destroy my family's reputation. He'd make sure that The Gypsy Royales were known only as a band of kidnapping thieves."

"But that's not true."

"He yelled at Gisella, saying she'd sealed her own fate—whatever that meant—and then dragged her out of the restaurant. I followed them out. He stopped at the street curb in front of a parked sedan. I pleaded my case at the top of my lungs, 'I love and respect your daughter. I'm hardworking and successful, and I want to marry Gisella.' He laughed in my face, called me a low-life, and said he'd never allow someone like me to marry his daughter. At that point, Gisella pulled out of her father's grip and yelled at the top of her lungs that she loved me and wanted to marry me. I reached my hand out for her, but the old bull forced her into the backseat of the Sedan. He slammed her door shut, got in the car, and they sped off."

"What'd you do? You rescued her, right?"

"I tried. I called her that night. Her phone had been shut off. I drove to her house. Two guards stood watch on her family's property. I mailed letters. They were returned. I went to our favorite café every day at noon for three weeks straight." Cosmo scooted his chair away from the table, causing the iron legs to screech on the balcony's tile floor. He walked to the edge of the balcony and leaned on its iron railing.

I joined him.

"After five months of not hearing from her, and my letters being returned, I figured she wasn't interested in me anymore. I couldn't get to her. I didn't know what else to do. I prayed for her protection and that she was happy."

"But—"

"A year later, Silver handed me a folded Bucharest newspaper, open to the engagement announcements. He pointed to a photo of Gisella standing next to Dragos Teszari, the son of Marius Teszari, the real estate and construction magnate. I was shocked. My swan looked defeated. No joy shined from her eyes. My poor angel's wings had been clipped. I could tell she didn't love him. They were to marry in two weeks."

Cosmo wiped his eyes and then gripped the balcony railing with both hands. The veins in his forearms swelled to the surface. "It had to be her father's doing, that bastard! It was one thing for the old bull to ruin my life, but another to ruin his daughter's."

I was angry too, but slowed my breathing.

Cosmo wrestled two men in front of a church. All three wore dark suits and ties.

"So, what did you do?"

"What I had to. I drove to her house. But just like before, the guards turned me away. I tried writing again. Again, the letters came back. On the morning of my true love's wedding, I put on my best black suit. Gisella needed *me*, not some trust fund twit. I hopped in my Fiat and sped to the Stavropoleos Monastery. The wedding was a big deal, so I had to park two blocks away. Luxury cars and security guards filled the streets. I filed in with a group of five walking up the steps to the front of the church. Within seconds, two guards nabbed me and forced me on the other side of the road. I fought them the best I could, but two more came. Her father left nothing to chance. All the guards had photos of me. The brut was sharp, a third-generation businessman. *Nemilos milionar*—a ruthless millionaire."

I followed Cosmo back to the table.

He chugged the rest of his water and then squeezed the plastic bottle until it crumpled. "The old bull died of a heart attack a few years back. Made all the papers." He tossed the bottle into the basket by the door.

"Wait—what about Gisella? What happened? Is she still married to the twit? She can't be happy. Let's find her on the Internet! You guys could meet again."

"Valthea—"

"They're probably divorced by now. You were her true love, not him. I bet Gisella dreams of you every night. Maybe she's on a social media site. I'm sure she'd be so excited to hear from—"

"Val—Gisella died."

My heart stopped. "What?"

"Happened about two months after her wedding. Abnormal heart rhythm."

"No—why? She was your swan princess, your soul mate. It was your destiny to meet."

"And we did." His eyes welled. "My angel's in heaven now. But in here," he patted his hand twice to his heart and whispered, barely able to speak, "I hold our memories, and I'll never let them go."

Cords of shock, sadness, and anger wrapped around me and bound me to my chair. I couldn't move.

"Valthea, the kind of love Gisella and I shared comes maybe once in a lifetime. I'm proud to say, we seized it wholeheartedly. I pray you have the courage to do the same when true love finds you."

SEVEN

The *Gypsy Royales* traveled caravan-style in four motor homes. I rode with Lumi and her parents, Gabi and Gheorghe, in the vehicle referred to as the *family van*. Apollonia and her fiancé, Strum led the way. Rosa and Big Bruno followed. Fourth in the tailgate rode Cosmo, Sorin, Dino, and Silver. Apollonia dubbed their vehicle the *testosterone trailer*.

First festival stop: Bucharest. I asked Aunt Sylvie to come to the second show when I'd be less nervous.

In keeping with first-festival-eve tradition, the men and women split up after dinner. The men gathered in the testosterone trailer for a night of poker and vodka. The women met in Apollonia's cramped living room for celebratory champagne and truffles and storytelling.

"Here's to the summer ahead." Apollonia raised her flute of champagne. "May our audiences be filled with plenty of people—with plenty of cash!"

We brought our glasses together. Lumi and her mom laughed along with Apollonia. Rosa wet her lips with the bubbly liquid and then put her glass on an end table, reaching instead for the box of chocolates. I sipped the drink, not sure I liked it.

Apollonia refilled her glass.

Gabi made a toast. "May this summer bring an audience that includes a wealthy man who falls in love with my beautiful daughter."

"Cheers to Lumi." Apollonia gulped her drink.

"And may he be a kind man," Rosa said, popping a bulbous truffle in her mouth.

My eyes met Lumi's. I knew she was already in love with her father's cousin, Dino. I'd seen a past vision of her meeting Dino in the middle of night for moonlit walks and kisses. I caught her writing her name over and over, as *Lumi Mitrea*. And when I'd read Dino's past, pretending to read his palm, Lumi was the blonde in the bar room who instigated trouble.

"Have you nothing to add to my toast, Lumi?" Gabi asked.

Lumi offered her bored expression.

I felt tipsy after one glass of the effervescent liquid. Although I drank wine a month ago, on my sixteenth birthday, I'd never liked the taste of alcohol. Lumi obviously did. A year older than me, she drank twice as much as I did, yet seemed unaffected. Rosa flittered about, high on cocoa and sugar.

To ease the tension coming from Lumi, I raised my glass. "To Lumi and her future husband, whoever he may be." From the corner of my eye I saw Rosa struggling with her fleshy hands to open another box of chocolates. "To Rosa, our beloved costume-maker. May she stay creative and her hands stay nimble." Everyone cheered. I finally felt like I was fitting in. "To Apollonia, our fantastic dance leader, we wish her joy and prosperity."

"Yes to prosperity!" Apollonia clanked her glass hard against mine.

"Woo-hoo!" Gabi howled.

Gabi and her husband Gheorghe tapped juice glasses in a toast. He told her he loved her and was thrilled to have another child with her after so many years.

I lifted my glass higher. "And of course, to Gabi, may she and Gheorghe have a healthy baby—"

Gabi's care-free expression flipped to shock. Hadn't Gabi announced her pregnancy? Uh, oh.

Lumi glared at her mother. Only the effervescent bubbles dancing in everyone's drinks could be heard until Rosa dropped her handful of chocolates into their box, cluttered with empty, stiff paper liners.

"Sister—why didn't you tell me?" Rosa reached past me and hugged Gabi, tears trickling down her cheeks. "I'm so happy for you." She took a step back and looked at her sister's belly. Her eyes now twinkled. She shook her head, smiling. "I didn't know you wanted more children."

Gabi fixed her eyes on mine. "We didn't want to tell anyone until we knew the baby was going to make it."

"I'm sorry, Gabi" I said. "I thought—"

"So, that's why you've been singing more and dancing less." Lumi grabbed an open bottle of champagne and took a swig. "You could've at least told your daughter before telling the outsider."

Gabi reached toward Lumi, but her daughter turned away and chugged more champagne.

"She didn't tell me anything," I said. "I just guessed. Your mom hasn't been as active. She didn't drink her champagne. And, uh ... she has that beautiful glow about her."

"Yes, I noticed it, too." Rosa stood next to me facing Gabi. "I suspected, but I didn't say anything."

"Please!" Apollonia worked her way into the middle of our huddle. "A baby is coming into our world. Let's drink!" She raised her glass and passed a freshly poured one to Rosa.

I was surprised to see tears in the serpent woman's eyes. Maybe Apollonia wasn't entirely filled with venom.

"Yes, yes," Rosa said. "Cheers!"

"*Salut!*" I tapped her glass.

"*Salut!*" Gabi giggled. "I *am* excited. The doctor said everything's all right. Baby's due in six—" She let out a loud belch. "I better lie down."

Rosa helped Gabi to the sofa.

"I'll make some tea." I filled the kettle and set it on the stove.

Apollonia wet a clean washcloth and sat next to Gabi. She smoothed her sister's hair back and held the cloth on her forehead. She seemed so kind. It was a pity Apollonia didn't drink champagne every day.

After a few minutes and a cup of tea, Gabi sat up. "I feel better. Now who's got a story that goes with both champagne and chamomile?"

Apollonia kissed Gabi's forehead and then stood. "I've a story, or rather, a topic. Kisses. Specifically," she said impishly, "first kisses."

"All right, listen up you young girls," Gabi said to me and Lumi.

"Please," Lumi mumbled. "I've already experienced many kisses."

"You better not have," Gabi yelled.

"Now, now. Let's keep the baby calm," Rosa said, sitting next to Gabi. "Let Apollonia have the floor. Go ahead, Sis, start us off with a story."

I sat on the overstuffed chair in the corner. Lumi sat on one of its arms.

Apollonia paraded around as best she could in the tight quarters, happy to hold court even with a bunch of women. "Okay, listen up girls. I've a theory about first kisses and their effect."

"Sounds scientific." Rosa bit into a gooey truffle.

Apollonia hissed her theory. "If a girl's first kiss is terrible, then all the kisses thereafter will be better because her expectations are low. The girl will think the best is yet to come. And eventually, it does."

Gabi held one hand on her barely bulging tummy. "That was the case with me!"

Rosa and Lumi laughed along with Gabi. I joined in too. I wanted them to think I knew a lot about kisses.

C.K. Mallick

"The other possibility is ... " Apollonia hiked her long skirt up a couple of feet, exposing her calf-high boots. She planted one foot on the arm of the chair where Lumi and I sat. "A girl's first kiss may be fantastic. Amazing."

Rosa snorted as she laughed. "That's how it was with my Bruno."

"How fortunate. Because when the first kiss is wonderful, a girl can fall in love on the spot. The boy could end up her first love and possibly her husband." Apollonia twirled a strand of her hair as if she withheld further romantic wisdom.

Her theory made me glad I was a late bloomer. I wanted my first kiss to be with Sorin.

Apollonia narrowed her eyes. "Ah, but first-loves rarely last. When it ends, the girl must go on with her life. The problem is that now she knows what it feels like to be in to be in love, to love, and be loved. She'll seek that same feeling for years, decades if necessary. If she doesn't find it, she may end up doing the worst thing of all. She'll settle for the wrong man."

I furrowed my brow. Aunt Sylvie never told me such things.

"Do you know what happens next, Lumi? Valthea?"

I nearly fell off the chair. It was the first time Apollonia called me by my name.

Lumi inclined forward, her boredom finally taking a back seat.

Apollonia paused for effect. "If the woman settles for the wrong man, the memories of her true love will haunt her, especially at night. At least in sleeping, her heart will feel fulfilled. Well, that's it. The end of my story." She took her foot off the chair. "Let's take a break." She sashayed to the kitchen and pulled a bottle of champagne from the kitchen.

Lumi hurried with her champagne glass to join Apollonia.

Gabi scurried off to the bathroom, holding her belly.

Rosa went to the kitchen and opened another box of truffles.

That's it? What about Apollonia's first kiss? What about the theory? Did Gabi agree? What about Rosa? Forget it. I rested back in the cozy chair and closed my eyes. What would it feel like to kiss Sorin?

"Who are you dreaming of?"

I opened my eyes.

Apollonia had boxed me in, standing in front of my chair with her hands planted on its arms and her face inches from mine. "You're thinking about kisses aren't you?"

"Get off of me." I went to push her, but she plopped down on my lap. "I said, get off!"

56

"Not yet, acro-rat." She hooked one arm behind my head.

I squirmed, trying to wriggle out of the chair. "Stop it, Apollonia. You're being weird."

"Don't worry," she whispered. "I'll teach you how to kiss. First you pout, then keeping your lips soft, you—"

"I already know." I thrust my body upward to slide her off my lap, but she made herself heavy and forced me back down.

"I bet you don't." She dug her fingers into my jaw and forced her lips to mine.

"Yuck!" I shoved Apollonia off me and hopped out the chair. She slid to the floor rug and stayed there, laughing.

Rosa poked her head into the living room. "What are you girls doing in here?"

"Nothing," I said.

Apollonia laughed harder.

Gabi came out of the bathroom.

I rushed in, locked the door, and turned the fan on for noise. I *hated* Apollonia. I wiped my tears and blew my nose. How dare she ruin my first kiss? It was supposed to be with Sorin. I splashed my face with cold water, dried it, and then stared into the mirror. *When* would I see something of that witch's past? When would I—

"You all right?" Rosa knocked on the door.

I came out of the bathroom. "Yeah. Thanks, Rosa."

Apollonia sat in the overstuffed chair, finishing another glass of champagne.

I forced a yawn. "I'm tired. Going to bed early. See you in the morning, everyone."

I walked the damp, dirt path back to the family van. The night's cool air felt divine after an hour in the viper's pit. I whispered aloud, "When I get an insight into Apollonia, I won't hold back. I'll de-fang her in front of everyone. She'll see ... she'll see that the venom she spits at me is nothing compared to what I can deliver."

EIGHT

The next day, everyone dressed and readied in their motor homes for the show. Costume changes took place in a small tent behind the outdoor stage where we performed. Lumi's dad, Gheorghe, the violinist, vacated the family van early to set up with the other musicians. I sat in the kitchen booth, looking into my portable mirror. I applied eye-shadow, filled in my brows, and swept on some blush. Like the others girls, I extended my black liquid eyeliner up and out, for a cat-eye effect. I couldn't stop smiling. Excitement for my first-festival-show shoved aside my rambling worries of what the summer would be like with Apollonia.

"I'm going to re-check the stage surface." Gabi gathered her dancing scarf and tambourine. "See you girls out there in twenty." She snapped the end of her scarf at Lumi.

"Ow!" Lumi grabbed her shoulder and scowled at her mother.

"Oh, that didn't hurt. But I *will* hurt you if you're late."

Gabi opened the door to leave. "Oh, hi, Sorin. Come in. They're almost ready."

"Hey girls."

"Hey." Lumi didn't look up, but continued applied her makeup in front of the large mirror hanging on the living room wall.

"Hi." I smiled.

"The festival is packed." He sat across from me in the booth, resting his forearms on the table, and clasping his hands together.

I loved his lean, well-defined arms.

"Nervous?"

"A little."

"Come outside for a second, Val."

"But I have to—"

"Just for a second."

I followed him to the door.

"Hey, Valthea—my mom will beat you if you're late."

"No she won't." Sorin held the door open for me. "Don't listen to her, Val. We'll be right back." He walked me a few yards to the path next to the motor home. "In case you haven't figured it out, Lumi and Apollonia are jealous of you travelling with us this summer. You're a ranked gymnast, and Cosmo gave you a solo. They can't compete with that. Just be aware, they'll try to psyche you out before the show and your act."

"Thanks for the warning, but Apollonia and Lumi haven't been exactly pleasant toward me in general." I shook my head. "But then, I've been through it all with competitive gymnasts. I've seen girls crumble laxatives into a competitor's breakfast before a meet so that by noon, they have to drop out. One time, an alternate gymnast put crushed glass in the top-ranked teammate's slipper. And some coaches get beastly. Not my coach, but this other team's coach berated his girls team with put-downs right up to when they lined up for their entrance walk. I've learned to keep to myself before competitions and shows."

"That's good. By the way, you look striking in your stage make-up. But you're prettier without makeup."

My heart skipped. "Thank you." I looked up at him. "And you, Sorin?" I asked, coyly. "What do you do to a new co-performer before a show? Keep her from getting ready so that she's late?"

"Feisty. I like it. Actually, Valthea, I like you."

I felt my face flush.

He opened his arms. "How about good-luck-hug?"

I stepped toward him, fantasizing a good-luck kiss.

"Hellooo-ee!"

We separated.

"Oopsy!" Silver strolled between us with his hand on the seat of his unicycle. "Did I interrupt something?"

"No," we said at the same time.

"*Merde!*" Silver said over his shoulder.

"*Merde.*"

"Sorin, what's *merde?*"

"Eet ees ze French word for poo-poo. It's a way of saying 'good luck.' Kind of like the American expression, 'break a leg.'"

"Oh." I smirked at his attempt at a French accent. "I get it."

He opened the motor home door. "Go on, finish getting ready. Otherwise, I'll stand out here and talk to you until we miss the entire show."

I walked up the steps. "See you out there. *Merde.*"

"You got it." He chuckled. "*Merde.*"

I closed the door behind me.

"He's such a flirt, isn't he?" Lumi said, straightening the seams of her fishnet stockings.

"Sorin wasn't flirting."

"Sure he was."

Lumi. She looked as she did now, seventeen going on twenty-seven. Crop top and jeans, strong chin, rare smile, and her signature dark roots. She and Dino made out while leaning against a bunch of garbage bins behind the bleacher stands at a festival. Trash and beer cans littered the ground around them.

"Just so you know, Valthea, Sorin flirts with *every* girl who gets called up on stage. You can't be gullible enough to think you two could *ever* be boyfriend and girlfriend. You're barely sixteen. He's almost eighteen. He can get hot girls who are older—older meaning experienced, if you know what I mean."

She doused her genie-styled ponytail with hairspray. "There's no reason for him to waste his time on an adolescent. There's always a bunch of sexy women watching our show who want to bed him."

I added another coat of mascara to my lashes. "I know flirting is part of show business. The girls in the audience are attracted to the male performers—probably more attracted to musicians than jugglers, don't you think?" I grabbed her can of hairspray and spoke over its hiss. "Girls probably flirt all the time with Gheorghe and Strum. And Dino."

The opening dance with the girls went great. No mistakes. I couldn't wait for Aunt Sylvie and our neighbor, Mr. Karl to see me perform the second show at two o'clock. I ran down the stage steps, around the corner, and ducked into the changing tent. I took off my corset, skirt, and peasant blouse. Underneath, I wore my solo costume: a sleeveless, tie-dye body stocking. I rolled down the ends of my tights from above my knees down to my ankles and pulled on the matching elbow-length mitts. Rosa designed the tie-dye theme to go with my rock-and-roll routine.

I ran back up the steps and then walked with pointed toes to my start position on stage. Facing away from the festival crowd, I posed, trembling with self-inflicted pressure, but also excitement.

Dino tapped his drum sticks together and counted, "One, two, three."

The musicians played a two-bar intro, and then I spun around, smiling. Arms stretch up. Arms press down. Lengthen. Step-hop, *chassé*, side leap, pivot-turn, step, switch leap, punch, straddle-jump, pose. I strutted to the upper, right corner of the stage in time with Strum's electric guitar riff—five, six, seven, eight. I paused, taking a deep breath. Next move—my second-to-last and hardest tumbling pass. I lifted my chest and then, while focusing on the opposite corner, slowly exhaled. I ran four strides into a round off, back handspring, double-back-tuck. The pass went excellent until the finish. I lost my footing, fell backward, and landed on my fanny. Quickly, I transitioned into a back roll to make it look planned. But then, I went blank. *Merde!* What was next?

Random muscle memory of playing around at the gym kicked in. I, the regimented and trained gymnast, started break-dancing. Already in a squat on the mat, I swung my legs out and around my body and whipped myself into a head spin. I dropped belly down and rippled backward like a worm. Dino switched his percussion to hip-hop.

The audience whistled and clapped. I stood, remembering the rest of the choreography. I flew into a series of front handsprings. After landing, I hopped into my end pose—a wide stance with one arm flung side, while the other hand strummed the final chord on an air electric guitar. Strum matched my move perfectly with his real electric guitar.

Applause and stomps vibrated the stage.

I smiled at the crowd, bowed, and then waved, exiting. Once in the changing tent, I changed into my dancing skirt, blouse and corset. No time to be upset about my screw up. I had to go out into the crowd and *read palms*. I zipped up my boots and stepped out of the tent.

"*Scuzați-mă?*" Cosmo grabbed my arm. "What was that nonsense?"

"Cosmo, I'm sorry. I blanked—"

"If you make a mistake, you pick up from where you left off. You don't make up entirely new choreography. What's wrong with you?"

"Cosmo," Strum said, walking up with the other musicians. "Give her a break. It worked out fine. We pulled it off. The crowd loved it."

Cosmo shot up his hand. "Silence! Valthea, your number is rock-and-roll. What was that crazy hip-hop stuff you did?"

"I don't know. It just—"

Cosmo's facial features went from down-turned and upset to upward and gleeful. "Actually ... ha! I loved it! It was *extraordinar, excentric, abracadabrant!*" He punched the air overhead. "We'll make hip-hop part of your act starting tomorrow."

C.K. Mallick

"You mean, change my routine?"

Gheorghe, the violinist, threw his hands in the air. "Change the routine? But we just learned our—"

"Come on, Gheorghe, admit it. You had fun up there."

"Cosmo, it's not an easy transition going from rock to hip-hop."

"True, Gheorghe, but you did it! You made the violin a wild instrument. I'm telling you—*extraordinar*! It's time you pushed yourself."

"It worked, Gheorghe." Strum put his arm around him. "I loved what you did. You reminded me of a mad fiddle genius ... or Itzhak Perlman meets David Garrett."

"Who?" Dino pulled a pack of cigarettes from his pocket.

Cosmo slapped Dino on the back. "Ha! Dino, that street sound you pulled out of your percussion—fantastic! And Strum, the heavy metal you did at the end was perfect. I want Valthea's solo to be a mix of Romanian folk, rock-and -roll, and hip hop. We'll meet at nine in the morning to fine tune."

"Come with me, Val." Cosmo walked me away from the musicians. "Today you showed me you're a quick study. You made the best of a mistake, and now we'll make it even better." He gave me a quick hug. "I need to go check on a speaker. You go have fun and make some money reading palms, okay? See you in a little bit." He ran twenty-feet and then turned around and yelled, "Valthea—I'm proud of you."

NINE

I stood on the grassy edge of one of the main festival paths. Hundreds of people flocked the park. I smiled at the mother of a family of four. She held two of her children by their shirt collars.

"*Scuzați-mă, doamnă,* ma'am, I'll read your palm and tell you—"

"Tell me what? That I'm going to have another kid? No, thanks."

"But I don't—"

The woman scuffled away with her brood.

I felt a tap on my shoulder. "Miss?"

I turned. "Yes?"

A couple in their forties stood in front of me with their arms draped around each other. The buxom woman wore a mini-skirt and a stack of gold bracelets on both forearms. The man's shirt, unbuttoned halfway to his navel, showed-off his dark tan. He held a cigar in his free hand. They smiled at me, glanced at each other, and then smiled at me again.

The woman spoke softly. "We've been searching and searching."

"It's true." The man nodded.

I studied their faces. "You ... you've been searching?" Could they be? My hope and pulse skyrocketed. "Searching for who?"

"Not for *who,* little miss, but for what." The man puffed his cigar.

The woman smiled sweetly. "He's embarrassed. He thinks cotton candy's only for little kids. But I love it."

"I'm not embarrassed. She can have anything she wants. So, Miss, could you please steer us in the right direction?"

I couldn't respond for several moments. I pointed. "Most of the refreshments are on that side. But um, before you go, I could read your—"

"Thanks so much." The man waved, cigar in hand.

I wiped my brow. Where were they? I wanted to yell at my parents. What was taking so long? Their lives should be okay by now. They should be making every effort to see me. I kicked a clump of dirt on the path. And why wasn't anyone letting me read their palm? My palms sweat. What if, when someone let me read their palm, I didn't have any visions? No. Pictures had to come. If not, I'd disappoint Cosmo. Grandmamma would gloat and harass me, and Apollonia would insist I sit on a loveseat and kiss old men. Worst of all, I'd feel like a fraud.

I cleared my mind and inched down the grounds, studying people's faces. Maybe my parents worked on week days, like most people. If so, they wouldn't attend a festival until the coming weekend. I looked for any potential suspects anyway. Within twenty minutes the festival goers blurred together, and my stomach went queasy.

"Valthea? Valthea Sarosi?"

I turned. "Yes?"

"I thought that Gypsy man announced you as one of his performers. I was sitting so far back, I wasn't sure I heard right. You and my son went to the same elementary school."

"Really?" I didn't recognize the drawn woman. She wore a faded pullover and a denim skirt two-sizes too big, cinched with a macramé belt. A floral scrunchie held most of her hair on the top of her head. "Who's your son?" I glanced around. "Is he here?"

"Somewhere. Can't miss him. He and his friends wear only black. My son's Fane. You remember Fane, don't you?"

I nearly choked. I hadn't heard that name since my first week in kindergarten. My mind drifted back to the day I met him. A day I'd remember for the rest of my life.

I was six. My kindergarten teacher marched my class outside to the schoolyard to play. This made me happy. I wasn't used to being cooped up all day. I sat on one of the playground swings and swung as high as I could.

"Hey, Valthea," said the third-grader named Fane. He and four other kids approached me. I didn't need visions to know Fane was trouble. "I heard the old woman who adopted you found you in the woods." He sneered. "Do you know why parents leave their babies in the woods?"

I dug my heels into the dirt to stop swinging.

"Because they don't want them. They hope a bear will eat their kid." He and his gang laughed and slapped hands in high-fives.

I stared at Fane, hoping to see through him. Beyond him. I wanted the mean boy to disappear. Suddenly, everything in front of me disappeared and gold and white light shone in my mind's eye. I wanted to stay in that peaceful, safe place forever, but within seconds, a scene appeared.

Musty smell. Heavy footsteps. ... A man with shadowed eyes corned nine-year-old Fane in a small dark room. The man loomed over him like a gigantic monster. Fane pleaded, "I'm sorry, Dad. I didn't mean to knock over your beer. It was an accident." "No, Son," his dad grumbled. "You were the accident." He slapped little Fane across the face and pushed him to the floor. Fane screamed, "Mom! Mom—" "Stop calling your mommy. You know she never comes." His father unbuckled his belt and yanked it out from the loops of his jeans He slapped the belt's end to the floor as if cracking a whip. Fane screamed, "Mom—"

I squeezed my eyes shut for several seconds, hoping to stop the vision. It worked. I stepped away from the swing and motioned for Fane to come closer. "I need to tell you something."

"Watch out," said one of the boys with him. "Her guardian's like an old a witch. Probably taught her magic. Careful, she could put a spell on you."

"Shut up! I'm not afraid of this puny girl." Fane walked toward me. "What do you want?"

I cupped my hand and whispered in his ear. "Make your dad chamomile tea. It'll calm him down. It'll help him from getting mad at you."

Fane backed away, nearly falling on his friends. "You don't know anything!" His eyes darkened. "You and your old lady are witches." He hurried off, his gang at his heels.

A week later our kindergarten teacher told us that Fane's father had died. After school, I walked into the house. Aunt Sylvie called me into the living room.

"Come," she said, sitting on the sofa. "We need to talk."

"Am I in trouble?"

"No, but I need to ask you some questions."

I sat in the tall chair across from her and folded my hands on my lap. I swung my legs, anxious for her to hurry and finish her talk.

"Valthea, remember when you told me an older boy named Fane bothered you?"

"Yes."

"You haven't mentioned him lately. Has he bothered you since then?"

"No." I stopped swinging my legs. Recalling the image of Fane's father's eyes, and the way the angry man hit and pushed Fane. It made me shudder.

"Valthea, I read in the paper that Fane's father died yesterday. He was poisoned."

"Poisoned? Like a rat or with a poison arrow?"

"Valthea, this isn't some story. It's real. A little boy's father has died. The police think that Fane or his mother poisoned him."

Like a rat.

"You told me before that Fane was mean to you, but you turned your cheek like they taught you at Sunday school. Afterward, you saw a scene of Fane's father hurting Fane. Do you remember?"

"Yes," I mumbled, feeling like I was in trouble.

Auntie studied my face. "Valthea, you know your gift is from God. You use it for good or stay silent. Good thoughts and words bring good deeds. Bad thoughts and words bring —"

"—bad deeds. I know. You told me a zillion times."

"Valthea, we are having a discussion. No attitude, please. Now then, what I need to know is if you said *anything* that might've, accidently, given Fane an idea or way to kill his father?"

"No." I squirmed on the seat cushion. "We only talked about tea. I told him chamomile tea would make his dad sleepy. Like you tell me when I'm jumping around at bedtime. You say it every night. I told him just like you tell me. I didn't tell him poison. I told him tea, Auntie." I punched the seat cushion and started to bawl. "I didn't do anything wrong. I promise." I covered my eyes.

"Oh, my dear, of course not." She got up and sat next to me. "There, there." She wrapped me in her arms and rocked us. "I know you would never intentionally hurt anyone. You can't even squash a bug. But children and adults, like you, who see what others do not, must mind their words carefully. Increased intuition is increased power. And child, that power is from God. He hopes you use it for good, and I do too." She smoothed my bangs to the side. "Child, you were made sensitive for a reason."

I finally calmed down and looked up my Auntie. "Was Fane's father allergic to tea?"

"Probably not, dear, but it *is* possible that Fane, or his mother, added poison to his tea or his beer or his supper." She kissed my forehead. "But your suggestion of herbal tea is a far cry from a plot to murder someone." She sat straighter but kept me close. "I want you to promise to come and talk to me right away when you have a scary or bad reading. We'll discuss it and decide together what to say or do." She shook her head. "You're very young, but we have to start now growing your wisdom. It cannot wait. You must learn the art of discernment."

Discernment. It challenged me at six years old and today at sixteen. The smell of roasting peanuts and the midday sun brought me back into the moment. "Yes, ma'am, I met your son a long time ago."

"You didn't just meet him. You influenced him." She pushed me backward. "Fane went to a juvenile correction facility because of something *you* told him to do to his father. Because of how my husband died, I couldn't collect on his life insurance policy." She pushed me again, harder. "You should've been blamed. You should've gone to jail. Then I would've gotten that money. I told the judge it was your fault, but I couldn't prove anything."

I stayed backed away from her. "Ma'am, you don't know what you're talking about."

"I didn't have my son for three years. When he returned, he wasn't my little boy any more. He was an angry twelve-year old man."

"Ma'am, you've got it all wrong. I remember *exactly* what I told Fane because he and his gang taunted me on my first day of school. I said one thing to him—*make your dad a cup of herb tea.* That's it. Tea."

"I don't believe you. Look at you ... reading palms. You're a witch. A psychic. You *knew* what my son would do, and you encouraged him. You're a despicable girl. Because of you, my little boy grew into an out-of-control young man."

"First of all, you're wrong about me. I only see the past. Second, if you loved your little boy so much, why didn't you find a way to stop your husband from beating him every night?"

"How dare you?" She slapped my face.

I cupped my cheek. Fane's mother stormed away. It was true what they say. The abused often become the abuser. I walked off the main path, passing the tent selling evil-eye jewelry, and sat on an old tree stump. I *hated* my gift.

"Excuse me, sugar?" A bleach-blonde woman wearing jeans and cowboy boots waved at me from the main path. "You're the palm reader, right?" The American in her mid-twenties sounded like she was from Nashville. A pretty brunette stood next to her dressed the same way. They stood frozen with wide eyes and perfect smiles, like two contestants in a Miss America pageant waiting for a judge's decision.

C.K. Mallick

"Be right there." I plodded over to them, not wanting to see any more visions. "A reading is fifteen *lei*. Tips are welcome," I mumbled.

"Great. No problem." The blonde's eyes sparkled. "I have a pile of them *lei* bills."

"Thank you." I folded the bills into my pocket.

"All right!" The brunette girl gushed. "This is going to be fun."

The brunette girl and a tall guy with a crew cut went into a jewelry store. After several minutes of surveying the glass cases, the guy purchased a heart-shaped pendant necklace. The brunette squealed and gave him a thumbs-up. "It's perfect!" The guy handed the pendant to the shop's engraver. "I'd like it to say, Kyle loves Jenny." The engraver nodded and took the pendant.

"Here you go, sugar." The blonde girl held out her hand, palm up. "My church is against fortune-telling, but I'm desperate. I need to know if the guy I'm in love with back home is also in love with me."

"By the way, I'm not a fortune-teller. More like a historian. My palm-readings reveal the past. Maybe your church doesn't mind that as much." I took her hand. "My name's Valthea. What's yours?"

"Oh, my goodness, where are my manners? Pleased to meet you, Valthea. I'm Jenny. This is Lisbeth. We're from Texas. You know ... the biggest state in America. Well, not including Alaska." She rolled her eyes while maintaining her pageant smile.

"I'm so glad your name is Jenny ... uh, I mean, I'm glad to meet you, Jenny." I glanced at her palm. "Yes, there is a man who loves you. His name's Kyle."

Jenny jumped up and down.

Lisbeth squealed and hugged her. "I told you he loved you."

"Goodness gracious. Thank you so much." Jenny pulled out a dozen *lei* in different denominations from her purse. "Here you go." She handed me the wad of bills. "You just made me the happiest girl in the world."

I fanned out the notes. "Wait, this is equal to about a hundred American dollars."

"Don't you worry, Valthea. My family can afford it."

Lisbeth nodded. "They can."

"Well, bye-bye now!"

Jenny and Lisbeth flashed their smiles, pivoted in unison, and headed for the beer stand. I folded the banknotes and slid them into my left skirt pockets.

"Handleser? Palm reader?"

I turned to the sound of the German-accent.

"I'd like my palm read."

The pear-shaped fellow, no taller than me, wore a well-tailored suit. He smoothed his broom-moustache with his extended pinky showing off a gold and ruby ring. His cologne wafted between us.

He stuck out his hand. "You know *handleser*, not everyone will tip as generous as the women who just left."

He grinned, but looked lecherous. His moustache and eyebrows resembled a squirrel's tail, but his aggressive manner reminded me of a badger.

"What'd you tell that *frauline?*" He raised one brow and reoffered his hand. "How about me?"

I didn't want to touch him. "The fee is fifteen lei."

He reached into his jacket pocket and then stopped. "First, let's see how good you are, Bendy Girl."

"Bendy Girl? Oh, you mean gymnast."

"Apparently you bend and tell people their future. Remarkable." He wet his lips with the tip of his tongue.

"I don't tell the future." I brushed my bangs down, noticing his stare.

"What was that mark?" He pointed at my forehead.

"Nothing."

"Interesting. Now read my palm. I'll evaluate your accuracy." He jutted his hand toward my chest, nearly poking me with his finger-tips.

"Hey—watch it."

He grinned.

I would've left if Apollonia hadn't stood next to the evil eye trinket stand, watching my every move. I used one finger to tilt *badger's* palm toward me.

A dark, stately mansion: antique chairs with clawed feet, rich-colored rugs, a polished table displaying sculpted figures of girls in ballet and acrobatic poses. A pungent men's cologne.

"I see a mansion with beautiful furniture, works of art and—"

"Don't insult my intelligence," Badger said, partially closing his eyes. His lids fluttered in a creepy way. "Anyone can guess such from the quality tailoring of my jacket. I want the truth." He jabbed his fingertips into my sternum.

"Ow!" I let go of him and crossed my arms in front of my chest.

"I barely touched you." He glanced from right to left.

"Yes, you did! And it hurt."

"It was an accident, I assure you." His grin frightened me.

"We're through here." I started to walk away, but spotted Apollonia still standing in front of the kiosk glaring at me. Why didn't she just go paint kid's faces? I turned back to Badger.

"We're almost through here. Palm, please."

Snapshots of his past played before me.

"You like to fight others—mentally, not physically. You're cunning with your extensive vocabulary in three, no, four languages. You enjoy besting others in debates, and you don't compromise your opinions. You'd never punch a man in the face because other methods of aggression and retaliation suit you better."

Pictures crawled to the front of my mind of Badger as a child. He sat cross-legged on the ground, smiling and dismembering insects. He threw stones at birds and little—

I dropped his hand and stepped away.

He laughed. "Fantastic, Frauline! I knew you weren't a fake." He slapped five *lei* into my hand.

"Sir, I told you before the reading, the fee is *fifteen lei*."

"You weren't that good, *handleser*. Maybe next time." He toddled off.

I tucked the bill into my right skirt pocket and ran to the nearest water spigots to wash Badger off my skin and his reading from my mind. I leaned over the three-foot spigot pipe to avoid the mud puddle moat. At least Cosmo would be happy with the money from the American. I turned the nozzle.

"Give me what's mine."

I recognized Apollonia's hissy threat. "What are you talking about?"

"The money."

"I don't owe you any money." I rinsed my hands.

"Yes, you do. I deserve the money from the man with the moustache. You didn't even want to read his palm. If it wasn't for me staring at you, you wouldn't have gotten a single *bani*. So hand over the cash."

"No." I looked at her over my shoulder. "I stayed with him because I'm a responsible troupe member and a professional." It was sort of true.

"Wrong!" Apollonia used her foot to push me to the mud.

"Hey!" I fell and then quickly stood, half-coated in muck and my blood boiling white-hot. I fired up to slap her, but she plowed into me, shoving me to the ground. My head barely missed the spigot's steel pipe.

Apollonia turned off the water, drilled her knee into my stomach, and reached in my pocket.

"Stop! You're hurting me. I'll give it to you."

"Make it quick." She brushed her hair off her shoulder and stood.

I held my stomach and stood. My soaked blouse clung to my back, and I smelled like a dungeon-rat.

"Hurry up."

I wiped my face and then handed Apollonia the banknote from the German man.

She snatched it. "*Five lei*? From that overdressed pig? I don't believe it."

"I'm going to Rosa's for a clean costume." I walked away.

"Liar!" Apollonia lunged at my back, making us fall to the dirt.

I shoved her side. "Leave me alone!"

"Not 'til I get my money." She grabbed me by the throat. "You think you're better than everyone, don't you? Well, you're not!" She reached into the pocket holding the money from Jenny.

"Yes!" Apollonia let go of me and stood triumphant. "Now I'll leave you alone." She kissed the wad of bills.

"Give it back! That money has nothing to do with you."

"See you later, mud-rat." She tucked the cash into her bra, stepped over me, and slithered into the crowd.

I walked to the nearest row of food vendors and slipped behind the rickety fencing, so no one would see me crying. Then I heard a yelling match break out, I peeked through a hole in the wood slates. Three guys in black tank tops, jeans, and sleeves of tattoos surrounded the cook at the gyro stand. I recognized the guy in front. It was Fane. The boy I knew from kindergarten had grown into a man with big shoulders and arms and— I backed away from the fence. Like his father before him, Fane wore shadowed eyes.

TEN

Cosmo scolded Apollonia and ordered her to stay away from me after the incident with the money and the mud. I appreciated the gesture, but kept my guard up. Snakes are known to slither underneath doors and slip through wall cracks.

I slept at my auntie's house instead of in the family van during our two-week stay in Bucharest. Auntie insisted, and I didn't mind. Cosmo and Sorin came over every night for dinner.

I liked seeing Sorin in the house I grew up in. After I hid my stuffed animals under my bed, I showed him my room. He liked the wall I'd plastered with *Cirque du Soleil* posters. He referred to my shelves and cases of gymnastic trophies and medals as impressive. Nawa, our crow, and Radu, the cat, took to Sorin and Cosmo right away. It's a good sign when animals like a person. Aunt Sylvie doted on Sorin like a mother does a first born. Fine by me. I hoped he'd become my boyfriend.

After Bucharest, our traveling caravan headed for the coast. We'd perform two days in Mangalia and then drive north to Constanta. Lumi insisted on riding with the guys in the testosterone trailer. Sorin showed up with his backpack, ready to ride in the family van and keep me company. We finally had some alone time—two-hundred-and-fifty-four kilometers of alone time. Alone, that is, except for Lumi's dad, Gheorghe, who drove, and her mom, Gabi, seating in the front passenger seat. Sorin and I hung out in Lumi's and my bedroom. We played cards and board games. I beat Sorin at cards, but he beat me at the board games.

"Val, we have an hour before we get to Mangalia. Is that enough time for you to tell me how you came to be with Miss Sylvie? Dad knows the story, but wanted me to ask you."

"Cosmo knows?" My heart sped.

"Yeah, but if you're uncomfortable we don't have to—"

"No, it's okay." I glanced out the window. We whisked passed a rundown strip mall covered in graffiti and stray dogs roaming about.

Sorin stacked two pillows under his head and lay back on Lumi's bed.

I sat crossed-legged in the center of mine. "Aunt Sylvie tells the story better."

"I don't need to be entertained. I just want to know everything about you." He rolled to his side, facing me. "Plus, it gives me an excuse to stare at you."

I caught a glimpse of my flushed cheeks in the wall mirror. "I remember her telling me the story as if it were yesterday." I took a deep breath and tuned into the memory. "One morning, Aunt Sylvie went into the woods to pick blueberries. It was the end of the season. She said the grassy path leading to the woods sparkled especially bright that day with morning dew. She claimed the birds sang more joyful, and that she felt a miracle was in the air. Like your dad, my auntie exaggerates."

He laughed. "My dad says he doesn't exaggerate, that he's just passionate about life. Go on."

"My Auntie said Nawa followed her into the woods, as usual. He flew overhead and perched on nearby tree while she picked berries. Her basket was half-full when she heard a baby cry."

"In the woods? Was it you?"

I nodded. "Aunt Sylvie dropped her basket and ran. She pointed forward, commanding Nawa to go to the cries. He flew ahead. She followed, pushing off tree trunks and grabbing branches to hurry herself along. Auntie stopped at a clear patch of woods where Nawa sat perched on a tree stump. In the center of the clearing was a white baby basket."

"Amazing. It figures your life began like a fairy tale, *prințesă*."

"Yeah, a *grim* tale of a baby left in the woods to be eaten by wolves and bears."

"Don't say that. It's truly a fairy tale. Think about it. Miss Sylvie's like a fairy godmother, and you are definitely a princess."

"I like that. But if so, you'd be in the tale too, because now I know *you*. Who would you be?"

"Hopefully a chivalrous knight or maybe a prince."

To me, he was both.

"What happened when Miss Sylvie saw you, a little baby in the woods?"

"Aunt Sylvie said the ground circling my basket must've been cleared by someone. There weren't any pine cones, pine needles, or branches cluttering the area. She saw Nawa perched on the tree stump like a royal guard, his black and indigo feathers gleaming in the sun. Auntie picked me up, cradled me in her arms, and carried me home singing that old Romanian lullaby, *Nani, Nani*. Nawa flew overhead."

"Remarkable. So then Miss Sylvie adopted you?"

"After months of legal clearing." I shrugged. "I still don't know who my parents are."

"There must've been *a* clue of who left you in the woods. Didn't Miss Sylvie check the area or—"

"I asked Auntie a thousand times if she had any idea who I belonged to. Were there any footprints, a snagged piece of clothing on a bush, or anything indicating who could've left me in the woods? She said our neighbor, Mr. Karl, went through the area later that day." I unfolded my legs and lay on my side, facing him. "Later, I ran searches on the Internet."

"Nothing's ever come up?"

"A couple of false leads. I've asked Aunt Sylvie, why would a mother leave a baby in the woods to die? She argued that my mother obviously didn't leave me in the woods to die. It was berry-picking season. My basket was in a conspicuous spot. My bottle was half-full and lay next to me as if I'd just been fed. She thinks my mother loved me, but for whatever reason, couldn't keep me."

Sorin sat up, reached over and took my hand. He kissed it. "I'm sure Miss Sylvie's right." He looked at me with warmth.

Sorin's touch, the way he gazed at me ... I felt comforted ... reassured.

He lay back down. "Did she tell you anything else?"

"Yes. Auntie said." I spoke in my best fairy godmother voice. "'You weren't wrapped in some old blanket and dropped into the woods. Why, no, you were placed in a ring of wildflowers.'"

Sorin laughed. "You sound just like her."

"'Why heavens, child!'" I hammed it up. "'A sunbeam had found its way through an audience of trees to shine on the exact spot where you lay.' When I was six-years-old, I asked her if the sunbeam looked like a circus spotlight. Of course, she said yes. I considered the sunbeam to be a sign from God. The circus was my destiny. That's the end of my story."

"*Great* story." Sorin scooted off Lumi's bed and sat next to me. "Valthea," he spoke quietly. "Have you ever had a boyfriend?"

"Uh ... no, not really."

"I really like our friendship."

Terrific. Was I destined to be one of those girls that guys liked only as *a friend*?

"But I want more." He kept his hands folded on his lap. "I want us to be boyfriend and girlfriend." He looked at me as if he'd asked a question.

Boyfriend and girlfriend! My skin tingled, my heart leapt, and my mind went crazy. I wanted to jump on my bed as if it were a trampoline.

"What about you, Val?"

I couldn't speak quick enough. "I want the same."

"Yes!" He hugged me tight, our chests pressing hard together. "You feel so good. I never want to let go of you."

"Me neither."

On the drive to Constanta, Sorin rode in the family van again. Although I lay on my bed, and he lay on Lumi's, I pictured us lying together on lounge chairs on the Black Sea's beach. I imagined us swimming in the salty water, embracing with our wet bodies, kissing each other's lips, necks, shoulders—

"Guess who I met today, Val?"

So much for my fantasy. "Who?"

"A physician visiting from America. He saw our last performance." Sorin continued typing something on his cell phone. "I'm looking him up online. His reputation's excellent." He set his phone on the end table and sat up. "This doctor juggles a little himself. Different, huh? He loved my act."

"That's wonderful, Sorin. Hey, I'm really excited about Constanta. I can't wait to swim in the Black Sea together."

"Me too, Val." Sorin rolled on his side and propped himself up on one elbow. "His name's Dr. Bander and he's head surgeon for the trauma center in a hospital in Florida. He told me that when he was in med school, one of his professors suggested he learn to juggle. Dr. Bander learned how, and now he encourages his students to do the same. Interesting, huh?"

I half-listened, visualizing our bodies becoming one with the sea.

"I handed him three tennis balls from my prop bag. He tossed pretty well."

I huffed and sat up. "A juggling doctor? I don't get it."

Sorin sat up and scooted to the edge of Lumi's bed. "Think about it—juggling increases hand-eye coordination and the ability to let go and trust. Dr. Bander also has his students practice sketching with both hands to increase ambidexterity. I'm going to start doing the same."

"You're going to start drawing?"

"Sketching ... doodling." He put his fingertips on my knees and mimed playing rapid piano notes. "Dexterity, Val. Makes fingers and hands nimble for surgery." He stopped tapping my knees and rubbed them for a second.

I wished he hadn't stopped. I liked the attention.

He grabbed one of Lumi's flat square pillows and laid back. He balanced the pillow on his middle finger and spun it around with his other hand. He kept it spinning. "I have to be ready. Pre-med. September's right around the corner."

"September? I knew you were filling out scholarship applications but—"

"I've been sending out apps for the past three months. One came through just in time for fall."

Sledgehammer blow to my heart. My life went from fabulous to sucking. "Oh. Good. Good for you. You're still going to come home and do the spring and summer festivals next year, right? Your dad already asked me to come back."

"No, this is my last tour of festivals. The college is in England, and pre-med's intense. I can't leave school for weeks or months at a time." He spun the pillow faster. "You don't know how much work it took to convince my dad that I needed to pursue my own dream. He *finally* accepted my leaving the troupe. He knows I want to help people. Someone else can take over when he retires."

"You don't have to be a *doctor* to help people. Singing, tumbling, and juggling make people happy and feel good. Entertainment is healing. Entertainment's good for one's—"

"—soul, yes, I know." Sorin kept his eyes on the spinning cushion. "I've heard it my whole life. Guess my dad's already fed you his favorite nugget of wisdom. Anyway, it's all set. I leave the first of September for London. Exciting, huh?" The pillow toppled from his finger and onto the floor next to my feet.

I kicked the pillow and walked to the room's closed accordion door.

"Val—" Sorin came up behind me and turned me around. "Why are you upset? I thought you'd be happy for me." He followed my eyes until I stopped avoiding his. "My going to college doesn't have to affect us. I want what we're starting to grow. I won't be able to leave school for weeks at a time, but I can fly home once a month or so, to see you."

I nodded, missing him already.

"There's so much I want to share with you. You understand the outside world and the crazy world I grew up in. Plus, I can't wait to know everything about you. We've only just begun." Sorin slid his hands down my shoulders, intertwined his fingers with mine, and drew me in close. Not a single point of light could fit between our hips and chest. His lips neared mine. He inhaled my breath ... my soul.

I inhaled his intensity.

"When we finally kiss," he whispered, "I know I won't be able to stop."

My chest heaved. "Then kiss me. Kiss me now." I closed my eyes.

"Sorin—" Gabi yelled from the other side of the accordion door. "Get out here and drive. Your uncle's falling asleep at the wheel."

ELEVEN

The first night in Constanta, the twelve of us made our way to the seaside resort's nightlife area. Constanta, like most of Romania, presented contrasts at every turn. We walked along the promenade, inhaling fresh salty air. We passed by a row of industrial buildings and a massive shipyard that dwarfed the town's beaches.

Cosmo pointed to the cruise ships docked at the port. "Now *those* ships will guarantee us plenty of festival guests."

"Yes, money, money, money," Apollonia cackled.

Within moments, we came to a long section of shops, bars, and restaurants.

Apollonia stopped in front of a clothing boutique. The center mannequin wore a yellow and white sundress. "That would look beautiful on me. I want to try it on."

I glanced at Apollonia's oversized handbag draped on her shoulder. Normally half-stuffed, it now laid flat against her side. She must've emptied it before leaving her motor home.

She pulled Strum into the boutique.

"*Hei, băieți*, you guys, look!" Silver pointed to a bar across the street. "Live music."

A four-piece band set up their equipment and instruments in the bar's streetside terrace. Silver sped ahead of us. "Who's game?"

"Me, but slow down," Dino said, trailing behind the high energy unicyclist.

Lumi stayed next to Dino.

"Okay, how about the rest of us?" Cosmo stopped and rubbed his hands together. "Anyone hungry?"

"I am," Gabi said.

"We all are." Gabi's husband, Gheorghe grinned and gently patted his wife's belly.

"We are, too." Big Bruno put his arm around Rosa.

"Actually, Dad," Sorin said. "There's a place I want to take Valthea."

"Excellent, son. Seize the moment. Constanta's a romantic town, when you're in love."

"Dad ... "

"Call my cell if you two want to join us after dinner." Cosmo smiled. "Valthea, I'm glad you're with us."

"Thanks. Me, too."

Cosmo and the others continued down the promenade toward more restaurants. Sorin and I ventured off onto a side path that led to *The Mermaid Café & Grill.* The open-air, seaside restaurant buzzed with couples, from their twenties to their seventies, displaying romantic affection. My desire to kiss Sorin amplified every second we were together. *When?* When would he kiss me?

After dinner, Sorin and I strolled back to the main street of the resort's village. We held hands without effort or nervousness. The evening's balmy air and random breezes added to our romance. We walked by a stone-front bakery with its door propped wide open.

"Yum, cinnamon," I said, inhaling.

"And peaches," Sorin added.

"Good nose."

"Thank you." He nodded. "It's not always a good thing."

Black rod iron balconies jutted out from several two-story restaurants and tourist shops. We passed by a noisy beach bar. It looked like a fun place but reeked of beer and grease. Sunburned beachgoers packed the place.

Sorin chuckled. "Now this is when it's not wonderful having a good sense of smell."

We crossed the street. When visions came to my mind from people walking past us, I pushed them away and turned my thoughts to the choreography of an old tumbling routine. No way did I want to be taken away from my precious present with Sorin.

"Val, no one will be back at the motor homes for at least a couple hours. We can go to the family van and relax in private for a while. If you'd like."

"I'd like."

We stopped at a café, ordered two flavored ice teas to-go, and continued toward the road leading to our motor homes.

"You know," Sorin said between sips. "Even though I'm excited about college, I don't like the idea of us being apart."

"I feel the same way. I want to be together. Yet, I'm also excited about my coach sending out audition tapes in September to a bunch of different circuses."

"You're not waiting for the school year to finish?"

"I'll do school online if I get in. I mean, *when* I get in."

"You'll get in."

"Thanks. Hey, Sorin ... I was wondering, how come you never talk about your mom? Did she and Cosmo have a bad divorce or something? Did it end because he was still in love with Gisella?"

"My dad told you about Gisella?"

"Yeah."

"Tragic, huh? My dad definitely knows what true love is. He's always tells me, *never settle, son. Never settle.*"

"My auntie lectures me about love, too. She believes in love-at-first-sight."

Sorin stopped us in the middle of the sidewalk. "What about you? Do you believe in love at first site?"

My heart felt like it would explode. "Uh ... do you?"

"Absolutely."

I swallowed. "Me, too."

"Good."

We walked to the curb, waited for several cars to pass, and then crossed the street. Did 'good' mean Sorin believed in love-at-first-sight, in general? Or was he hinting that he felt something when he first saw me? I sucked down a third of my ice tea.

"So, Sorin, you must take after your mom. Did she have blue eyes, too? You don't look typical *Roma.*"

"You don't either."

"I think you look like a young King Arthur from the time of Camelot."

"I like that." Sorin pulled me to the side, letting a rowdy group pass by us. "Let's sit over here for a minute."

We sat on a concrete garden bench in front of a floral shop. We watched as a couple, conversing with English accents, exited the shop. The man handed the woman a single red rose. They kissed and walked away, arms around each other.

"Val, there's something I want to tell you. But I need you to promise you won't judge anyone else involved in what I'm about to tell you."

"Uh ... all right. I promise."

"Cosmo's not my real dad. He adopted me."

What? "You were adopted, too?"

"Yeah, and, like you, I was abandoned. Cosmo adopted me."

"You're kidding? Oh, my God. How old were you? Where'd he find you? Why didn't you tell me?"

"I've wanted to tell you." He looked down at his tea, stirring it with his straw. "I was four. My parents brought me, my older brother, and my little sister to the Bucharest Spring Festival."

"Where we met?"

"Yup. The three of us kids rode ponies, ponies, watched stilt-walkers, and saw a Gypsy show on stage. I remember because the Gypsy girls danced with tambourines, and my sister had her own mini-tambourine at home. Anyway, after a while, our parents went to a food stand. My older brother was supposed to watch me and my sister. I saw a man walking a bear cub on a leash. I left my siblings and followed them around a corner. When I turned around, I didn't know where I was. I cried until a girl in a Gypsy costume offered me a cookie."

It was my vision! "Sorin, this is a major. I can't believe you waited to tell me this. What happened next?"

"The girl picked me up and carried me, saying she'd help me find my parents."

"So, she took you to the front of the park, to security."

"Actually no. Carrying me, she ducked behind a fence and ran to a motor home, way in the back of the park somewhere. It started pouring rain. I remember the sound on the vehicle's roof."

"Rain, or no rain, that girl wasn't helping you find your parents, at all." I gasped. "It was Apollonia, wasn't it?"

Sorin held up one hand, as if to stop me. "Remember what you promised."

I fumed. "No judgment—but—she *did* kidnap you. What a snake."

"No. Apollonia explained everything to me when I turned ten. She said that she'd seen me with my family and then shortly thereafter, she saw my parents grab the hands of my siblings and hurry off to the exit. Valthea, she saw them leaving, without even looking around for me. They'd left me there on purpose."

"And you *believe* her?"

"Yeah. She might not have made the best choices, but she was a kid. She didn't know what she was doing."

"She didn't know the difference from right and wrong? She didn't think to take you to security and have them announce a lost child over the loud speaker?"

"Back then, not all festivals put up loud speakers. Cosmo called the police station, the orphanages, and child services for weeks after that. He even took out ads in the paper. With no leads, and no legitimate bites, he finally managed to adopt me."

"You didn't know your last name?"

"Cosmo said it was a long name that I couldn't pronounce and he and Aunt Gabi couldn't figure out what I was saying."

"Cosmo did everything he could, of course." I stood, walked to the trash can ten-feet from the garden bench, and pitched my drink. I took my time walking back. "So. Apollonia snatched you up and carried you to a motor home. It rained. Then what?"

"I fell asleep on the couch in the living room. The next day, Apollonia told me she looked for some kind of identification in the neck of my shirt, inside my shoes, and in my jacket pockets. That's where she found a note."

"What'd the note say?"

"That I was a good kid, and whoever found me, please take care of me. The upsetting thing is, is that my parents didn't sign their names. At the bottom of the paper they wrote, 'Parents of Sorin.' All I have from my original family is that note, the clothes I wore, and the toy stethoscope around my neck." Sorin got up and tossed his cup in the trash can.

I didn't believe for one second that Sorin's parents wrote such a note. Apollonia wrote it and hid it that first night. I was sure of it. I looked up. The stars didn't twinkle like they had minutes ago. I didn't want Sorin to hate me for accusing his family. I let go of pushing forth for the truth—for now. I held Sorin's hand. "At least you're safe."

He shifted to face me. "Thank you, Valthea. Thank you for understanding. I feel extremely lucky that Apollonia found me that night. If not, I would've ended up in an orphanage."

"You mean blessed. If my auntie hadn't found me in the woods and adopted me, I would've ended up in an orphanage or dead."

Sorin drew my hands to his lips and kissed my fingertips. "I'm glad we met at a festival instead of a children's home."

We walked.

"Sorin, if your parents left you on purpose, there must've been a good reason why they couldn't keep you. You were a cute kid."

He smirked. "And how would you know that?"

"Oh—" Oops. "Just guessing. Are you still trying to find family?"

"No. I've come to peace with it. The Dobra's love me and care for me. And Cosmo is the greatest dad in the world."

I stopped walking, rose onto my tip toes, and kissed Sorin on the cheek. "Thanks for sharing your story with me."

"Thanks for the kiss."

"You're welcome."

We had turned off the main road and come to a fork in the path.

"Which way, Sorin?"

"Left."

"Sorin, may I share a secret with you."

"Sure. I can keep a secret."

"I can *read* people."

"I noticed. You're very perceptive."

"No, not just perceptive. I'm clairvoyant. I can see people's past."

He stopped. "You're serious."

"Yes."

"That explains a lot." He led us to the right, down a brightly-lit cobblestone street. "So ... what's it like?" He grinned. "Have you read me?"

"I don't always see things. My gift isn't predictable. In a way, it doesn't matter. For the most part, people already know the answers to the questions they'd ask me. They just want someone else to say it out loud. I can't control what part of a person's past I see. I just hope to bring a little comfort and reassurance to the people I do read."

"What about my past? What have you seen?" Sorin faced me, grabbing my shoulders. "That's why you said you knew my parents wanted me. You *saw* them. Tell me, Valthea. Tell me everything, no matter what you saw. I can handle it."

"Sorin. I've barely seen any visions of you. Believe me, I've tried. Other than seeing you study for school, I've seen you only as a toddler with a teen girl giving you a cookie and carrying you away. But you already know that."

"Nothing about my parents?"

I shook my head.

"That's all right. No big deal."

"Yes, it is, Sorin. I know what it feels like not to know. I wish I saw something for you."

We came to the road leading to our motor homes.

Reading people's past was not only a lone experience, it made you feel alone ... isolated. It's like seeing stars in the sky that no one else sees. I looked up to the Constanta sky and searched for the brightest star. If I could see only *one* more vision for the rest of my life, I wished I could see why Sorin's parents left him.

"Here's a story for you, Val." Sorin chuckled. "My dad told me that my first three days with his family, I only ate, cried, and slept. I wouldn't talk or play. Then one morning, he sat with me on my blanket and juggled mini-beanbags. He said it made me laugh. He did this for seven days straight. By the eighth day, I'd become a happy kid. We've laughed together ever since."

"That's great material for a juggler's bio, assuming Apollonia told the truth."

"Val, come on. I'm telling you, Apollonia adored me. She dressed me up every day like her little doll."

"Okay." I play-hit him. "Forget all that. I'm happy she found you, and I'm *extremely* happy we met."

"Me, too *prințesă*. Me, too." He put his hands on my shoulders and petted my arms lightly, from my shoulders all the way down to my fingertips.

I wanted him to grab me in close and kiss me, but we'd reached the grassy lots with our motor homes.

"Come on." Sorin took my hand and led me to the family van.

It took me several tries to unlock the door. Once in, I took off my sandals, and Sorin slipped off his deck shoes.

"Valthea—" Sorin locked his eyes to mine, took my waist in his hands, and backed me out of the entranceway and down the hall. "I'm attracted to you, every part of you."

The rise and fall of my chest revealed the quickening of my breath. Maybe the natural display of my excitement excited Sorin, just like Cosmo's story of how Gisella's excitement further excited him.

Sorin pressed his hands against my bedroom door, his arms on either side of my face. He leaned in, inhaled my scent, and then kissed me. I instantly left the real world and entered the surreal. Sweet kisses led to juicy kisses. Juicy kisses led to ferocious ones. Our bodies merged into an abstract sculpture of two lovers gift-wrapped around each another. The interlaced position cut off some of my hip and shoulders' circulation, but I didn't care—it added to the excitement. My head went light, my skin moist. Sorin and I united into a single flame. No, not a flame—an undulating torch of fire caught in the howl of a summer night's wind. I wanted the thrill to blaze through me, always and forever, never extinguishing.

"After you, *prințesă*." Sorin opened my bedroom door.

I approached the bed, part feline, part woman. I lay next to him, curving my body in a way I hoped made me look alluring and at least eighteen.

He turned on his side to face me. His eyes traveled from my face, down my body, and then back up to my eyes. "You're not only sexy, you're beautiful." He separated strands of my hair with his fingers, smoothed them down my shoulder, and then leaned in to kiss me.

"Wait—" I put my hand to his chest. "I'm not ready to go all the way. I like you, and I'm attracted to you, but I want to save—"

"I know, I know." Sorin let go of me and rolled onto his back. "You want to save yourself for that one special one, your wedding night, your soul mate. I know. It's a girl-thing." He sat up on the edge of the bed and exhaled heavy. "It's hard, but I'd rather you be that kind of girl instead of the one who's already slept with five guys before they've turned twenty. Just know, I'm going to have to pull myself away from you sometimes, like when we're kissing and things get hot and heavy. Like *now*." He stood. "I need a cold soda. Want one?"

"Sure."

He opened my bedroom door. "And don't worry. I still want to be your boyfriend."

"And I still want to be your girlfriend."

"Good."

A minute later, Sorin returned with two sodas. I sipped mine. He guzzled his. We set our bottles on the bedside stand and lay down. We hugged and kissed playfully for several minutes, while half laying on each other. Making out with Sorin was now my absolute favorite thing to do. After we French-kissed for a bit, the heat between us burned hot again. I rolled Sorin to his back, climbed on top of him, and held down his wrists. A surge of power gripped me—part cat, part goddess. I lowered my forearms to either side of his face and purred content over my man prey.

"You're more than I ever expected, Valthea." Sorin's pupils widened. His breath quickened. "Hey, Val."

"Yes?" I kept my voice low.

"Whisper something into my mouth. Anything. I want to feel your words slide down my throat."

TWELVE

A jazz festival occupied the main park in Constanta on Sunday, granting our troupe a day of leisure. Everyone planned to meet at about noon at *Modern,* a large beach in the middle of the city. The guys took off at eight in the morning to play soccer. Rosa and Bruno went out for a buffet breakfast. The rest of the troupe slept in. I decided to go to church by myself.

Aunt Sylvie would've loved Saint Mina's. The Orthodox Church could've been from a fairy tale. It sat on the edge of an aqua blue lake surrounded by tall, Grimm Brothers' fairy tale bushes. It's pointy tower shot skyward. Chocolate-colored wood encased the exterior of the building. Inside, sprays of morning light, myrrh incense, and quiet spirituality, created a confection of peace.

I knelt and prayed. "Dear Father, thank you, for my health and for my auntie's health. Please keep her healthy and happy while I'm away this summer. Thank you for the opportunity to perform with the Royales and for bringing Sorin into my life. Father, I'm in love with him, and I want us to be together forever." I sighed. "If it is Your will. As always, please guide me to use my insight in the right way." I crossed myself and whispered, "In the name of the Father, the Son, and the Holy Spirit, amen."

After the service, I stepped out from the dimly lit church and into a bright summer day. I couldn't wait to go to the beach and swim in the water with my champion.

"*Scuzați-mă,*" barked a woman behind me.

Two elderly ladies circled around and stood in front of me. The thin one, with gray curls peeking out of the edges of her headscarf, whispered, "We stopped you because—"

The meatier woman, with a wrinkled potato face, didn't whisper. "Your womanhood bled through your skirt. We thought you should know."

I subtly smoothed the back of my skirt with one hand. My heart stopped. Oh, God, no—not today.

"Lucky for you, I've good eyes for an old woman. We'll walk you to the church's facilities."

"No thank you. I'll go home." I turned the back of my skirt to the side and let my shoulder purse cover the soiled area.

"Is this your first?" the gruff lady asked. "You a late bloomer?" I didn't answer.

"So you are." She folded her arms. "Lucky for you, I tell it like it is."

"Louisa, please don't—"

"I really need to go." I eyeballed the sidewalk across the street.

The lady named Louisa stepped forward. "Some say it's a joyous day. You're a woman now. They say it's to be celebrated, but I don't agree." She snarled. "Your blood coming warns that you're no longer free. Your innocence and childhood is instantly over. This is why some call it *the curse*."

"Oh, Louisa, please!" The tiny lady tugged on Louisa's shawl.

"She must know, Emmie." Gruff Louisa put her face to mine. "From now on, you must protect yourself from men until the day you marry. And when you do marry, more freedom slips through your fingers. He's the man. You've the monthly blood. Children follow. Prepare to worry and toil the rest of your days."

The old woman's warnings went down as unpleasant as cod liver oil. "I've got to go. *Le revedere*, bye." I walked away, taking small steps and trying to keep my legs close together.

Once back at the family motor home, I tore off my clothes and hopped into the shower. How unfair. I needed to dress like a girl in mourning for a week every month, to be sure blood never showed through on my clothes. If I were home, Auntie would cheer me up, bringing out her old circus books and photo albums. She'd make me hot cocoa and butterscotch pudding with nutmeg sprinkled on top. Radu would curl up next to me on the bed and purr until I napped. Nawa would caw and do clever things to entertain me. Why did this stupid thing happen today? I cried so hard, I peed. My blood-reddened pee streamed to the shower floor, mixing with my fallen tears, and swirled down the drain. I yelled up to the bathroom ceiling, "This day sucks!"

Afraid Sorin and everyone would return soon, I hurried out of the shower and dressed. I folded some toilet paper into a makeshift pad and placed it inside my underwear. I hunted for pads in the bathroom cabinet, every drawer in the trailer, and under each bed. I went back into the bathroom and pawed under the sink one more time. How could Gabi and Lumi be out of pads at the same time?

C.K. Mallick

I gripped the bathroom sink and looked into the mirror. Although I didn't believe in curses, it felt like a second one struck with my next thought. I had to ask the most evil woman on the planet for the most embarrassing thing in the world. I pushed off the sink and stormed out of the family van, slamming the door behind me. My heart thumped harder and harder as I headed across the grassy lot toward the den of the wicked sorceress. Strum had parked their motor home fifty-feet away from the rest of ours. Apollonia had claimed she needed quiet to catch up on her beauty sleep. Ridiculous. She needed inner beauty.

"Apollonia ... Apollonia!" I yelled, knocking on her door. If she didn't answer in three seconds, I'd walk into town and—

The door opened. "Oh. You." Apollonia folded her arms and leaned against the door frame. She looked sallow and mundane in her beige, Japanese-style robe with no makeup and stringy hair. She reminded me of a geisha before her wigs, makeup, and charms. "How interesting," she hissed. "I'm supposed to stay away from you, yet here you are, at my doorstep, first thing in the morning. What the hell do you want?"

"It's not that early. It's almost ten-thirty."

"Whatever! What are you doing here?"

"I need something," I mumbled.

She narrowed her eyes.

"I need a ... a ... um—"

"Stop acting like an orphan, and come in. I need my coffee." She left the door open and walked inside.

I kept my legs close together walking up the steps. I trembled, alone for the first time with the sorceress in her den.

Apollonia stood in her kitchen in front of the stove. She turned the flame up under a kettle on the back burner, and then faced me, leaning against the side counter. She slid a cigarette from her tarnished silver case. She lit it, sucked in a slow drag, and then exhaled in my direction.

I coughed.

"You've already been to church?" she asked, going to the refrigerator.

"Yes." I stayed by the door.

"Then you don't need cash." She poured five spoonsful of sugar into her cup. "So?"

"Um ... "

Apollonia struck a spoon on the counter's edge. "Valthea—I'd like to relax with my coffee and cigarette this morning alone. Stop wasting my time, and tell me what you need."

"A pad." My words drowned under the hot kettle's whistle.

"A *what*?"

"A *pad*," I yelled, but didn't need to. Apollonia had picked up the kettle.

She froze in place, poised as if a plot brewed within her mind. Without a word, she poured the boiling water into a French press.

I perspired. My insides cramped. Cigarette smoke filled the tiny kitchen adding to the claustrophobic atmosphere. I wanted to get what I needed and run.

Apollonia smoothed her robe and sat on the bright side of the kitchen booth as if taking her place on a throne. She slid the ashtray from the back of the table to the center. Blinding sunlight shot through the window. It washed out the color in her face and lightened her jade eyes to the to the yellow-green of emerald tree boa constrictors.

"You started your period today?"

I looked to the floor.

"Wait a second—is this your first time?"

I glanced up.

She gleamed. "At church?"

"Yeah."

She burst out laughing.

"Forget it!" I spun around, flung the door open, and ran down the steps and out into the grassy field. As I ran, the folded toilet paper in my underwear worked its way upward, to the back of my waistband. I reached around, pulled out, and threw it to the ground. I hated my period already.

"Hold on—" Apollonia yelled. "I've got what you need. Come on back before the guys come home."

I looked over my shoulder.

The witch waved me back.

Merde! Sorin couldn't see me like this. Neither could Cosmo or anyone else.

Once inside Apollonia's motor home again, she locked the door and led me to the tiny bathroom. "Before my morning coffee, I'm horrible to my fiancé, too." She smiled her fakest smile. "Don't feel special."

But I did feel special. Apollonia was *always* horrible to me.

She held her cigarette to the side and grabbed a box from the cabinet below the sink. "Here. Tampons." She put the box on the counter and pulled out a white stick. "Stick this inside you. It'll absorb the blood. I'll leave you so you can concentrate." She laid the stick on the counter and left, closing the bathroom door behind her.

I opened the door and stuck my head out. Apollonia was halfway to the kitchen. "Apollonia, do you have any pads, instead?"

She turned, exhaling smoke as she spoke. "If you want to be an entertainer, you must wear tampons. Now hurry up. I want you out of here so I can relax."

"What about woman cloths. Do you have any of those?"

"That's it." Fury on her face, she stormed toward mme. She shoved me from the doorway. "You've wasted my entire morning." She threw the cigarette into the toilet. "Just another reason I don't like needy newcomers. I'm not here to hold your hand. Now stick this thing up you."

"No. I don't know how, and I don't want to. I want a pad."

"I don't have any pads. Pull down your panties and spread your legs. I'll do it for you."

"No!" I pushed her away and went for the door.

She grabbed me and shoved me against the wall, slamming my back against the towel bar.

"Ow!" I cried.

"Shut up! You're not hurt."

"Get away from me!" I ran out of the bathroom and out of the motor home. I leapt from the top step to the ground, landed weird, and fell forward on my hands and knees. I quickly jumped up and ran fifteen-yards before Apollonia called me back.

The beige-robbed sorceress stood on the top step of her doorway. "Here—" She threw a square box my direction. It hit the ground and bounced. "Take it." Apollonia then turned and slithered back inside her den of darkness.

I walked to the box. Pads. I looked up. Apollonia watched from a window. I ran with the box to the family van, ignoring the blood trickling down my inner thighs and the tears blurring my vision. I never wanted to see Apollonia again, and I never wanted to use tampon sticks. I didn't care if I was the only circus star who wore pads and insisted her costumes be black or dark red.

By one o'clock, the troupe showed up at *Modern* beach. Hundreds of vacationers lounged in the rows and rows of rentable beach umbrellas and lounge chairs. Others played and swam in the water or stretched out on towels on the sand. Cosmo rented four umbrellas, each with a pair of lounge chairs. He, Rosa, Big-Bruno, and pregnant-Gabi sat together under one umbrella, feasting on chicken salad and pita chips. Lumi lay on a lounge chair with her umbrella closed. The guys played Frisbee in knee-deep water, forty-feet from shore.

Sorin called me moody because I wouldn't go swimming. He didn't understand. Cursed is different than moody. Stupid *red-tide* situation. Sorin and I could've floated in the water together, swam, and shared salty kisses. But instead, I lay on the chair next to Lumi, praying direct sun would dry up my uterus and stop this thing called menstruation.

That evening, Cosmo reserved a terrace table at a popular Greek restaurant. I bought postcards from its mini gift shop to send to Aunt Sylvie, keeping my promise of informing her of the cities we traveled. I wrote about the shops along the promenade, the beaches, and St. Mina's, but not a thing about my womanly passage.

Sorin and I joined the others on the restaurant's upper terrace. The air felt balmy and divine. My maxi-pad felt bulky and awkward. We sat at a long dinner table. Our drinks came within minutes.

Apollonia raised her pink-colored cocktail. "I'd like to toast Valthea on her special day."

Everyone held up their glasses.

I glared at her. She wouldn't dare ...

"First, a riddle," Apollonia articulated her words. "What famous body of water in the Bible does Valthea relate to starting today?"

"Huh?" Dino mumbled.

"I don't get it." Silver scrunched his face.

"The *Red Sea!*" Apollonia blurted. "Valthea became a woman to-day. She started her—"

"Shush!" Rosa smacked her sister's wrist. "Leave her alone."

"Why? We're celebrating." Apollonia's laugh rose to a shrill.

Hate wound in my stomach like a tornado. I wanted to fling my fork at the evil witch. I leaned toward Sorin and whispered, "I'm leaving."

He grabbed my arm before I could stand and whispered back, "Leave now and she wins."

He was right. I scooted my chair in.

Cosmo's fist hit the table. "Enough, Apollonia!" He nodded to Strum. 'Take your fiancé out of here before I kill her."

Apollonia brushed her long hair from her shoulder and smiled. "I'm going out to smoke." She looked down her nose at me as she and Strum passed by.

Sorin placed a hand on my knee. "Stay cool, Val ... let it go."

I trembled with rage. The rest of the troupe sipped their drinks, shot me looks of concern, and read their menus. Their distress made me feel better. Apollonia was one of theirs. I was the outsider.

Minutes later, Sorin leaned into me again and whispered, "She's coming back. Why don't *you* make a toast? Show her what kind of a woman you are."

I took a breath and picked up my virgin daiquiri. "Everyone, I'd like to make a toast."

Strum and Apollonia continued toward their seats.

"Here's to *The Gypsy Royales*! Thank you for welcoming me into your troupe, not only as a performer, but now as a full-fledge woman."

The troupe clinked glasses and cheered.

Apollonia almost tripped over her chair.

Cosmo strode from the head of the table over to me with his beer held high. "Here's to Valthea." He put his free hand on my shoulder. "She's survived our crazy and dramatic family. God love her!"

"*Salut!*"

"*Salut!*"

"Cheers!"

Cosmo tapped his bottle to my glass. We drank, and he hugged me with one arm. "I love you." He kissed my forehead and then strode back to his chair.

I wanted to cry. I used to imagine my mother saying, "I love you", before leaving me in the woods. In real life, no one but my auntie ever uttered the words. But now Cosmo did. I loved him for that, and I loved him, too.

Lumi walked up to my chair as our waitress placed plates of calamari, olives, hummus, and bread on the table. "Want to go to the ladies room?" she asked.

"Sure." I wanted to check on my womanly state anyway.

When I came out of the bathroom stall, Lumi stood in front of the mirror brushing her hair. I washed my hands.

She spoke to the mirror we faced, "Where'd you find tampons anyway? Mom and I are out. Did you go to the store? I hate buying those things. I feel like everyone's staring at me."

I pulled a lip gloss out of my purse. "I went to Apollonia. She gave me a tampon and a box of pads."

"Really? That's weird. Maybe she keeps a box of pads around in hopes that her period will magically return"

"Return?" I put on some gloss.

"She doesn't get her period anymore."

"I didn't know that."

"Why do you think she doesn't have any kids?" Lumi stuffed her hairbrush into her purse.

"How come she doesn't get her period anymore?"

"I don't know. No one tells me anything."

"Strum knows she can't conceive, and he doesn't mind?"

"Guess not. They've been engaged for two years."

A surge of unfamiliar, yet powerful energy permeated my mind and spread into my body. I finally had the ammunition I needed to cage, de-fang, and drain Apollonia of her venomous words and ways. Tons of clever and mean things to say to her flooded my mind.

"Ready?" Lumi asked.

I grinned and zipped my purse shut. "*Absolut.*" I checked my hair in the mirror one more time. I didn't recognize myself. Distortion, worse than any funny mirror at a carnival could produce, reflected back at me. Vengeance and ill-intention blotted out my bright eyes and light-hearted glow. I rewashed my hands to get rid of the grotesqueness. It stunned me how easy dark and negative thoughts could take over.

Lumi and I left the bathroom and returned to the table.

Sorin pulled out my chair. "You okay?"

"Yeah, thanks."

Apollonia forked some calamari and glared at me from across the table.

In a blink, visions of Apollonia's past appeared.

Apollonia, ten years ago, twenty-something. ... She lay in a heap on her bathroom floor, crying from her gut. A river of blood came from her nightgown. "No, no!" she wailed, sounding like a mother elephant, gorilla, or cow, stripped of its offspring so their young could be chained and used for kiddy rides, butchered for a souvenir hand, or dished out as veal parmesan. I shuddered. *Apollonia's cries were that of a mother who never had a chance to love her baby. She had miscarried.*

The vision altered. ... Apollonia lay in a hospital bed. Strum sat next to her. When the nurse left the room, room, Strum unzipped his jacket and pulled out a white kitten. He placed it in Apollonia's outstretched hands. The gray splotch on one side of its head looked like a beret. Apollonia cuddled and

93

kissed the kitten. She kissed Strum and held the kitten close to her bosom, gently rocking back and forth. "There, there," she sang softly. "It's all right. I've got you. There, there ... "

Recent. Apollonia and Strum walked from Strum's car toward the house. Night time. No else one around. "Why?" Apollonia cried, slurring her shouts, and barely able to walk a straight line. She carried an open bottle of vodka. "Why does God hate me? All I ... all I ever wanted was a child. Just one." She dropped the bottle and collapsed into Strum's arms. He held her for a moment, and then scooped her up, and carried her as if he'd done it many times before.

"Hey, acro-rat, everything all right down there?" Apollonia slapped the table and let out one of her classic cackles.

I didn't look away from Apollonia, but remained poised. For I no longer feared the snake. I pitied her.

THIRTEEN

Cosmo yelled, "Circle time, everyone. Last show of the summer!" Cosmo took my hand, starting the circle.

The troupe gathered and continued forming a circle behind the festival stage. Cosmo scheduled Brasov, the Dobra family's hometown, as the last city. Only I needed to say good-bye at the end of the day.

Rosa walked up and took Cosmo's other hand.

Sorin ran up and clasped my free hand with his. I wanted to cry. Would Sorin and I ever perform together again?

Silver stepped into the circle between me and Sorin. "It's been fun, Val."

My heart cracked. "Greatest time of my life."

Cosmo closed his eyes. "Thank you, God, for the exceptional people surrounding me on this fine day. What a fantastic troupe! Help us put on a great show, and please be with my family, and extended family after today as we go on with our lives." He squeezed my hand. "May this not be the end of summer, but the beginning of a wondrous fall filled with new friendships."

After a ripple of amen's and high-fives, Cosmo clapped his hands and yelled, "Places everyone!"

Everyone dispersed to the prop box, the dressing tent, and the base of the stage steps.

"Here," Apollonia huffed, handing me a scrap of paper. "Miss Sylvie called earlier. Don't throw it away. She made me write her message verbatim because she's going to ask you for it later. What a suspicious old woman. Like I wouldn't tell you she called." She continued walking toward the dressing tent.

Did Apollonia really think I wouldn't tell my auntie how mean she'd been to me? Small-brained-snake. I read the note:

> Mr. Karl and I will be at the bus station. Can't wait to see you.
> Miss you.
> -Auntie.

I studied it. The distinct handwriting style looked exactly like the writing in the note that Sorin's parents left with him.

"Two minutes to our marks!" Cosmo yelled. "Have a great show, everyone!"

I ran to the other side of the stage. "Sorin!"

He held three bowling pins in each hand. "What's up, Val? You're pretty happy for it being our last day."

"I'm not happy about that at all. I'm happy for what I've discovered. Look—I'd had my suspicions, but now we've proof."

"Val, you're right about a lot of things, but can we talk after the show?"

"Just take a quick look." I held up the note from Apollonia. "Recognize this writing?"

"Places—now!" Cosmo yelled.

"I'll look later." Sorin kissed me on the forehead. "Better hurry to the other side."

I tucked the note into my pocket, ran behind the stage to the platform's steps, and lined up behind Apollonia and the other girls. I stared at the back of Apollonia's head. I couldn't wait for Sorin to know the truth about his childhood.

After the show, we took our bows and exited the stage. The musicians packed up their instruments and Sorin and Silver packed their clubs, balls, and Frisbees into mesh bags.

"Sorin."

"Hey, Val."

"Here." I handed Sorin the handwriting the message from my aunt that Apollonia wrote down. "Really look this time."

Sorin unfolded the note.

"Apollonia answered Cosmo's cell phone right before our show. She wrote the message from Aunt Sylvie." I pointed to the note. "Look at her handwriting. In what other note, that you've read a million times, do you remember seeing this kind of writing? Apollonia doesn't dot her *i*'s like normal people. She draws circles. In the note your parents supposedly left with you, the writer also drew circles."

Sorin handed me the note and then slung his bag of props over one shoulder. "You're reaching, Val." He put his arm around me and walked us toward the back lot. "I know you don't like Apollonia."

"What does that matter? She *hates* me. It's not the point."

"No, Val. You're frustrated. You've no clues to find your parents, and you're—"

"No, Sorin, forget all that. Don't you want to know who your parents are? What really happened that day?"

He stopped and faced me. "Babe, you make an adorable Sherlock Holmes, and I appreciate you wanting to help, but a lot of people make circles instead of dots."

"Maybe, but how many people make circles, *and* over-sized capital I's, *and* cross their T's with a sharp downward slash?" I held the note in front of his face.

He glanced and then kept walking.

"Sorin, let's confront her. I mean, *you* confront her. Ask her directly. Did you take me from family?"

"Valthea, to be honest, I don't want to ignite a major drama. I leave for college next week."

"Exactly. You could find out the truth before going away. Confront Apollonia."

"Val, stop. Don't you think I've already considered the possibility that Apollonia stole me that night and forged that note? Sure I did. But I decided years ago, that even if she did stoop that low, my biological parents didn't look very hard for me. If they really wanted to, they could've found me. I don't care anymore. Cosmo's my dad. The troupe is my family. I've accepted it. I hope you can, too."

I couldn't. I tossed the note into a nearby trash barrel. Seeing past events taught me many things about people or as Aunt Sylvie called it, human nature. People aren't always ready to act on the information given to them. Timing affects everything. It'd only be a matter of time before Sorin saw the truth.

My bedroom looked exactly as I'd left it. Why would it look any different? I was the one who left my home to travel with a group of strangers. I scooped up the Cinderella pillow and lioness stuffed animal from my bed and carried them to my closet. Over the summer, I performed a solo in eight different cities across the country. I read palms of nice people and mean ones, and I became a woman. I opened my closet, dropped the pillow and stuffed animal into a half-full, clear, plastic storage container, and snapped the lid shut. During my time with the Royales, I also defended myself against a begrudging wolverine with a cane and a venomous, green-eyed sorceress. But most significant of all, I met, kissed, and fell in love with my soul mate.

The lioness looked up at me through the container's clear top. As a kid, I never let my auntie store dolls or animals in a closed box. I didn't want them to suffocate. Cute notion coming from a kid, but silly from an adult. I slid the container under my hanging clothes and shut the closet door.

"*Dejun,* Valthea. Breakfast!"

C.K. Mallick

"Be right there." I headed down the hall, but then turned around and went back in my room. I threw open the closet door, pulled the lioness and cub from the Tupperware-like coffin, and placed them back at the head of the bed.

The kids at school acted the same as they did in May. I'd called my friend, Lyla every other week over the summer. I told her about the American cowgirls I met at the festival, of Apollonia, the cruel beauty with a haunting cackle, and Sorin, my boyfriend and champion. She listened to my stories with enthusiasm, but then interrupted me rattling on about the same things she always did, her controlling parents, crushes on cute boys, her clothes and hair. I felt like I'd grown up, leaving her behind, but she was still my friend. Coach Muzsnay responded to my heightened zeal at gym practice and singled me out from the rest of *The Lionesses* team. He'd always seen my future in the Olympics, until I turned fifteen and grew two-inches. The growth-spurt threw my timing off and slowed my progression. Plus, five-feet, six-inches was tall for an Olympic gymnast. I cried for two days and then got over it. My dream had always been the circus anyway. My height saved me from delaying it four years. Coach Muzsnay videotaped my routines and played them back for me. My teammates didn't hide their jealously. I stayed friendly, but focused. I had goals, and those goals called my name every second of every day.

Sorin and I communicated in every way possible. Sometimes by phone calls or texting, other times we FaceTimed or Skyped, but my favorite were the video chats.

I adored seeing him and loved when he kissed his *iPad* pretending to kiss me. I printed out his romantic emails, held them in my hands, and read them like the old-fashioned love letters Aunt Sylvie stored in boxes, but wouldn't let me see. Could two human beings keep a relationship alive through emailed love letters, cell phone kisses, and video camera dates? I prayed so. If not, Sorin and I could end up facing the blank screen of a lifeless love.

By the end of October, our conversations dwindled to three, sometimes two, times a week. He needed more time to study. I needed time to perfect my audition DVD for circus scouts.

Aunt Sylvie yelled from kitchen. "Val. Telephone. It's Sorin!"

"Coming!" I ran downstairs.

"Oh, Sorin," Aunt Sylvie sighed, standing next to Nawa's cage. "It's wonderful to hear your voice and know that you're doing well at school. I'm so proud of you."

I walked toward her, one hand reaching out for the phone.

"Valthea's here, and she's excited to talk to you."

"Auntie, don't say that." I reached for the phone again.

"Here she is." She handed me the phone.

I grabbed the phone and shooed her into the living room.

"Oh, you're fine dear." Aunt Sylvie smiled on her way to give them privacy.

"Hi, Sorin." I sat on the nearest bar stool. "Why didn't you call my cell phone? I'm sorry about Auntie keeping you on the phone."

"I called that phone on purpose. I wanted to say hello to Miss Sylvie. So, how are you?"

"Good, but I haven't heard from you in a week."

"And I haven't heard from *you* in a week." He chuckled. "My dad says you and him are emailing each other. I'm glad. It takes pressure off of me. He doesn't understand that I can't call him morning, noon, and night. He wants to talk every day."

"Cosmo and I are similar that way." I used to wonder if Cosmo could be my father. We both stood with our backs arched the same way, laughed like hyenas at good jokes, and hated onions. I'd eliminated the idea because like Sorin, Cosmo and I didn't resemble each other. Besides, Gypsies are known to *take* babies and children, not give them away. "I've good news, Sorin. Coach Muzsnay sent an audition DVD of me to eight European circuses and shows. One he sent to a former student, the choreographer for *Sky Brothers Circus*. Not that she'll show favoritism, but he said she'll at least watch more than the first thirty-seconds because it's from him."

"That's great. Good luck."

"He says we should hear back by November." I hopped off the stool. "I pray one of them picks me."

"November? That soon?"

"Most shows need to be cast by December. Isn't it exciting?"

"Sure, except I thought of a way for us to be together."

"You're going to pursue your degree online and travel with me?" I held my breath.

"Nice idea, but no. Listen, Val, I've got a study group in fifteen minutes. Let's talk later about your idea of joining the circus."

"It's not an idea, Sorin. It's my dream. It's real, and it's almost here."

"I thought that maybe—"

"You've a study group at ten at night?"

Aunt Sylvie walked into the kitchen and filled the tea kettle with water.

Timing.

"It has to be at ten. Some classes don't let out until nine. Why are you upset?"

I kept my back to my auntie and wiped a sprinkling of tears from my face. I whispered, "Because we never have enough time to talk anymore. I always feel rushed with you."

"Aw, babe. Let's talk or message tomorrow night, okay?"

I wanted to tell Sorin that I missed him desperately, but I didn't want to sound like an eleven-year-old girl with a crush. "Okay."

"I miss you. X-O, *prinţesă*."

"X-O." I hung up and headed out of the kitchen.

"Hold on, there." Auntie followed me into the living room. "You spoke with Sorin on the phone, yet you don't look happy. What's wrong?"

I stopped at the base of the stairs. "Everything's fine. He has a late study group, and Ive an early gym practice." I walked up the stairs.

"Don't be too hard on yourselves. Long-distance relationships are challenging."

"I know, Auntie." I leaned over the upstairs railing. "We're fine. We're following our dreams without being weighed down by emotions."

"Emotions like *love?* Valthea, love doesn't weigh you down. It builds and lifts you up. On the other hand, impatience, jealousy, and fear of abandonment will weigh heavy on the heart."

"Who said anything about love and the heart? Cosmo? You two should understand how impossible it is to balance career and love. Goodnight." I started to go into my room, but stopped. I turned around and walked back down the stairs into the kitchen.

Auntie stood in front of the stove, staring at the whistling kettle. I turned off the stove and set the kettle on another burner. "I'm sorry for what I said about you and Cosmo. I guess I'm afraid Sorin will forget me and how great we are together."

"Nonsense." She poured the boiling water into two mugs of chamomile. "Bring the dish of mixed nuts, please." She walked past me toward the living room, a cup in each hand.

I set the nut dish next to the mugs on the coffee table. A dog, or maybe a wolf, howled outside. I parted the bay window's drapes and pressed my forehead to the cold glass, hoping to see it. The robust moon glowed red-copper.

"Cosmo didn't say anything and you don't confide in me, but a mother knows things. I can tell how much you feel for Sorin and how he feels for you."

I turned from the window.

"It seems like you're putting a fence around your heart." She wrapped both hands around her tea mug as if warming them. "Sorin adores you. I can hear it in his voice on the phone. I saw it in his eyes at the bus station. He's in love with you, Valthea."

I wanted to believe Sorin was still in love with me. The row of trees lining our backyard stood tall and silent like armed soldiers who slumber while standing guard.

"Valthea, you two are friends and you're in love."

Radu wove in and around my legs. I picked him up and cradled him like a baby. "It's not fair, Auntie."

"What's not fair, dear?"

"That my dream career takes me far away from my dream guy."

FOURTEEN

"*Stai jos.* Come sit." My auntie walked into the living room where I played with Radu. "We need to have a serious talk." She patted the couch cushion next to her.

"Wait." I pushed my sweater sleeves up. "Watch how Radu flips in the air." Serious talks from my Aunt Sylvie were never good. I dangled a feather cat toy four-foot in the air. Radu jumped up and swatted it. "Radu's practically a circus kitty."

Aunt Sylvie sat primly, crossing her ankles. "Speaking of the circus, Mr. Muzsnay called."

"He did?" I darted around the coffee table and sat next to her. "What'd he say? Was it about my audition CD?"

"Yes."

"Yes!" I punched the air above me. "Which circuses liked me?"

She lowered her eyes.

"Oh." I froze like an ice sculpture to keep the dagger of rejection from piercing my heart and bleeding me to death. "My life is over. They don't want me. I'll never be a—"

"Valthea, please. Let me finish. Six of the circuses and shows declined, but two asked Coach Muzsnay for a second DVD. So, he sent the longer version that you two made."

"Thank God." My ice shield melted. My numbed heart beat strong again. "Which two?"

"*Presto,* the show in Athens."

"That's the magic show with a couple of aerial acts."

"Yes. The second one is *Sky Brother's Circus.*"

I bounced on the sofa cushion causing Aunt Sylvie to bounce, too. "That's the one I want!"

She grabbed my forearm, stilling me. "We need to discuss the three possibilities. *Presto, Sky Brothers Circus,* or trying again next year."

"We can't even let ourselves think of that last possibility."

"Fine. I know how you are about positive thinking. The possibility is there, but we won't focus on it." She folded her hands on her lap. "If you join the show in Greece, you'll leave mid-February, learn your numbers, and perform from April to—"

"April to June." I used my hands if a wall calendar hung in front of me. "Two shows a night, except for Good Friday. I memorized everything."

102

"There's no touring because it's a stage show, but you'd still leave home, live with strangers, and perform as a professional. It's a less drastic booking than signing a nine-month contract with *Sky Brothers Circus*."

"I like drastic. I want it."

"Of course, dear. If *Sky Brothers Circus* hires you, you'd leave the first of January. After six weeks of rehearsals and two weeks of shows in Sofia and Bulgaria, you'll begin touring."

"Yeah, I studied Sky Brothers. They tour nine countries, March through November. The founder's grandson is the current director. There are no animal acts. They do matinees four days out of six. Mondays are black. That means there are no shows."

"I know what it means." Auntie furrowed her brow. "It's a rigorous schedule, dear. Don't think it'll be easy."

"The more shows, the better. I hope they pick me. Did Coach say anything else?"

"With the show in Greece, you'll do school online and room with other girls in bunkers. With Sky Brothers, you're assigned a tutor, and you'd share a motor home with roommates."

"My dream is nearly here!" I sprung to my feet, wanting to race up and down the neighborhood like a roadrunner. "I can't believe it, I mean, I *do* believe it! I sat, seeing my Auntie tear up. "Don't worry. Whether I end up in Greece or touring Europe, I'll visit you a lot."

"You can't, Valthea. You can't just leave any time you please. It's show business. In fact, once you sign a contract, you can't leave unless there's a dire emergency."

"Then I'll save my money and send you plane tickets."

She wiped her eyes with her handkerchief. "You know I won't fly. If Sky Brothers chooses you, I'll take a bus and visit you in Bulgaria. If you end up in Greece, Mr. Karl and I will drive one weekend to see you." She put away her hanky. "Tsk! We don't know anything yet. And here I am crying and getting your hopes up."

"You're not getting my hopes up. My hopes have never gone down." I opened the bay window curtains. The oaks and beeches stood scantily clad in a few sepia leaves and some completely naked. When I was little, I'd wished that the fallen autumn leaves would stay bright lemon-yellow, pumpkin-orange, and apple-red. I imagined them in a cartoon, dancing a jig with the wind over snow mounds and frozen ponds, mimicking their lily pad sisters which glided across lakes in the summertime. But nature follows its destiny. Every year, the fall colors dropped and decayed. What was my natural destiny?

If the *Presto* show in Greece hired me, I could see Sorin every month from October to February. If *Sky Brothers Circus* hired me, and I toured with them, I'd only see Sorin at Christmas and his summer break. If no one hired me, we could take turns visiting each other every month. Whichever way the wind blew, I'd experience something great and miss out on something great. Nature. Destiny.

December first. December second. December sixteenth! Winter vacation finally arrived. Auntie and I'd travel the next morning to Brasov. I couldn't wait to see Sorin. I sat on the bay window seat, petting a purring Radu. Snow fell earlier than normal. Mini snow puffs, speckled with bits of twig, balanced on the bushes behind our home. They reminded me of the powdered-sugar cookies served at holidays and wedding receptions.

I laid Radu on the blanket next to me and went to the kitchen. "Auntie, let's bake powdered wedding cookies to bring to Cosmo and Sorin tomorrow."

She poked her head out from behind the pantry door. "Wedding cookies? That's subtle."

"No, I'm *not* hinting. It's a holiday cookie, too. Italian's serve them at Christmas-time."

"Of course, dear." She giggled, taking the flour form the fridge. "I just happen to have all the ingredients, just like you and Sorin have all the ingredients for a wonderful marriage."

"If you're going to say that when we give them the cookies, let's not make them."

"I won't need to say a word. The morsels will speak for themselves."

Early the next morning, we traveled by bus to Brasov with a suitcase and two tins of cookies.

"Take the window seat, dear." Auntie waited for me to slide in. "I'll most likely nap."

After an hour of asphalt highway, the morning clouds lifted, and the sun came out as we drove into a small town. The buildings and church rooftops glistened with a clean layer of snow. Quaint shops flaunted yellow and purple pansies from window planters. Snow-speckled grassy hills rolled in the background. I wanted to inhale the crisp freshness of the outdoors until a worry crept in, casting a shadow on the postcard village. Would Sorin be happy that *Sky Brothers Circus* loved my tapes and hired me? Or would he be upset I hadn't told him sooner?

"We'll reach Brasov in twenty minutes. Ah," Auntie sighed. "Christmas near the mountains ... how lovely."

I pulled out my wool cap and makeup compact from my handbag. I opened the compact and examined my face in its mirror.

"Your makeup's fine, dear. It's as in tact as it was five minutes ago. Remember, Sorin won't be at the station when we get there. He's flying in from England today."

"I know. Bruno's picking him up from the airport." I blended my eyeliner with my finger. "Auntie, please don't mention anything about my getting into the circus until I've a chance to tell him."

"What?" Auntie shifted in her bus seat and glared at me. "You haven't told him yet?"

"I will as soon as I see him." I snapped shut my compact.

"I'm disappointed, Valthea. I need to know you've the sense and courage to make responsible choices. You're about to leave home for eleven months and travel around Europe with complete strangers."

"I said, I'd tell him."

"It's not the point." Auntie sat straight in her seat again. "Why would you withhold such news anyway?"

"I want to tell him in person."

"What about Cosmo? Have you told him?"

"I will." I pulled on my wool cap and tucked in my hair. "After I tell Sorin."

Our bus pulled into the Brasov train station. Cosmo stood on the sidewalk smoking and talking on his cell phone. He waved, seeing us exit the bus. "*Alo, alo,* my two favorite ladies!" He tucked away his phone. "How was the trip?"

"Fine. Thanks for picking us up."

Cosmo greeted Auntie with a kiss on either cheek and then gave me a big hug.

"My car's right here." Cosmo pressed his key chain and the trunk to his Maserati popped open. He'd parked in the fire lane. He fit our suitcases into the trunk. "Ah, Valthea, we missed you so much. Well, mostly me and Sorin." He opened the car doors for me and Auntie.

"Thanks." I slid in the backseat. "I didn't think you meant Apollonia and Grandmamma."

"Ha! Listen to her, Sylvie. Our girl's grown into a beautiful and funny woman."

"Yes, my girl has." Auntie fastened her seatbelt.

Cosmo sped through the snow-dotted countryside, while he and Auntie talked about Gabi's pregnancy, his rental business, and how empty the house seemed without Sorin.

"Is he in from England yet?" Aunt Sylvie asked, reading my mind.

"He should be home by now. Bruno left an hour ago for the airport."

What if Sorin wasn't as excited to see me as I was to see him? What if he was furious I hadn't told him about the circus? *Think positive, Valthea. Think positive.* I sat back in the heated leather seat and stared out at the hills. I released my worries and imagined them floating out of Cosmo's car and drifting away like lacey snowflakes.

Cosmo pulled into his home's two-car garage. "Welcome to the Dobra House. You each have your own room. Sylvie, Gabi has the extra bedroom for you, and Val, if it's okay, you'll stay in my den on the sofa bed."

"That's great," I said, looking past him for Sorin.

"We appreciate your generous hospitality," Auntie said. "Thank you."

We slipped our boots off at the door and walked into the house through the kitchen.

Cosmo shouted as we walked into the foyer. "Guess who I brought in from the cold? Where is everyone? They must be in the movie room." He helped Aunt Sylvie with her coat.

"Valthea!" Sorin rushed toward me from the side hall.

Seeing him, I realized I missed him more than I could miss anything in the world.

He kissed me, picked me up, and spun me around. "Valthea!" He craned his neck to Aunt Sylvie. "Hi, Miss Sylvie."

"Hello, dear. We'll hug later. Don't drop her."

"My boy will never drop her," Cosmo said, offering his arm. "Coffee, Sylvie? Let's give these teenagers some time." She looped her arm in his, and he escorted her toward the kitchen.

"I missed you." I tried not to cry.

Sorin lowered me. "I missed you, too." He held me at arm's length. "Thank God, we've two weeks together." He stepped in close, his lips nearly touching mine. "Let's be greedy and spend the entire time together."

I loved how Sorin expressed his affection for me without restraint.

He helped me take my coat off and hung it next to Aunt Sylvie's on one of the wall hooks. I quickly took off my scarf and fluffed my flattened hair.

"Whoa, Val. Your hair. It's white."

"It's platinum, platinum-blonde. Do you like it?"

"Yeah, I mean, I'll have to get used to it. Why'd you dye it?"

"My yellow-toned skin blended with my light brown hair and eyes. I want a distinct look now that I'm in *Sky Brothers Circus.*"

"They already hired you? Wow. Congratulations." He didn't smile. "I don't want to talk down here. Let's go upstairs to my room." Once upstairs, he shut the door and we sat on his bed. "When'd you find out?"

"I didn't find out definitely until two weeks ago."

"Two weeks?" He stood. "Why didn't you tell me sooner? You could've warned me. Christmas won't be the same now."

"Why?" I took his hands. "We still have most of the holiday break together."

He jerked away. "When are you leaving?"

"Well, uh, the circus opens in Bulgaria in February. Rehearsals start in January."

"*When*, Val? When do you leave Brasov, this house, and me?"

"New Year's Eve."

Sorin walked to the other side of his bedroom.

"Why are you upset? I thought you'd be happy for me. There's no difference with my leaving in January for the circus and you having left in September for college in another country. But, yeah, I should've told you sooner. I'm sorry. It all happened so fast. I wanted to—"

"No, Val." He spun around. "There was nothing fast about this. You told me you wanted to be in the circus, and you are. It's no surprise, and it's not sudden." He walked back to the bed and sat next to me. "I'm upset because I figured out a way for us to see each other twice a month from January all the way to May."

"How?"

"Rocket science. I bought plane tickets. The first six are wrapped up as your Christmas present." He gripped his head with both hands. "Why'd I have to meet you *this* summer?" He dropped his hands. "We should've met when I was already a doctor and you were through with your circus obsession." He walked to the bedroom door, locked it, and then laid next to me on sat his bed.

I didn't know what to say. I lay down, facing him.

For several minutes we pet each other's arms and shoulders while kissing. Sorin's azure eyes faded to gray. "Truth is," he whispered, "I'm proud of you. I love you, and I'm happy for you. I just want to make sure we stay together."

"Me too, Sorin. That's why this whole thing is hard. I want to be together. But you can't turn your back on your calling to be a doctor, and I can't give up my circus dream. Plus, traveling throughout Eastern Europe with a famous circus increases the chance of me and my parents finding each other."

Sorin pulled me on top of him. I relaxed my full body weight onto him. We blended in our matching pair of dark blue jeans and navy sweatshirts.

"Babe, why are you crying?" Sorin smoothed my hair down past my shoulders.

"In two weeks we'll be apart again."

He held me tighter. "I miss you already."

"Sorin?" Aunt Sylvie called, tapping on his door. "Valthea?"

We hopped from the bed. Sorin ran to the door. I stood nonchalant in the middle of the room. He looked at me, I nodded back, and he opened the door wide. "Come in, Miss Sylvie."

Aunt Sylvie looked at Sorin and then at me. "Valthea told you the news?"

"Yes ma'am. I'm happy for her."

She nodded. "That's because you're a fine young man. Listen, your father's asking for you and Valthea to join us in the kitchen. I'll tell him you'll be down in five minutes." She started down the hall and then stopped. "Sorin."

"Yes, Miss Sylvie?"

"Keep the door open."

"Yes ma'am."

Ten seconds later, Sorin pulled me around behind his open bedroom door. He put his back against the wall and pulled me into him. He devoured me with his eyes for several seconds before kissing me with full passion.

He stopped suddenly. "Val, you *know* we can make this work." He kissed my shoulder.

"How? How can we stay close when we're a thousand miles apart?"

"I'll change the tickets. I'll visit you on my breaks in the spring, summer, and winter. I'll fly to wherever your circus is playing. There's always a way."

I wanted to continue swimming in the azure of his eyes, but I looked away. "We need to go downstairs or Cosmo will come up here."

"Thirty more seconds, and then we'll go down." Sorin planted a desperate kiss on my lips and then French kissed me. His tongue pet and caressed mine. I could barely breathe with Sorin's chest pressed hard to mine and his tongue reaching for the back of my throat. The raw vulnerability made me shiver. I waited as long as I could before surfacing for air. When I did, he sucked in my last breath, causing my legs to give out on me. He held me tight and blew a gust of life into my mouth. I was rescued. But with the blow came lust. It trickled and then poured in, down, and through my body. New found ecstasy captured and carried me out to sea with the command of a rogue wave. Powerless to resist, I let go and floated underwater, more than willing to drown in pleasure.

FIFTEEN

A tap at the door woke me. I stretched out on the den's sofa bed. "Who is it?"

"Wakey, wakey."

"Sorin?" I bolted up from the bed.

"May I come in?"

"No! I mean ... wait one second." I put a mint in my mouth, chewed it up real quick, and then laid back down, smoothing my hair on my pillow. "Come in."

"Merry Christmas Eve, babe." He walked in and planted a kiss on the small V birthmark on my forehead.

"Merry Christmas Eve. I love your sexy morning voice. Hey, why are you already fully dressed? Doesn't matter. Let's snuggle anyway."

"Val, we can't snuggle, as much as I want to. Half my family is downstairs finishing their third espresso. I'd like you to get up, and dress warm. We're going hiking."

"Hiking? No, it's too cold."

"There's barely an inch of snow on the ground." He yanked my bed covers off.

"Hey!"

"There's someplace special I want to take you."

"Really? Where?"

He opened the door. "A place I loved as a kid. I'll wait out here while you get dressed." He closed the door behind him.

I slipped on a second sweatshirt, pulled jeans on over my flannel shorts, and put on a pair of thick socks. I swung open the door. "Ready. Just need a cup of coffee."

"I've coffee and hot chocolate in thermoses in my backpack downstairs. It's with our coats and boots in the kitchen."

"You're like a boy scout in the morning."

"I'm excited about where I'm taking you."

"Me too," I said, following him down the dark toffee wood stairs. "Now that I'm awake." With Sorin, it didn't matter where he took me or what we did. Fun and romance always traveled with us.

We made our way through the kitchen without much fuss from my auntie, Cosmo, or the others. Once outside, Sorin led me through his backyard and down a path leading to a steep trail, lined with tall, fragrant pines. The morning sun, the hot cocoa, and goofing off along the way, helped make the thirty-five-degree air more than tolerable. After a bit, we stopped and gulped more caffeine.

"Val, the place I'm taking you is sacred to me. As kid, I used to go there to get away, and to think about stuff. And pray. Although my family never went to church, when I was little, Rosa read me stories from a children's Bible storybook. I liked the stories. It showed pictures of people praying by trees, rocks, ponds and in the desert. So as a kid, I prayed outdoors. I still do."

"I understand. I grew up going to church every Sunday with Aunt Sylvie, but I like praying best walking in the woods. I feel connected, especially in the morning."

"Yeah, mornings are the best out here, too. I mean, look around. It's like we've become a part of nature's secret world."

Troupes of evergreen trees stood tall, decorated with shimmering smidges of frost. A banditry of chickadees collected in bushes chock-full of red berries. In the distance, a stag and a doe chewed on tufts of winter grass. A rabbit caught my eye as it darted around an oak and then hopped into the thick of the woods. I hoped to see a lynx that morning, since it was my favorite animal, but glad we didn't, after seeing the deer and the rabbit.

We hiked another ten minutes. A gigantic blue spruce met us at the end of the trail.

"Awesome, huh?" Sorin pointed. "This tree is like the avatar of the forest." He pressed back a section of the spruce branches. "After you."

I walked through the narrow space and followed Sorin up a six-foot bank.

"Ta-da!" He opened his arms wide, presenting a mini-world centered on a boisterous brook. Sunbeams shot through a column of trees, making its water sparkle as if stirred with gold glitter. Blinding white frost and neon green moss covered the brooks' edging rocks.

"Sorin, this place is precious."

He stepped behind me and put his arms around my waist. "I knew you'd like it. Princesses love fairy tale lands."

"Yes, we do. *And* I love those cat tails. They look like circus batons, tipped in dew drops instead of rhinestones."

"With your imagination, you could be the next creative director of *Sky Brothers Circus*."

"I'd love that. Maybe someday." I slipped out of his arms and snapped photos of chipmunks chasing each other around a hollow tree stump to the left of the bank. I crept toward them holding up my cell phone. They scampered away. "Darn."

"Don't worry. There's plenty of wildlife here. Give me your hand."

I tucked away my phone and took Sorin's hand. We climbed to the top of the rocky ledge near the brook. Sunshine and blue washed away the last bit of Christmas Eve's lavender dawn.

Sorin pointed to a pair of hawks circling each other in the sky. "They mate for life, you know."

"Really? I like hawks and the way they glide across the sky. They make you want to fly."

"*You* probably will in the circus."

A party of blue-jays screeched from their position in the pines behind us. The blue-crested birds hopped from branch to branch, sending dollops of snow crashing to the ground.

"Thanks for coming here with me on Christmas Eve." Sorin hugged me into his side.

"It's gorgeous. Thanks for wanting to show me. Why didn't we come here before?"

"Guess I wanted to save this place for a morning like this." He pointed to the stretch of land to the east. "Someday I'm going to build a house on that piece of property. In the meantime, we can visit this area and another special place I'm taking you."

We walked, glove and glove, down a wide trail connecting to a road. Our boots crunched atop the gravel and snow.

"Sorin, we could've taken your dad's truck up here."

"Not to the brook. Plus, hiking's more fun. Come on." We walked faster, and then he stopped me. "Valthea, close your eyes." He covered my eyes with his frost dampened gloves and steered me around a corner. "Behold!" He removed his hands. "Our very own chalet."

I opened my eyes.

An adorable brown-stone cottage sat tucked in the center of sage-green fir trees and white berry bushes. Butterscotch and white rocks made up the home's chimney and framed the arc around its front door.

"What do you think, Val?"

"Its—"

"I would've brought you here this past summer, but the roof was being repaired. My family uses this place for visitors or as a hang out after cross-country skiing and summer picnics."

"It's incredible."

We walked the frosty stone path to the front door. Sorin dug into a window planter and pulled out a jumbo jingle bell. The bell's velvet ribbon connected it to a single, brass key. The sound of him unlocking the door could've woken an entire neighborhood. I wondered if the hawk, chipmunk, and deer held their breath, as I did in anticipation of entering Sorin's special place.

We walked through the arched doorway and into a quaint living room. Sorin yanked off the plastic sheets covering the sofa and two chairs and tossed them aside. The furniture's chocolate, gold, and marshmallow-colored fabric exuded warmth and coziness. Persian rugs covered part of the wood floor. The butterscotch and white stone fireplace took center stage and anchored the room with character and strength.

"We need some light." Sorin swept back the window's drapes.

I stood between the two chairs and turned around in place. "This cottage, it's right out of a Hans Christian Andersen tale."

"That's fine, as long as it's one of his stories that don't end in tragedy."

"Oh, no. This is definitely a happily-ever-after kind of cottage."

Sorin pointed to the adjoining kitchen's ceiling. "It needs a few repairs and a good cleaning. The electricity is turned off right now. I'll start a fire." He threw several logs into the pit from a stack next to the fireplace. He squatted down and held a lit rolled newspaper under the logs.

A family is riding in a car: The mother sits in the passenger seat clinging to a child's sweater. The scene appeared in black and white except for the tomato-red sweater the mother held. Tears streamed down her face. Two children, a boy about ten and a girl about six, slept in the backseat with their seatbelts on. The father leaned into the steering wheel as he drove in the pouring rain. He furrowed his brow. "One more light after this one coming up, and we'll be back at the festival grounds. This time, I'll search with the security guards. Honey, you stay in the car with the kids. If we don't find him, we'll check those side streets again. You've called the police station. All we can do now is look for him and pray." The mother kissed the sweater. "That's all I've been doing. Praying for our Sorin's safety."

C.K. Mallick

The reading took my breath away. It was Sorin's family! I wanted to tell him immediately, but the vision continued.

Sorin's father stopped at a red light. The rain poured hard on the windshield, making the road in front of him barely visible. A semi-truck barreled down the crossroad on his right. Sorin's father's light turned green. He drove forward. The truck hadn't slowed down. "We'll find him, honey," Sorin's father said. "Don't worry, we'll—" The semi-truck ran his red light and—wham! He broadsided Sorin's family's car. It crumpled like a collapsed accordion. Flames burst. A blazing fire.

No! Oh, my God, no. My knees buckled. I clutched the back of one of the chairs and sat. How would I, how could I tell Sorin? I caught my breath. Should I tell him?

"That should do it." Sorin brushed his hands off on his jeans. "Hey, check out these pictures." Sorin handed me one of over the dozen framed photos crowding the fireplace mantle.

I tried to sound cheery. "You guys leave a lot of pictures here."

"Yeah. Dad's Mr. Sentimental. He needs pictures of his family everywhere he goes."

I stood and joined Sorin by the fireplace. "I like that about Cosmo." I swallowed hard. God, guide me. *Please.*

"Look at my dad in this picture. It was taken twenty years ago. He was quite a stud." In the photo, a muscular Cosmo wore a tank top and jeans. He stood with his arms crossed and smiling big. Sorin put down the picture and picked up another. "This is me when I was eight." Sorin wore red shirt and pants, holding up his arms, a ping pong ball in each hand. "I'd already been juggling on stage for a year."

"You were a cute kid."

He put it back. "Let's lay on the couch. Now we can relax and snuggle."

"Are there any blankets?"

"In the bedroom closet."

"I'll get them." I went into the bedroom and took a couple of deep breaths. Sorin's family being killed was the saddest vision I'd ever seen in my life. I thought of the chipmunk by the brook to keep myself from crying and returned with a couple of blankets.

Sorin scooted the couch closer to the fireplace, and we lay in each other's arms under the blankets.

"Val, what do you want in the future, besides performing in the circus? We've never talked about it. I mean, do you want a family? Kids?"

"Yeah." I kissed his nose. "Your nose is cold. I guess that's good; they say if a dog's nose is warm, he's sick."

"I consider myself more wolf than dog, but don't change the subject. Back to my question, please."

"Okay, okay. I want to perform as long as I can and then maybe choreograph or become a creative director of a circus. I want a family, too. But I don't want to marry just anybody. I want to marry for love. What about you?"

He kissed my nose. "Your nose is freezing."

"Don't change the subject."

He laughed, pulling me closer. "All right. I want to be a physician. I want to marry a girl I'm wild for, who's also my best friend. I want to build a home on that property I showed you. Two kids, a golden retriever, and a tuxedo cat would complete my ideal."

"Sounds ideal." A reading interrupted my daydream ...

A year ago: Inside the fairy tale cottage, Sorin pulled the plastic from the sofa and chairs like he did when we stepped into the cottage. He spoke to a girl about sixteen with long, black hair. Pretty. She wore a suede fridge jacket.

He said, "Dorina, break out the hot chocolate. It's freezing in here."

The girl's eyes lit up. "Let's spike it! Got anything in the cupboard?"

Strong emotions like jealousy always cut short readings. I slid out from Sorin's arm and sat up, facing him. "Who's Dorina? I didn't know you liked the Pocahontas type."

"Dorina? How do you—oh. You saw something."

"Yeah."

He pushed off the sofa, chuckling. "Is this what it's going to be like having a girlfriend that's a psychic?"

I followed him to the fireplace. He picked up a framed photo and handed it to me.

"Is that her?"

The girl I'd seen in the vision posed in a group photo with a snowy background. Cosmo, Sorin, and Lumi were in it along with two other adults.

C.K. Mallick

Sorin took the frame from my hand and placed it back on the mantle. "Val, Dorina's my cousin. Her family visits every other winter to ski."

"Okay. I didn't know."

"There's a lot you don't know. So, guess what? You're going to start asking me stuff instead of seeing my past and jumping to conclusions. He grabbed one of the sheets of plastic and covered a chair. "I must be crazy letting myself fall in love with a clairvoyant."

"Sorin, I only see bits here and there, not everything. But going forward, I'll ask you questions instead of assuming." I wrapped my arms around him. "I couldn't help it. The image threw me."

He stopped covering the chair. "Then we'll create new images." He picked me up over his shoulder and carried me to the couch. We laughed at first and then kissed while intertwining our bodies. After several heated minutes, Sorin called a coffee break time out. He said I drove him crazy. That made me happy.

Sorin sat up, took the muffins he packed from the backpack, and handed me one. I poured coffee into the lids of the thermoses and Sorin took a sip. He held up his cup up and swayed side-to-side. He belted out a drunken pirate rendition of *Oh, Come all ye Faithful*. I sang along like a pirate's wench, but couldn't stop laughing.

The fire's last spark dwindled after our second chorus. Sorin rubbed my arms.

"You're shivering. Let's get you home." He put the fire out completely and shut the curtains. "Next time we're here, there will be photos of us above the fireplace."

"I can't wait to come back in the summertime." I helped cover the sofa and chairs.

"You mean, when you're no longer touring with *Sky* and I'm no longer in school or interning?"

"That seems so far off."

"We'll find a way to come here for a few days. Don't worry. This place will always be here for us. Remember, once a month we're going to meet. We're going to stay in love forever."

"Yes, we are." I prayed the notion possible.

SIXTEEN

We left the cottage and hiked down the trail back to the Dobra house. I spotted two big sitting rocks on the side of the trail. *Timing.* "Sorin, can we take a break? I need to talk to you."

"Sure." He dropped his backpack and sat on the less smooth rock. "What's up?"

"A vision came to me of your past, or rather, your family's past."

"My family's?"

I took a deep breath. "Yes."

"You mean my family with Cosmo or the family that left me at the festival?"

I looked him directly in the eyes. "Sorin, your family didn't leave you. Your parents loved you very much and—"

"Valthea." He stood. "If you're trying to be nice and make me feel better about what my parents did, don't."

"No, Sorin. This is real. Please sit."

He slowly sat.

"That afternoon at the festival, you, your brother, and your sister were supposed to stay near the food stand while your parents paid for snacks and drinks. But you followed a dancing bear and its trainer, slipping through the crowd. When your parents turned around, you weren't there. They scolded your siblings, and then quickly circled the area, calling your name over and over. Your father reported you missing at the festival's security booth and called the police. The security guys searched the park. But they didn't find you because you weren't—"

"Because I wasn't *in* the park. Apollonia had already taken me behind the scenes, to Grandmamma's motor home, at the edge of the woods."

"Right."

Sorin pushed off his rock and walked fifteen-feet away before stopping. He kept his back to me. "Go on."

"Your parents took your siblings by the hand and hurried to the parking lot. Your mother prayed out loud. Your brother and sister cried. Together your family walked up and down the rows of cars, shouting your name and looking for you."

Sorin turned around and walked back toward me.

"It started to rain. Your family didn't stop looking for you. They kept on." I paused. "When they didn't find you, they decided to drive to a nearby neighborhood."

Sorin sat on his rock facing me, his eyes glazed over.

"Now it was pouring so hard that your father could barely see to drive." I swallowed. "They were stopped at a light when a semi-truck, coming from the other direction. Oh, Sorin," I sobbed. "I'm so, so sorry."

He grabbed my shoulders. "What Val? What happened? *Tell me.*"

"The truck driver didn't slow down." I shook my head, tears streaming down my cheeks. "He ... he ran the light."

Sorin choked back his tears. "Did anyone—"

"No. The impact happened instantly. But they didn't suffer."

Sorin didn't utter a sound or move.

I gently put my hands on his knees. "I'm sure they're in heaven together now."

Sorin's eyes flooded with tears. "It's not fair."

"No. It's not."

Sorin folded forward, his arms and head landing on my lap. He wept without a sound.

We hiked home in silence.

Sorin thanked me for telling him what I saw. He confessed he felt relief knowing what happened to his family, that they loved him, and they didn't leave him.

I was glad for Sorin. But now, I asked myself a new question. Were my parents alive or dead?

By eight o'clock Christmas morning, the kitchen had been a buzz for hours. The aroma of cabbage and sausage and cinnamon and baking apples filled the Dobra house. Sorin and I met at the top of the stairs. He looked cute in his flannel pajama bottoms and long-john shirt. He brushed my bangs back and kissed my forehead. "*Craciun Fericit, prinţesă.*"

"Merry Christmas, to you, my handsome knight."

We headed downstairs.

"Good morning, sleepy heads." Aunt Sylvie slid a covered baking dish into the oven and set the timer. "*Craciun Fericit.*"

"Merry Christmas, Miss Sylvie." Sorin kissed her on each cheek.

She hugged him and then me, her hands still in oven mitts.

"*Craciun Fericit,* Auntie."

"You too, dear."

The kitchen door leading to the garage swung open. "Merry Christmas, everyone!" Cosmo stomped his feet on the mat and stepped inside. "Hey, Silver," he yelled past us. "Enough juggling. Give me a hand with the wood."

Silver put the three glass ornaments he juggled into a box on the dining table and raced by us.

"I'll help you guys." Sorin followed Cosmo and Silver out the garage door.

Once the guys stacked wood next to the fireplace, and Lumi and I set the table, Gabi announced, "Everyone, go clean up. Our feast will be ready in thirty minutes. Don't be late."

Sorin and I met at the bottom of the stairs thirty minutes later. He looked fine in his crushed-velvet jacket, turtleneck, and straight-legged jeans. I felt beautiful, like a champion's princess, in the dark-red velvet dress Aunt Sylvie made me for Christmas. She insisted I opened the gift early.

"You look stunning, Val. I'm getting used to the white hair." He petted one of my sleeves.

"You mean platinum, but thanks." I kissed his cheek. "And you look very elegant."

He gave a tug on his jacket. "Never been told that before."

"Why does every guy in this family wear black boots?" I pointed to his shoes. "If you traded those in for a pair of Beatle boots, you'd look like an English rock star from the nineteen-sixties."

Sorin looked confused. "What are beetle boots?"

"Boots like *The Beatles* wore." Cosmo stood at the top of the stairs, handsome in his military-style jacket and black jeans. His high turtleneck and precision-shaved goatee accentuated his sculpture-worthy face. "Beatle boots are pointed." He stamped down six stairs, punctuating his march in time with each syllable. "They come to the ankle." He stamped down two more steps. "They're mostly black." He jogged down the next four in quick succession. "But we *Romas* prefer a heartier version of boot." He jumped to the floor from the remaining step, clicked the angled-heels of his boots together, and bowed.

I clapped.

"That's my dad," Sorin said. "Subtle. Not dramatic at all."

"Ah, true," Cosmo laughed. He threw his arms around me and Sorin and walked us to the kitchen. "Wow, Valthea, you look like a movie star."

"Thanks Cosmo. You look very handsome."

"Yeah, Dad. You look elegant."

"Thank you both. Not bad for a forty-something-young guy."

Auntie stood near the kitchen entrance. "Not bad for any age."

"*Aleluia!*" Cosmo shook his hands overhead. "It *must* be Christmas. Miss Sylvie paid me a compliment."

"Honestly." Auntie rolled her eyes.

Cosmo took Auntie's hand and kissed it. "My darling Sylvie, you look beautiful as usual, inside and out."

"Such a charmer. Please, go sit down." She gestured toward the dining room. "We're bringing out the food."

My time was nearly up. I needed to tell Cosmo I made it into a circus and couldn't perform with his troupe in the spring or summer. I prayed he wouldn't be furious.

The Dobras', Auntie, and I gathered in the dining room. Two sets of Christmas dishes and antique crystal stemware made for an eclectic, although homey, dining table. Multiple strands of white lights hung along the back wall.

Lumi put two baskets of knotted holiday bread on the table. Cosmo stood at the far end opening a bottle of *Tuica*, a plum brandy.

A loud commotion and Grandmamma swearing came from the kitchen.

"She'll quiet in a minute." Cosmo set a bottle of white wine on the table and opened it. "You see, Lumi and Apollonia are Grandmamma's pets."

"I'm her favorite." Lumi scooped up a handful of nut-covered chocolate balls from a glass dish.

"Every year Apollonia says she's staying for Christmas, but then leaves with Strum on Christmas Eve night to go to his folks' home." Cosmo uncorked a bottle of red wine and set it next to the other open bottles.

"So no Apollonia on Christmas day?" I tried not to smile.

"Thank God." Lumi poured herself a glass of wine. "Whenever she's around, she has to be the center of attention, or she'll cause trouble. She's a predictable pain."

Cosmo took the bottle of wine from her hand. "Go easy there, Lumi. On your Aunt Apollonia and on the wine."

Rosa and Gabi paraded into the dining room with dishes of cabbage rolls and sour soup with meatballs. Sorin took the heavy dish from Gabi and put it on the table. I helped Rosa with hers. Bruno carried the silver platter holding the roasted pig with an apple in its mouth. Grandmamma scuffled next to him, directing his every move.

"Every year she go." Grandmamma grunted like a hog. "Every year."

Bruno set the platter in the center of the table.

"Forget her, Grammy," Lumi said, kissing the old woman on both cheeks. "Christmas is wonderful, thanks to you."

The old grump smiled. Her eyes twinkled below their hoods.

I marveled how God granted even the most miserable of souls on Earth at least one person who could soften their heart. I figured Grandmamma hated me, but I didn't hate her. I'd seen an insight from her past weeks ago. Through it, I learned Grandmamma grew up poor with no education. She went without so her children could eat a hot meal a day and grow up strong. Later, her husband, Cosmo's father invested in a home and then another and another, turning their life around. Maybe Grandmamma hated me because I was an outsider, or because Cosmo favored me. Or because Sorin, the family's golden boy, was in love with me. Or so I hoped. At least Grandmamma would rejoice when I announced a circus hired me and I wouldn't be around anymore.

Gabi sat closest to the kitchen. She tapped her water glass with a knife. "Can we please sit down at the table like civilized people and enjoy our Christmas meal?"

Grandmamma sat at one head of the table and Cosmo at the other. Sorin and I sat next to each other with our knees touching under the tablecloth.

Auntie and I'd placed a young oak branch in the center of the dinner table, in keeping with orthodox Christmas tradition. We decorated it with sprigs of holly and gold bric-a-brac. The display represented baby Jesus and new hope. Some people believed the branch tradition survived the year's communist-ruled Romania because of its subtlety. My auntie believed the tradition survived because of what it symbolized in the hearts of the people.

"Sorin," I whispered. "What do you think of the centerpiece Auntie and I made?"

"I love it. It adds spirit to the room. Just like you do. I'd like the branch, and you, to become a part of my Christmas tradition."

"You mean like next year, here, with your family?"

Sorin whispered, "Next year, and for years beyond with me."

I flushed and whispered, "I'd like that."

Grandmamma slapped the table. "Stop whispers."

"Sorry Grandmamma." Sorin squeezed my hand under the table.

"Sorry, Mrs. Dobra," I said.

"May I bless the food, Grandmamma?" Bruno asked.

She pointed to Bruno. "Bruno do blessing."

I closed my eyes to pray, wanting to fantasize a future Christmas with Sorin. Instead, visions from Grandmamma's past showed up.

Fifteen years ago, she sat where she did today. The dinner table shone like polished hazelnuts. The man I'd seen in Cosmo's childhood reading, Cosmo's father, sat at the other end of the table. Toddler Sorin sat in a booster chair between him and Cosmo. The old man cut Sorin's food into pieces while making animated faces and funny sounds. Sorin gurgled and kissed his grandfather back without prompting. Rosa, Apollonia, Gabi, and Gheorghe sat at the table, too. Grandmamma coddled over Lumi and smiled throughout the vision.

Everyone in the past vision naturally looked younger and less worn—except Cosmo. Interesting. Other than some gray hair, he looked practically the same. Aunt Sylvie once told me that people grow old when they lose their sense of humor or stop seeing wonder in the world. She claimed gratitude erased years from a person's face and spirit. Although my auntie didn't tell jokes, she giggled about something every day. She also never tired of the miracles found in nature. My mind trailed off. Hmm. Aunt Sylvie and Cosmo would make amazing grandparents.

"Amen," Bruno bellowed.

Everyone said 'amen' and made the sign of the cross. Within one second, Silver and Gheorghe began yelling across the table, Bruno stabbed a meatball and popped it into his mouth, and Dino downed his wine. He poured his second glass as Rosa and Cosmo burst out laughing at some inside joke.

Lumi yelled from the other side of the table. "Val, stop hogging the *piftie*."

The jellied dish, made with pork, beef, and tons of garlic, sat smack in front of my plate. It wiggled with every bump of the table. "I'm not hogging it. I don't even eat *piftie*."

"Then pass it this way. I'll eat your share. I'm starving."

"You've been eating a lot lately," Dino grumbled.

"No I haven't."

Cosmo scooped up a ladle of soup. "Be in shape by January third. We booked a gig at Ishta's home. Val, you can join us. Maybe a shorter version of the piece you did over the summer. What do you think? School doesn't start back until the fifth, right?" He dunked a corner of his bread into his soup and took a bite.

I felt Sorin's eyes on me.

Auntie stopped buttering her bread.

"Sorry, Sylvie," Cosmo said. "You and Val discuss it first."

She smiled at Cosmo and then whispered to me, "No more putting it off. I'll make a toast and then you will."

"Can't I wait until after the *cozonac* cake?"

Auntie straightened and held up her wine glass. "I'd like to make a toast. Thank you all for inviting me and Valthea to join you during this sacred time of year. Good tidings to all. God Bless, and *Craciun Fericit!*"

"Merry Christmas!" several said at once.

Auntie took a sip and then glared at me.

I slowly held up my glass. "I also want to make a toast. Or kind of an announcement. I ... I made it into *Sky Brothers Circus.*"

Gabi and Gheorghe clinked glasses. Silver whistled. Rosa, Bruno, and Lumi clapped their hands.

Cosmo leapt from his chair and hurried around to where I sat. "Bravo! Fantastic! Superb!"

I stood and hugged him. He reacted exactly how I would've wanted my own dad to react.

"Cosmo, being with you this summer made it possible."

"Ah, Valthea, it was you. The circus people loved *you.*" He kissed my cheeks and then strutted back to his chair. "How about that, everyone? My precious ones are fulfilling their destiny. Sorin's on full scholarship in England, and Valthea, at sixteen, made it into a European circus." He wiped his eyes. "They may be living far away, but I'll feel them close in my heart." He raised his glass. "*Salut!*"

"*Salut!*" Everyone cheered.

Sorin whispered, "I want to feel you close in my heart."

I did too, but would it be enough?

Sorin and I stood on the sidewalk where the bus heading to Bucharest parked. Aunt Sylvie already sat in her seat. Diesel fuel triggered nausea and tears.

"Take a deep breath, babe." Sorin hugged me close. "Thank you again for the photo disc you made of us. It's my favorite Christmas gift since Dad gave me a bike when I was five."

"Being with you is my greatest present." I snuggled in the warmth of his coat. "I can't wait to visit the brook and the cottage again."

The bus driver shouted, "Leaving in two minutes. Two minutes!" He stamped out his cigarette and climbed into the bus.

A dozen people near the bus hugged, put out cigarettes, and grabbed their bags.

Sorin kissed me on the lips and then kissed both my hands. "I care about you, Valthea." He tucked my bangs under the edge of my cap. "If you need a good listener, money—*anything*—you call me. You're my best friend. I *love* you."

"You're my best friend, and I love you." I stood on my tiptoes, slid my hand to the back of his head, and pulled him toward me. Before I could kiss him, he pressed in closer and kissed me first.

"Let's go, kids," the bus driver yelled.

"Sorin, listen. You must leave the station. Once I'm on the bus I don't want to see you standing on the sidewalk and waving good-bye. It's too sad."

"But, Val, I want—"

"Promise me?"

"All right."

I kissed him and then ran up the four bus steps. The driver pulled the metal lever and closed the door. Sorin stood on the edge of the sidewalk facing the bus.

"Sir," I said to the driver. "Please open the door for a second."

"Miss, I've been patient. But I am on a schedule."

"Please?"

He grabbed the lever and pulled open the door.

I ran down the steps and held the rail bar, letting my body swoop forward toward Sorin. He held my waist and kissed me.

"All right, young man," the bus driver yelled past me. "Buy a ticket or step away."

Sorin stepped back onto the sidewalk. "I heart you, Valthea."

"I heart you, Sorin."

"That's terrific," the bus driver grumbled, pulling the lever, and closing the door.

I hurried to my seat next to Aunt Sylvie and faced the window. Our bus pulled away from the curb and headed toward the main road.

Sorin stood by the bus station sign, waving good-bye like I asked him not to. I smiled and waved, glad that he did.

PART III

SKY BROTHERS CIRCUS

SEVENTEEN

"The Muzsnays are here," Aunt Sylvie yelled from the foyer.

I picked up Radu from the kitchen floor and kissed the top of his head. "My little Radu." I scratched the hefty orange cat under the chin and he closed his eyes and purred. "I'm going to miss you." I kissed his head once more and then set him in front of his food dish. Nawa perched on his kitchen stand. I smoothed his feathers with two fingers. "Nawa ... Keep an eye on Auntie for me. I won't be back until next winter." I wiped my eyes, grabbed my purse from the kitchen table, and walked into the foyer.

"Button your coat," Auntie huffed. "I'm not going to see you for a long time. You need to stay well."

I hugged her "Thanks for letting me do this. You're the best parent a girl could have."

She hugged me in silence and then blurted, "Enough sentiment. I'll see you in five weeks on your opening night." She shooed me toward my suitcases. "Time to get on with your new life." She tightened the tie on her cardigan. "Don't keep Coach and Mrs. Muzsnay waiting. They're nice enough to let you ride with them."

I slung my duffel over my shoulder. "They're going to see relatives in Bulgaria anyway."

"Still, move along. Show appreciation." Aunt Sylvie avoided sentiment by acting ornery. She opened the front door and January's cold whooshed inside.

Coach Muzsnay stood at our doorstep with his hand up, about to knock. "*Buna dimineata*, Miss Sarosi."

"Good morning, Coach Muzsnay."

"Now, Miss Sarosi, don't you worry about Valthea. She'll be fine. Your girl's quiet, but smart. She's more aware of what's going on around her than most people."

"*Da*, that she is." Aunt Sylvie led us outside.

Coach put my suitcases in the trunk of his car as Mrs. Muzsnay rolled down her window.

"Good morning, ladies. Are you excited, Valthea?"

"Yes ma'am. Thank you for inviting me to ride with you."

"We wouldn't have it any other way."

Coach held the back car door open while Auntie and I hugged good-bye one more time. She shivered in my arms. "You're freezing, Auntie. Go inside."

126

"I'm fine, dear."

"I'll call you tonight."

"Don't forget, Valthea."

"I won't." I slid into the back seat and then faced backward when Coach pulled the car out of our slushy driveway. Aunt Sylvie stood at the door step waving. I put on a brave face and waved good-bye, panicking inside.

After five and a half hours and one espresso stop, we drove up to Sky Brother's property. I read the frost-topped sign aloud, "Welcome to *Sky Brothers Circus.*"

We parked in front of the main office and walked in. The secretary introduced me to my chaperone and tutor, Alin Ganea. Miss Alin's sister was Katja Ganea-Brennan, Sky Brothers choreographer and former student of Coach Muzsnay. She sent her regards to the Muzsnay's and me. She'd arrive in town in time for orientation that night.

Coach and Mrs. Muzsnay hugged me good-bye. I promised to email them about rehearsals and my new life. They'd see me perform in March, when the circus toured Bucharest.

Alin Ganea, the forty-something, brusque, and rather masculine-acting woman told me to call her simply, *Alin*, not Miss Alin. We loaded my suitcases into a van and drove less than a mile to a field with motor homes, campers, and vans.

"Twenty-seven vehicles." Alin pointed to the last one in the second row. "That's where you'll live."

We carried my bags across the crunching layer of snow to my new home, identifiable by its collection of *Hello Kitty* bumper stickers. I followed Alin up the steps. The community area of the motor home was laid out much like the family van I'd traveled in over the summer, only more upscale. The dining booth set across from a small, but complete and modern kitchen. Built-in couches with tan and blue seat cushions faced each other. A TV, suspended by brackets, hung high in the corner. The hallway led to the bathroom, closets, and bedrooms.

"Girls, this is Val. Val, this is Li and Bai. I'll put these in your bedroom." Alin took my bag and headed toward the back of the motor home.

"My name is Valthea. Hi." I took off my coat and boots.

The girls wore faded black sweat suits with their hair pinned tight into a bun. Each held a pug in their arms.

"I'm Bai," said the girl on the left.

The other girl held up her snorting, short-muzzled dog. "I'm Li, and this is Bert."

Bai held her dog out toward me. "And this is Ernie. Do want to hold him?"

"No, that's okay. Hello, Ernie." I waved to the pup. "Wait a minute. Bert and Ernie? Like from *Sesame Street*? I watched that show as a kid. *The Count* is still a Romanian favorite."

"We learned English by watching *Sesame Street* before going to first grade." Li kissed her dog's face. "I liked Bert the best."

Alin slid into one side of the kitchen dining booth. "Can we please sit during these niceties?"

The girls put their dogs on the floor and slid into the other side of the booth.

Alin patted the cushion next to her and then pulled a toothpick from her flannel shirt pocket. "Sit, Val. Let's get these initial introductions out of the way." She grumbled, "Eight years already. I don't know how I do this."

I didn't want to sit next to the gruff woman, or do anything she said. Why did *she* need to be my tutor?

"We're foot-jugglers," Bai said.

"I've never seen a foot juggling act in real life."

I remembered something Coach Muzsnay told my gymnastic team about the children training for Chinese acrobatic shows. Someone in my team complained about Coach modifying our diets. He said we were lucky. Chinese acrobats had to perform their routines perfectly to earn dinner. I looked at Bai and Li.

Eight rows of a dozen slight-bodied Asian girls in long-sleeved red leotards lined up in a huge gymnasium. Li stood in the front line. Bai stood two rows behind her. A pair of coaches and a man and a woman, wove through the mass. The man's brows stayed pinched and his jaw held tight. The coaches selected Li, Bai, and two other girls, and then dismissed everyone else.

Li and Bai wore matching chartreuse body stockings. They lay on a bench-like apparatuses using their feet to juggle and toss large paper fans. They passed the fans back and forth, flipping them in the air. A panel of serious-faced judges sat at a long table.

A day later, the girls stood on a platform, holding up silver medals. It wasn't the Olympics, but a prestigious world competition.

Later that night, Li, Bai, and the male coach who selected them from the audition, met in his office. He yelled something in Chinese and then snatched the silver medals from the girls' hands and threw them on the floor. He shoved Bai against the wall, grabbed her head with both hands, and pounded it against the wall three, four, five times.

I couldn't bear to watch. I squeezed my eyes shut, but the vision persisted.

Li screamed and yelled for help. The coach let go of Bai's head and slapped Li across the face. He shoved her hard, slamming her into the wall. She crumpled to the floor, landing next to the unconscious Bai. The coach yelled Bai's name and something else in rapid fire Chinese. He then began kicking Bai. Li yelled and flung her body over her friend's. The man with the tight jaw didn't stop. He kicked Li in her ribs and then the back of her head. Someone knocked on the door. The violent man turned away from the girls, lying in an immobile heap. He smoothed his hair back and unlocked the door. The female Chinese coach pushed past him and ran to Bai and Li. He exited without a word.

I covered my eyes. Why God? Why do you show me such horrible things?

"What's wrong with you?" Alin asked.

"Nothing." I sat on my hands and smiled at Li and Bai. "I can't wait to see your act. I'm sure you two are great."

"They're okay," Alin mumbled.

"You're wrong," I said. "Theirs is a featured act with Sky Brothers. They must be great."

Bai opened a package of Twizzlers. She peeled a few strands from the pack and then laid the rest on an empty plate in the center of the table. "Want some?"

"Thanks." I peeled off a piece of licorice.

"What about you?" Li asked. "You're in the clown act?"

"Are you fifteen, like us?" Bai asked.

"I'm sixteen, and I'm a gymnast, not a clown."

"Maybe Val, but you're in the clown act." Alin aimed her chewed toothpick at me. "This year, one of Sky's entry level characters is a dancer-acrobat ingénue. That's you. The clowns are Emeric and Pauly. Emeric's a slim six-four, and Pauly's—"

"Pauly's a midget," Bai said, chewing her licorice.

Li nudged Bai. "She means he's a *little person.*"

"Alin, are you sure I'm the clown act? In my audition DVD I did advanced routines on the uneven parallel bars, the beam, and—"

"Doesn't matter. You're not part of a circus family, and you're not a world competition medalist." Alin dropped her toothpick into a Styrofoam cup on the table. "Your job is to excel in the act you're assigned and the one you're understudying. You're here because my sister believed you could handle both. If you can't, I suggest—"

"I can, Alin. No problem."

"I like your hair," Bai tied a piece of licorice into a knot and then took a bite. "It makes you look twenty-five."

"Twenty-five?" Did Sorin think I looked old?

"Move it," Alin said, shoving me toward the end of the booth. "Let's get you to wardrobe. Time for your costume fitting."

I quickly slid out of the booth, imagining gorgeous costumes in rich, dark colors. *Dark*, because I still refused to wear ...

"See you later, Valthea," Bai said.

"Bye. Nice meeting you two."

"You mean four!" Li held up one of Bert's front paws.

Alin drove us less than a mile from the motor home parking lot to the wardrobe building. We walked through the front door and down the main foyer. "The wardrobe master is an American and a real character." Alin winked. "If you know what I mean."

"I heard that!" A robust black man with a shaved head sashayed toward us from a side hallway. He shined with exuberance. "True, I am a fabulous character."

"This is Val." Alin took a wide, manly stance.

"Welcome, young lady. My name is Carlo Reye. You may call me, Carlo Reye." He chuckled.

I stepped in front of Alin. "Nice to meet you, Carlo Reye. My name is Valthea."

"Pleasure's mine, Valthea."

Carlo Reye is six-years-old, in kindergarten. He left the boy's table and walked to the girl's table. "Who'd like a party gown for their doll?"

The ten girls in the classroom yelled, "Me!"

The squatty kindergarten teacher, all jowls and hips, wagged her finger at Carlo. "You," she said. "Go back to the boy's table. Leave those fabric swatches and art supplies for the girls."

"But Miss Thornton, I can make party dresses!"

"No, you can't. Not in my classroom."

Carlo Reye sat quietly in his chair at the boys' table.

Miss Thornton walked up behind him. "You need to toughen up and start acting like a young man." She grabbed the back of his chair and shook it hard.

One of the girls cried, "Stop, Miss Thornton! Stop!"

Miss Thornton didn't stop. Her face turned bright as a poison dart frog. Little Carlo Reye couldn't hang onto his chair any more. He slid forward, banged his mouth on the table's edge, and fell out of his chair. Carlo Reye's head hit the chair next to him. He cried, holding his head with both hands, curled up on the floor. The children huddled behind their tables. The one heavy-set child in the class ran up to Carlo and knelt beside him.

"Are you okay?" She blotted his bleeding lips with a fabric scrap.

Mrs. Thornton yelled, "Get away from that queer! He has terrible, terrible cooties."

The next morning, sunlight streamed in through the row of windows in Carlo Reyes' classroom. The children hunched over their desks', holding pencils, and writing on big pieces of paper. The classroom door swung open. A slender woman with huge eyes and a stylish black-and-white suitdress stood at the doorway. She resembled Diana Ross. The teacher's jowls jiggled as she stood.

"How dare you barge into my classroom? I'm in the middle of—"

"Of what?" the Diana-Ross-woman yelled.

"Ruining my son's life?"

The teacher's frog-like eyes bugged.

The Diana-Ross-woman continued. "Miss Thornton, if you ever say anything inappropriate or nasty to Carlo Reye again, I'll make another appointment with your principal, and you will be fired. Children," she spoke softer, facing the class "If Miss Thornton forgets to tell you, I'm telling you—you are all God's children. It doesn't matter what you look like or what talent you choose to develop. You can do anything you put your mind to. This is America, children. America." She waved to Carlo Reye. "Son, I'll pick you up at two."

"Ready, Valthea?"

"Huh?" I blinked several times. "Yes, Carlo Reye. I'm ready."

He looked past me. "Alin, you may leave us now. I'll escort Valthea to the cafeteria when we're through here."

"All right ... Lady Carlotta." Alin imitated Carlo Reye's walk as she headed down the hall.

"Don't call him that." I yelled at her back. "His name is Carlo Reye."

She glanced over her shoulder. "Listen to you." She walked away. "Catch you later."

"Carlo Reye, why do you let her call you names?"

"Doll-face, I appreciate your allegiance. But I pay no mind to name-calling."

"But it's not right."

"True. But Valthea, do you really think secure, confident people belittle other people?"

"No."

"Okay, then. End of today's life lesson." He flung one end of his scarf over his shoulder. "On to more important things. Your costume. This way, please."

We pressed on down the hall until he stopped at a huge set of double doors. He faced me and raised one eyebrow high. "I hope you're ready. Because when it comes to costumes and design, I don't play. This isn't a closet in the back of your local theatre, honey. *This*," he said, busting the doors wide, ushering me through, "is the circus!"

I gasped, stepping into the warehouse filled with rows and rows of sparkling, sequined jackets and bodysuits, jeweled leotards, and rhinestone gowns with ostrich feathers. Huge overhead panels of skylights covered the ceiling. Rare January sunshine beamed in, reflecting off the layers of spangled and boa-draped costumes.

I held out my arms, rotating them side to side. "There are prisms all over me."

"Of course! Rainbows dance in here!" He swept one arm to the side, presenting more of his vast warehouse. "You are surrounded by the best! Come along."

I followed the wardrobe master down aisles of costumes arranged and labeled by act, color, and size. We brushed by net tutus, soft feathers, and satin capes.

"It's like all these costumes are anxiously waiting to be zipped onto a body so they can come alive. They're masterpieces."

"True, true. You know, Valthea, in the circus world anything can happen. You can do whatever you put your mind to." We turned right onto the next aisle. "You could end up a Sky Brothers sensation with star billing."

I took a breath. "I look forward to that day."

He gave me a sideways glance. "Confident, eh? Good. Makes dreams more likely to happen." He picked up a strand of my hair. "Hmm. I'll get one of the stylists to change it to a golden-brown. Your character is like a sprite. Platinum is way too harsh." He let my hair fall back on my shoulder. "Now then, your size is right over here." He pointed toward the costumes ahead of us.

"How do you know? You haven't measured me yet."

"Doll face, you're dealing with a master. You're a European thirty-four. Besides, diamonds always fit."

"Diamonds?"

"Easy, girl. You'll be wearing rhinestones."

"I know." I faked a chuckle. "Just kidding."

Carlo Reye slid four hanging leotards with attached skirts to one side of the aluminum rail: two dark red, one black, and one white. Matching sequins covered the front of the costume's bodices.

"Since your role is both dancer *and* acrobat, I can't dress you in a tumbler's unitard *or* a ballerina's tutu. So, *voila!*" He held up the white version of the skirted costume.

I blanched, staring at its sheer skirt.

"Snowy white; it'll accentuate your character's innocence."

EIGHTEEN

Sky Brothers Circus orientation took place in the main auditorium. The secretary I met that afternoon passed out rehearsal folders to the cast and crew entering the building. I hugged the folder to my chest and walked in. Nearly fifty people, in groups of two and six, nearly filled the lower east rows of the stadium-style seating.

"Valthea!" Bai waved from their third row seats.

Li pointed to the seat next to them. "Saved you a seat."

"Thanks." I ran up the steps and sat with them. "Where are Bert and Ernie?"

"No animals allowed." Bai shrugged. "Weird for a circus, huh?"

Li pointed to the performance ring. "Wait until you meet the choreographer, Miss Katja. She's so nice. And there's Mr. Sky."

Nik Sky, director of *Sky Brothers Circus*, and grandson of its founder, stepped into the center of the ring.

"*Dobar vecher! Vitejte!* Good evening and welcome." He spoke into a microphone headset, welcoming us in his parent's languages of Bulgarian and Czech. Fortyish, he resembled a Hollywood director with his wire-framed eye glasses and khaki fishing vest. He continued in English introducing his secretary, who'd I'd met earlier, the chief of operations, who was his brother, and then Miss Katja and Carlo Reye. He introduced the stage manager and his assistants and the tent master and his crew. I caught Carlo Reye's eye and waved at him. He waved back.

Nik Sky scanned the stands. "The staff will come around in a minute and meet you."

Li whispered, "I heard Mr. Sky's first wife divorced him when she became pregnant. She was a Hungarian Gypsy. She never let him see the child."

"But now he's married happily with three children," Bai added.

Li whispered, "There are stories about who his first wife was, and what became of her and the baby."

"Welcome to the circus!" One of the brothers from the Ukrainian teeter board act said, leaning forward from his seat in the row behind us.

Bai and I turned.

"It's a world within a world," the Ukrainian said, sitting back as Nik Sky spoke.

Bai and I faced front.

"Here's the lineup for when each will rehearse," Nik Sky began.

"The exact times for rehearsal are in your folder. Besides this space, we've a number of practice rooms." Nik Sky had an easy, genuine way of speaking in front of a crowd. He held up his clipboard. "Starting at eight in the morning until one, it'll be teeter board, adagio, clowns, and ladder-acrobats. Rehearsing from one until seven will be high-wire, the aerial silks. ... "

Nik Sky, decades ago, nine-years-old. He skipped along a dirt path, around what must've been Sky Brothers old home grounds. He shouted hello to a wire-walker practicing on a low cable. He skipped on and waved to a spry older woman carrying fabric bolts of bright satin. He stopped at a sectioned off area where a man worked with eight poodles in various colors and sizes. The dogs hopped up on their individual wooden crates, one-by-one. The last and smallest dog in the semi-circle lineup, a scruffy, brown poodle, missed his attempt to jump up on his crate. The dog trainer yelled, "Stupid dog!" With a riding crop in hand, the trainer approached the little dog. "Stop!" Nik shouted. "No beatings! My dad said so." "Hush kid," the man growled. "I can replace this idiot mutt faster than you can wipe your girly tears. And don't go running to your daddy, or I'll come get you. You're not the director yet."

"I'm not afraid of you. I'm going to buy that dog." Little Nik turned and ran down the dirt path.

A hearty-looking man working with an elephant is in a fenced enclosure. The elephant's ears were speckled and frayed along the edges. "Look, Dad," twelve-year-old Nik said to the man standing next to him. "He's using a hook." The man, his dad, yelled at the elephant trainer. "Hey—no hooks. You know the rules." The elephant trainer yelled back, "I'm doing what I got to do to keep this bull in line." His dad yelled back, "And I'm doing what I need to do to keep you in line. And I say, no hooks."

I looked at Nik Sky, standing in the ring with his staff.

A teen-aged Nik Sky. He wore jeans, a long sleeved T-shirt, and wire-rimmed glasses. "Egon," Nik said to a man hosing down an empty tiger cage, "I know you love and care for your cats."

"They are my children, Nik." "Yes, but tell me honestly, Egon, don't you wish they'd never been captured and were free in the wild instead of being forced to jump through our fire hoops?"

"Yah, Nik, of course," Egon said. "But people like animals in circus. No animals, no money." Nik's serious face brightened. "I don't know. We'll see about that."

Now I understood why Nik Sky chose to direct a people-act only show. His childhood experiences ignited a vision for his role as the future director of *Sky Brothers Circus*. Not only did he keep his vision, he managed the courage to bring it to fruition. In my nine-and-a-half years of clairvoyant readings, I'd never seen anyone blend success and compassion as well as Nik Sky. I studied the man with disheveled, dirty blond hair with a humble, yet strong stance. I liked him. He acted as director of his circus' talent and crew, but also like a grandfather elephant, protecting and caring for his family.

Nik Sky continued with the orientation. *"The Wheel of Destiny* will use this auditorium from seven on." He lowered his clipboard and smiled at his staff members standing at the ring's edge. "All right, gang. Go meet and greet our new family."

Miss Katja glided up to the first row and sat with the Russian adagio couple. The pretty, mid-thirties-year-old blonde moved with the grace and command of a gazelle queen. Like me, she rimmed her light brown eyes with dark eyeliner. I wondered ...

"Hi, Li." Miss Katja sat between me and Bai. "Hi, Bai. *Alo,* Valthea."

"Hi, Miss Katja," they said.

"*Alo,* Miss Katja." I quickly pulled a bobby pin from my bun and pinned my bangs up and to the side. "I'm very happy to be here."

"Wonderful. I look forward to working together. You know, Valthea, we've a lot in common. Bucharest is also my hometown, and I'm sure Coach Muzsnay told you I trained with him for many years."

"Yes, ma'am. He speaks highly of you."

"That's nice. He's a good man and a great teacher. Just to let you know, in this circus when we work in a group, we speak English. When it's the two of us, we can converse in Romanian."

"Okay." She didn't even glance at my birthmark.

"Emeric and Pauly, your co-actors, are performing at a children's charity tonight."

"We told Valthea about them," Li said.

Miss Katja smiled. "You'll meet them tomorrow morning. They'll introduce you to your act, and then you and I will meet in the afternoon." She pointed to the folder. "It's all outlined in there." She stood, posture perfect. "Welcome, Valthea. I'm glad you're here."

"Thank you, Miss Katja." She climbed two rows higher and introduced herself to the high-wire walkers from Poland.

I ripped the bobby pin from my bangs and forced it open until it broke in two. *All* my wishes didn't need to come true in one day. Soon, it'd be easy for my parents to find me. *Sky Brothers Circus* traveled Eastern Europe for nine months. My face would be on the website and sometimes in newspapers. They'd see my photo and recognize themselves in me. Yes, I not only believed it possible, but knew in my heart my parents and I'd be reunited.

NINETEEN

I walked into Rehearsal Room C forty-minutes earlier than scheduled to meet with the clowns. Folding chairs and a few barstools lined the back of the room. Full-length mirrors plastered the opposite wall, and gymnastic mats covered a third of the floor. I worked out and stretched for thirty minutes and then sat on one of the barstools, toweling off. The door swung open at two minutes before nine.

A long-limbed man with a hook nose stepped inside the rehearsal room. He looked me up and down, grinned, and then strode past me toward the mirrors. "*Bonjour, Mademoiselle*, Valentina." He dropped his backpack on the mats. "*Je suis*, Emeric."

I stood. "*Bonjour. Je suis*, Valthea."

He spun around. The grim lines of his face turned upward, and his eyes brightened. "*Ooo ... parle vous Francais?*"

"No, but I speak English."

His smile turned downward and his turquoise eyes grayed and retreated under heavy lids. "English? *Alors quoi?* Who cares? " He faced the mirrors, pounded himself in the chest, and then flicked his hands overhead. "What about ze French? What about respecting France?"

"*Bon jour*, Emeric. Good morning, Valthea." A little man entered the room. He carried himself tall despite his waddle. "I'm Pauly." He extended his hand up to me.

"Hi," I said, shaking hands like an American.

Pauly set his wallet, keys, and cell phone on a folding chair and then walked toward the front of the room. "Guess you've already met Emeric."

"Pauly doesn't speak *François* either," Emeric said with his strong accent. "Ee's from Cal-i-fornia. I put up wiz 'im because ee's damn good clown."

"A damn good and tolerant clown." Pauly nodded.

"*Ale!*" Emeric jogged ten-feet onto the mats.

Pauly headed in the opposite direction towards a closet door.

"Valentina, you are in ziss act." Emeric shooed me away. "Go help Pauly."

"My name's Valthea." I ran to the closet.

Ceiling-to-floor shelves housed all kinds of props, from maracas and neon orange street cones, to plastic flowers and rubber chickens.

Pauly handed me a droopy laundry bag and then grabbed several signs attached to wooden stakes.

"Pauly, I can carry some of those, too. This bag is as light as a feather."

"Look inside," Pauly said, grinning.

I opened the bag and peeked in. Pauly and I burst out laughing.

"Stop playing around," Emeric yelled, shadow-boxing. "Zare's work to do."

Pauly and I placed the stake signs into a red, white, and blue barrel at the edge of the mats.

Emeric pumped out a series of double and single arm push-ups. After thirty, he sprung to his feet, brushed off his hands, and then leaned into me whispering, "No more pushups. It might excite you."

I stepped back.

"Don't pay attention to him." Pauly muscled his way in between us like a protective bulldog. "He's arrogant, and he flirts."

Not wanting Emeric's remarks to bother me, I imagined him as a goofy cartoon. "It's okay Pauly. No big deal. He's just being ... uh, French."

Emeric rolled his eyes. "Oofa."

Pauly chuckled. "Valthea, I think you're going to do fine amongst us circus folk." He paced. "All right, here's the overview of our act. You play a dancer-acrobat determined to practice her routine. Emeric views himself a debonair clown and vies for your affection on three different occasions."

Emeric smoothed his graying hair back with both hands, looking into the mirrors. "I *am* debonair."

"Right," Pauly said over his shoulder. "Going on, Emeric interrupts you three times. First, he brings you flowers, then a box of chocolates, and then an engagement ring. My role is to sell you various types of magic feathers which enable you to ward him off. Your character's goal is to finish your routine."

"Feathers?"

"Yeah." Pauly used his hands to explain. "When Emeric presents you with a gigantic bouquet of flowers, I walk by holding a sign that says, *sword feather for sale*. You take the sword-feather and slice the heads off the flowers."

"But it's not a real sword. It's a feather, right?"

"Oofa! Trick—trick bouquet. You slice ze heads off ze flowers. I drop ze bouquet, and run out of ze ring like crazy person."

C.K. Mallick

I pictured the scene. "Does the audience laugh?"

"But of course." Emeric rolled his eyes.

Pauly continued, "You start your routine again from the beginning. You get two bars further, before Emeric returns. This time, he offers you a four-foot-wide, heart-shaped box of chocolates. You refuse them. He trips, drops the box, and the chocolates spill everywhere. Heartbroken, he crawls on his hands and knees, picking them up."

"Pauly, wait—when do I learn *exactly* what I do? When do we start practicing?" My palms sweat. "I've never done any acting before, and I've never been an acrobat in a clown act. I want to be believable. I need to be perfect."

Pauly smirked. "You gymnasts are all overachievers, aren't you? Don't worry, Valthea. We'll practice our act hundreds of times before we open. You'll be perfect. Each and every bit of choreography will be locked solid in your muscle memory." He pulled a sign out from the barrel. "Going on. While Emeric's picking up the spilled chocolates, I walk by dragging my drawstring bag and holding up *this* sign."

I read it aloud, *"Tickle Feather for Sale."*

"I sell you an ostrich feather, and you use it to tickle Emeric. The tickling drives him bonkers. He shields himself with the lid of the chocolate box, blocking the tickling feather. You toss the feather and begin your routine again. You almost finish, but Emeric marches into your spotlight, drops to one knee, and holds up a rubber diamond engagement ring the size of a bicycle wheel."

"That's funny. Do I buy another feather?"

"Yup. This time it's a black crow feather. The sign I hold up will say, *knife-feather*. When Emeric sees you holding the *knife-feather*, he scrabbles to get away. You run toward him. In eight counts, you hop on his back, hug him tight, and—" Pauly made a gurgling, dying sound as he drew the edge of his right hand across his throat from left to right. "You slice."

"Whoa, that's pretty violent."

"It comes off comically. Kids laugh."

"Let me get this straight, Pauly ... I hop on Emeric's back, hang on by hugging him, and then pretend to slit his throat with the crow feather."

"You got it. Three parts—hop, hug, and slice."

"Hop, hug, and slice."

"Don't worry, Valthea." Pauly folded his arms across his petite barrel chest. "I'll make sure you remember how to cut Frenchy's throat."

140

"Not funny, Pauly. And Val." Emeric lightened his voice, "I make sure it'z exciting to hop on my back." He blew me kisses. "Muah-muah, my little ingénue."

"Knock it off, Emeric. Valthea, I apologize for my fellow clown." For the first time, I noticed Pauly's eyes weren't brown, but hazel.

Cement pole lights lit an employee parking area behind a shopping mall cinema. Tall palm tree branches swayed in the night breeze. Four teenage boys hung out around a black Monte Carlo, laughing and passing around a bottle of liquor. The back door of the cinema opened. Pauly, about seventeen, exited the building alone. The boys surrounded him within seconds.

"Well, what do we have here?" one of them said.

Another piped in, "Which dwarf are you? Bashful or Grumpy?"

The shortest guy in the group approached Pauly. "I'd leave you to someone your own size, but none of us are your size." The punk pushed Pauly to the ground. The four guys crowded in, taking turns kicking and ...

"Stop!" I cried.

Emeric jumped back. "Sorry Valentina. I like to play around. Don't vorry, your not my type. I like big chest girls or sexy, like ze Spanish acrobat sisters."

"Don't be a jerk, Emeric. And her name is *Valthea*." Pauly dropped the sign he held into the barrel. "You all right?"

"Yeah." I crossed my arms in front of my chest. "Just thinking of something else." Carlo Reye taught me that confident people don't need to degrade others.

"Do you need a break, Valthea? Food and drink machines are in the hall."

"A break? Already? Oofa." Emeric threw his arms in the air.

"No, Pauly, thanks. What happens after I *hop, hug, and slice*?"

"You finish your routine. You curtsy. The audience applauds. You exit. I walk by the *dead* Emeric carrying a sign that says, *healing feather*. I wave a pink, poufy feather over his body, and he awakes. He does a back roll, jumps up, and is all better."

"I hope you're not shy, Valentina. In ziss act, our bodies always touch. With ze tickling-feazer you straddle me on ze ground. With ze knife-feazer you jump on my back, and you hug me close."

"Honestly, Emeric." Pauly planted his feet wide and his fists on his hips.

"Vell?" Emeric exaggerated a wink. "Can you handle it, Val?"

C.K. Mallick

Emeric. He stood in front of a mirror in his motor home bathroom securing a toupee. Strange. Emeric wore a bald cap for his clown act—but he was already bald.

"*Oui*, Emeric, I can handle it because I'm a professional."

Pauly reached up and patted my shoulder. "*Touché.*"

"*Un professionnel?*" Emeric pulled a pack of cigarettes from his backpack. "No. Naïve. Romanian gymnast at sixteen is naïve as Parisian child of nine. You probably never kiss a boy in your life."

Sorin wasn't a boy. He was a gentleman and my champion.

"*Bon.* Enough." Emeric spoke with his un-lit cigarette in his mouth. "Smoke break."

"Valthea, you want a soda?" Pauly grabbed his wallet from the barstool by the door.

"Sounds good." I studied our reflections in the mirror. Emeric strode across the room, all legs, nose, and insecure-based arrogance. Pauly stood eyelevel with a barstool, radiating a presence five-times his stature. And then there was me, the girl on the mats. The *Bendy Girl*, the plain biscotti who overachieved all she undertook to prove her worth and forget she was an unwanted orphan.

Yeah. I fit right in.

TWENTY

I entered the low-lit auditorium for my first understudy rehearsal with the *Divas of Silk* act. A two-foot-high wall encircled three-quarters of the performance ring in the center of the building. Two crew guys worked securing cables with duct tape along the base of the wall. Someone tinkered on something in the rafters overhead. Inside the ring, a man of about forty, wearing a baseball cap and work gloves, tugged and positioned three, twenty-five-foot-long silk ribbons hanging from the ceiling.

I sat on the ring's wall, extended one leg to the side, stretched over it, and then did the other leg. Maybe I'd become good friends with the girls in the trio, and we'd hang out and do stuff together. The candy-red exit sign at the east door illuminated the wall clock underneath it. *Almost three.* I rubbed the calluses on my palms.

"Ye understudyin' the silk act?" The man positioning the silk ribbons asked.

"Yes, sir."

"Call me Fossey. Ye know, in me mother's day, girls climbed and posed on natural fiber ropes. Today, there's these stretchy Lycra scarves." He smoothed one of the red bands. "Ever been on one?"

"I watched some *YouTube* videos. The artists made it look so easy"

"Yeah." He walked over to where I sat while tightening his walkie-talkie with a screwdriver. "Ye'll learn to climb, wrap around, and drop and roll from these bands. It's a class act."

"I can't wait."

"Ye look familiar. First year with us?"

"Yes. My name's Valthea. I'm new. Have you been with Sky Brothers awhile?" "Aye, years."

"Do you use harnesses or nets for the aerial acts?"

"Mostly harnesses. It's nice. The wires are invisible to the audience, and my crew controls them by remote. Nets are used for flying trapeze and the high wire walkers." A call came through on Fossey's walkie-talkie. He pressed a button. "Be there in a wee bit," he said, his Irish accent strong. He tucked the screwdriver in his tool belt. "Back to work for me. Welcome, Valthea."

"Thanks. Nice to meet you."

Fossey went over and helped the guys securing cables to the ring's curb.

The east door swung open and a stream of light filtered into the ring. I stood at attention before it slammed shut. Three girls, each a different height, walked toward the ring. The exit sign lit their silhouette, creating red auras around them.

Miss Katja entered a moment later. "Fantastic!" she yelled. "Our first rehearsal and everyone's on time." She flipped on the house lights and walked down the aisle to the center of the ring. She held a clipboard and a ring of keys. "Good afternoon, girls. Let's take a minute to get to know each other before we start." She glanced at her singing cell phone. "I've got to take this. It may be a minute. Please introduce yourselves." She pointed to Fossey. "Meet Fossey, tent master and my husband."

He looked up and saluted.

"He's here if you need anything." She answered her phone and walked toward an exit door.

"I'll start." The statuesque redhead's beauty mark above her upper lip, thick, arched brows, and sultry voice reminded me of a hot 1990's actress. "I'm Beata. I'm from Poland, and I'm twenty-eight. Let's see ... I love Thai food, long walks on the beach, and—"

"Men!" said the petite blonde girl.

"It's true." Beata batted her eyelashes.

I joined in their laughter.

"What's your name?" Beata asked.

"Valthea. Valthea Sarosi."

"Have you worked a ribbon before, Valthea?" she asked.

"No, but I'm a quick learner."

"You'll love it, darling. At five-foot-nine, I have to love it. Not many acts for an Amazon acrobat." Beata planted her hands on the rolled-down waistband of her sweatpants. "Welcome to Sky Brothers, darling."

Beata as a child. She played in the snow with her older brothers, laughing and throwing snowballs. Eleven. Her mother drops her off at early morning gymnastics practice. "I'll see you after school, Beata," she said. "Remember, you can do anything you put your mind to." They hug and kiss good-bye. Fully-blossomed at sixteen, Beata sat with her family at the dinner table, to a meal of a steaming roast chicken, potato dumplings, and green bean/almond casserole. An apple cake, displayed on a cake stand, and a silver coffee canister, sat on the adjacent buffet table. Her family took turns going around the table, sharing about their day and then discussing current world events.

Viewing pleasant pasts, like Beata's, refreshed my optimism about people and life.

"I'm Stasya," the petite blonde said. "I'm seventeen and from a small town outside Moscow. Where are you from, Valthea?"

"Bucharest." I'd never met a tan, pixie-like Russian girl before. Stasya reminded me of a Malibu Barbie Doll, or perhaps Tinker Bell.

Russia. Midday, overcast and cold, no snow, lots of wind. Stasya and a girlfriend, both fifteen, skipped their afternoon ballet class. They walked along a quiet street with a handful of shops. "Hey, Tamara," Stasya said. "Let's stop for some hot cocoa." "Great idea. I'm freezing." A man wearing a wool cap and an army-green field coat crossed the street and walked toward them. Stasya and her friend picked up their pace. He ran up toward them. The girls ran, but the man grabbed Tamara around her arms and waist, and carried her into the nearby alley. Tamara screamed and cried for help. Stasya ran after the man, hitting him repeatedly on his back. "Let her go!" Stasya yelled. The man swatted Stasya away, throwing her backward. She got up and ran to the nearest shop. "We need help—hurry!" She tugged on the shopkeepers arm. "A man grabbed my girlfriend. You have to stop him!" The man held his ground, in the middle of his store, and asked, "Is the man tall, with a wool cap and an army jacket?" "Yes! Hurry. Come on." The shopkeeper yanked out of Stasya's grip. "I can't help you. I don't have a gun." The woman standing next to them shoved the shopkeeper against the checkout counter. "Coward! Then call the police. You." She took Stasya's hand. "Come with me." The woman hurried Stasya into her car parked in front of the shop. She turned her vehicle around, slammed on her car horn, and kept her hand on it while driving into the alleyway. The man with the wool cap hopped off of Tamara, pulled up his pants, and ran away. Tamara lay crying on a crumpled cardboard box. "Chert poberi! Dammit!" the woman swore, putting the car in park. Stasya jumped out of the car and ran to Tamara. The woman followed, uttering, "We're too late."

Weeks later. Stasya knelt at her bed, crying as she prayed. "Father, please forgive Tamara. It's not her fault. If that man hadn't ... hadn't been bad, she would've never hung herself. She was a good girl. She loved You, Father. Please, I beg You." Stasya sobbed. "I beg for her forgiveness. Let me help her

145

now. I couldn't help her then." Stasya sobbed for several moments and then prayed, "Lord Father, please protect me and the rest of my girlfriends. Help us to see clearer and to avoid trouble." She made the sign of the cross. "In the name of the Father, the Son, and the Holy Spirit, Amen."

My prior optimism crumpled like the cardboard box in my vision.

"I like Thai food, too, and performing on the silks." Stasya beamed. "I *love* being high in the air."

"I'll tell you why you love being up high," said the third girl of the trio, a stunning brunette with a thick Bulgarian accent. "You're shorter than everyone, except for the midget clown. When you're up high, no one can look down at you." She undid her hair clip and tousled her long black hair. The side spotlights cast electric blue on her mane and turned her eyes the color of sapphires. She smoothed and re-clipped her mane, smiling as if pleased with her cleverness.

I disagreed with the Bulgarian girl. Intertwined with a ribbon, hanging sixty to hundred-feet in the air, allowed Stasya a higher and wider point of view. She probably felt safer and in more control than she did on the ground.

"Daniella," Stasya said, gesturing to me. "Introduce yourself to Valthea."

Daniella slid into a split. "I don't waste my time talking to understudies who are clowns."

I stepped in front of her. "I'm a nationally ranked gymnast in a damn good clown act. You should respect Emeric and Pauly. They're excellent at what they do. And Pauly's not a midget. He's a—"

"Don't tell me who to respect."

"Easy, Daniella," Beata's throaty voice carried admirable command.

Daniella snickered. "I'm surprised Miss Katja chose this girl to understudy our act. The silks require skill and grace"

"I've both, and I'm standing right here, so talk to me directly." Fabulous. Another beautiful bitch has come into my life. Why couldn't more attractive girls be nice, like Beata and Stasya, or like Cosmo's Gisella who was considered *more angel than girl*? What would Apollonia and Daniella do when their pretty faces faded, and they couldn't get away with being snide and snobby anymore? I doubted they would end up sweet and wise like Aunt Sylvie.

Daniella wheezed. "Where's my inhaler?" She rummaged through her gym bag. "I had it in my hand coming in. *Where* is it?"

"We'll find it." Beata circled Daniella, moving shoes, and looking under our gym bags.

Stasya retraced our steps from the ring to the exit door.

Fossey stopped what he was doing and helped look. "Bloody high risk, she is," he mumbled. "Bloody high risk."

"Help them!" Daniella yelled at me, holding a hand to her chest and breathing hard.

"What does it look like?"

She wheezed. "Idiot!"

"Sit, darling." Beata took Daniella by the shoulders and sat her on the ring's bank"

"Getting upset only makes breathing harder," I said, looking around the floor where we gathered.

"Don't talk to me." Daniella barely drew in her next breath.

Miss Katja entered the auditorium through the south door.

"Daniella's having an attack," Beata yelled. "We can't find her inhaler."

"My spare is in the dressing room." Daniella wheezed. "In the jeweled box by my makeup."

"I'll get." Beata ran toward the exit.

"Breathe easy, Daniella." Miss Katja sat next to her. "I'm right here."

Six-year-old Daniella sat on one end of the living room couch. Her step-father sat between her and her mother, his new wife. He handed Daniella a beautifully wrapped present. "This is for you. I'm your new father, and I'll always take care of my good, little girl." Daniella opened the present. Her eyes lit up as she lifted an expensive-looking princess doll from its box. At nine, Daniella's father gave her a cocker spaniel. At twelve, he gave Daniella new bedroom furniture for Christmas. When Daniella turned fourteen, she begged to go to a circus boarding school. Her father finally agreed. "I'll miss you so much, my little princess." He held her tight in a long hug at an airport. Daniella's mother stood in the background. The worn woman would've been pretty if she gained fifteen pounds. Away from home, Daniella garnered little attention from others. She played up her asthmatic condition when not training. Wheezing here, trying to catch her breath there. This manipulation worked. Daniella drew oodles of caring females and a pile of lustful males feigning concern.

I watched Daniella monopolize Miss Katja's attention. I always thought it unfair how the one who misbehaves and connives received more attention than the one who's quiet and does the right thing.

"I found it!" Stasya yelled, running from the east door. She handed the gizmo to Daniella.

In moments, Daniella breathed fine.

"Excellent. We're going to get started," Miss Katja said, standing. "Daniella, sit this first one out. Beata and Stasya, I'll talk you through the choreography. Valthea, watch it once, and then we'll get you up there. We've five weeks before our pre-opening gala. We need to be perfect in four."

"Hi *prinţesă.*, I miss you so much. What have you been up to?" Tonight Sorin appeared Face-time on my phone.

"I miss you too, my champion." I filled him in on my latest rehearsal schedule and told him about Daniella using her asthma as an attention getter. I told him how much I admired Beata's ribbon act, wishing I could learn it one day. He listened patiently, then apologized that we couldn't see each other until spring break due to his studying twelve-hours a day and weekends. All too soon, we said our goodbyes. We kissed the phones and his face was gone. I missed him already. Thank goodness my rehearsals kept my mind busy and my soul soaring.

Pre-opening night fell on the seventh of February. Our audience consisted of family, friends, and the circus' board of directors and investors. There were numerous heated dressing rooms adjacent to the arena. Once Sky Brothers began touring, the cast would dress and do their makeup in their motor homes. The silk trio girls and I used one of the smaller heated rooms. We sat in a row at a makeup table facing bulb-lit mirrors. Beata sat at the end nearest the door, followed by Daniella, Stasya, and then me.

"Nik Sky wants to add an aerial act next season." Daniella put down her eye shadow brush and gazed at herself in the mirror. "A *solo* aerial act."

"You've a pretty good shot at it if you keep your asthma under control." Beata centered her sequin choker. "Not me. With my height, it's the silks, a quick-change act, or a theatrical piece with clowns."

"Please," Daniella said, putting on mascara. "One clown per dressing room." She leaned into the dressing table, looking past Stasya and Beatta. "Oh. Valthea. Sorry. I didn't mean that as a cut to you. After all, circuses always need a clown or two ... or three."

"She's not really a clown." Stasya lined her eyes with a black khol pencil. "She does advanced aerials."

Daniella elbowed her.

"*Smotret!* Watch it—I could've poked my eye." Stasya rubbed her shoulder. "What'd you do that for, anyway?"

"Remember your loyalty."

Stasya glanced at me in the mirror.

"Stop bickering, darlings. It's draining before a show." Beata flicked her hand.

"Sorry." Daniella dusted on a glittery powder. "I find it exhilarating imagining our future days as stars with the circus. Stasya, you should stop feeling sorry for clown-girl and think about your future."

"I do think about my future. I want to marry, live in a real home, and have children." Stasya dropped her tube of eyelash glue to the dressing table. "Ugh. Why can't I talk and put on false lashes? There's glue all over my lid."

"I'll help." Daniella pulled Stasya and her chair out away from the table, and then facing her, sat on her lap.

"Don't sit on me."

"I'll be done in a second." Daniella dabbed Stasya's eyelid with a cotton swab and realigned the strip of false eyelashes. "All better." She kissed Stasya's eyelids and then eased off her lap. Daniella caught me watching her in the mirror. The weasel's smirk grew.

I loaded up my makeup puff with powder and pat my nose. *Merde!* I quickly grabbed my towel.

Stasya giggled like a pixie. "That's a lot of powder." She picked up a can of aerosol hair spray and sprayed her bangs back.

"Told you she was a clown." Daniella laughed until she wheezed. "Hey—stop spraying!"

"Sorry. I forgot to go into the hall."

Daniella snatched her inhaler from the rhinestone box setting on the dressing table. The vixen sucked on it as if she'd almost lost her life.

"You okay?" Beatta asked.

"I am now." Daniella snarled at Stasya. "In the future try thinking before you do stupid things."

"I said I was sorry."

Daniella ... one year ago. She stood in a crowded dressing room wearing last season's silver and black costume. One of the girls sitting at the dressing table saturated her up-do with hairspray. Daniella pushed her, wheezing and gasping for air.

"I told you—spray in the hall!" She grabbed her inhaler and sucked on it. A manager poked his head in the room and yelled, "Places!"

Daniella shoved the hairspray girl out of her way and ran into the hall with the other girls. A few minutes into the act, Daniella fell from the lower part of her silk, ten-feet to the ground. The spotlight quickly switched focus to a clown on the opposite side of the ring. The circus medics ran to Daniella, lying in the dark. They wrapped her ankle and placed ice packs on either side of her knees. "You're lucky," one medic said. "You could've fallen from the top of your ribbon."

"Let me ask you a question, Valthea." Daniella wore the crazed look of a carnivorous weasel. "Which of the three of us do you think Nik Sky would pick for a solo aerial act?"

Jozef, the stage manager, knocked on our door. "Twenty minutes to show."

"Thanks Jozef," Beata yelled and then glanced at Daniella. "Don't get into this now. We only have a few minutes."

I quietly covered my birthmark with concealer, knowing how I would answer Daniella's baited question.

"It only takes a second to answer."

Beata darkened her beauty mark with eyeliner. "Tell her what she wants to hear, Val."

"I think Stasya would make a beautiful soloist and cover act on the circus program. Except it sounds like she'd rather have a family."

"What makes Stasya so great?" Daniella tore of off her wool shrug.

I continued. "Beata would also make a superb soloist. She demonstrates mathematical exactness on the ribbon."

"*Da.*" Stasya nodded.

I made purposeful eye contact with Daniella. "You never worry about Beata messing up or, you know ... falling."

"Yeah," Stasya said. "Daniella, remember last year when you—"

"Shut up, you twerp." Daniella pitched the cap of her lipstick bullet at Stasya's head.

"Why are you throwing things at me?" Stasya scooted her chair away from Daniella's, closer toward mine. "It's not a secret. Everyone knows you fell last year."

"Shut up, Stasya. You, too, clown-girl."

"No. I haven't finished." I straightened my costume tiara. "As far as I go, I know I'd be an excellent choice for a solo because I've solid skills, I'm a quick-study, and healthy."

Daniella squirmed in her chair. "All right. You've said your thoughts about everyone except me. Not that I value your opinion, but you might as well finish."

Predictable weasel. ... "Okay, Daniella. You're pretty. You've stage presence, and you're punctual. But if I were a circus director, I'd be afraid to hire you because of your asthma. You're a bloody high risk. You put yourself and others in danger."

"It's true." Stasya perked up. "She fell last year."

"Shut up!" Daniella shoved Stasya to the floor and started choking her.

"Stop!" Beata and I yelled, dashing over to them and pulling Daniella off Stasya.

Beata pushed Daniella toward the door. "Get out of here!"

"No. I need to finish my makeup." Daniella turned and sauntered over to her chair.

"I hate you!" Stasya ran to the bathroom on the other side of the room. Beata ran after her.

I picked up Stasya's velour sweat jacket from the floor.

"See what you've done, clown-girl?"

"You mean what you've done." I glared at Daniella, hoping the gold in my irises would burn the blue in hers. "I'd never treat a teammate like you just did." I ran to the bathroom to check on Stasya.

"Teammate?" she yelled to my back. "This isn't grade school, and you're *not* Stasya's teammate."

I peeked inside the tiny bathroom. "Are you all right?" I handed Stasya her jacket.

Stasya took it from me and balled it up, placed it under her head, and then leaned against the wall. "I can't stand her."

"Stasya?" The weasel spoke sweetly, burrowing her way into the bathroom.

Beata held up one hand. "Daniella, get out of here."

"Stasya," Daniella continued, "I'm sorry that Valthea didn't say you'd make a great solo star. She's cruel and selfish. Forget about her." Daniella opened her arms. "I'll take care of you."

"You've done enough caring for one day." I wanted to smack her.

Stasya scooted further away from Daniella. "Stay away from me."

Daniella tipped her chin up and pivoted away from Stasya. "I need to finish pinning up my hair." She exited the bathroom.

She didn't fool me. It was a retreat.

Beata came in. "Stasya, if you're okay, we should finish getting ready. Show starts in five minutes."

"I'm fine."

We helped Stasya up and followed her out of the bathroom.

The four of us primped in silence at the dressing table. A streak of light from the half-open bathroom door reflected on the floor space behind our dressing table and chairs. I too reflected on what lay behind the scenes at *Sky Brother's Circus*. I thought about traveling with *The Gypsy Royales* and being part of Coach Muzsnay's *Lioness Gymnastic Team*.

I studied with Coach Muzsnay since I was nine. Although being part of the *Lionesses Team* provided a sense of belonging and family, many of my teammates whispered behind my back. I didn't come from a normal family. Traveling with *The Gypsy Royales*, I felt welcomed and loved by Cosmo, Sorin, and Rosa, but the negativity from Apollonia and Grandmamma never stopped. My current family with *Sky Brothers Circus* included a rough chaperone, an arrogant clown, and a wheezing witch. But it also included a four-foot, protective friend, a dashing wardrobe master, and an encouraging choreographer.

I realized two things gazing at the eighty-watt beam highlighting the floor behind me. First, in every "family" there are people you get along with and people you don't. Second, my true family, Aunt Sylvie, Radu, and Nawa, were pretty great.

I closed my makeup bag. Two of my three childhood dreams had already started to manifest: I'd found my soul mate, and I was in a circus. I still needed to find my parents. I smoothed down the sheer panels of my skirt and then checked the back of my costume in the mirror. Being in the circus was great, but becoming a soloist was my true dream. All I needed was an opportunity to prove myself.

"Places for Valthea!" Jozef yelled, knocking on our dressing room door.

"Thank you." I headed to the door. First step—to be one of the *Divas of Silk* as soon as possible. I shoved Daniella's chair out of my way and exited the dressing room.

TWENTY-ONE

Pre-gala opening night finally arrived, along with an all-white bouquet of flowers from Sorin. I caught my reflection in the dressing room mirror while inhaling the freesia, jasmine, and sweetheart roses. I didn't look like an orphan or a clown in my moonstone-white costume and rhinestone tiara. I wore my gold-brown hair slicked into a bun. Wisps of crystals glued to my cheek-bones shimmered. Black eyeliner and thick false-lashes turned my eyes the color of spun gold. I kissed a cluster of Sorin's jasmine, set the vase on my dressing table, and headed down the floor-lit hall to my waiting place at the east side of the ring.

Emeric and Pauly finished their clown bit, waved at the applauding crowd, and then scurried to their starting places for our act. I walked with pointed toes into the spotlight. Once at my mark, the D.J. waited the choreographed three seconds, allowing the clowns to saunter into the ring. The heat from the lights pounded my shoulders and back. Those three seconds felt like thirty. I couldn't swallow. Was I panicking? I caught a whiff of jasmine and thought of Sorin—the balm to my nerves.

The waltz from Tchaikovsky's *The Sleeping Beauty* began. I danced, turned walkovers, and then whipped out a series of front handsprings followed by a front aerial. When I landed, Emeric ran toward me with the oversize bouquet of flowers. He fake-tripped and I hopped into a punch-front-tuck to land on the other side of him. The audience laughed on cue.

The *Sky Brothers Circus* musicians followed Emeric and Pauly's stunts, punctuating their antics with percussion and horns. We made it smoothly through our entire number from start to finish. I bowed and exited, and Emeric and Pauly finished the healing feather gag. My adrenaline continued to race in the dim backstage area.

I'm in the circus, I punched a fist into the air. *I'm really in!*

After intermission, I tucked behind a curtain panel, careful to hide my blaring white costume. I wore it throughout the show until the grand finale when the cast paraded around the ring. Fossey stood a few feet away from me, keeping an eye on his crew. I marked the *Divas of Silk* choreography with my hands.

"Good for ye," Fossy said, his Irish accent thick. "Always studyin'."
Fossey's mother was from Spain, but he grew up in his father's Ire-

land. "Believe it, or not, I know what it's like. Before workin' the tent, I roller skated with me cousin on a small platform thirty-feet in the air, liftin' and twirlin' her. Adagio routine. Good to go over what ye'r understudyin', especially ones ye've a chance of performin'."

"You think I've a chance?"

"Sure, lass. Everybody knows Daniella's pushin' it with her asthma. If she gets upset, throws a tantrum, or gets a few whiffs of aerosol spray, she has a breathin' attack. Never mind she's always losin' her inhaler. Bloody high risk, she is. Bloody high risk."

I watched Daniella perform. "I've seen several of her asthma attacks."

"No denyin' her loveliness, yet some nights she's not strong. Her beauty and charm helps carry her."

I scratched the calluses on my palms. I always worked my butt off. Nothing ever helped carry me.

Fossey raised one of his bushy black brows and looked at me out of the corner of his eye.

"What?" I asked.

"Ye'r strong. Ye work hard. In the clown act, ye've skill and timing. When ye rehearse the silks ye look tense."

"I do? I can't. I need to be great on the ribbon."

"Then relax, lass. Let yer body become one wit that piece of Lycra out there. It'll change yer performance. Ye'll see."

"Become one with the silk?"

"Ye got it." Fossey winked and walked away, answering his walkie-talkie.

The following night, I went to the dressing room early, did my makeup, and then relaxed and wrote postcards to Sorin, Aunt Sylvie, and Cosmo. The silk girls strolled in at their usual time.

"You're ready early," Daniella hung up her coat. "You know, being early doesn't make you better."

Beata laid her coat over the back of her chair. "No drama tonight, please."

"Or any night," Stasya mumbled, taking off her boots.

Daniella sat at the dressing table in front of her makeup box. "Be quiet, Stasya."

Stasya flinched. "Don't talk to me."

I scooted my chair over, making room for Stasya in case she wanted to get away from the evil weasel.

Stasya glanced at the space and then at me. She pulled her chair out from under the makeup table.

Daniella grabbed her wrist. "Where do you think you're going? Stay next to me."

"I'm not your dog. I'm going to sit next to Valthea." Stasya pulled out of Daniella's grip and dragged her chair next to mine. "I bet Valthea's going to be Sky's next solo aerialist."

Daniella said nothing, which worried me. The coy beauty unrolled her brush case and slid out a six-inch long powder brush. Unlike my makeup brushes, all of hers matched with their solid blond wood handles and dark brown brush hairs.

"Stasya," she said in a baiting tone. "You're still my best friend, aren't you?" Daniella's dimples showed. They always did when she faked a smile.

Stasya continued sponging makeup on her face and didn't reply.

"I said, *aren't you?*"

Beata slapped her hand on the table. "Leave her alone, Daniella."

In an instant, Daniella jumped up and grabbed Stasya's ponytail. Chairs crashed. Daniella flung Stasya to the floor, sat on her, and whacked her across the face with the wooden end of her powder brush. She dropped the brush and started punching her.

Beata and I pulled Daniella off Stasya and dragged her to the other side of the room. Daniella made it to her feet, but Beata grabbed her from behind and held her in a bear hug.

I ran to the crying Stasya. I tucked my gym bag under her head and held a small towel under her nose. "Keep your head up. I'll be right back." I opened the door and yelled down the hall.

"Josef, we need a medic!" I left the door open and ran back into the dressing room. I wet a fresh washcloth, knelt next to Stasya, and held it under her bleeding nose. I smoothed the hair from her face. "It's okay. The medics are coming." Blood and marks covered Stasya's face and forearms.

"You've done it now, Daniella." Beata held the beast tight. "They're going to fire you."

Daniella struggled to free herself. "Nik Sky wouldn't dare. My father's on the board of directors. Nothing's my fault anyway. This wouldn't have happened if Stasya hadn't sided with clown-girl. Right, Stasya?"

I stayed crouched near Stasya, my eyes fixed on the blue-eyed Bulgarian.

Daniella's strength caught up to her rage, and she busted out of Beata's arms.

"Back off!" I stood, ready to fight.

Beata tackled her.

"What's going on here?" Miss Katja and the circus medics ran into our dressing room.

The medics pushed their gurney next to Stasya, laid her on it, and then placed icepacks to both sides of her face.

Beata kept hold of Daniella as they up stood.

Miss Katja put her hand on Stasya's shoulder. "You'll be okay, Stasya. The medics will take care of you."

The two young men rolled Stasya out of the dressing room as Beata let go of Daniella.

Daniella brushed her tangled hair back. "Why medics? What's the big deal?" She put her chair upright, sat in it, and re-pinned the sides of her hair.

Miss Katja stood behind us, looking into the mirror. "It's over, Daniella. Your bad behavior is intolerable."

"I don't know what you're talking about." Daniella picked up her powder brush from the floor. Dried blood speckled the blond wooden handle. "We were fine until Valthea came and tried to take over by pitting us against each other." She wiped her brush handle with her towel and then used the brush to powder her nose. "Everything is Valthea's fault."

"*Nothing* is my fault. You're a freaking sociopath. Minutes ago, you beat up your best friend and you're showing no remorse."

"I am not a—"

"*Stai!*" Miss Katja held up one hand. "Stop right there. We'll discuss everything after the show. Stasya's in good hands and on her way to hospital. Meanwhile, we've a show to do. You three need to clear your heads, finish getting ready, and go into the ring and give your best performance ever."

"Absolutely." Beata nodded.

I blotted my face with a towel, trying not to smudge my makeup.

"Valthea, your understudy will perform your act tonight. You'll be on Stasya's silk."

Guilt diffused my elation. I didn't want to replace Stasya or ever see her hurt.

Miss Katja leaned against the door. "I'm staying right here until show time."

"I opened the closet and took out the purple sequined leotard in my size, ready in case of an emergency ... ready for an opportunity to shine. The moment should've been my happiest, but it wasn't. I changed out of my white skirted leotard and slipped on the costume. Time to refocus. In twenty minutes, I'd be forty feet up in the air in front of a live audience. I closed my eyes and visualized a perfect performance. The silk and I are one. ...

The ringmaster bellowed, "Ladies and gentlemen, watch now as the three ribbons dangling from ceiling come alive with the acrobatic finesse of our three lovelies. Beata Walcheska from Poland, Daniella Nemska from Bulgaria, and tonight, replacing Stasya Kokoveva, Valthea Sarosi from Romania. I give you—Divas of Silk!"

Psychedelic lights ricocheted across the audience and throughout the auditorium. Rainbow colors swirled around our ribbons and splashed the ring's floor. The conductor raised his baton and led the orchestra in an East Indian sounding version of the Rolling Stones song, "Get Off of My Cloud." Beata, Daniella, and I entered the ring like rock stars. We climbed, wrapped, and unrolled from our ribbons in sync and with precision and flair.

The silk and I are one, I told myself. The silk and I are one. The audience applauded several times during our routine. Toward the end, we wrapped our ribbons around one arm, ran three counts, and then with crew assistance, flew through the air in succession. The crowd loved it, I loved the crowd, and my destiny loved me.

TWENTY-TWO

After every show, the *Sky Brothers Circus* artists loop the ring in a finale procession and then file out act-by-act. I paraded, waved, and smiled along with Beata and Daniella as part of the *Divas of Silk.*

Beata peeled off her costume mitts as soon as we entered the low-lit, backstage area. "Good work out there, Val."

"Thanks. It felt great."

Daniella yanked off her Velcro choker.

"Valthea," Miss Katja yelled over the clumps of performers making their way down the hall to their dressing rooms.

"Be right there," I yelled back. I cut in front of the Ukrainian teeter board brothers and met Miss Katja at the back wall. "Hi Miss Katja. How were we?"

"Let's walk," she said.

Uh, oh. I swallowed hard.

We followed the two guys from the *Wheel of Destiny,* Sky's final act.

"Val," she said slowly, "I realize tonight was your first time on the silks in front of hundreds of—"

"Miss Katja, I promise I'll get better. I'll practice extra on Mondays, and I'll—"

"Val, listen. Nik and I demand excellence from every artist in every show. It doesn't matter what's going on with a performer's personal life, at home, or in dressing room. The old adage is true—the show must go on."

"I'm sorry. I did the best I—"

"You were excellent."

"I was?"

"Yes. In fact, Nik and I learned a lot about you tonight. Not only do you stand up to bullies and defend your friends, yet in a moment's notice, you can pull it together and perform your heart out." She stopped in front of my dressing room. "Nik and I see great potential in you, Valthea."

"Thank you. I'm striving to be a soloist."

"I know. You remind me of myself at your age. By the way, Stasya's doing great. Nothing's broken. Doctor said she's fine for Sunday. You've four more days on the ribbon, and then you're back with Emeric and Pauly."

Although happy for Stasya recovering, I wanted to cry.

I walked into our dressing room early on the Sunday of Stasya's return.

"*Scorpie.*" I kicked Daniella's shoes out of my way and stood in front of her station. "Hag." A ball of anger burned my throat like a jumbo raw onion. The short-winded weasel held claim to one of the three ribbons that I wanted and better deserved.

Daniella's four-by-four inch rhinestone box shimmering under the mirror's bulb-lights caught my attention. I took out the inhaler and closed my fingers around it tight. What'd happen if I hid it? I scanned the room. Beata and I tidied the dressing room the night before. Beata had made a welcome back sign and taped it to Stasya's mirror. I'd placed a planter of white daisies in front of her makeup kit. With the exception of the negative cloud surrounding Daniella's station, cheer and warmth bounced throughout the room. I dropped the inhaler into its jeweled box. Forget it—you reap what you sow. Reading people and seeing their past taught me many things. The main lesson being that every choice made in the present affected the future.

I moseyed to my station and shoved my gym bag under the dressing table and sat. Applying the ballerina-style makeup for my role in the clown act psyched me up for the day's matinee. Matinees drew oodles of kids, and Pauly said children kept clowns employed. I loved their laughter.

"Valthea!" Stasya ran into the dressing room. "You're here early."

I jumped out of my chair and hugged her. "Stasya! How are you?"

"Great, physically, although I'm dreading eight months of you-know-who—*wow!* Daisies!" Stasya leaned over her chair and inhaled the full bouquet. "I love them."

"They're from all of us." I sat. "I'm glad you're okay."

"Thanks." Stasya hung her coat on a wall hook and then walked up to Daniella's station. "You know I hate her, right?"

"Forget her." I ducked my head under the dressing table and dug through my gym bag for my extra box of bobby pins. "Focus on you and the audience's excitement to see you."

"Great welcome back sign. Who drew our caricatures?"

I sat up in my chair. "Beata did. I didn't even know she drew. Hey Stasya, let's trade places so you don't have to sit next to Daniella."

Stasya scooted her daisies and makeup kit over three-feet. I switched our gym bags under the table. We applied makeup in peace for fifteen minutes before Beata and Daniella walked in.

"Darling!" Beata bent over and hugged Stasya. "Welcome home, your *real* home." She tossed her beret onto the dressing table. "No more laying around for you."

"Resting is boring. I can't wait to get back in the ring. Hey—thanks for the sign and the flowers. I'm saving the card forever."

"We're going to have an awesome matinee today, I can feel it." My upbeat moods annoyed Daniella.

Daniella snarled at Stasya in the mirror. "I don't care where you sit." She dropped her gym bag next to her chair. "Hey—" She banged her fist on the table. "Where is it, clown-girl? What've you done with my inhaler? I never leave the box open, and it's not in the box."

What? Where'd it go? I put it back in its box. "I don't know where it is."

"You conniving sneak!" She grabbed my hair, forcing me to stand.

"Let go!" I pried her fingers open and pushed her away.

Daniella tripped over her chair and fell back. Like a ravaged animal, she pounced to her feet and swat at me. "You took it!"

"*Przestan!*" Beata shouldered us apart. "Stop!"

"Not until clown-girl gives me my inhaler. I know she took it."

"I did not."

"I said, stop!" Beata pointed to our chairs. "It's almost show time. Both of you sit and finish getting ready."

Daniella set her chair upright, but she didn't sit. She slowly unrolled her brush case.

Once again, my stomach knotted up before a show because of the brunette vixen's spoiled-brat behavior. I shoved my makeup kit toward the mirror. "Daniella—why do you always have to ruin everything? I've worked my whole life to be in a circus. Finally my dream comes true, and I'm so happy. But not for long, because every day you waltz in here, and within seconds, you ruin the thrill for all of us. I can't stand it anymore, and I can't stand you."

"I don't care what you can and cannot stand. You've been coming here early for weeks, waiting for the perfect moment to steal my inhaler. You're hoping I've an attack so you can take my spot. Well, it's not going to happen. Beata, please make clown-girl return the inhaler that my medical doctor prescribed."

I glanced at the weasel. "Good thing you've a rich step-daddy on the board of directors. Any other circus wouldn't hire you, with or without your asthma."

"How dare you! And how do you know if he's my step-dad or not?"

Didn't Daniella ever mention it?

"Hold on." Beata held up one hand. "Valthea, sorry to ask, but have you seen or accidently moved Daniella's inhaler?"

"There are no accidents with her." Daniella heaved. "She's calculating. And Valthea, stop looking at me like you know things." She pushed me.

I grabbed hold of her shoulders, and she fell with me to the floor. She swiped her nails across my face. I shoved her off me and flipped her on her back. She started to wheeze.

"Your asthma, again?" I stood and stepped away from her. "Where's her inhaler?"

"Here!" Stasya handed Daniella her inhaler. "I found it under your towel."

Daniella shoved the contraption in her mouth and after several good breaths, said, "No, Stasya. I looked under my towel. It wasn't there." She scowled at me.

Stasya busied herself, setting the chairs upright and pushing them into the table at our stations.

Beata helped Daniella to her feet. "Easy now, relax, and breathe. Valthea, grab a can of cold soda from my cooler and put it on your cheek."

I did. The cold re-flared the sting from Daniella's claws.

"You thief!" Daniella yelled between puffs. "You knew you were caught, that's why you put it under my towel."

"No, I didn't. You must've—"

The dressing room door swung open. It was Miss Katja and the stage assistant, Jozef.

Daniella put her hands behind her back, hiding the inhaler. "What—no knock, handsome? You trying to catch me naked?"

Daniella, a petite, nine-year-old. ... It's nighttime. She has her own bedroom. She's lying in bed with the covers pulled up to her eyes. Her fingers shook, gripping the blanket's satin edging. She breathed short, rapid breaths.

C.K. Mallick

The bedroom door opened slowly. A nightlight in the hall outlined the tall figure of a man in a bathrobe. He whispered as he entered her bedroom. It was her step-father. "Daddy's here to see his good, little girl." He closed the door behind him and locked it.

I wanted to butcher the part of evil men which harmed children. No wonder I loved animals and being outdoors. Nature held no evil past.

"Daniella," Miss Katja said, standing next to the stage manager. "It's over. We're sending you home. I'm sorry."

"Sorry for what? What's over? What are you talking about?" Daniella slipped her inhaler into its box. "Everything's fine."

"Afraid not." Jozef stood behind her. "I'm walking you out. Sky's orders."

"Impossible. My father—"

"Listen, Daniella," Miss Katja spoke calmly. "Nik Sky and the board of directors can no longer employ artists who aren't of sound health or who send other artists to the emergency room. You've had a good run. Now it's over."

"No! This isn't happening. I ... I don't understand." For two seconds, Daniella's facial expression held no sign of maneuver or scheme. But then her eyes narrowed, and she cocked a sinister smile. "Or maybe I do understand. It's because of *her*, isn't it?" She pointed to me.

Jozef took her by the arm and led her to the door. "No, Daniella. It's because of you."

She screamed, "How could you, Miss Katja? You're horrible. *Tnen ca yehachen!* You're a dyke like your sister!"

Miss Katja put the inhaler in Daniella's purse and handed it to her. "Try to leave with some dignity."

"I'll take her to the office to sign release papers." Jozef walked her to the door.

"Beata? Stasya?" Daniella shouted over her shoulder. "Tell them! Tell them how Valthea caused all the problems."

Miss Katja closed the door behind Josef. "All right, here's the deal. You three are officially the *Divas of Silk*."

I could barely breathe. "Do you mean for the rest of the tour, or until you find a replacement?"

"For the rest of the tour."

Beata whistled like a fan at a soccer game. Stasya clapped like a joyful pixie.

Miss Katja rolled up Daniella's brush case and packed in her kit. "Valthea, cover those scratches and then add the silk diva makeup colors. Mark through the choreography twice." She hung Daniella's gym bag on her shoulder and picked up her packed makeup box. "Girls, the past is the past. Right now, there's only this moment." She opened the door. "I believe in you three. Now go out there, and give your audience the best matinee ever! Oh, and Valthea—"

"Yes, Miss Katja?"

"Take the center silk."

"Yes, ma'am."

She exited.

The center silk! I opened my palette of eye shadows, picked up my makeup brush, and faced the newest member of the *Divas of Silk* in the mirror.

TWENTY-THREE

Sorin called me for our Face Time session at midnight. I put a pillow on my stomach and then rested my iPad on it.

"You there, babe?" Sorin looked sexy unshaven and wearing a black muscle-tank top.

"Yeah, just getting situated."

"Now I see you. Hot as usual. Geez, *prinṭesă,* I really miss you."

"I miss *you*, Sorin, and I've exciting news."

"Tell me everything." He tucked several pillows under his head and lay back on his narrow dorm bed. "Any more trouble from the Bulgarian girl? Hey—are you in a different room? I don't recognize the background."

"There'll be no more trouble from Daniella. And yes, I'm in a different motor home, and I've new roommates. That's part of what I wanted to tell you."

"By the way, Val, it's great to see you two days in a row."

"What are you talking about? We didn't Face Time yesterday."

"I saw the *YouTube* video of you filling in on the ribbon. I check Sky's website every couple days."

"You do? You did?"

"You're amazing, babe."

"Really?" I couldn't help but smile.

"Big time, really."

"Good because Daniella was fired. I'm in the silk act *permanently*."

"Congratulations! I'm happy for you."

"Thanks. Next week, we'll be in Bucharest. Aunt Sylvie will see me as a *silk diva*. I wish you could be there."

"Me, too. But remember, I'm super proud of you." Sorin lay on his side.

I did the same and then kissed his image on my screen. "I miss you, so much Sorin."

He kissed his screen. "Miss you more. Let's stay online until we fall asleep. I want to kiss and touch you all night. I can't wait any longer. I need to sleep with you."

Aunt Sylvie insisted she and Mr. Karl meet me for breakfast the morning of the first matinee in Bucharest. I couldn't wait to see them and for Auntie to see me as a professional circus performer. I waited at a center table in the cafeteria tent sipping hot cocoa. About half the cast members ate early breakfasts on matinee days. Others slept in, stayed in their motor home and made their own coffee. I liked the homey feeling of someone else making me a warm meal. Fourteen people came through the food tent before Aunt Sylvie and Mr. Karl entered.

"Auntie!" I ran up to her and Mr. Karl and greeted them with hugs.

"It's so good to see you, dear."

"It's *great* to see you, Auntie. You too, Mr. Karl."

"Valthea, dear, you're too skinny."

"I'm not skinny, I'm fit."

"I look forward to seeing your show," Mr. Karl spoke in his usual quiet voice.

"Thanks, Mr. Karl. What would you two like for breakfast? French pastry, eggs Benedict, feta quiche? They make everything, although most of us can't indulge in a lot of what they make. The musicians and crew are lucky. They can—Auntie, why are crying?"

"You look so grown up." She wiped her eyes with her handkerchief.

"That's because I am. I'm sixteen-and-a-half."

Mr. Karl pulled a folding chair out for me and one for Aunt Sylvie. "You girls sit and visit. Syl, would you like eggs Benedict and a coffee with cream?"

"You know me well." Aunt Sylvie giggled like a smitten girl.

"What'd you like, Valthea?"

"Oatmeal with cinnamon. Thanks, Mr. Karl."

"So, dear, tell me how your studies are coming along with Miss Alin."

"Auntie, I'm in the circus, and you ask me about school work?"

"I'm still your parent. I need to make sure—"

"Alin says I'm an excellent student. We meet four times a week. She checks all my homework and then gives me new assignments, blah, blah, blah." I sipped my cocoa. "I can't wait for you to see the show and tell me what you think."

"I'm sure I'll love it."

Mr. Karl set our breakfasts on the table.

I scooped up a bite of oatmeal and then dropped my spoon into my bowl. Sorin!"

Sorin stood at the food tent entrance, disheveled from travel, but gorgeous. He spotted me. "Valthea!" He dropped his duffle bag and ran toward our table.

I almost fell, running toward him. We met halfway and embraced. He picked me up and spun me around.

"Sorin, oh-my-God! I can't believe it."

He laughed.

"I thought you couldn't get away until spring break?"

He kissed me a bunch of times and then lowered me. "I wanted to surprise you."

"Well, you did."

"I'll get your bag." Mr. Karl, walked up to us. He and Sorin hugged, patting each other on the back. "You two go sit with Miss Sylvie." Mr. Karl continued to the front of the tent.

"Okay, thank you." Sorin took my hand. We walked so close to each other, we nearly tripped over each other's feet.

"Auntie—did you know about this?"

"Yes, dear. Good morning, Sorin."

"Good morning, Miss Sylvie."

Mr. Karl returned to the table. "Valthea, since you stay at home while your circus is in town, I thought it best to invite Sorin to stay with me. That way, you kids can be near each other when you're not performing."

Sorin took his backpack from Mr. Karl. "Thank you again, Mr. Karl."

"How perfect. I'll get to see you at the beginning and the end of each day." I turned to Mr. Karl. "Thank you so much. Great idea."

"And babe, don't forget. I'll be in the audience for all your shows."

"*Alo, alo, alo!*"

The howling *hello's* came from the entrance. I turned. "Cosmo?"

My second favorite man in the whole world darted toward us. "My Valthea!" Cosmo sang, hugging me strong. "I had to come. Ha! Look-both your Dobra men are here to support and celebrate your rise to circus fame."

My spirit soared. Thank you God.

My matinee performance reflected my elation of knowing four dear people sat in the audience, watching me perform. Afterward, they met Miss Katja and Fossey, Beata and Stasya, Emeric and Pauly, and Bai and Li. I loved the people in my life meeting and liking each other.

After the night show, Cosmo drove us in his rented SUV to a nearby restaurant. He ordered us a special bottle of Cabernet and an extra basket of the fresh-baked bread.

"This is a special night." He raised his glass. The room's blood-red walls and dim, amber lighting cast an old world glow to the ever-exotic Cosmo. "To friends, family, and health!" We tapped glasses and drank. "And to Valthea." Cosmo added, with theatrical flair. "Her journey has taken her from tumbling in her backyard, to a prestigious act in one of Europe's most popular circuses. Here's to your continuing success. *Salut!*"

"*Salut!*" Mr. Karl and auntie chimed.

Sorin kissed my shoulder and raised his glass.

After the delicious and celebratory dinner, Sorin and I went to the movies. Basically, we sat in the back row and made out for a few minutes every half hour. Halfway through the film, Sorin snuggled close and whispered in my ear. "Valthea, I want you to know, I love *us*. Being with you, my soul mate is always incredible. I love you."

I wanted to cry. I wanted to shout for joy. I wanted to run into a round-off, back-handspring. ... I turned my face to his, until our lips nearly touched, and whispered, "I love you, too."

"We're the luckiest people in the world."

"I agree."

"And Val—"

"Yes?"

"I got to tell you, you're amazing in the ring. I believe in you and your desire for a career with the circus."

Sigh. Finally. "Thank you, Sorin. That makes me happy."

"Good, because your happiness makes me happy, and when I'm happy, I get hungry." He kissed me on the cheek. "I'm going to the food concession. Want anything?"

I couldn't even think of eating. "Yes, please. Twizzlers."

"You got it. *Anything* for my soul mate." He walked down the cinema's carpeted steps and then turned toward the exit door.

I was thrilled Sorin loved me, but now wondered: did Sorin see me more as a career girl than his future bride? I prayed he saw me as both.

TWENTY-FOUR

I lounged on my bed, scrolling through the dozens of cell phone photos Sorin and I took during our Bucharest time together. The "fun" ones included us swinging from tree limbs in my back-yard, him feeding Nawa, and me after a show in full costume, riding him piggy back. My favorite photos showed us kissing in front of the big top, leaning on trees, and at cafés. We wouldn't see each other again until his college's spring break—four weeks away.

I turned off my phone, sat up, and peeked out the window over my bed. No sun, only gray. A green road sign read: *320 kilometers to Budapest*. I lay back down. Hungary was the third country on Sky Brothers tour. I'd spend a lot of time stuck in a motor home over the next eight months. It'd be easy to fall glum and forget the thrill and privilege of living my dream. I pushed open the curtains, pulled my hair into a ponytail, and walked into our motor home's main living area.

"Beautiful day, isn't it?" I said.

Beata stood at the counter making sandwiches for the two crew guys who often rode with us and took turns driving. "Sure, Val, if gloomy is your favorite color."

I opened the fridge and took out the carton of eggs. "Days like this inspire me to bake. Anyone for homemade carrot cake with maple cream cheese frosting?"

Slovakia followed Hungary, followed by Poland. Sorin's spring break fell on the same week we played Krakow. Fossey and Miss Katja offered the extra bedroom in their motor home so he could be near me—but not too near. I waited for his arrival at the train station.

"Sorin—" I waved my arms. "Over here!"

We wove through the crowd toward each other until we inter-locked in a hug and kiss. The noon-time travelers split around us like the fever of stingray we'd seen in the shallow coast of the Black Sea.

"Let's get out of here," he whispered. "I want to stretch out my legs and hang out with you."

I led Sorin out of the station. Within ten minutes, we stood in the center of the town square, waiting in line at a blue trolley stand for a hot pretzel. The elderly lady working the stand pointed to our choices: salt, poppy seed, and garlic. Sorin ordered salt. I ordered poppy seed, but then changed to salt for obvious reasons.

That night, we went to a cavernous cellar bar, swirling with clove cigarette smoke, and rocking to Elvis Presley's *Hard Headed Woman* from a jukebox. The exposed brick and Persian rugs stretched over its wooden floors and set the scene for the bar's dozen vintage pinball machines. Sorin stood behind me, coaching me. After several games, he moved in closer. He kissed my hair, shoulders, and the back of my neck.

"A little shiver from my girl?" He whispered, gripping the sides of the machine and working the levers. "I'm glad pinball excites you."

I turned around in his arms to face him. "It's not pinball that excites me."

"Me neither, *prințesă*."

Red and violet roadside wildflowers greeted our circus caravan on the outskirts of Berlin. Fossey and his crew set up the performance tent within a day and a half on the mowed field. The field allowed ample space for patron parking, our tent (which sat fifteen-hundred people) and a back area for our twenty-seven motor homes. We opened Berlin on May first to a sold out crowd.

On our second day performing in Berlin, one of the assistant stage managers knocked on my motor home and handed me two-dozen monster yellow mums. "These are for you, Val. And girls," he said to me, Beata and Stasya. "It's twelve-forty. Twenty minutes 'til show time. See you out there." He walked away, talking into his headset.

I smelled the flowers. "They've no scent, but they look spectacular." I set the heavy vase on the kitchen table.

"*Mamusie* ... mums. What a unique choice." Beata cupped her hand under one of the flowers. "I pictured Sorin more of a rose guy. College must be expanding his culture and mind."

Stasya snapped a few pictures with her cell phone. "Are they from Sorin?"

"Of course," I said without thinking. "Who else?"

Beata held the door open. "Show time, girls. Let's go."

I called Sorin during intermission. "Sorin, I'm glad you answered. I thought you'd be in a study group or something."

"Val! *Cum esti*? How are you?"

"Better now. We haven't spoken to each other all week."

"I know. I'm sorry. I wanted to call, except when I only have a few minutes it's harder to call than not. I don't like to cut us off. Plus, I can't concentrate to study after talking to you."

"You exaggerate, Sorin. Listen, intermission's almost over—"

"That means you've only a minute to talk."

"I called because I couldn't wait to thank you."

"For what—answering the phone?"

"No, Sorin, you know. What you sent ... the flowers."

"I didn't send any flowers."

Merde. "Aunt Sylvie must've sent them then."

"Wasn't there a card?"

"I didn't take time to look."

"Maybe someone in the circus has a crush on you."

"No ... "

"Val, we're still exclusive, right?"

"Of course. Why do you even ask that?"

"You've some pretty friendly photos on Facebook."

"What about yours with girls in your room and in bars?"

"There are two girls in our study group, and those photos were shot in the library and restaurants. I do have to eat, you know."

"And I have to go."

"Wait—answer me. Are we still exclusive?"

"I thought we were, but since you keep asking me, I wonder if you still want to be."

"I definitely do. *Te iubesc,* I love you, Val. I *heart* you."

"I *heart* you too, Sorin."

"So we're good then?"

"Yes." *Good* except that the guy I was in love with lived seven-hundred miles away.

Stasya stood at the kitchen table holding her boots in one hand and a belt in the other. "*Ewe pa?* Again? Yesterday mums, tonight irises. How come you get so many flowers? Are they from Sorin?"

"I don't know. I can't find a card with those either."

"Twice no card?" Beata zipped up her boots. "Strange. Men love credit for their gifts. Speaking of men, Stasya and I've a date tonight with two, tall German men at a jazz club. Miss Katja and Fossey are joining us."

"You're meeting the men you talked to during intermission?"

"That's right, darling."

"Then Stasya, you should be happy. I get flowers, you get dates."

"Except that I'm nineteen, Beata's twenty-eight, and we're single. You're sixteen with a steady boyfriend."

"Sixteen-and-a-half, with a boyfriend I hardly see."

Beata stopped at the door. "That's right. Welcome to the circus, Valthea. If your guy's not in the circus you're in, it's *always* long distance. If family and friends don't visit you, you don't see them until December."

"It's the only part of the circus I don't like," I mumbled.

Beata set her purse on the counter and walked to the kitchen booth where I sat. "Are you sure there's no note?"

"I've an idea." Stasya whipped the greenery out of the mum arrangement and stuck her hand into the vase. She pulled a small, soaked envelope out and held it up. "Got it!"

"Brilliant." Beata handed her a dish towel.

Stasya blotted the note and then passed it to me. "Maybe the flowers are from two different dirty old men. They're probably over forty and chubby."

"Nothing wrong with forty," Beata said in her throaty voice. "I've dated some very interesting middle-aged men."

"I know a handsome forty-year old that's super fit." I opened the envelope and pulled out the wet card.

Stasya's eyes bugged. "Am I the only one who hasn't dated an old guy?"

"I didn't date him. Cosmo was the director of the troupe I traveled with last summer. This note's blurry. I'll try to read it. It's mostly in English.

Frauline Valthea, It's always a pleasure to see you perform. You're a ...

Something, something acrobat—I can't read that part. I think it says

... and a beautiful young woman. Yours truly ...

I laid the card on the table. "It's a short name, too wet to decipher."

Beata picked up the card. "No clear name?"

"What about these?" Stasya lifted the vase of irises overhead. She unpeeled a two-inch square note card taped to the bottom of the vase.

"My goodness." Beata took the card from Stasya and handed it to me. "You're a regular card sleuth."

C.K. Mallick

"It's from the same guy.

Frauline Valthea, there are no flowers as intriguing as you. I hope my gift of flora brings you pleasure. Yours truly, Halse."

I laid the second note on top of the first. "His name's Halse."

"You've a smitten German fan." Beata grabbed her bag. "How fun."

"It's weird." Stasya switched the notes around on the table. "Seems like they came in the wrong order. In the first note, the guy said it's always good to see you perform, like he'd already seen you perform."

"Maybe his English isn't as good as yours, Stasya." Beata nudged her toward the door. "Let's go. We're late."

"Don't worry, Val. I'll continue my detective work later."

After they left, I studied the cards.

It's always a pleasure to see you perform.

Did this fan come to every show? Was it a fan? Maybe Sorin was right. Maybe one of the cast or crew had a crush on me, except there weren't any Germans or Swiss on tour with us this season. Who else could it be?

Stasya led the way out of the big top after our Wednesday matinee finale. "Hurry up! It's a gorgeous day. I'm going to get my lounge chair and lie outside and get tan."

"That sounds a lot better than napping in a motor home." Beata quickened her step and peeled off her costume mitts.

"Hey, Val—" One of the assistant stage managers pointed to the fold-out table near the exit. "Take those on your way. The flowers are yours, too. They came during the show."

Two boxes, one long and one smaller and flat, lay next to a tall vase of sunflowers with heads the size of tea saucers.

"We'll help you." Beata picked up the vase. "I *love* sunflowers. If I could only find the equivalent in the human kingdom. You know, a tall man with a sunny disposition."

Stasya tucked the flat box under her arm, and I carried the long box. We walked through the mowed field to our motor home.

Stasya held the door. "Do you think they're all from your mystery fan?"

"I hope they're from Sorin."

Beata set the sunflowers on the kitchen table between the mums and the irises. "My God, we live in a greenhouse." She slid into one side of the booth. "Open your gifts, Val. I'm not doing anything until you do."

"Me neither." Stasya sat next to Beata. "This is fun, even if they're all for you."

I read the card tucked in the sunflower's vase. "These are from Halse.

> Frauline Valthea, I hope you've enjoyed the flowers I've sent thus far. Sunflowers remind me of you reaching for great heights. Congratulations on how far you've come. Have a great show tonight. Kindly, Halse."

Beata rest her forearms on the table. "Seems he's following your progress."

"Val," Stasya leaned into the booth. "Did you get flowers while in the clown act?"

"No."

"Maybe your fan's some cyber guy who's never even seen our show. Maybe he keeps tabs on you through the circus website and videos."

Beata slid the long, white box toward me. "Many things are possible, Valthea. You might as well sit and open your gifts."

I sat opposite the girls and then removed the envelope taped under the long box's pale pink satin ribbon. "It reads, *Prinţesă* ... " I exhaled.

"They're from Sorin." I cradled the box to my chest and continued reading aloud.

> "I want our hearts close even when we're afar. I miss and love you, my Circus Superstar. Love always and forever, Sorin."

"Aw ... " The girls sounded in unison.

"I love Sorin more than ever and more than anything." I pulled one end of the bow, and the satin strands cascaded to the sides like ballet slipper ribbons. I let the lid slide to the floor. A dozen, long-stemmed, pink roses lie inside the box like an ensemble of pink-haired, lithe ballerinas waiting to go on stage.

Beata reached across the table and tipped the box. "Long-stemmed roses? Your Sorin has taste."

I scooped them up and inhaled their petals. My entire being ached for my soul mate.

"Open this one." Stasya placed the flat box to me. "It's probably from Sorin, too."

I laid the ballerinas in their bed of tissue.

"No, Valthea. Those beauties need water." Beata slid out of the kitchen booth.

"Thanks." I handed Beata the box. "This is the best day ever. I feel so close to Sorin." I untied the dark brown cord cinching the flat box, took off its lid, and unfolded the tissue paper. "Pretty ... " I held up a gold-and-white print, silk scarf. A note dropped out.

"That's not your average scarf, darling." Beata placed Sorin's vase of roses on the table. "That's a *Hermès* designer scarf." She picked up the fallen note.

"Expensive." Stasya reached across. "Who's it from?"

"You read it, Beata."

"Fraulein Valthea— "

Beata looked up.

I folded the scarf and put it back in its box. "It's not from Sorin, but it's still a gift, and I'm thankful."

Beata continued:

"I invite you and your girlfriends from the ribbon act to a special dinner."

She glanced up. "He's trying to gain trust through your friends."

"Keep reading!" Stasya pushed the roses out of her way.

"A reserved table will await the three of you at the five-star, Brandenburg Berliner at ten o'clock after your show tonight. All I ask is that you wear the scarf I sent you. Yours truly, Halse."

She set the note on the table. "It's not a romantic dinner with Sorin, but it's an opportunity for exposure and culture."

"And good food." Stasya took the scarf from the box and wrapped it around her neck.

I unpeeled the dinner vouchers from the bottom of the box, and held them up, fanned out like cards. "Dinner, anyone?"

That night, we caught a ride into town with the Ukrainian brothers from the teeter-board act. Stasya told them of Halse, and they shared their stories of nice and peculiar fans. I tied Halse's scarf to my purse strap. It didn't feel right to wear it around my neck or anywhere touching my skin. The guys dropped us off at the entrance to the restaurant. Two model-looking blondes in black minidresses greeted us at the doors. Once inside, the *maître d'* led us to our table. Four gold pillars squared the soft-lit dining room, decorated with gold-framed mirrors and black linen covered tables. My eyes darted from mirrors to tables trying to figure out which man could be Halse. The *maître d'* stopped at the center-most, conspicuous table. He and two waiters pulled out our chairs and lay black linen napkins across our laps.

"Your waiters will return in a moment." The *maître d'* bowed slightly and walked away.

Beata whispered, "I could get used to this."

"Me, too." Stasya pointed. "Look up." A crystal chandelier's tierof dangling icicles cast rainbows of light on us and our table. Stasya eyeballed her place setting. "Which fork do I use for which dish?"

Flatware, stemmed glasses, and gold-crackle-edged plates sat before each of us.

"Watch and copy me, Stasya. Although my auntie and I rarely went to fancy restaurants, she taught me about dinner etiquette."

"Girls," Beata tilted her head. "Halse's is probably watching us from in there."

A group of distinguished-looking men conversed and drank from snifters and highball glasses inside a dim-lit, glass-enclosed lounge, two tables to our right. The collection of sounds within the restaurant dizzied me. A Strauss waltz streamed from built in speakers. Two waiters poured sparkling water into our crystal-cut glasses. Another waiter de-corked a bottle of French champagne.

"Val?" Beata held up her champagne flute. "The toast isn't complete until you actually drink to it."

"Right, sorry." I picked up my glass of champagne and took a sip. Its effervescence tickled my cheeks, but the unpleasant taste made me think of Apollonia.

"Darlings," Beata said, leaning in. "Which man do you think is the mysterious Halse? I hope he's sexy." She held the stem of her flute. "What about the dark-haired man sitting behind you, Val? Well-tailored suit, expensive watch ... "

A handsome young man sat with a woman over twice his age. He kissed her sun-spotted hand.

"I don't think so, Beata."

Stasya passed the basket of bread. "Okay, then check out the lounge. How about the one with the red face and comb-over? He looks like a stalker."

Beata twisted around in her chair. "He's not paying attention to us."

"Maybe it's the tan guy with spiky hair."

"Seriously, Stasya?" Beata rolled her eyes. "He's so effeminate. I say the lone-wolf at the far end of the bar could be Valthea's man."

"Not her man, Beata—her fan." Stasya gulped more champagne.

A waiter walked up to our table and recited the evening's specialties. The girls ordered rabbit smothered in a garlic cream topping. The image disturbed me, so I ordered a potato and asparagus dish.

Beata and Stasya wanted to sit at the lounge after dinner. I agreed and drank flavored club soda while they downed shots of peppermint schnapps with two men visiting from Sicily. The bartender asked what we were doing in town. I told him, and he told me he wanted to be an actor. I looked into the mirrors behind him for any suspicious men in the dining room. No one stood out.

Beata paid with the vouchers, and we took a taxi back to our motor home. We spent over two hours at the *Brandenburg Berliner*. If Halse was there, he didn't reveal himself.

"Ta-da!" Stasya and Beata yelled when I walked into the living room.

"What's going on?" I stood in my bathrobe, towel-drying my hair.

"This!" Stasya presented a four-foot-long, brown gift box sitting on the couch between them. An orange satin bow topped the package. "We signed for it while you were in the shower. It's from Halse. It came with this." She handed me a small chocolate-brown envelope.

Beata moved to the arm of the couch. "Come sit, Val. This must be something fantastic."

"I wish we could meet Halse." Stasya scooted over. "Maybe he's not weird, but shy."

"Either way, darling, he's definitely generous."

I sat between the girls, ripped open the envelope, and read aloud.

> "Fraulein Valthea, you clever girl. The scarf tied to the strap of your purse was ingenious."

"He was there!"

"I knew it!" Stasya bounced on the couch.

"If only I'd seen him, I could've read him. I mean ... we could've read his body language and seen if he was a freak or not."

"Please, Valthea, it takes more than a moment to know a freak."
Beata rest one arm behind me. "This guy could be anything from a
nice, old gentleman to *Deutsch* Mafia."

Stasya lit up. "That's a scary, yet exciting thought."

"Another possibility is that ... " Beata lowered her voice, "This
man could be your father."

My heart stopped.

"I suppose it's possible." I set the gift box on the floor. "But if
Halse was my father, wouldn't he run up to me after a show, hug
me tight, and tell me how relieved he was to find me after years of
searching for me?"

"Maybe he's easing in to meeting you." Beata spoke matter-of-
factly. "Maybe he didn't introduce himself right away because, as a
father, he felt embarrassed and ashamed he'd abandoned you and,
or, your mother when you were a baby."

Somehow what Beata said made sense. She and Stasya knew my
background.

"Finish reading the note." Stasya leaned in and looked over my
shoulder.

"Okay, um ...

It's a perfect time for Sky Brothers Circus to leave Germany.
I've discovered a lovely prima ballerina who dances in the Stuggart
Ballet. I apologize, but I'm intolerant of mediocrity and disdain
complacency."

I looked up at the girls. "What's he talking about?"

"I'm not sure, darling, but he's probably not your father."

I read slower.

"You won't perform much longer with Sky Brothers Circus, with
your waning talent and Nik Sky's standard of perfection. Frauline
Valthea, you're a— "

I crumpled the note and pitched it down the hall. "What a
jerk!"

Beata swore something in Polish and retrieved the note I tossed.
"Val, the man obviously knows nothing. Your skills are constantly
improving, not waning." She smoothed open the note. "I want to
see what else that thug wrote ...

Frauline Valthea, you're a disappointment."

My blood boiled.

"My exquisite ballerina is sheer perfection at sixteen and is the new object of my affection. I've sent you a "grand finale" gift which will add class to you and your inevitable departure from the circus. Auf Wiedersehen, Halse."

"*Idiota.*" Beata balled up the note and threw it in the kitchen trash can.

Stasya smacked the gift box. "Open it, Val. Let's see this un-classy guy's classy gift."

I slid off the orange satin ribbon. "This Halse person gives back-handed-compliments and direct cuts in the same breath. Daniella used to do the same to you, Stasya."

"Mean and manipulative." Stasya helped me remove the box lid.

I broke the seal on the tissue paper, gripped the smooth leather handles sticking up, and then stood, holding up Halse's gift: a *Louis Vuitton* monogram duffel bag.

"*Zartujesz?* Are you're kidding?" Beata pet the bag. "This is quite a farewell gift from someone who thinks your talent is waning."

"He's telling me to pack my bags, that my career's over."

"Bully," Stasya grumbled.

"I know why we've never met Halse—" Stasya hopped off the couch and faced me and Beata. "Because there is no Halse. The mystery fan isn't a man. It's a *girl*. It's Daniella!"

"Daniella?" Beata and I said in chorus.

"Think about it. In one of Halse's notes he refers to the silks as ribbons. Non-circus people call them scarves and silks, not *ribbons*. Also, Halse, I mean, Daniella set you up. She flattered you and then made herself mysterious to intrigue you. Now she's going in for kill. She wants to destroy your self-esteem."

"I don't know ... "

"Think about it. Why would someone write a condescending note and send an expensive bag if they were truly done with you? No. I'm telling you, it's Daniella. She wants you nervous and para-noid that Nik Sky is about to fire you. She wants you to screw up in the ring. She wants you to fall, like she did."

I negated the image of falling from my mind.

Beata shook her head. "I disagree, Stasya. No way in hell would Daniella spend over a thousand dollars on a designer bag unless it was for herself."

"Sorry, Stasya, I lean toward Beata's logic. To me, Halse profiles the classic, obsessed and sadistic fan. I'm going to nap and forget about Halse." I went to my room, lay on my bed, and closed my eyes. I imagined Sorin holding me in his arms. Thank God, we'd see each other in Vienna in three weeks. My heart pounded, this time not with love for my champion, but with fear of the phantom Halse.

TWENTY-FIVE

orin arrived the day after our circus train of motor homes rolled into Austria. Fossey picked him up from the airport and delivered him to my door step. Sorin never skipped on intensity when hugging me. I loved being wrapped in his arms and hearing his rapid heartbeat. It made me fearless to express my feelings.

"I missed you so much, Sorin. I don't feel like the house I grew up in is my home anymore. I feel like you're my home."

He kissed me. "That's exactly how I feel, Val. Guess that means we've been homesick for each other." He held my hand and we walked toward the food tent. "Do you think if you saw me every day you'd still be into me? Or would you get tired of me?"

"I'd probably get tired of you."

"Val—"

"Kidding! I'd continue being in love with you." I wished I could see Sorin every day. "What about you?"

"I'd stay in love with you, too. So, tell me, what else is going on in your life?"

Not wanting to spoil our time together, I didn't mention Halse. "You know, what you see on Sky Brother's website. I really love performing."

"I'm happy for you. Val, since you're off tomorrow, I'd like to take you to the Vienna Woods Park. I rented a convertible."

"How fun." I rose up on my tiptoes and planted a kiss on his lips. "I'll pack a picnic."

The next morning, Sorin drove up in a dark blue metallic *Porsche Panamera*. Like father, like son. The Dobra men liked sexy cars. We sped around winding roads, long straight-aways, laughing as we sang made-up lyrics to the Austrian pop music playing on the radio. I felt like a character out of a vintage film, wearing cat-eye sunglasses and my hair in a high ponytail with a scarf tied around it. Sorin's smile shined whiter than usual without competition from his eyes, hidden behind a pair of dark *Ray Bans*. I loved my champion. I just loved him.

Sorin parked at one of the main three rivers of the Vienna Woods. We carried our picnic basket and blanket past a patch of periwinkle and ochre wildflowers to a secluded, shady spot. We positioned the blanket under a pair of willow trees lining the river, and lay down. Thick woods stretched behind us, twenty-feet away. Midday sunrays bounced off the river and shot between the willow's vines, casting us in stripes of gold.

"It feels good to relax with you." Sorin put one of his legs over both of mine.

We lay on our backs with our arms over our heads. I held his hand nearest me. "I love my life right now. Being with you is divine." The willow vines swayed in rhythm with the wind. "I know—I'll make us willow-wreaths."

"I'd like that later. Right now I'd like to kiss you." He covered my body with his, and we kissed for several minutes. My thoughts traveled far from willow wreaths. Sorin rolled off me, kissed my forehead, and sat up. "I need to take a break and calm down."

I loved that Sorin lost himself with me.

He pulled a bottle of chilled Chardonnay from the picnic basket. "Snuck this in." He opened the bottle and poured us each a glass. "*Salut!*"

"*Salut!*"

I finished most of my wine, although I didn't care for it. Sorin drank two glasses and ate two and a half sandwiches.

I stretched out on the blanket and fell into a deep, brief nap. When I woke, Sorin lay on his side, staring at me. "For you, *prinţesă.*" He tucked two sprigs of white, star-shaped flowers into my hair. "I found them growing over there." He pointed to the right of our blanket. A napkin-full of the sprigs lay between us.

I picked a sprig from the napkin. "Edelweiss ... " I took a whiff. "They smell divine."

"Yeah, well, you look divine." He kissed my lips, my neck, and my throat. He aroused much more than my interest.

A loud rustling came from the woods. I sat up. "Did you hear that?"

Sorin helped me stand. "That was no bunny rabbit."

"Are there bears here?" I whispered, not sure if I should move.

"Maybe, but there are definitely wild boar, and they're aggressive. Let's go somewhere else."

I quickly packed the wine.

Sorin tossed the remains of his sandwich toward the woods. "Whoops. I probably shouldn't have done that." He picked up the blanket. "Food will only make the bear want more."

"Bear? I thought you said boar."

"I meant boar." He laughed, taking the basket from me.

"It's not funny."

We ran with our stuff toward the dirt parking lot. Sorin laughed most the way. "Don't worry, Val. It was probably *Big-Foot*."

"Ha, ha."

We threw stuff in the back of the car and hopped in.

"Hurry, Sorin. Put the top up before a bear or whatever jumps in the backseat."

Sorin started the engine and the car top lifted up and came forward, swallowing us whole. After a few minutes of driving, Sorin made up a story of a Big Foot monster eating the rest of his sandwich and tucking sprigs of edelweiss behind its ears. I loved how Sorin, the serious med-student, acted goofy around me. The goofier he acted, the more special I felt.

The next morning, Sorin and I met at one of the picnic tables outside the food tent. We sat next to each other on the table, our feet resting on the sitting bench.

My already-puffy eyes welled. "This is so hard, Sorin. I wish your school wasn't in England."

"I wished your circus only played in England." He kissed my shoulder. "Val, we need to Face Time at least once a week. I must see you, not just talk and write."

Fossey drove his truck up on the dirt path that ran along one side of the motor homes. "Mornin', kids," he yelled through the open passenger window. "Ready, mate?"

"Yeah."

Sorin and I stood and hugged. He kissed my birthmark. "*Te ador, prințesă.*"

"*Te ador*, my champion."

Sorin put his duffle bag in the back of the truck, kissed me once more, and then got in.

Fossey put his truck in gear and then drove toward the circus grounds exit. They barely made it a hundred yards, when Sorin stuck his head and arms out the window and waved.

I waved back and blew him a kiss. They rounded the corner leading to the highway.

"Please, God, keep our love true and make it last forever."

That evening, an assistant manager knocked on our motor home door earlier than normal.

"Come in," Beata yelled.

She, Stasya, and I sat at our kitchen table booth applying our performance makeup.

"You're early. We still have thirty minutes before—oh." Beata nudged me. "Flowers."

"They're for you, Valthea." The young man placed a glass bowl of petite, white flowers on the table. A twine of sky-blue ribbon and a willow vine encircled the bowl. "See you girls in thirty at the tent." He exited.

"I can't believe it!"

"Why?" Stasya huffed. "You always get flowers."

"You don't understand. These are edelweiss, and there's a willow wreath-crown wrapped around the bowl." I took another whiff. "God, I love him. Yesterday, at the park, I was going to make Sorin a willow wreath crown. But when that whole bear scare, boar-thing happened that I told you about, I didn't have the chance."

"You're lucky." Stasya shook her head. "Your boyfriend leaves in the morning and sends you flowers in the afternoon."

"Sorin's smart. His visit's over, and he doesn't want Val to forget about him."

"I'll never forget about Sorin." I peeled the folded mini-card from the side of the bowl and opened it. "Oh." I felt nauseous.

"What's wrong, darling?"

"Let me see." Stasya reached out her hand.

My hand trembled as I handed it to her.

She read it.

"Fraulein—

Wait ... I thought Halse was over you and into some tutu chick?"

I trembled. "Why'd he send edelweiss? How'd he know? I mean, who sends someone a willow wreath? Halse must've been there."

Beata spoke softly. "Val, you're shaking. Don't be upset. The willow vine isn't necessarily a crown or a wreath. It could simply be decoration."

"Why'd he send anything?" Stasya held the note with both hands and read.

"This week, your circus is in my mother's homeland. I couldn't resist sending you her favorite flower. My nostalgia is not for you, but for her. I'd a free moment, as my ballerina injured her back in a car accident and can no longer dance. Don't expect anything more from me. Be smart and consider another career. Athletic entertainers need to plan for injuries. Auf Weidersehen, Halse."

C.K. Mallick

"I don't like it. He's peculiar and creepy. He badgers you and then belittles you. He says he's done, no longer your fan, yet he writes and sends you his mother's favorite flower."

"Not *he*, Beata." Stasya raised her voice. "*She*. I'm telling you, it's Daniella."

I pushed the bowl of edelweiss to the back of the table. "I don't think Halse is Daniella. But whoever he is, something's not right."

TWENTY-SIX

In the middle of the afternoon, on non-matinee days, most circus artists and crew members shopped for necessities, or relaxed in their motor homes, watched movies or napped. I needed a walk to clear my head of Halse.

I spotted Fossey patching a tear in the back of our performance tent. "Need some help?"

"Sure, lass. Ye can pass me a few pieces of duct tape. Want to finish up before the rain comes." He shot me a look of curiosity from under his black brows. "What's on ye mind?"

Fossey, like a handful of acquaintances in my life, "read" people quite well. Were they simply observant and concerned? Maybe, like me, they possessed psychic skills but didn't want to admit it. Aunt Sylvie claimed intuition resided in everyone in various degrees. Were high degrees of paranormal talent inherited? I passed Fossey a piece of tape and told him all about Halse.

"So, what do you think?"

"Aye, Valthea ... fans can be bonkers. But the edelweiss coincidence—that's highly unusual." He held his hand out for another piece of tape. "I can see how it'd make ye a wee uncomfortable."

"More than a *wee*." I handed him a six-inch strip of tape. "What should I do?"

"Use common sense. Be aware ... cautious. Don't give oot personal information and don't walk aboot town alone. If he says *anythin'* that makes ye uncomfortable, ye come to me straight away." He looked to the sky. "Clouds rollin' in quick. One more piece should do it."

I passed him the piece I prepared. "Thanks, Fossey. Guess I needed to talk to someone besides Beata and Stasya. The three of us can get kind of dramatic. I feel better."

"Course ye feel better, lass. Ye talked to an Irishman."

"Fossey, please don't tell Miss Katja. I don't want her to worry."

He looked at me sideways, his bushy brows pinched together. "I don't keep secrets from me lady. *Ye* need to tell her."

"If he contacts me again, I promise I will."

Fossey wiped sprinkles of rain from his brow. "We finished just in time."

I handed him the tape roll. "See you, Foss." I ran in the light rain to my motor home, changed into a comfy sweat suit, and then stretched out on my bed. I picked up my cell phone and speed-dialed number one.

Sorin answered after four rings. "Hello?"

"Hey, it's me."

"Me who?"

I felt like I'd run full speed into a gymnastic vault, instead of bounding from its springboard and landing on top of it in a pretty handstand. "Me, *Val.*"

"Valthea!" Sorin yelled over the noise in the background. "Sorry, I'm at lunch and this place is packed on Fridays. Plus, I don't get caller I.D. here. How are you? Still in Bosnia? Doing anything fun there?"

"We left Bosnia four days ago. It rained a lot, but we hit the cafes and drank too much coffee and ate too much baklava."

"Where are you now?"

"Serbia. We're here through September." I took Sorin off speaker. He sounded like he was at a bar. "Last night, the girls and I went to one of Belgrade's famous floating nightclubs. It was awesome. Actually, we've gone two nights ... in a row. Where are *you*? Sounds like you're in a bar?"

"Hardly. Lunchtime at a busy fish and chips place. Hold on a second—hey, Brigit, order me the same. Okay, I'm back. So what's up?"

I hopped off my bed. "I didn't know something had to be up for me to call. And who's Brigit?" I paced in a U-shape around my bed.

"A girl in my study group. And no, Val, nothing needs to be up for you to call. Did you play my voicemail last night?"

"Yeah, did you hear mine this morning?"

"No, I was studying. Yeah, *sweet*, Brigit. Thanks. Listen, babe I've only thirty minutes to eat and dash back to class. Can we talk tonight—no wait, Monday night?"

"Sounds like Brigit's more than a study partner. You never call me *sweet.*"

"I was referring to *sweet* tea. Come on, Val. We need to trust each other."

Tears streamed down my cheeks. I wished I sat next to Sorin eating fish and chips, laughing, kissing, and being close. "I'm sorry. I trust you. I just miss you so much."

"I miss you, too. Monday night we can Face Time as long as we like."

I nodded and then choked out my words. "I can't wait."

"I love you, *prințesă*."

"I love you, my champion."

We hung up. I crawled into bed and pulled the sheet over my face. I didn't care if my slobbery cries left mascara ink-blots on the white cotton. I missed him. Why couldn't I have both my guy and my career in the same place at the same time?

"*Moskva's* or *Café Mirjana*?" Beata asked, waiting by the door for me and Stasya.

We showered and changed in a hurry to get out and enjoy the day after our flawless Sunday matinee.

"Both are close by and serve homemade Serbian food and offer Sunday specials." Beata sounded delighted with her find.

"How about *Café Mirjana*?" Stasya grabbed her purse from the counter.

"Fine with me. I'm starving." I followed Stasya out.

"Valthea—" An assistant manager stopped us halfway. "Before you take off, there's a guy who wants to meet you. He's in the concession tent."

"Is he tall and blond?" Stasya asked.

Butterflies danced in my stomach imagining a visit from Sorin.

"Or," Beata asked, in her low voice. "Does he speak with a German accent?"

The thought of Halse squashed the butterflies.

"Neither," the assistant said. "But this guy watched the show and won't leave until he meets Valthea."

"What's he look like?" Stasya asked.

"An American. Short ... about seventeen, great leather jacket. He's in a circus."

"Come along, girls." Beata led the way. "Let's check him out. Maybe he'll whet our appetite."

A dozen patrons lingered in the concession tent buying T-shirts, coffee tumblers, and circus programs.

"Is that him?" Stasya gasped. "The guy with the snow cone?"

Beata grinned like the Cheshire cat. "Very attractive. Rugged."

A fit-looking guy, my height, stood across the tent at the program booth holding a snow cone. Spiky gel-styled hair and strong cheek bones, he wore dark blue jeans and a black leather jacket. He waved. Definitely American.

The American knelt at a grave site with his face buried in his hands. Behind him stood a row of adults and a group of boys from eight to eighteen-years old. Everyone wore black and most had black hair. "Carpe, Carpe," he whispered, touching the gravestone.

A deafening roar of motorcycles blasted through my head.

"He's cute." Stasya giggled.

Beata nudged me forward. "Go, have fun."

"No, Beata. I've a boyfriend, remember?"

"I didn't tell you to make out with him. Although I'd like to. Just go talk to him. You need connections in the circus world. Our contracts don't auto-renew, you know. Go. We'll wait by the car. If we don't see you in ten minutes, we'll know your networking."

"I'll be there in five minutes."

"Sure, Val." Beata smirked. She and Stasya exited the concession area.

I felt naked in the middle of the tent.

The American guy walked toward me. "You're Valthea Sarosi, right?"

"Yes. Hi."

"I'm Excel." His sleeve rubbed against the side of his jacket as he extended his arm. Leather against leather sounded sexy. He took his time releasing my hand.

Why'd the butterflies reserved for my champion dance in my stomach?

"I loved your act, Valthea. You looked great, although you're more beautiful close up and without stage makeup."

"Thank you." I liked hearing my name with an American accent.

"Thanks for seeing me. I had to meet you." He looked around. "Do you have a boyfriend or someone waiting for you?"

"I do have a boyfriend."

"Oh, then he's here. I'm sure he watches every show. I won't keep you."

"You're not keeping me. He's in England, at college."

"A long distance relationship ... I'm surprised. If I had a beautiful girl like you, I would've taken my courses online."

"My boyfriend's pre-med. He can't take all his classes online."

"Pre-med?" Excel smirked. "Guess you two have a lot in common." He held up the snow cone, his hand wet and sticky-looking. "If I'd known I'd see someone today who inspired me, this melting snow cone would've been a rose. I didn't want to greet you empty handed. I think I should toss this."

"Thank you for the thought."

He walked to the nearest trash can and threw it away. He wiped his hands on his jeans as he walked back. His chocolate-brown eyes stayed fixed on mine. Why'd this guy make me nervous, and why'd I like the feeling?

"You don't seem to be a jaded circus girl or a gymnast with an attitude. I'd guess you to be a *good-girl*. A good girl is rare in the circus world."

A good-girl? Was it a bad thing?

"Valthea, I don't why, but I'm definitely drawn to you. I'm comfortable around you. I believe we were meant to meet. Do you think that's weird?"

I felt uncomfortable, but intrigued. Do Americans always say everything they feel to strangers? "I—" Another insight. ...

Engines roared loud and unnerving. A huge wire ball sat in the center of a circus ring. The wire shined like polished silver under the overhead lighting.

"You're different, Valthea. Circus girls are often full of themselves or locked into their family." He cocked his head. "You hungry? We could go for an early dinner and talk some more. I'd love to get to know you. Your circus doesn't perform tonight. We can go anywhere you want."

"I don't know anything about you." His insights didn't reveal his character, or whether he was a *good guy* or a *bad boy*.

He straightened and put his hands behind his back. "I'm Excel Perez of the *Perez Riding Family*."

"What do you ride?"

"Motorcycles. You haven't heard of us? How long you been in the circus?"

"It's my first year, and I'm not from a circus family."

"The schooled variety. Not me. I grew up in this world. My dad, uncle, three brothers, and two cousins—we all ride. Youngest one's fourteen. My dad's over forty. Sometimes our act is called the *Globe of Death* or *Globe of Steel*. Whatever you want to call it, seven to eight of us ride loops, up to sixty-five miles an hour, in a sixteen-foot-wide steel mesh cage. Picture that, Valthea." He grinned. "Right now, we're touring with *The Bertinelli Circus*. Our next stop's Hungary. I drove an hour to see Sky's circus because my family's touring with you next season."

"You are? I didn't think Nik Sky had decided yet on which acts he wanted for next—"

"Nik might call our act, *The Sphere of Steel*. You're touring next year, too, aren't you?"

"I'm not sure." Why hadn't Miss Katja talked to me and the girls? I wanted to leave Excel, sprint to her motor home, and ask her.

"Please let me take you to dinner," Excel said, lowering his voice. "I bet we've a lot in common, like our dreams and our future in the circus." He put his hands in his pockets and stepped back. "Don't think I'm weird for saying this, Valthea, but I've a good feeling about you. I think we should be friends."

I guess he could be my friend. Miss Katja and Fossey were probably eating dinner anyway. I'd ask her later about next season.

"We can go to *Café Mirjana*. They've Sunday specials, and my roommates are going to be there."

"Great." Excel hugged me for a quick, strong second.

"Excuse me ... " The concession manager walked up to us. He spoke to Excel. "You're one of the riding Perez's, aren't you?"

"That's right." Excel shook the manager's hand. "I'm Excel Perez."

"Is your family being considered for next season?"

"Uh ... " Excel glanced at me and then grinned. "We're in!"

"Confirmed, already? I'm surprised. Well, good. I like your family's act. I look forward to your family touring with us." He nodded once and then headed to the roasted peanut station.

I wanted to be known, like Excel, by everyone in and out of the circus world.

"Valthea, I hope you're not afraid of motorcycles. Mine's parked out front. I'm a safe driver and brought an extra helmet."

"A motorcycle?"

"Don't be nervous. I passed *Café Mirjana* on my way here. It's literally five minutes away. Maybe ten. What do you say?"

"I say, it's good to have friends in the circus."

"Smart girl."

We walked to where he'd parked his bike. He handed me the extra helmet, and I put it on, knowing it'd flatten my hair.

He mounted the bike and tapped the space behind him. "Sit close, and hang on."

Why didn't I think ahead of time of how close our bodies would be?

He looked at me through the helmet shield. "Hop on."

I straddled the bike, scooted in close, and put my arms around him and his leather jacket. Excel revved the engine. I felt like I was cheating on Sorin, but I had to sit close and hang on, or I'd fly off the bike.

We rode out of the parking lot and onto the two-way street. Within moments, the wind knocked out my worries. The faster he went, the more I liked it. The more I liked it, the more I relaxed. I felt one-hundred-percent in the moment and completely free.

TWENTY-SEVEN

Excel and I walked into *Café Mirjana*. I scanned the dozen and a half tables and booths. "I don't see my roommates."

"Maybe they went somewhere else. Let's sit here." Excel gestured to an available booth. We sat on opposite sides.

A waitress walked up, put a basket of bread on the table, and recited the specials.

My thoughts drifted to Sorin. Sorin ate lunch with girls in his study group. It was no big deal, my sharing a meal with fellow circus talent.

"I ordered for you, Valthea."

The waitress walked away.

"But you don't know what I like."

"You'll like what I ordered. Trust me." Excel leaned forward. "We're so far away from each other. I want to have a nice conversation with you about our circus goals. I don't want to yell. I'll come sit next to you." He slid out from his side of the booth.

Heat shot through my body. Was it nervousness or something else? "Uh, sure." I scooted toward the wall. His knee bumped mine when he slid in. He smelled of lime and leather. Fresh ... manly.

Excel told me about his family, growing up in the circus, and the different injuries he suffered riding.

"Is *Excel* your stage name?" I sipped my sparkling club soda, ordering flat water a better choice for avoiding burps.

"It's a nickname." Excel chewed on some bread. "My full name's *Excelsior*. It means onward and upward in Latin. Radical, huh? My father's Mexican, and my mother's from California. She named all of us boys after Latin words and phrases. She's kind of out there. My dad agreed to the names because they sounded Spanish."

"What are your brother's names?"

"*Tanto, Cito, Infinitum*—we call him *Finney*. Enough about me. Tell me about you and your family. What was it like growing up in Romania? What are your parents like? Your English is really good, by the way. Any brothers or sisters? How'd you end up in the circus? Heck, tell me everything today even if it's while we're eating, and you've a mouthful of food."

I let out a nervous laugh and looked away.

"What's wrong?"

"Nothing." I wished Sorin sat next me, and we were eating together and sharing stories.

Excel rubbed my shoulder. "If you're nervous, don't' be. You can trust me."

I'd never seen such long eyelashes.

The waitress placed four platters of food in the center of our table.

As Excel served some of each dish onto our empty plates, I told him briefly of Aunt Sylvie, my gymnastics team, *The Gypsy Royales*, and Sorin.

He set down the serving spoon, leaned toward me, and kissed my cheek. "I couldn't help it." He leaned away, holding up his hands.

My chest went from warm to hot. "Excel, I told you, I've a boyfriend."

"I didn't mean to offend you. You're sweet and pretty and feel like family ... like a sister."

I disregarded his kiss on my cheek, afraid of seeming juvenile.

"I bet you're the kind of girl who wouldn't hurt a fly. I've always been keen to a person's character and street smart. For some reason, my sensing things about people went to another level after my brother died two years ago." He wiped his eyes and took a gulp of his soda.

"Sorry you lost your brother."

"Thanks."

"What do you mean by 'sensing things'? Do you see visions, hear things, or what?"

His eyes widened. "I wish. No, I only sense what people are about and what they want."

Thank God.

"I used to be a cocky kid, flipping my dirt bike in the air and racing around." He looked at me sideways and grinned. "Okay, I'm still cocky, but I'm picky who I hang out with." He scooted closer to me. "This time I'll ask. May I kiss you before we eat?"

I scooted away. "No, Excel. I'm here as a friend only. We're just having lunch."

"Let's kiss each other's cheek, like you Europeans do."

"Europeans do that when they greet each other, not before meals."

"No fair! We didn't kiss when we met. You owe me. Don't be a stuck-up Euro-babe."

"I'm not a stuck up Euro-babe."

Excel rested his folded hands on the table. "Valthea, would you like to pray with me before we eat?"

Excel threw me at every turn. "Sure, as friends sharing a meal." I folded my hands on my lap.

Excel spoke quietly. "Thank you God for this food. Thank you for bringing my new friend, Valthea and I together today."

I gave thanks for the food and then prayed for more insight. Over the years, I learned that most people are better in certain life roles than others. Excel appeared to be a good son and devoted brother, but that didn't guarantee he'd be a respectful, platonic friend. Aunt Sylvie had taught me not to rely on visions. She insisted I think with my head and listen to my heart. Since I couldn't figure out this motor-cycle-riding-guy, I'd have to apply another one of Auntie's favorite sayings: Time tells all.

"Amen. Let's eat." Excel rocked the booth, digging into his meal. He scoffed down his food in silence for several minutes and then washed a mouthful down with some soda. "I've an idea. My mom and I are going to the *Smederevo Castle* on the Danube tomorrow. She's always wanted to see it. Why don't you come with us? My mom's always surrounded by us guys. She'd love a girl around for the afternoon."

"I don't know ... "

"Are you one of those boring circus girls who hide in their motor home when you're not performing? Come out. Live. See the sights. My mom wants some pictures of me and her together. Don't you want photos to send to your Aunt Sylvie?"

"I should send her photos."

"Great! I'll pick you up in my mom's rental car at ten o'clock in front of Sky's main tent."

The next morning, at ten-fifteen, Excel rode up and parked his bike in front of the big top.

"What happened to the rental car and your mother?"

"I know, bummer. She didn't feel well. I promised her we'd take lots of pictures. It cheered her up."

"If it's just us, I only want to be there an hour and come home."

"Don't be a drag, Valthea. Let's take the day and have fun."

"One hour, or you can go alone."

"Have it your way." He grinned, bur his glare remained angry.

We rode along the Danube to the *Smederevo Castle*. It didn't take much to imagine myself entering a fairy tale with the castle fortressed by a stone wall. We walked the path leading to the front of the fortress. Excel's high energy and sunny optimism made me forget about his pushiness and made the adventure fun—until he tried to kiss me.

"Excel—I told you—we're just friends. I want to go."

"I'm sorry. I was wrong. I assumed that you're lonely like me. You're supposed boyfriend lives a million miles away. I like you, Valthea. You're different from any girl I ever met. I'll leave you alone if you want. But your boyfriend should've never left you alone."

"You don't know anything about me and Sorin. Take me home."

"Why, so you can mope in your motor home and wonder what your boyfriend does every night? Valthea, we're standing in front of a castle. A castle! You grew up with them in Romania, but I didn't. Please, Valthea? I'll behave. Let's take some pictures, and then we'll go." He handed me his phone and then ran twenty-feet to the castle's doorway. He posed like a gorilla and then like a sword fighter.

I snapped a dozen shots. "Those were funny. Your mom will probably like them."

"She'll love them," Excel yelled, running down to where I stood. "I can't wait to tell her all about you."

What'd he tell her? He didn't know anything about me—unless he *could* see things and wasn't telling me.

"You're turn, Valthea. Give me your phone."

I handed him my phone. "A few, then we go."

"Deal."

I walked up to the castle and posed in front of its ivy-covered wall.

"Great," he yelled. "Now do something else."

I hopped up on a ledge, folded my arms across my chest, and focused miles away. The breeze blew my hair from my face.

"Do some smiling."

I hopped down and leaned against a stone wall, my palms to the rock wall. I smiled, not for Excel, but for my auntie and Sorin.

"Those were gorgeous, Val. Send all of them to my phone."

I walked down the path toward Excel and took my phone from him. "Thanks." I walked passed him toward the parking lot. I wiped away wishful tears, wishing it were Sorin and I creating memories at a castle. I wanted us to collect tons of memories that'd one day be considered ancient.

"You're going to send me some of those pictures, right?"

I kept walking down the stony path.

Excel ran past me, and then stopped in front of me, blocking my way. "Valthea, *please* send me the photos." He leaned in and whispered, "You're the prettiest girl I've ever seen."

Excel ... not long ago ... he sat at an outdoor café with a gray-eyed blonde. She wore a white ruffle blouse. A double-decker trolley went by. Its billboards were in English, its ads speckled with the British pound symbol. Excel looked the girl straight in the eye. "I think you're the prettiest girl I've ever seen." She blushed, and looked down, smiling. He kissed her neck and then whispered, "Don't worry. I won't rush things with us. You're too special to me."

A row of snow-lined, brick-front shops. ... Excel walked hand and hand with a girl wearing a plaid cinched coat, The shop windows displayed Christmas lights and decorations. Several showcased a menorah. Excel turned to the girl. "Mattie, I don't want to be intimate with you unless we're exclusive." The girl giggled, wrapped her arms around his neck, and kissed him. She then took his hand and led him two shops down, to a red brick apartment building. She pulled a set of keys out of her shoulder bag.

Excel and I walked to the parking lot. We stood on either side of his motorcycle.

"Val, I don't want to rush things with us. You're too special to me. I also don't want to be intimate with you unless we're exclusive."

I shook my head in disbelief. People glamorize psychics who see the future. But like history teaches us, knowing the past helps predict the future. I took a breath. "Excel, there will *never* be any form of intimacy with us."

"Valthea, you're obviously naïve about romance and the ways of the world. That's all right. I'm patient and determined."

"And you're delusional." I unhooked the extra helmet from his bike and pulled my hair back. Sure, Excel told me he liked me, thought I was pretty, and looked forward to our touring together. But I never expressed the same to him. Besides, he was wrong. I wasn't naïve. I felt blessed. My first boyfriend happened to be my soul mate.

He stopped me before I put on my helmet. "I almost forgot to tell you."

"You're stalling, Excel. I want to go."

"Would you listen for a second?" He spoke through gritted teeth. "You're so uptight."

Like a cautious lynx, I quieted, keeping my eyes on him.

He took a breath and smiled like a kid again. "My dad called Nik Sky last night. And guess what? He wants a silk act for next season. How about that?"

"Why didn't you tell me this right away?"

"You were too tense. Anyway, my family will be around next week to sign contracts. Sky's probably having you sign, too. I'll text you and we'll meet up."

My mind raced ahead, imagining a second season touring with Sky and working with Miss Katja and the girls. A second season meant more people would see my photo on the web, in the paper, and in the circus program. More people—like my mom or my dad. They'd be proud. They'd wish they never left me in the woods. I imagined them running up to me after a show and hugging me tight despite my sequined costume scratching their arms. They'd tell me they loved me, that they searched for me for years, and that they were sorry they ever left me. If that happened, I promised myself I'd forgive them.

"We're going to have a great time touring together." Excel straddled his bike and put on his helmet.

I did the same. Maybe Excel *wasn't* mean, but a hot-blooded, Latin-American and a high strung adrenaline-seeking stunt rider. Maybe he'd be a good circus contact.

We rode along the Danube, my mind far from the sunny day, curling roads, and edging wildflowers. Instead, I thought about boys. I concluded there were two types. One type took a girl's breath away, forcing her to gasp, or inhale with excitement. This charming player, or hot "bad boy," made sure the girl knew—*he* was special. The second type of guy made a girl sigh, or exhale slowly, feeling enchanted. This dreamy, or "good guy" with values, always made sure his girl knew—*she* was special.

Which did I prefer? No question. Sorin.

TWENTY-EIGHT

The thrill of surprise made me grateful for my ability to read the past instead of seeing into the future. Four days after the *Smederevo Castle* excursion, Fossey delivered a grand surprise from the airport. Sorin.

During Sorin's three-day stay, we strengthened our bond by whispering sweet-everything's into each other's ears and discussing our future together. The residual effect of my champion's visit continued after he left. We needed the interlude of bliss and kisses to hold us through mid-December, nine weeks away. My cheeks glowed, my step bounced, and I craved sweets. High on love, I walked down the center of the food service tent between the two rows of fold-out tables and chairs occupied with lunching performers and crew.

Carlo Reye walked toward me carrying his lunch tray. He tipped his head in greeting.

"Afternoon, Valthea Sarosi. Great matinee today." The costume master's tray held chocolate-topped cream puffs, a slice of a hazelnut torte, and a jumbo cherry tart.

"Thanks, Carlo Reye." I pointed to his tray. "Are you going to have some lunch with that dessert?"

"Dessert first, I always say. God forbid I miss out on the best part of the meal because I'm full."

"I like your logic."

"Naturally. Enjoy your lunch, doll-face."

"Enjoy your dessert." I resisted the dessert bar and stepped up to the sandwich counter. "I'd like a Mediterranean wrap, please."

"Val!"

I turned.

Excel strutted through the food tent like he owned the place. Leather jacket, black jeans, big grin. Although I appreciated his exuberance, his place in my life continued to be crystal clear—acquaintance.

"Hi, Excel." I didn't greet him European style. "Is your family with you to sign contracts today?"

He looked me up and down. "Thigh-high boots with shorts in September. Love the look. Good thing I'm too young to have a heart attack."

What seemed cute or charming a week ago now seemed predictable and well-rehearsed. "Wool leggings aren't sexy." I avoided eye contact. "I've already ordered. Go ahead."

"Great, I'm starving." He leaned into me. "Starving for you."

I stepped back. "Excel—quit making those remarks. I'm tight with my boyfriend. And that's that. Got it?"

"Settle down. I'm fine with that." He spoke to the woman making my sandwich. "I'd like the same as Valthea, without the onions. Got to have fresh breath for my sweetheart." He held up his hands. "Kidding!" He laughed and then nudged me, trying to get me to join in.

Instead, I side-stepped. Excel laughed about everything. Was it because he was from America, or do people from California laugh all the time? I glanced at the tent entrance where Emeric and Pauly sat with the two Spanish acrobat girls who performed the ladder-balancing act. Pauly didn't laugh at everything, and he grew up in California, and he was a clown.

Excel carried his lunch tray and followed me to a middle table. He sat across from me. I ate in silence. He commented on numerous cast and crew members, speculating on who he thought were sleeping together.

Pauly and the Spanish girl named Lola walked up to our table. "Hi, Val." Pauly nodded to Excel. "Excel."

"You two know each other?" I asked.

Pauly didn't smile. "We did a season with a New York circus a couple years ago."

Excel sat back in his chair, looking over Lola, and wetting his lips. "Pauly and I've something in common. We're both unforgettable, but in different ways. What about you, pretty girl? *Hola. ¿Cómo se llama?*"

"Lola," Lola answered, making goo-goo eyes at Excel. She conversed in Spanish with him until a commotion at the front made us all turn.

Emeric knocked over a couple of folding chairs and chased the other ladder-acrobat around a table. The girl laughed and rattled off something in broken English. Emeric picked her up and ran toward us.

"Let's go, Pauly. *Allon-y!* Time for ze amusement!" Emeric winked at Lola. "Lola, you can carry Pauly." Emeric turned around and headed for the exit. "*Allon-y! Allon-y!*"

C.K. Mallick

Excel faced Lola. "*Mamasita,* don't you think you deserve a younger, more able man to show you a good time?"

"Back off, Excel." Pauly stepped in front of Lola. "What are you doing here, anyway? Valthea has a boyfriend, and you're not part of our circus."

"Don't worry, little man. We're just having some lunch."

"Val, you all right with him here?"

"Yeah, Pauly, thanks. We're just talking."

"All right." Pauly reached up, took Lola's hand, and led her towards the exit.

Lola peeked around and blew Excel a kiss.

I glared at her. If Lola and Excel wanted to hook up, fine. But don't disrespect my friend.

"Where are your roommates?" Excel asked, looking around the tent.

"They went for facials."

"Perfect. Hurry and eat." Excel took a huge bite of his sandwich. "We can go to your place and listen to my new iPod tracks."

"No, Excel. I like to chill out on my own between matinees and night shows."

"You can chill on your own when you're dead." He leaned forward and whispered. "Truth is, Val, I need to talk to someone I trust and don't feel comfortable talking here."

"Why, what's wrong?"

He wiped invisible tears from his eyes with one hand. "After my brother, Carpe died in the ring, I've had anxiety attacks. You know, about racing my bike in the cage. Sometimes it feels like its closing in on me. It's intense, Val. A lot can go wrong."

"You can't think that way, Excel. You must visualize everything going smoothly."

"See? You say all the right things." He exhaled. "I need someone to talk to. Then I'll feel better."

"Why don't you talk to your family? I'm sure they'd—"

"No, we never voice our fears. My father forbids it. We practice and work out every safety detail. Period. No discussion."

The more I found out how other people lived and treated each other, the more I appreciated the way Aunt Sylvie raised me. "Five minutes. That's it. We'll talk in my motor home. Nothing else. And then you go. Got it?"

"Got it."

200

We walked the dirt path to the lineup of parked motor homes. Once inside mine, Excel slipped off his boots and threw his leather on the couch.

I hung my jacket in the closet.

"Your room this way?" he said, heading toward my bedroom.

"No, we're going to talk in the kitchen."

"But I want to lie down," he yelled from the hall.

"No, Excel." I followed him into my room.

He set up his iPod on the end stand in seconds and then laid down.

"Gee, make yourself comfortable." I stood at the end of my bed with my arms folded.

"Thanks." He turned the volume up and rested his head on my stack of pillows. "It's Spanish pop. Like it? I bet it'd turn Lola on."

I rolled my eyes. "Turn it off and get off of my bed."

"You're so uptight. Come lay next to me. I want to tell you how many colors I see in those beautiful eyes of yours."

"You obviously feel better. You can go now."

"Your eyes have gold, bronze, and even specks of yellow."

"Take your iPod. I'm seeing you out." I pivoted toward the open door.

He grabbed my arm. "You can't tease a guy and not follow through."

I yanked my arm free. "*What?* You're delusional. Get out—now."

"Don't play naïve, Valthea. No one will see it that way. You ate lunch with me. You invited me into your home. We're lying on your bed together."

"Wrong. I'm standing, and you're leaving."

He took me by my shoulders and threw me on the bed, forcing me on my back.

"Stop it!"

"Quiet." He held down my wrists. "I promise you'll love it."

"Get off me." I pushed my hips upward to buck him off.

He clamped my jaw with one hand and forced me to face him. "We are doing this rough or sweet. It's up to you."

"No!" I screamed.

"Shut up." He covered my mouth. "You know you want me."

I pulled his hand from my mouth and screamed, "Stop! *Help!*"

He unbuckled his belt. "Fine. Rough and fast."

I wriggled to the side, gripped the glass candle jar from my bed stand, and flung it at the window. It smashed the glass and went through.

"*Mierda!*" Excel hopped off me and the bed. He hunched over, fumbling with his pants, and staying clear of the window. "*¿Estás loco?*"

I ran out of my motor home to the one nextdoor.

"*Anatoly, Anatoly!*" I banged on the Ukrainian's door. "*Anatoly!*"

"You blew it, Val."

I turned.

Excel sauntered down my steps. "We could've had something wonderful." His once bright grin now appeared lewd.

"Get the hell out of here, or I'll report you."

He walked by me, zipping up his jacket. "Nothing to report. You changed your mind. That's all."

"Liar!" The sound of his leather jacket made me cringe. "I never—"

"Pity." He paused. "Your virginity really appealed to me."

"You don't know anything about me."

"Got to go. I'm worked up and need a sure thing." He waved with his back to me and headed to the visitor's parking lot.

I trembled, walking back to my motor home. Not ready to go back inside, I sat on my steps. How could I've been so naïve? He needed to talk ... he was afraid to ride in the wire cage ... What a jerk! I should've never ridden on his motorcycle or—

"Valthea!" Pauly hurried toward me. "I was looking for you." He stopped in front of the candle jar lying on its side on the ground surrounded by shards of window glass.

"What is all this?" He glanced up at the hole in my motor home's window. Are you all right?"

"I had to make some noise. Excel wouldn't leave."

"Where is he?"

"Gone."

"I went back to your table, but you guys had left. The guy's no good. Did he—"

"No. But he tried."

"That bastard!" Pauly fisted one hand. "Listen. Don't say anything to your roommates or anyone else. Gossip goes crazy in our little circus village. I'll report him and take care of everything, including your window."

"Pauly, what am I going to do? I want to tour with Sky next year, but I can't stand the thought of being around Excel."

"He's not touring with us next year. Nik wouldn't hire the Perez family."

"But Excel told me—"

"Excel lies." Pauly sat on the step above mine and put his arm around me. His hand nearly reached around both my shoulders. "It's okay now, Val. You don't have anything to worry about. Nik ran a background check on Excel months ago because of rumors. He won't hire the Perez's because of Excel's reputation. Nik Sky's good that way. He doesn't care how fantastic an act is. He puts us, his family, first." He removed his arm and then chuckled. "Nik's like a big, ol' grandfather elephant, always looking out for everyone."

"I'm so embarrassed, and I'm angry."

"Val—It's not your fault. Excel's a jerk."

I wiped my eyes. "Yeah, but what if I'd been single and fell for Excel, and then later found out that he'd used me? I don't know who I'd hate more—him or me?"

TWENTY-NINE

Skilled athletic prowess and magnetic stage presence make for a good circus performer. Adding laser-like focus made them a consistent one. Two hours after the episode with Excel, I slipped into my *Divas of Silk* costume and walked out into the ring with Beata and Stasya. I executed the ribbon choreography with complete precision. Focus.

After the show, I showered and brewed some tea. Beata and Stasya went out for a late dinner. My cell phone vibrating on the kitchen counter made me jump. It was a text from Pauly.

"Dinner, my treat. B there in 5."

I texted back. "Thx, no. Long day."

Pauly wrote, "More reason for fun & I don't want to eat alone."

My protective bulldog. "OK. Give me 15."

I pulled an orange tunic sweater over a gray camisole and leggings, unlocked the door, and then sat at the kitchen booth in front of my makeup mirror. I brushed on a gloss color to match my sweater and then ducked under the table to retrieve the tube of mascara that had rolled off.

The motor home rocked like someone had walked up the aluminum steps. The door creaked. Pauly, or whoever it was, didn't say hello. I looked up from underneath the booth. I didn't see anyone. My heart raced. I sat up slowly, slid out of the booth, and backed down the hall. I pulled a full-size umbrella from the hall closet and clutched it like a saber.

"Who's there?"

Pauly walked in. "What are you doing, Val? Choreographing a new clown act with umbrellas instead of feathers?"

"Why didn't you knock?" I tucked the umbrella back into the closet. "You scared me."

"Why'd you leave the door open after a day like today?"

"You're right. Guess I do need to get out and clear my head."

"Hey, Val, I need to apologize."

"For what?"

"The whole thing with Excel could've been prevented. I didn't know he was hanging around until I saw him in the cafeteria with you. I should've warned you."

"No, Pauly. I was naive to think we could've been circus friends."

"The kid's always been trouble, Val. He's a charmer. Guys like him. Old ladies adore him. Little boys worship him. He's not to be trusted, and he's far from being boyfriend material."

"Like most guys in the circus, I'm sure."

"No—like most guys everywhere, but not all guys. Anyway, forget him. Don't waste another thought on the dude."

I locked up, and Pauly and I walked to the grassy area where the cast and crew parked the cars they had rented or towed behind their motor homes.

"Thanks, Pauly, for taping up my window."

"No problem. It'll be replaced tomorrow."

Pauly opened the car door for me and then went around to his side. He drove, sitting on a thick pillow and working the gas and brake pedals through the hand controls built into his custom-designed stirring wheel. "Tonight, I want to take you to *Vuk Bistro*. Some of the cast are already there. We'll have a glass of wine, some good food ... "

"Food sounds good, but wine makes me sleepy."

"Then vodka. One drink and very weak."

"I'm amazed how much vodka circus people drink." I lowered my window. "I could never drink a lot and turn aerials the next day."

"The Russians and Ukrainians can and do. But then they drink vodka like Italians drink wine and Americans drink beer. It's part of the culture. Good news for us—no matinee tomorrow. Speaking of Russians, have you ever tasted a *White Russian*?"

"No."

"I'll order one for you tonight to sip on. It'll be the second time you've experienced *a first* with me." He stopped at the street light.

"What was the first?"

He exaggerated a sigh. "Ah, how soon they forget."

I smacked his shoulder playfully. "Tell me. And drive. The light's green."

He worked the gas pedal lever. "You and I performed together in your first act, on the first night, in your first circus."

"You're right!"

He shook his head and smirked. "Tall people. ... "

We arrived at *Vuk Bistro* in twenty minutes and immediately ordered our drinks and dinner. Pauly ordered cheesecake and strawberries for dessert. Within minutes, he stood holding his stomach. "Never eat fast."

"I don't."

"Yeah, well, easy does it with your drink. I'll be back in a few minutes." He headed toward the restrooms.

I quickly ordered two more drinks, instructing the waitress to make them twice as strong. Kahlua, vodka, and milk tasted like dessert.

I gulped down one of the two drinks while watching the Ukrainian brothers from the teeter board act clear space at the back of the restaurant. The four brothers moved a couple of tables and a bunch of chairs to one side. They toasted and downed two rounds of shots. Two of the guys stepped into the cleared area and kicked up into handstands.

Pauly returned. "Check them out."

I tucked a paper napkin into my empty drink glass and pushed it next to the plate holding my barely eaten dinner. "Pauly, what are they doing?"

"Post-show entertainment. Handstand-pushup contest."

"Let's go back there and watch."

Pauly glanced at my glass. "I'm glad to see you're taking your time with that drink. I only ordered it for you because of what you went through today. Don't get any ideas. This isn't a habit we're making together."

"I know. Thanks. I'm happy to be out."

Pauly signed for the bill without looking over the check and picked up his drink. "After you."

I felt like a grown up, walking with a drink in my hand toward the back of the restaurant.

Two of the Ukrainian brothers pushed up and down in perfect handstand position. Anatoly, the biggest brother, and the spotter for the teeter board act, counted the repetitions. One brother executed seventeen pushups before his sweater slid down and covered his face, revealing his eight-pack abs. A curvy redhead walked up to him, bent over and air-kissed his stomach. Half the twenty-or-so people who'd gathered, whistled and cat-called.

The other brother hopped down from his handstand. "Too drunk for handstand." He smoothed his hair back with both hands. "My brother wins."

I applauded along with the crowd.

The winning brother kicked down from his handstand, spotted the redhead, and walked over to her, pushing up his sleeves. They barely spoke before they started kissing. He pressed his face into her copper-colored hair and whispered something. They laughed and kissed some more.

I studied the curvy woman. If guys thought brunettes were smart, and blondes were fun—what were redheads?

"Silk girl!" Anatoly yelled, pointing at my drink. "You drink milk?" He then spoke in a sing-song tone. "*Not too tough.*"

"Anatoly, this isn't just milk." I downed the entire drink and set the glass on the table next to me. "Whoa." I paused for balance and then pulled off my bulky sweater and handed it to Pauly. "Here." I walked up to the cleared area.

"Valthea—" Pauly held my sweater in one hand and his drink in the other. "What are you doing? You just finished a White Russian, and you don't even drink."

"I'm fine. I got this." I kicked into a handstand.

The fourth brother kicked up next to me. Upside down, he shouted, "Let's go milk-girl!"

The gathered patrons clapped and counted along, some in Serbian, some in Russian, and a few in English.

"*Jeden, dva, tri. ...*"

"One, two, three. ... "

The room spun. I concentrated on keeping my core tight and the pads of my hands and fingers pressed to the wood floor.

"*Sem, vosem. ...*"

"Seven, eight—"

"Scoot over, midget," someone shouted."

I kicked down from the handstand and then reached for Anatoly's arm to steady myself. I didn't feel so good. "Where's Pauly?"

The fourth brother kicked down from his handstand.

"You ruin our bar," the man shouted again. "You're all a bunch of circus trash."

I spotted the belligerent man. He sat at the bar wearing a wrinkled trench coat. I guessed him to be about sixty, and a drunk, from his haggard face and slumped over body.

Pauly stood next to him. "What's your problem, mister? If you don't like—"

"You threatening me, shorty?" The man looked down at Pauly.

Within seconds, the four Ukrainians had banded together and positioned themselves between Pauly and the mouthy drunk.

Anatoly's voice bellowed. "You disrespect him, you disrespect me. We drink. We play. But we act nice. You act nice, or we throw you out."

The drunk slurred his words. "You think you're ... you're special because you jump in the air or flip around? Nah. ... You're just tent people, walking on wires and swinging on bars." The liquid in the man's rock glass sloshed from rim to rim. "Circus trash. All of you. Get out of here. Go get a real job." The man nearly slid off his barstool.

Pauly waved off the drunk and joined me at a small table along one wall. My stomach felt horrible.

The teeterboard brothers dispersed, flirting with barmaids, or stepping out the back door with cigarette and lighter in hand.

Images of the drunken man's past flashed through my mind. When they stopped, I ignored the sick feeling in my stomach and walked up to him. "Sir, just because you didn't become a priest like your father dreamed, doesn't mean others shouldn't enjoy the dreams they've made come true."

Pauly tapped me on the shoulder. "We should go, Val."

I spoke over my shoulder. "Okay, in a minute."

The man held on to the edge of the bar. His forehead and mouth wrinkled and contorted. He seemed to be struggling between shouting obscenities and breaking down and crying.

"Sir," I continued, "for your information, being in the circus *is* a real job. We've all trained for up to eight hours a day since we were six-years-old. We've given up carefree childhoods and normal adult lives to become the best in our demanding and dangerous fields."

Pauly tapped my shoulder again. "That's good, Val. Let's go. The vodka's making you brave."

"Okay, in a minute." I stayed with my feet planted in front of the now speechless boozer. "You see, sir, we're not like most people. The luxury of a thirty-year career isn't an option. We're athletic artists. We're lucky if we make it past five years."

The man's face seemed to age with each word I spoke. He finished the last of his drink and stared at the bottom of his empty glass as if an intoxicating love affair had suddenly ended.

The teeterboard brothers and some new patrons gathered around us. My palms sweat. I could perform in front of a thousand people, but

I shook speaking in front of even three or four. "Going forward. ... "
I knotted my sweater around my waist. "I'd appreciate it if you never
again call me, or any of my colleagues, circus trash. Because there is
nothing trashy about us or what we do." I turned to Pauly "Now we
can go."

Pauly led me away from the bar.

"Hey," the drunk yelled to our backs. "How'd you know my father
wanted me to be a priest?"

Pauly and I turned.

He slurred, "My brother put you up to this, didn't he? Where is
that low-life?" He sat half-off his bar stool. "I like booze, gambling, and
women. I could've never become—how'd you know?"

"No worries, old man," Pauly said. "This Romanian guesses all
kinds of stuff after vodka and vertical pushups."

"Oh. *Romanian.*"

Pauly and I left the back bar and walked to the front section of the
restaurant.

"I need a coffee before driving." Pauly gestured to an open table.
"Let's sit for a minute."

The waitress came right over.

"American coffee, please. What do you want, Val?"

"Ginger ale."

She returned with our drinks in a couple moments.

I sipped my soda. "Are you still dating Lola?"

"Nah. She's not interested in me that way." He strained a happy
face. "That's how it is with me and girls. I'm friend, novelty lover, but
never boyfriend. No getting around what I am."

Despite the league of White Russians I'd consumed, a vision came
to me crystal clear.

Pauly knelt down on one knee in front of a woman who towered over him.
She looked five-ten, not including her platform heels. Bleach-blonde. Sultry-
lined eyes. Pauly pulled a small blue velvet box from his jacket pocket, held
it up in presentation, and then opened it. The box held a teardrop diamond
engagement ring.

Pauly perspired. "Natalia, will you marry me?"

The statuesque woman let out a throaty laugh. "You not serious? On
knee, you like bookaska, a little bug."

Pauly cheeks flushed a furious red.

Natalia sang, "Bookaska, bookaska!" He started to stand, but she pushed him playfully, and he lost his balance and fell on his rump. Natalia shrilled louder than before. "Funny clown! Affair not serious, only fun game."

Pauly stood, planting his feet wide. He clutched the velvet box and puffed out his chest. "Nothing is funny, and it wasn't a game to me."

I wanted to cry, and I wanted to write a book. Maybe if people, kids and adults, knew how much their words affected others, they'd think before they spoke. I'd seen in my years of visions how detrimental, and haunting, cruel words and bullying affected others. Reading people's past also enlightened me to how far a smile, encouraging words, and expressed belief in someone, carried a kid, a man, a woman. It was simple, but it was also easy. I could do more. I could be nicer, more thoughtful, and more generous with my smile.

The waitress brought me another ginger ale and poured fresh coffee into Pauly's empty cup.

"You know, Val, people being politically correct and calling me a *little person* doesn't change anything. I'm still a midget, dwarf, freak, or whatever else they call me behind my back."

"No Pauly, you're far from being a freak."

He raised his hands and shook them like a vaudeville performer, razzle-dazzle-style. "*Dat da!*" He lowered his arms and sat back. "Face it, Val. Circuses have provided a hunky-dory, semi-protected community for outcasts like me for generations"

"Come on, Pauly. People aren't as bad as they used to be. Besides, if you're a freak, then I am , too."

"Hardly." He batted our table's salt shaker back and forth on the table from one hand to the other. "Come on. Gymnasts, contortionists, wire walkers—you guys are all athletes."

"Professional athletes are trained freaks." I gulped some soda. "We're circus mammals taught to amaze at any cost."

He stopped the salt shaker mid-slide. "The difference is—you've choices. I was born this way. I'm limited."

"This isn't the nineteen-thirties. You can be an engineer or an accountant or—"

"*Me*, in an office all day?"

His joking made me feel better. "Pauly, there's three ways that I'm weird. My parents abandoned me in the woods when I was a baby. I see visions of people's past. And I've a—"

"You think you're the only person on the planet whose parents couldn't take care of their kid? It happens in America, too."

The waitress stopped at our table. "Another coffee and a ginger ale?"

"Yes, please." I answered for both of us.

"As far as you seeing stuff, I figured from some of the things I've heard you say, a little Gypsy rubbed off on you."

"Nothing rubbed off on me, Pauly. I've read people since I was five." I swept my bangs off my forehead. "*And* I was born with this."

"What? High-arched eyebrows?"

"No, the birthmark on my forehead."

He leaned forward. "There's nothing on your forehead. Maybe a scratch. I don't know. It's dark in here."

"How can you not see it?" I stood quickly. "Whoa." I sat.

"I think I'd better take you home."

"No. I've to go to the ladies room and make sure it's still there."

"Val, let's go. You can check it when you're home."

I left the table and walked straight to the ladies room. Three low wattage bulbs lit the two-stall bathroom. I leaned over the bathroom sink, practically pressing my face to the mirror, and brushed my bangs side. I squinted. I could barely see the little pink birthmark on my fore-head. *No* ... I wanted to cry. It was my only link to my— I quickly turned on the faucet and splashed my face to quell my queasiness.

Where was my mother? I needed to talk to her, see her, and understand why she did what she did. I dried my cheeks and eyes with a wad of brown paper towels from the stack on the counter. What if my mother moved to America or Australia? I threw the towels in the trash can, feeling sicker by the second. No, my mother wouldn't do that. It wouldn't make any sense. It'd be too hard to find me. You don't leave someone you love and move to another country. I looked in the mir-ror and gasped. I loved Aunt Sylvie, Sorin and Cosmo and yet, I left them.

I prayed my mother wasn't like me, or rather, I like her. I pushed into an empty stall, lifted the toilet seat, and threw up.

THIRTY

Fossey always set up a pathway of Tiki lights leading from the motor homes to the food tent. The lights helped when cast or crew craved snacks in the black of night. Beata, Stasya, and I decided blueberries and whipped cream would help us sleep. We looped arms, and like silly little girls, pranced down the path.

Stasya giggled. "I feel like we're off to see the wizard, in *The Wizard of Oz.*"

"Which character would you be, Stasya? Scarecrow, Tin Man, or Cowardly Lion?"

"I don't know, but Beata would be the Tin Man. She's tall and the coldest."

"Ha, ha. Funny, funny," Beata said, deepening her voice.

"What about you, Val? Who'd you be?"

"I don't know. What do I need more of, brains or courage?"

"Val, darling, it's been nearly two months since you've heard from Halse. Do you miss his attention?"

Whiplash. "Uh ... no. Not really."

"Not Halse, Beata," Stasya whispered. "Daniella."

My cell phone rang. I unhooked my arms from the girls. "Auntie, what's wrong? You never call after eight."

"Everything's fine, dear. Can't an old woman call her famous circus daughter?"

"I'm not famous yet, and you're not old."

"Tell your auntie 'hi' from us," Beata said.

Stasya waved and they continued toward the food tent.

"Beata and Stasya say hi."

"Tell the sweet girls hello from me."

"I will. So, Auntie, how are you? Your blood pressure? Your hip? Hope you're not working as hard as you always do."

"No worries, dear. Are you in Albania yet?"

"We rolled into Tirana today. Did you get the fabric I sent from Czech? What about the buttons from Vienna? Did you like them?"

"*Da*, yes, *multiumesc*. I loved everything. But the money you sent me, I put aside for you."

"No, Auntie, that's for you. I want you to buy something nice, something you want."

"Can you hear Nawa? He's cawing away. He knows I'm talking to you. You two have been connected since that afternoon we found you in the woods."

"You mean *morning*. You told me you found me in the morning."

"Yes, yes ... guess I'm getting a bit old. But I'm hanging in there, like Radu. The big tom's moving slower these days, but he continues to purr like a lion. We nap on my chair by the big window every afternoon. The sun warms our joints. Ah, enough of my old age gripes. How are you? No injuries? Staying strong?"

I waved to Emeric who walked by flirting with one of the costume assistants. "Yeah, the hamstring I pulled is almost totally healed. I still wrap my wrists, but that's it. Auntie, we could've talked about this in the morning. Why'd you call?"

"Did you talk to Miss Katja today?"

"Not really. First day in town, everyone's setting up. Why?"

"She wanted my permission to train you for a new act and for you to potentially tour another season with Sky Brothers."

"Really? You gave her permission, right? What's the act? It is on the silks?"

"Miss Katja will give you the details, but yes, I gave my approval."

"You're the best Auntie! I need to find Miss Katja immediately. Can we talk tomorrow?"

"Of course, dear. Go. I love you."

"Love you, too, Auntie. Bye." I hit *end call* and then speed dialed number-three.

Miss Katja confirmed what my auntie said. She wanted to choreograph a routine for me on the aerial hoop—*a solo!*

Fifteen minutes later, I sat at Miss Katja's kitchen table in her and Fossey's motor home. I tucked my hands under my thighs to avoid fidgeting or picking my calluses.

"I'm about to make some tea. Would you like Earl Grey, chamomile, or green tea?" Miss Katja placed a plate of pumpkin spice cookies in front of me. "Fossey stockpiles tea."

I thought of Grandmamma Dobra's tea stained teeth. I thought of Fane and his father and the chamomile tea. "Uh, Miss Katja, do you have anything besides tea?"

"Juice, almond milk, hot cider. ... "

"Cider, please. Thank you."

She poured me a glass and set it on the table. "What do you think about learning a routine on the hoop?"

"I love the idea. I'll learn whatever you give me in time for next season."

She made herself tea and sat across from me. "Before next season. We need to be nearly perfect the first week of January to audition for Nik."

"That's in four weeks." I bit into my cookie. Part of it crumbled, sticking to my lips. I wiped my mouth with a napkin and then brushed the spillage on the table into another napkin. "Sorry."

"*Nici o problemă.* Cookies always crumble." She took my balled up napkins and tossed them in the trash. "To be ready, we must train in December, during our holiday break." She sipped her tea. "I called Coach Muznay. He said we can set up and practice in his gym. Fossey will rig up a hoop. We'll train four hours a day, five days a week, which still allow us time with our families. Luckily, we both have roots in Bucharest."

"My auntie would say we're blessed, not lucky. Thanks for believing in me, Miss Katja."

"We'll see how much you're thanking me when I'm putting you through conditioning drills on your holiday. Sorin coming home for Christmas?"

"Yes. We haven't discussed it yet, but we'll probably take turns visiting each other. That is, on the days I'm not training with you." I washed down a bite of cookie with cider. "I can't wait to train for the new act. Sorin will understand."

Miss Katja warmed her hands on her mug. "You know, maintaining a fantastic personal life, while having a career, is harder than any act in the ring." She sighed, smiling. "But it's worth the effort. Of course, I married Fossey, the love of my life and my best friend."

"You two are perfect together. Plus, you're both in the circus." I slid out of the kitchen booth and rinsed out my glass.

Miss Katja set her mug in the sink. "Valthea, other talent will be competing for your same solo spot in Sky Brothers Circus. There's risk in not signing with another circus for a guaranteed act. You need to be the best and the most exciting. Nik expects excellence and something fresh in every headliner. The good news is, he usually agrees with my opinion regarding aerial acts." She looked me square in the eye. "But if we fall short of his vision, it won't matter how much influence I have. Do you understand?"

"Yes."

Miss Katja walked me outside.

I inhaled the crisp October night air, wrapping my scarf around my neck. "What about Beata and Stasya? I heard there'd be a silk act."

"A flying silk act. Nik signed two guys from England. I tell the girls in the morning of his decision to let go of the trio. But don't worry, Beata and Stasya have time to send out audition discs, and I'll make a few calls for them. With you, if Nik changes his mind or decides on another act, we'll be forced to scramble to find you work. You always have the option to go home."

"No way. I want to stay in the circus."

She smirked, zipping up her sweat jacket. "I figured. Since most circuses have contracts signed before January, you may end up working piece meal. A theatrical production here, a party there, perhaps a music video. ... "

"So nothing's for sure?"

"Afraid not, Val. Not in life and never in show business. But if you give the hoop your best shot, and Nik picks up the act, you're on your way to a chunk of fame and limelight. Solo acts guarantee more photos, articles, and more features on our Facebook page and website."

More exposure is what I need. A thousand times, I played out the scene in my head of meeting my parents after a show. I imagined sitting at one of the long tables after an evening performance and signing circus programs for kids and adults. A man and a woman walk up to me and they hand me their program. I'd ask their name or who the program is for. They glance at my forehead and smile. Tears roll down their face. The woman says, "Please write it to Mom and Dad." I spring from my seat, run out from behind the table, and wrap my arms around them. The patrons in the tent cheer. My mother and father tell me they're sorry, and they've searched for me for years.

"*Iubesc stele* ... look at all the stars." Miss Katja pointed to the navy sky. "So beautiful. It's nice having the motor homes away from bright city lights."

I searched the shimmering constellations for the big dipper.

"Valthea—"

"Yes?" I scanned the sky.

"Do you understand the risk involved with this plan?"

I faced her. "Yes. Nik Sky must contract our act."

"Exactly. It's important you think it over. You don't have to answer tonight."

C.K. Mallick

I didn't need a shooting star or any other sign. I knew my answer. "Miss Katja, I know greatness requires great risk and a leap of faith. I'm willing to take that risk, and I'm all about faith."

"That's my girl." She hugged me.

I looked over her shoulder and up to the sky. There it was—the big dipper. Its stars twinkled, as if winking at me.

The next day, I dialed Sorin for a Face time call. Within moments, he appeared.

"Great timing." He combed his hair back with one hand. His eyes sparkled despite our two-dimensional phone screens.

I told him about the new solo act and Miss Katja's plan to coach me over winter break. "Val, I'm sure Mr. Sky will pick up your act. You're phenomenal, and Sky Brothers needs a sexy girl in the air."

"I don't know about sexy, but thanks." Sorin calling me sexy thrilled me.

"You're on your way to becoming a star, babe. I only wish you were in an English circus. Then I'd see you more. Thank goodness I'm prepping for tests, or I'd never survive our eight-and-a half week countdown."

I touched the screen as if touching his face. "That's so long. We're here until the end of the month, and then we go to Macedonia, and then Bucharest. I *love* being in the circus, Sorin, but I do miss you desperately."

"Cameras and phones don't cut it. I need you in real life. I need to kiss you ... touch you. In fact—" The screen jarred as Sorin stood. "I'm going to fly to Tirana next weekend."

"Really?" I kissed my iPad over and over, smudge on top of smudge. "I can't wait!"

"I can justify the trip. You relax and energize me. I'll study while you perform. Then when I come back, I'll be refreshed."

"Are you sure, Sorin? How expensive—"

"Don't worry. Dad has mileage built up on his card. He insists I use all of it to visit you."

"Cosmo's the best."

"I'll only have two days, Val. I'll study when you're performing. But otherwise, I'm not letting you out of my arms."

Sorin arrived two days later and kept his word. We stayed inter-locked nearly his whole visit. Although he had to sleep in Fossey and

216

Miss Katja's motor home, he came over both mornings with a bowl of fruit from their fridge. We'd sit on my bed and feed each other pineapple wedges, strawberries, and grapes. How great it'd be to wake up every day with Sorin. We made dinner after the evening shows and ate it in my bedroom while watching movies. Well, part of movies, anyway. After Sorin left, it took two days of constant application of *Vaseline* on my lips to heal their love-chapped state.

We performed our last show of the tour on November thirtieth. For nearly a year, I'd worked and traveled with a great group of people. I'd miss them, but remained hopeful I'd be contracted another season, like Miss Katja, Fossey and his crew, Pauly and Emeric, and Carlo Reye. Beata and Stasya secured steady work within two weeks. The three of us vowed to remain active social media friends.

On December third, I met Miss Katja at Coach Muzsnay's gym in our hometown. Miss Katja paced a section of gym floor.

"For the next four weeks, we'll train five hours a day. Your holiday time with your auntie will be in the evenings and on Sunday."

"I really appreciate this, Miss Katja." I jogged in place, warming up. "By the way, Cosmo and Sorin are coming here the last two weeks of December, instead of me and Auntie going up to Brasov."

"Perfect. You'll have training, family, and boyfriend time."

Fossey dragged a thick gymnastic mat from the side of the gym and positioned it under the hoop he'd rigged in the center of the gym. "Hoop's ready."

"Thanks, Foss. Now, Val, picture the hoop hanging four times higher. It'll be at sixty-feet for most of your act. We start low for you to get the feel of the apparatus. Hang from it. Play. Improvise. Do whatever for about twenty minutes. Get to know that steel circle, how it moves, how it doesn't. Then we'll do basic maneuvers, and then we'll take it higher. Good thing is, many of the moves you performed on the ribbon transfer to the hoop."

"Except with the hoop, there are times I completely let go."

Fossey held the hoop for me. "Here ye go, lass: thirty-six-inches of circular solid steel. I'll be working yer cable."

I wrapped my fingers around the bottom curve and pressed my palms to its cold smoothness. I piked at the hip and swung, pulling myself up through the center of the hoop.

C.K. Mallick

After my twenty-minute play time, Miss Katja coached me for an hour with the hoop ten-feet from the ground, and then another hour at twenty-five. Catching my breath and listening to instruction happened in the air with me sitting on the hoop's bottom curve. She didn't allow my feet to touch the ground for three hours.

Miss Katja, the gazelle queen, stood graceful and proud.

"Excellent for first day. Let's keep going."

The next sequence started with me standing beneath the hoop. I stood in ready position, my arms hooked around the steel. She nodded, and I ran six strides and then bound into alternating leaps.

"Strong core," she yelled. "Focus."

Fossey worked my cable, raising the hoop into the air. I sailed through the gym, arched body, pointed toes, flying over a landscape of floor mats, balance beams, and bars.

I shouted, "I love this! I love being in the air!"

THIRTY-ONE

Christmas morning, Aunt Sylvie made Cosmo, Sorin, and Mr. Karl sit at our dining table while she and I served spicy espresso and fresh-baked *cozonac*. Auntie's version of the pantone-like cake included chestnuts, cocoa, and raisins. I sat in my chair next to Sorin.

"Sylvie, your *cozonac's* heavenly." Cosmo served himself another piece. "Tastes exactly as Christmas should."

"Thank you. The crackling fire you and Mr. Karl built makes this room as toasty as Christmas should be. And Sorin, your ePod music's lovely." Auntie cooed. "It's mystical, almost spiritual. Who's singing?"

"It's an *iPod*, Auntie."

"I'm glad you like it, Miss Sylvie. It's Loreena McKennitt. This is her Celtic winter album."

"Speaking of spirits ... " Cosmo slid a bottle of *palinka* from a brown bag. "Why wait until dinner to celebrate with cheer? I'd like to make a toast this morning. What do you say, Sylvie? May I serve everyone a sip?"

"I said spiritual, not spirits." Auntie nibbled on a bite of cake. "Honestly, Cosmo. Alcohol in the morning?"

"It's eleven o'clock, Sylvie, and you wake up at five. It's practically your late afternoon."

Sorin put his fork down. "Miss Sylvie, I've a toast for tonight, or rather an announcement. I'd like to make it this morning instead of waiting, if it's alright with you,"

Aunt Sylvie glanced at him with a fond expression. "Well, in that case, it *is* almost noon."

Mr. Karl patted her hand. "Least the kids have some food in their belly."

"Cake is not food."

I removed five sherry glasses from the cabinet and set them on the table. They were prettier than our shot glasses.

The doorbell rang.

"I'll get it." I scooted out of the dining room and into the foyer. I opened the front door to a delivery girl standing on our front porch holding a clipboard and a vase of black roses.

Black?

"Are you Valthea Sarosi?" The scrawny twenty-year-old had a worn, gravelly voice.

"Yes."

She set the vase on the porch table left of the door and handed me her pen. "Please sign on the last line." She held her clipboard out flat.

"Who are these from?"

"There's a card attached. Someone from Germany."

My face went hot despite the bite in the frosty morning air. "I don't want them." I snapped. "Send them back." I handed her the pen.

She didn't take it. "Please, Miss, you can throw them away if you want, but I need a signature to get paid."

A scene of the girl's recent past. ...

The young woman sat at a table, spoon feeding a chubby baby. The baby gurgled with joy, trying to clap its hands together and missing each time. A woman of about forty, yelled at the young woman.

"You need meat on your bones. Why aren't you eating?"

"Ma, I don't make that much money. But look, baby Aurora's healthy. That's all that matters." She kissed her baby's cheeks.

I quickly signed my name on the sheet attached to the clipboard. "Sorry I didn't sign right away. The black roses threw me."

"Yeah, unusual choice for the holidays." The young woman tucked the pen in her clipboard, turned, and headed down the porch steps. "Merry Christmas."

"Wait! I've something for you. I opened the front door wide. "Come inside."

"I can't. I've more deliveries."

"I'll be quick." I ran to the kitchen.

Aunt Sylvie yelled from the dining area. "Valthea, who is it?"

"A friend." I backed up to face the dining room. "Auntie, may I give away one of the cakes you made for neighbors and visitors?"

"Of course, dear. Anything you'd like."

"Thanks." I wrapped one of the *cozonac* cakes in tinfoil and slid it into a paper bag, along with a half-pound of deli meat wrapped in white paper. I grabbed three jars of blueberry jam from our stock pile and put them in a separate bag. I hurried to the front door.

"Here!" I handed the young woman the bags. "We've extra." I shrugged. "Some of our relatives couldn't make it today. Merry Christmas to you and your family."

Her hollow eyes brightened. "Thank you so much. Merry Christmas to you, too."

I followed her out the door and pointed to the paper bags. "Your baby can have some of the jam I put in there. My auntie doesn't add any sugar."

"How'd you know I've a baby?"

"Uh ... uh ... there's a smudge of baby food on your coat."

She scrunched her chin to her chest and brushed off nothing. "Yeah, with a little one there are always souvenirs. Thanks for the goodies." Her face lit up. "I appreciate it." She carried the bags down the porch steps to the delivery van parked at the curb.

I snatched the note card from the rose vase.

> Frauline Valthea, I think of you often, even though you've lost your splendor and are no longer a magnificent rose in your circus. At least you try. Glückliches Weihnachten ... Merry Christmas, Halse.

"I have *not* lost my splendor." I walked the black bouquet to the side of the porch to our garbage can, knocked its lid off, and dumped his note and the roses inside.

Returning to the dining room, and sitting next to Sorin, helped me release my anxiety regarding Halse.

"Which friend was that, Valthea?" Aunt Sylvie asked.

"No one you know. A new friend."

Cosmo walked around the table, placing a half-filled sherry glass in front of each of us. "Now that we're all here, I've three toasts. Actually, I've twenty."

"Twenty?" Mr. Karl picked up his glass.

"He exaggerates." Auntie shook her head. "As usual."

"Believe it or not, Sylvie, I could come up with twenty toasts. I feel that blessed."

She reached across the table and laid her hand on Sorin's. "It's rare, Sorin, but when your father says things like that, I remember why I tolerate him."

"Ha! Don't listen to her, son. She loves me." Cosmo raised his glass. "For my first of three cheers, I'd like to congratulate my son for successfully completing his first semester of his second year at the university. To Sorin!"

"To Sorin," I said, louder than anyone.

The five of us tapped glasses and then sipped the *palinka.*

Cosmo continued. "To Valthea, who's completed her first circus tour. *Salut!*"

"*Salut!*" Auntie and Mr. Karl said in chorus.

Sorin leaned over and kissed my cheek.

"For my third toast, I thank the gracious Sylvie for spending the last three days and nights preparing a Christmas feast for us to enjoy this afternoon. *Crăciun Fericit!* God bless."

"To Auntie!"

"*Crăciun Fericit!*" Mr. Karl raised his glass.

"To Miss Sylvie!"

Mr. Karl finished his drink. "Sorin, did you have a toast?"

"Yeah, an announcement. Let me lower this volume." Sorin adjusted his iPod and then stood at the table behind his chair. He held up his sherry glass. His hand shook. He tucked his other hand in his back jean pocket.

Uh, no ... did Sorin need to announce something bad? Did he quit school? I prayed he didn't lose his scholarship. I wished I could read Sorin on command.

"Valthea Sarosi ... "

I twisted in my chair. What's he—

"You're my girl, and I love you." His voice trembled.

My heart pounded.

He pulled his hand out of his back pocket and presented a red velvet ring box. Butterflies in my stomach went crazy flying every which way. He placed the box in my hand. "With this, I promise to remain true to you."

Auntie gasped and pressed one hand to her heart.

Sorin bent over and kissed me. "Open it, babe."

I held the velvet box near my heart and lifted the lid. "Oh, Sorin!"

"It's a promise ring." He pulled out his chair and sat facing me. "Valthea, I promise you my love and my loyalty."

I wrapped my arms around his neck and kissed him. "I love you too, and I also promise my loyalty." I kissed him again and then sat straight, holding out my hand. The heart-shaped, pink-sapphire ring gleamed. "It's beautiful, Sorin. Perfect. *Thank you.*"

"Bravo!" Cosmo shouted.

Mr. Karl tapped his knife to his glass.

Auntie crossed herself and wiped away tears.

Sorin removed the ring from the box and slid the promise ring onto my right, ring finger. "*Eu ador.* I adore you."

"*Eu ado te.*" We kissed, and I held up my hand for everyone to see.

"Lovely," Auntie said, coming around the table to us.

"I know we're young, Miss Sylvie, but I pledge my heart to Valthea. God willing, the next ring I give her will be an engagement ring." He flashed a smirk, his azure eyes shined.

Auntie lit up, about to burst with joy. I thought she might break out into a jig.

"Double bravo!" Cosmo shouted and then sang like an opera star, "*To my son and Sylvie's daughter—la, la, la! A couple made in heaven, la, la. la!*" He bent over and hugged me and then Sorin. "I love you two so much. Love—love—love! You mean everything to me."

Auntie handed Cosmo her hanky. "Here, dear."

Cosmo stepped back. "Sylvie, I'm a man! I don't need a hanky." He snatched the handkerchief from her outstretched hand and grinned. "But I am a passionate man!" He wiped his eyes with it and then waved it overhead.

We laughed a second round when Sorin grabbed Auntie's handkerchief from Cosmo and imitated him. He tucked the hanky into his dad's shirt pocket and then put his arm around him. "Hey, Val, you know if things go my way, this is your future father-in-law." He tilted his head toward Cosmo. "What do you think?"

"Being family with you two would make me the happiest girl in the world."

Cosmo turned to Aunt Sylvie. "Sylvie, this is my happiest day until our Sorin and Valthea marry. After that, it'll be when we've grandbabies!" He kissed us both on the cheek. "And Mr. Karl, I promise you, I am not exaggerating as usual."

Auntie's cheeks flushed. "Oh, grandbabies ... what a scrumptious thought."

Cosmo stepped up to Aunt Sylvie, pulling her hanky from his shirt pocket and then using it to blot the corner of her eyes. "My passionate, passionate Sylvie ... "

"Oh, stop." She shooed him away. "You're still silly after eighteen years."

"Of course, I am! Why should I ever act old?" He tossed the hanky into the air, caught it, and then with a bow, handed it to her.

"I like the way you think." Mr. Karl poured Cosmo more *palinka.* "*Salut!*"

"*Salut!*" Cosmo threw down the shot. He set his glass on the table and reached for my hand. He held it up, letting the light coming in from the window catch the pink sapphire's sparkle. He kissed my hand and offered it to Sorin. "My boy has excellent taste, doesn't he, Sylvie?"

"Yes, the ring's exquisite."

"Ha! I was referring to Valthea."

Mr. Karl chuckled. "Cosmo, you're a charming, handsome fellow. Why are you single?"

Cosmo's face paled. "It's not by choice, believe me. Years ago, I met the one I wanted to spend my life with. Tragically, I lost her. Since then, I've met many women. None as sweet or enchanting as my girl. My Gisella's inside beauty quadrupled her outside beauty. Because of her, I know what is possible. I can't settle for anything less."

"Yeah, Mr. Karl, my dad wants another beautiful angel."

"No, I don't need a woman in my life. I'm happy on my own," Cosmo said, lying. "Family's enough for me." He took a deep breath and clapped his hands. "And what a wonderful family I have. Love is all around me!"

Auntie whispered, "Love is all around you, too, Valthea."

"I know." I leaned into Sorin. "My life is perfect."

THIRTY-TWO

Four weeks of intense training made for a stronger body, hardened calluses, and a wrapped ankle due to a miscalculation. I waited center-ring in Sky's hometown auditorium in Sofia, Bulgaria for my audition. I tightened my wrist wraps and stood in ready position.

"Ready when you are, Kat," Nik Sky yelled from the tenth row of the bleachers. His wife and three kids sat in the second row.

I glanced at Fossey. He nodded, holding the remote that worked my safety harness. Although he triple-checked everything, I had to force the image of falling from my mind. The thought can haunt an aerialist to their death if they let it. Miss Katja trained me to focus on feeling the hoop in my hands, against the back of knees, the crook of my ankles, or wherever my body connected with it.

Miss Katja stood at the edge of the ring. "Ready when you are, Nik."

"Great. Let's rock and roll!"

The circus DJ and a lighting assistant came in for my audition to work my music and the spotlight. When the music started, Fossey raised me and my hoop toward the ceiling. I performed the first minute-and-a-half of my routine with grace and precision. After the second chorus, I rested my hipbones against the bottom of the hoop for a half-a-second. Prepping for my next move, I planned to flip around, let-go, and then re-grab the hoop, but flipped slower than usual. I tried to re-grab the top of the hoop, but missed.

One of Nik's kids screamed.

Fossey worked the remote, causing my harness to jerk, but it kept me from falling. The save forced my ribs to strike the steel hoop, knocking the wind out of me and jarring my spine. I pushed aside the pain and pulled myself up to a long-body position. The rest of the choreography flowed without flaw. I hit the last pose tight and on cue. One beat later, the lighting tech killed the spotlight. One count. Full house lights up.

Nik Sky and his family applauded.

Fossey lowered me and the hoop a foot-and-a-half from the ground. I stepped away from it and wiped my sweat and tears with my leotard sleeve.

"Ye all right?" he whispered.

I nodded and unfastened the wire from my harness belt.

He tucked the cable behind a hook and set down the remote. "Don't worry." He put one arm around me and hugged me from the side. "Routine's good. He knows ye've another month to polish."

Good sucked. Only *excellent* was excellent. I tore off my Velcro wrist wraps.

"Stand proud, lass."

Nik Sky walked down the stairs to the edge of the ring where Miss Katja stood.

"What do you think?" she asked. "Remember, we've four weeks until pre-opening."

"Let's ask my kids." Nik Sky gestured to his family. "What'd you think, kids? Was it exciting? Was Valthea fun to watch?"

"Yeah!" shouted his youngest son. "I want a big hula hoop."

His daughter looked up at her mother. "Mommy, she's pretty. Will she fall again?"

Miss Katja stepped forward. "Hanna, she didn't fall. She's safe and did a great job."

Sky's teenaged son came down from the stands and stood next to his father. "I thought it was cool. I liked the music and Valthea's hot."

"Excuse me, Nik, honey." Mrs. Sky waved. "Sunday brunch ... we need to leave in five minutes to make it to my mother's on time."

"I'll be ready in two."

Nik Sky would determine and deliver my future in two minutes?

"Kat," he said, "super job working with Valthea." He faced me. "And Valthea, super job working with Miss Katja."

I knew where this was going. ...

"Well, my kids said it all, and I agree. And now I'd like to say, welcome Valthea to your second tour with *Sky Brothers Circus*."

My knees almost buckled. "Really?" I trembled. "I mean, thank you. Thank you, Mr. Sky."

"Thank you, Valthea." He turned to Miss Katja. "And for the new season's theme, I'd like to promote Valthea as *Girl-Raven* ... if that's all right with you, Valthea."

"Sure." I didn't care if Nik Sky promoted me as a Big-Foot on an aerial hoop. I'd a solo in the circus!

He illustrated his vision using his hands. "I'm setting you up to be a teen idol. Picture it, Val, you as *Girl-Raven* in a slick black costume performing hoop to a sexy rock song. Your photo will be one of four in the collage used to promote the new tour. That collage will also be the new program cover. You'll be plastered on YouTube, billboards in fourteen different countries, and of course, our website. I'm calling the new show, *Rock the Tent Down.* Tagline—*Exquisite meets Audacious.* How about that, Kat?"

"I love it, Nik. Brilliant as always."

I liked the theme, but I loved the plan for lots of exposure.

Nik Sky pointed to his older son. "My son's reaction was perfect. That's what I want—teens going gaga over Valthea, I mean, *Girl-Raven.* Kat, I need you to bump up the choreography. Make it edgy. Send rehearsal videos every day to my phone. We need quantum improvements within two weeks."

"Absolutely, Nik."

He pushed up his glasses. "I want our audience packed with teenagers. Valthea, as *Girl-Raven.* You can make that happen."

"And she will." Miss Katja put her arm around me.

After Nik Sky and his family left the auditorium, Miss Katja gave me a hug.

Fossey slapped my hand in a high-five. "If anyone can make someone a circus star, it's Nik Sky."

"Fossey's right. I hope you're ready. We've a lot of work ahead of us."

M-am născut pregătit ... I was born ready. "Miss Katja, I promise you, *Fata-Raven, Girl-Raven,* is ready."

Five-and-a-half weeks later, we opened *Rock the Tent Down* to a packed auditorium. The Bulgarian press posted all positive reviews. We performed in Bucharest three weeks later. The first show felt like opening night all over again with Aunt Sylvie, Cosmo, and Mr. Karl in the audience. During intermission, after the well-received first half of the show, Emeric and Pauly performed funny bits in and around the seated audience.

I stood at the edge of the ring, out of sight, five minutes before the second half of the show began. As Girl Raven, my costume included a pair of larger-than-life black feather wings. Carlo Reye and his team embellished the wings and my jet-black body stocking with purple rhinestones. I wore a black, shag-cut wig highlighted with purple glitter.

I chalked-up my palms. Although the audience laughed at Emeric and Pauly, I heard only the muffled sound of my hands clapping off excess chalk. The white particles floated in the air, like glistening magic dust in the ring's catches of spilled light.

The crew guy working my cable signaled me. I nodded. He spoke into his walkie-talkie, and I stepped into the shadowed ring.

The ringmaster's voice bellowed throughout the big top. "Laaadiees and gentlemen! Boys and girls! Children of all ages ... " The handsome man's jodhpurs gleamed. His jacket tails sparkled with rhinestones. "Combining flexibility, daring, and passion, our next performer makes the steel ring in the air her personal moon in the sky. From Romania, *Sky Brothers Circus* presents air acrobat extraordinaire ... " He took off his top hat and raised it toward the tent's ceiling. "*Val-thee-a Sa-ro-see—Girl Rave-en!*"

Bam, the spotlight flipped on.

I executed a chain of eight turns. My wings fluttered and beat with sound and momentum behind me. I finished center ring, slipped out of my vest of wings, and grabbed the bottom of my hoop, suspended from the tent ceiling. I kept my body long, and my toes pointed, as the spotlight followed me up toward the tent ceiling. My routine took place at sixty-feet for two-and-a-half minutes. The audience applauded after each of my showiest maneuvers.

For the final minute of choreography, my crew guy lowered me until my feet touched the ground. I held on to the hoop overhead and wound up my body. As the hoop rose higher and higher, I unwound, spinning faster and faster until my body resembled a raven feather caught in the midst of a tornado. Moments later, my rotations slowed, and my body morphed back to a seventeen-year-old girl in a circus costume. I pulled myself up to sit on the lower curve, and then lay back over it, hands-free, in an arched position.

Wild applause followed.

I held the seductive position for two counts. On count three, the music finished and the spotlight shut. Cheers and whistles rippled through the blacked out tent and right into my soul. The spotlight flipped back on. I sat up and smiled, waving to my fans. The crowd loved me. I loved them. And I loved feeling invincible.

THIRTY-THREE

The next morning, I went with Miss Katja and Fossey to a nearby diner café for breakfast. My tutor, Alin and her girlfriend, Pami, one of Sky's lighting technicians, walked in five minutes after we ordered.

"Top-of-the-morning-to-ye, ladies." Fossey stood and waved them over to our half-circle booth.

"And a great morning at that." Alin slapped a half-folded newspaper on the table. "Check the rave review from the *Bucharest Herald*." She and Pami took off their jackets and sat with us.

"They better rave." Miss Katja put down her coffee and picked up the paper. "This is our best show ever."

"Valthea, where's your auntie?" Pami asked. "Isn't she joining us this morning?"

"She had a doctor's appointment." I stirred my oatmeal. "Blood pressure checkup, or something."

Alin stopped our waitress. "Two coffees and two specials, please."

Pami pointed to the newspaper. "Val, you're highlighted in the article."

"I am? Miss Katja, read it out loud."

"Our little star!" Fossey ruffled my hair.

I leaned away. "You better not have jelly on your fingers."

"I don't, but I can arrange it, lass." He picked up our table's jar of strawberry jam and wiggled it while crossing his eyes.

"You're goofy."

"*Goofy?* Aye ... and to think, just last night I told Kat I wished we'd a daughter just like ye. Then ye go and call me goofy." Fossey faked a pout and set the jam next to the honey.

"Okay, I take it back. Jelly or not, you and Miss Katja *would* make great parents."

"Aye, that's more like it." He grinned. "And ye'd make any parent proud."

I'd eliminated Miss Katja and Fossey as parental suspects because they weren't the type to leave a baby in the woods, and they never said anything about my birthmark. Secretly, I wished they were my parents.

"Let's see what the Herald has to say." Miss Katja read:

"The Sky Brothers Circus is known for thinking outside of the box, with their removal of animal acts, extensive charity involvement, and recent creation of Sky Power Jewelry for girls. Besides being on the cutting edge, this circus puts on a spectacular, fun-filled show."

Pami sat back as the waitress served her and Alin's food. "That review will *definitely* boost Bucharest ticket sales."

"Absolutely." Miss Katja continued:

"Their current show, Rock the Tent Down, includes entertainment geared not only for children and adults, but teenagers. Teens, normally too impatient for rope walkers and too cool for clowns, will love Sky Brothers Circus's daring and sexy acts like: Wheel of Destiny, Globe of Death, and Girl-Raven."

Miss Katja looked up. "How about that, Val? Your act is sexy."

I blushed. "I like reporters."

"No, you like good reviews." Alin took a bite of sausage. "But watch out. There's always a flip side."

"Alin, don't be negative." Pami nudged her. "It's a wonderful review. Let her have her moment."

"More coffee?" The waitress stood at our table holding the coffee pitcher.

"Yes, please." Miss Katja laid the newspaper flat on the table and pointed. "*Three* photos. That's good coverage."

Fossey tapped his mug. "And Miss, may I've more hot water for me tea?"

"Of course." The waitress freshened up the coffees and then glanced at the newspaper and looked at me. "You're the circus star from here, right? Are you *all* from the circus?"

My stomach knotted. Was she a fan, or did she consider us circus trash?

Alin spoke up. "We're all from *Sky Brothers Circus*. Sitting right here at your table is Sky's director of choreography, its tent master, and one of our lighting designers. And this, one of our stars, Valthea Sarosi, *Girl-Raven*. I'm her tutor."

"Nice to meet all of you. Amalia, my daughter, envies you, Valthea. She takes gymnastics at school." The waitress fixed her eyes on my *Sky-Power* bracelet. "She has one of those bracelets and has started collecting the charms."

My bracelet held twelve of the twenty-two charms modeled after Sky's various circus acts. "That's great. Which ones?"

"The trapeze charm, the girl on the hoop, and the ringmaster."

Alin pointed her fork at me. "Valthea posed for the aerial hoop girl charm, *and* she performs it."

"Yes, I know. I can't wait to tell Aimilia I served breakfast to Valthea Sarosi and members of the *Sky Brothers Circus*. We're coming to Saturday's matinee. She's so excited."

"Bring her to the program signing table after the show. I'd love to meet her."

"That'd mean the world to her." The waitress said to Fossey, "I'll be right back with that hot water." She headed toward the kitchen.

"Don't let a little fame go to your head." Alin took another bite of sausage. "Remember, it's always temporary."

I wouldn't let it go to my head, but I liked being sort of famous.

Miss Katja turned a couple pages of the newspaper and re-folded it. "Look—here's a separate little bio and a photo of Valthea." She read:

"This year Sky Brothers Circus makes Romania proud, featuring one of Bucharest's own—Valthea Sarosi, aka Girl-Raven. The seventeen-year-old's aerial hoop routine is set to Heartbreak, by Def Leppard, and opens the second half the show. As her music blasts through the arena tent, the teen flies like a wild raven in, through, and around her steel hoop positioned sixty-feet up in the air. Valthea Sarosi attacks her routine filled with spins, flips, twists and splits and all at break-neck speed."

"I didn't start at break-neck speed."

"They'd never believe that." Pami punctuated her point with one hand. "You make it look easy. Read on, Katja."

"In the second part of her routine, Valthea Sarosi sails above the crowd, hanging from her ring of steel—a daring, sequin-clad temptress. At seventeen, Valthea is an aerial solo-ist, spokes model for Sky Power Jewelry, and a young lady on her way to a brilliant future. She's also an example of old-fashioned family values. While Sky Brothers tours Bucharest, she stays with her guardian, Sylvanna Sarosi in their quaint home on Teodora Street. Bucharest can be proud of Valthea Sarosi, the quintessential role model for young girls and aspiring gymnasts."

C.K. Mallick

Miss Katja handed me the newspaper. "Now *that's* great press."

I set the paper on my lap. "Why'd they say where I lived? Auntie's old. I don't want anyone bugging her."

Alin pushed her plate away and pulled a toothpick from her shirt pocket. "Did you *tell* the reporters you stay with her every night and that you lived on Teodora Street?"

"Yeah."

"Then get over it. It's your fault. Besides, anyone can find an address off of the Internet. Why are you complaining? You got your wish. You're a star. You kissed away your privacy a year ago."

Our second Sunday in Bucharest was Carlo Reye's birthday. After the day's matinee, Nik Sky surprised him with a party, complete with catered food and drinks. Most the cast and crew hung out over two hours, until nearly dusk. Fossey drank only part of a pint of ale, knowing he offered to drive me home. I wrapped up a piece of the birthday cake for Aunt Sylvie.

Miss Katja and Fossey played the oldies radio station, like they did every time they drove me home after a show. They sang along to a U2 song, "*Sunday, bloody, Sunday. ...* "

I sat in the backseat of the truck, looking out the window. "Why do you guys always play oldies? Why not try pop or alternative music?"

Fossey glanced in his rearview mirror. "Because oldies make us feel *youngie*."

"Oh, is that it?" Miss Katja rubbed his shoulder. "I've tried to figure that out for years." She kissed his cheek.

He glanced at her, and in that split second, they looked at each other like they were the only two people in the world. They were still in love. I prayed Sorin and I'd always be in love. I leaned forward toward Miss Katja's seat. "What *I* can't figure out is how come we never met before? Miss Katja, your condo's five minutes from my house."

Fossey glanced at Miss Katja. Miss Katja didn't say anything.

"How come I've never bumped into you at the market, the movies, or anywhere?"

"I bought the condo when I was twenty-one, Val. Stayed there only in December, and like you, I started touring at sixteen. I wasn't around much."

"It would've been neat if we'd met."

232

She turned around in her seat. "But we're in each other's lives from now on."

"Unless I'm not hired for the next tour."

"Doesn't matter. We'll never lose touch because we're *friends*. And with me, if I say you're my friend, its forever." She winked and turned back around.

I liked the promise of forever. It made me feel safe, warm, and loved. I guess being abandoned as an infant increases your hunger for someone, or *something*, to be forever.

Fossey held Miss Katja's hand. "Like it er not, lass, I'm yer friend, too."

"I like it." I lowered my window. The early evening's misty air kissed my face. I wondered if maybe Miss Katja and I'd bumped into each other before but didn't know it. For that matter, I could've walked by my biological parents on any street, in any market, on any given day over the last ten years and not known it.

"Air's pleasant tonight, aye?" Fossey said, glancing at me through the rearview mirror. "Sun felt good today after four days of cold rain."

"I want to walk the rest of the way home."

"It's pretty foggy, lass. Cars might not see ye walkin' long the road."

"I'll walk on the pedestrian path between the road and the woods. I'm tired of being cooped up. I want be outside."

"Do the street lights reach that path?" Miss Katja asked.

"Yeah." They sort of did. "Miss Katja, it was *sixty* today. This is March. It may go down to forty-degrees tomorrow."

"I don't know."

"*Please?* I'll be home in less than ten minutes."

Fossey shrugged. "We're less than a quarter-mile from her mum's. It's up to ye, Kat."

"Fine," she sighed. "But stay where it's lit. Not too close to the road and not in the woods."

"Thanks, and don't worry. I grew up with these woods. I know them inside and out."

Fossey pulled to the side of the road. I slung my gym bag over my shoulder, held the wrapped piece of cake in one hand, and hopped out of the truck.

Miss Katja lowered her window. "I'll call Miss Sylvie and ask her to turn on the backyard lights. Shoot me a text when you're home safe."

"I will."

"And Val, watch where you walk. Forests change."

As soon as they drove off, I walked ten-feet and straight into a muddy patch of dirt.

"Great ... on my favorite pair of boots." I scraped the mud chunks off with a stick and then tromped on into the woods.

Miss Katja must've phoned Auntie as soon as they drove off. Our backyard lights already glowed in the forest in front of me, about a soccer field away. Light from the street posts filtered in behind me, illuminating my path and creating an eerie atmosphere.

I sang, steering clear of prickly bushes and stepping over fallen branches.

"Sunday, bloody Sunday. And the battles just begun. ... "

I looked up, trying to remember the rest of the chorus. The coming night's moon hung heavy above the pine tree tops. Few leaves remained on the slim beeches and knotty oaks. As a kid, I called the old oaks, *kings*, the beech trees, *queens*, and the tall pine, *knights*. I sighed, remembering the arbor royalty.

"Good evening, Valthea."

My heart flipped. I turned around.

"*Endlich* ... finally. Valthea Sarosi." The squat man before me spit out his words.

"Who—" I dropped the cake and my gym bag and ran towards home. The kingdom of trees blurred in my peripheral as I ran faster and faster. My foot caught on something, and I tripped and fell.

The German caught up to me and grabbed my hair. "Got you."

"Let go!" I reached behind my head to pry off his grip.

"Remember me, *Bendy Girl*?" His chortle sounded coated with phlegm. He yanked me backward by my hair. "You read my palm last summer."

Badger?

He lunged at me from behind, and I fell forward. He landed on my back, smashing my ribcage and knocking the wind out of me.

"*Jungfrau*, my virgin." He rolled me over.

I shoved the beast to the side and ran.

"*Stoppen jungfrau!*"

"*Fire!*" I yelled, "*Fire!*" Aunt Sylvie told me that people won't leave their houses when someone yells *help*. Yell the word, *fire* and people come out in droves. "*Fire!*" My feet slid out from under me. I landed on a wet carpet of pine needles. I scrambled to my feet.

Badger shoved me to the ground. He sat on me, digging his knees into my ribs. "I've waited a long time *frauline*."

I squirmed. "Get off me! *Fire! Fire!*"

"Shut up!" He covered my mouth. "You ungrateful—*ow!*"

I bit the meat of his palm and then batted at his face, jutting my hips upward to buck him off.

A crow's caw sounded. Twenty feet past Badger, a black bird flew in our direction.

Badger held down my wrists and dropped his chest to mine. His broom moustache smelled like blue cheese. "You'll not escape again."

"Get off!"

"I'm here. *Ihre Halse.*"

"*Halse?*"

"You expected taller? More handsome?"

The crow cawed again, sounding nearer. With all my might, I shoved Halse off me and stood. He grabbed my ankle. I yanked out of his grip and kicked him in the chest, forcing him to the ground. I waved my arm in command. "Come, Nawa!"

Instead of flying in the direction I ran, Nawa flew past me, screeching and flapping his wings hard. I stopped and turned to command him to follow. Halse stumbled backward, looking up at Nawa, but didn't cover his eyes in time. He shrieked like a wild animal. Nawa perched on the fallen man's face, pecking at it with his beak.

"No, Nawa! No!" I ran toward them and shooed Nawa off Halse. My childhood pet obeyed and flew to a tree stump a few yards away.

Halse lay curled up on the ground, covering his eyes. Blood spewed from between his fingers. His cries of pain curdled my stomach.

Nawa perched triumphant on the stump. Blood splotched his ebony and indigo feathers.

"*Valthea!*"

I turned, hearing my auntie's voice. Our yard lights outlined her and Mr. Karl as they ran toward me. "Auntie—"

"*Die vogel!*"

Auntie screamed. "No!"

I spun around. Halse stood hovering over the tree stump where Nawa had perched. Halse's trench coat partially covered the stump. He stabbed the trapped mound beneath it with a knife.

235

"No!" I cried.

Halse covered his blackened eye with one hand. Blood striped his face. With his free hand, he drew a gun from a well-hid holster and walked passed me toward Aunt Sylvie and Mr. Karl. He sputtered, "No bird or *alten*, elders will keep me from my Valthea."

I inched backward toward the tree stump. I shook, pressing one hand down on my pet's coat-covered carcass while pulling out the knife.

"Wait, sir!" Mr. Karl held up his hands. "You need help. Put the gun down. We'll call a doctor, save your eye."

I approached Halse from behind, trembling.

"You two shouldn't have come." Halse fired two shots and aimed again.

Hop, hug, slice. I jumped on Halse's back, wrapped an arm around his neck, and drew the knife's blade from left to right across his throat.

Halse gasped and gurgled.

I hopped off Halse and backed away.

The man dropped to his knees, swayed once and then fell forward, face down.

My ears rang. I looked at the blood-wet knife in my hand. Oh, my God ... I'd executed on Halse the same choreography I'd done on Emeric a hundred times in the clown act.

"*No. ...*"

I turned.

Mr. Karl knelt on one knee, holding a limp Aunt Sylvie in his arms.

THIRTY-FOUR

alse fired two shots that night in the woods. Neither bullet hit Mr. Karl or Aunt Sylvie. But the horror of what could've happened hit my auntie straight in the heart, causing her to faint. Although the judge ruled Halse's death an act of self-defense, Auntie blamed herself for everything. She thought it her fault for wanting me to come home after shows, for my joining the circus, and even for encouraging me to play in the woods when I was a child. I told her nothing was her fault. I reassured her that we were alive and unharmed today because she taught me not to rely on my paranormal gift, but to use instinct, heart, and reason in all important situations.

When the head detective on the case came to our house, Aunt Sylvie put on a pleasant face. We served hot coffee and fresh-baked muffins in our dining room. I sat at the table, wishing the whole night never happened.

"This is a short visit, Miss Sarosi. I'm here to update you on our findings." The detective placed two manila envelopes on the table. He drank his coffee black.

"We found a silver, four-door Mercedes Benz parked on the side of the road near the crime scene. It was registered to Halse Herrmann. Valthea, we believe he intended to follow you home. He changed his plan when you exited Fossey Brennan's truck and walked through the woods. This Herrmann guy was a wealthy businessman with a fantasy-filled mind. If he'd been a professional criminal, I guarantee, we wouldn't be having this discussion."

Auntie closed her eyes. "Dear God."

I reached across the table and placed my hand on hers. "It's over now, Auntie."

The detective smirked. "Miss Sarosi, these muffins are delicious. Tons of berries, just the way I like them." He chewed a hunk of muffin and then brushed off his hands. He opened one of the manila envelopes.

"Here is some of what we found on a bulletin board in Halse's Berlin home." The detective slid out photos and scooted the pile to the center of the table. "We also found a slew of news clippings and copied magazine articles. Valthea, you weren't the only one pinned up on his wall." The detective held up the other envelope. "Herrmann followed the careers of other teen girl entertainers and sent them gifts, like he did you."

Auntie pressed a hand to her heart. "The whole thing is frightful."

"You're right about that." The detective set the second envelope down and gestured to the basket of muffins. "Mind if I've another?"

Auntie passed him the basket.

I fanned out the photographs. A dozen were of me and Sorin. Others captured me performing with the clowns and with the girls on the silks. Four showed me eating dinner with Pauly. There were only a few of me on the hoop. I slid one out from the rest and studied it.

"And I thought it was a bear." I tucked the photo of me and Sorin on our picnic in Vienna under the pile.

"*Bear?* What are you talking about?"

"It doesn't matter now, sir."

Aunt Sylvie stood. "Detective, thank you for your visit, but I no longer want to think or talk about that man or that night anymore. Valthea will wrap the rest of the muffins for you."

"I'm sorry, Miss Sarosi. I didn't mean to upset you. But thank you for the muffins." He gathered the photos and stuffed them back in the envelope. "I wanted to reassure Valthea that what she did was a good thing. We've plenty of proof that Halse Herrmann planned to defile and kill many teenage girls."

Auntie wrapped her arms around her center and left the room.

"Please, detective, don't say anything else. I'll pack these for you and be right back." I scooped up the muffin basket and went into the kitchen.

I quickly wrapped the remaining muffins in tin foil, threw them in a paper bag, and went back to the dining room.

The detective stood at the buffet table, spreading out the various newspapers Mr. Karl dropped off over the past week. He chuckled. "Who comes up with this stuff?"

> 'Circus teen saves guardian! Circus aerialist defies death on ground! Circus star kills fan!'

"These are great."

"I try not to read them. Here are your muffins. You're all set."

"Thank you. Hey, how about this one?"

> 'Acrobat cuts stalker's throat!'

"That'll grab a reader's attention. You're really famous now."

"Not the way I hoped." I showed the detective to the door and locked it behind him.

I gathered the newspapers from the buffet table and dumped them in the recycle bin. I stared at the newspapers and cried. *Newspapers ...* we used to save them to line the bottom of Nawa's perch. I let out an exhale I'd held for days. That night in the woods, three entities died: Halse Herrmann, Nawa, and the innocent Valthea.

The shareholders of *Sky Brothers Circus* voted for my understudy to take my place for two weeks. Three days is the normal bereavement allotment, but the shareholders wanted steady ticket sales and for the press frenzy to calm down. Nik Sky called daily to check on me. He said he couldn't wait for me to come back. Miss Katja and Fossey stopped by after shows to visit with me and Auntie. I missed Sorin and couldn't wait until his visit in five days.

I counted down the days until my champion's arrival. On the first day, Auntie and I looked through her old circus photo albums together. She told the stories I'd heard a hundred times, but never tired of hearing. On the second night, Mr. Karl joined me and Auntie for dinner. For dessert, we made his favorite—*Amandina* cake. The rum and caramel soaked chocolate nut sponge cake turned out divine, and we all indulged. Afterward, Auntie recounted funny stories of me growing up with Nawa and Radu. Storytelling and laughter brought the warmth and joy, missing since that night in the woods eleven days ago, back into our home. Quality-time with my auntie snapped me out of self-pity and reminded me of my many blessings. I'd a warm home, food in my belly, and people I loved and who loved me.

Three days later, the only parent I ever knew died of a stroke.

THIRTY-FIVE

Many Romanian artists, writers, and political legends lay buried in the exclusive *Bellu Cemetery*. Although famous for its artful graves, monuments, and sculptures, I saw it for what it was—a place for the dead. Crooked trees with leafless branches surrounded the cemetery's misty grounds. They conjured up images of witches with long arms and bony fingers, looming over tombstones. Why'd it have to be a gray morning in March instead of a sunny afternoon in June, or better yet *never*?

Aunt Sylvie's favorite shop keepers, her berry-picking group, and close neighbors and friends, encircled her gravesite. The presence of Coach and Mrs. Muzsnay and Mr. Karl calmed me. Earlier, I thanked Miss Helga and my old childhood friend, Lyla for paying their respects. Although *Sky Brothers Circus* toured Hungary at the time, and none of my circus friends could attend, Nik Sky, Miss Katja, Fossey, and Carlo Reye sent flowers. I received a Bonsai plant from Pauly and his new, *steady* girlfriend. I appreciated those attending the funeral, but wished no one had. I wanted to lay next to my auntie's grave and weep until sleep relieved me.

Sorin held my hand and kept me steady throughout the funeral ceremony. He prevented mourners from zapping the last droplets of my energy by greeting them for me.

Sorin and Pauly were the only people alive who knew of my gift. *Gift*? What gift? My ability to read people's past hadn't led me to my parents. It didn't keep Apollonia, Daniella, or Excel from harassing me. No vision warned me that Halse was *Badger*, an evil man with a plan to defile and kill me in the woods. And no insight alerted me to the hour or day when my auntie would have a stroke.

The bishop from St. Gheorghe's led the funeral service. He donned the traditional black robe and boxy orthodox headpiece. His deep baritone voice added to the finality of his words.

"May Sylvanna Sarosi's memory be eternal. Amen."

People tossed flowers on the lowered casket. A woman I'd never seen before stood on the other side of the gravesite. The overcast day didn't dull her well-coiffed, orange hair. Her coat's high fur collar accentuated her severe jaw line and thin lips. She tossed the calla lily she gripped onto the casket. Who was she? And who was the elderly gentleman standing next to her? He tossed his white carnation and then wiped his eyes.

A reading, my first since that night in the woods, came to me. ...

The mystery woman as a girl of seven ... pale skin and bright orange pigtails. She sat under a canopied bed, on a white, eyelet bedspread, across from a five-year-old girl with blonde curls. French provincial furniture and framed Degas posters of ballerinas furnished the room. The girls played with an array of expensive-looking dolls and stuffed animals with detailed faces. "Szus'," the younger girl cried, "give me back my dolly!" Orange-haired Szusanna hugged the doll tighter. "No! I'm the older sister. I get more toys." The younger sister reached for her doll. "But it's mine." "No!" Szusanna slapped her little sister across the face.

The slap startled me and pulled me from the vision. Within the next second, another demanded my attention. ...

Szusanna and the younger sister looked eighteen and sixteen. Szusanna stood on the back terrace of a mansion smoking a cigarette. The younger sister walked by carrying a soda. She wore capris, a shirt knotted at her midriff, and a pair of cat-eye sunglasses. Her hair had turned a gold-ish color.
"Come sit with me, Szus'. Tell me what friends you want to invite to my birthday party."
Szusanna followed her sister to the open-air, mosaic-edged swimming pool. The younger sister stretched out on a lounge chair.
Szusanna hovered next to her, yelled, "I don't care about your stupid party. I'm sick of everyone giving you praise and attention when you do nothing to deserve it."
"Szus', why are you upset? Mom also gave you a party on your birthday."
"I'm not talking about birthdays. I'm talking about every day. Mom and Dad favor you, and it's not fair. I hate you!" Szusanna bent over and jabbed the lit end of her cigarette into her sister's thigh. The girl shrieked, pushed Szusanna away, and ran toward the house.

I looked at the mystery woman. No *way* was she friends with my auntie. But if she wasn't her friend, then who—

"You all right?" Sorin kissed my hand.

"Not really."

He put his arm around me. We watched the flora pile up and cover the black earth cross atop my auntie's casket.

I whispered, "Who's that red-headed woman? She wasn't at the service."

"The one with the scowl on her face?"

"Yes. I saw past visions of her, and nothing that explains why she's here. Sorin, what if it's not Aunt Sylvie she knew, but—do I look like her?"

Sorin pulled me in close. "This is an emotional time for you, babe. You're vulnerable. But I'm happy to report, you don't look like anything like that woman."

"That doesn't mean we're not related."

Minutes later, Sorin and Cosmo flanked my sides as people passed by offering their condolences. Some of the funeral attendees I'd see back at the house for coffee and pastry. Some let me know they couldn't make it because they had to go back to work. Whichever—that was fine. Aunt Sylvie wasn't fussy that way.

"I'll wait by the car," Mr. Karl said.

I hugged my auntie's dearest friend. "We'll be right there."

"That woman," Cosmo mumbled. "She looks familiar."

"Which one?" Sorin and I said at the same time.

"That one." Cosmo tilted his head toward the redhead. "Or maybe not. I can't place her."

Szusanna stood twenty-feet away. She glanced at us and then headed in the direction of the parking lot. The stately gentleman followed.

"I'll be right back."

I caught up to them. "*Scuză mă ... salut.*"

They turned around.

"Thank you both for coming today. I'm Valthea Sarosi. Sylvanna Sarosi was my guardian. How'd you know my auntie?"

The woman looked me up and down. "I'm Szusanna Stanasila." She tugged at one of her fur cuffs. "This is Mr. Emil."

The elderly gentleman tipped his head and smiled with warm eyes. "Miss Valthea, I'm sorry for your loss. Miss Sylvie was a dear—"

"But now we must go," Szusanna said. "I've another appointment."

"Another appointment? My auntie's funeral was an appointment to you?"

"Very well, Valthea. You've my condolences. Come along, Mr. Emil." Szusanna pivoted and continued on toward the cemetery's parked lot.

Mr. Emil whispered, "We're at *five Aleea Modogan.* You must visit as soon as possible."

"Why? Who—"

"Mr. Emil!" Szusanna yelled. "I'm waiting."

"Remember—*five Aleea Modogan*," Mr. Emil said once more, before turning and walking briskly Szusanna's way.

Eighteen-year-old Szusanna ... she stood in a sun-lit foyer. She looked about to leave, with one hand on the entrance door handle. A middle-aged woman's firm voice sounded from another room in the house. "Why must you always stir up trouble?" Szusanna let go of the door and whipped around. "Me? I'm not the one who's pregnant." The woman yelled back, "Your sister's a good girl." Szusanna's cheeks burned red and her eyes glint of jealousy. "Why do you and Mom always defend her? I'll show you what a bad girl she is before she disgraces our whole family." The middle-aged woman stepped into view drying a cooking pot with a dish towel. Szusanna raged on. "I'll show you, Auntie. You'll see."

I couldn't breathe. Szusanna's *Auntie was my Aunt Sylvie.*

THIRTY-SIX

Three days under my bed covers didn't bring back my auntie, diffuse sadness, or reveal how Szusanna Stanasila knew the woman who adopted me. Cosmo tried comforting me by saying, *time heals*. Of all people, he should've known the cliché was a lie. Time only allowed me more time to shed a river of tears.

Cosmo and Sorin stayed at my house after the funeral. Mr. Karl joined us for breakfast each morning. The presence of these three gentlemen provided warmth and comfort during the saddest and emptiest days of my life. On the third night, I told Cosmo of my ability to see the past. He confessed he suspected as much. I read people's palms without looking at their palms. On the fourth morning, I woke to the sound of a text message from Miss Katja.

"Valthea — how are you? Ready to tour as a star again? Nik wants you to return early for a charity in Hungary. Airline ticket coming via email. Hope you decide "yes." If so, see you in 3 days! Miss Katja."

"It's time, Radu." I kicked off my bedcovers causing Radu to spring from the foot of my bed to the corner chair. He meowed. "That's right. Time for me to go back into the ring." I stepped into my bedroom slippers. "Auntie would be disappointed if I gave up on my dreams." I pulled on my housecoat. "Time to put my life in order. First thing I need to do is find out why that orange-haired woman at the funeral called *Aunt Sylvie, Auntie*."

I skated down the hall and then stopped to look over the wood railing. Cosmo, Sorin, and Mr. Karl sat at the dining table eating breakfast. A thousand times I'd stood in the same spot and yelled to Aunt Sylvie that I'd be down in a minute for breakfast.

"Good morning," I called.

Cosmo stood and waved his napkin in the air. "*Bună Dimineața! Our princess awakes.*"

Sorin scooted out of his chair. "Morning, Val."

"Come, join us." Mr. Karl gestured to the readied place-setting next to him.

Dear Mr. Karl. He handled the paperwork involved with the funeral and all of auntie's affairs. She'd left me the house, a decent savings account, and a taped-up box to open on my eighteenth birthday. Mr. Karl said the bank needed me to sign some papers. To

244

do so meant I acknowledged Aunt Sylvie's departure. I hadn't been ready, but now I needed to complete all unfinished business within three days.

"Would you like a cheese or a meat pie?"

"Neither, thanks, Cosmo. I'm not hungry. I received a text from Miss Katja. I'm back in with Sky. I leave in three days."

"That's wonderful," he cheered."

Mr. Karl shot me a thumbs-up.

"If you're good with the idea," Sorin said, "I'm for it."

"Thanks. I *am* excited. But first, I need to visit that woman from the funeral and find out her story."

Cosmo drove me and Sorin in his Maserati to the *Piața Victoriei*, in the heart of Bucharest. I sat in the passenger seat.

"Maybe that man, Mr. Emil, told me Szusanna's address because she's Aunt Sylvie's niece, and he wants us to connect."

"Possibly," Cosmo said. "That way, you're not alone. Although, you'll never be alone, you'll always have me and my son. Right, Sorin?" He glanced in the review mirror.

"One hundred percent." Sorin leaned forward, rubbed my shoulders, and then sat back in his seat. "What if Miss Sylvie never mentioned anything to you about Szusanna because they'd a falling out?"

"Ah, but son, Valthea met Szusanna at the funeral and glimpsed into her past. The woman's beyond unpleasant. My Sylvie was the sweetest woman in the world." Cosmo wiped his eyes. "She'd a strong exterior and a grand heart. She'd never tolerate a woman like this Szusanna, even if they were relatives."

"Wait a second, what if it's Szusanna who avoided my Auntie?"

"Maybe." Cosmo stopped at a street light. "Sylvie never told me of her family."

"Don't feel bad, Cosmo." I glanced up at the name of the street. "If I asked questions about her family, she changed the subject. It seemed to upset her. I let it go. Doesn't matter. Today, we're going to find out exactly who Szusanna Stanasila is, and what happened between her and my auntie."

Cosmo turned down *Aleea Mogdogan* and then slowed almost to a stop. His face paled to snow-leopard-white.

"Dad, why are you stopping? We're almost there."

C.K. Mallick

"Cosmo, don't worry," I said, "I'm not afraid of this lady or whatever she says to me."

"Of course you're not, precious one." Cosmo continued driving forward. "Everything will be fine." He pulled up in front of the wrought iron gate and spoke into the speaker box, saying my name.

After a few moments, the gate opened. We followed the gravel road past a fountain, a greenhouse, and a guard cottage. Mammoth shade trees surrounded the property. We drove twenty feet past the front entrance of the well-kept, Neo-Romanian, three-story mansion.

"Definitely old money right, Dad?"

Cosmo mumbled, "I suppose." He shifted the car into park.

Sorin took my hand in his as soon as we got out of the car. He smoothed his thumb over the pink sapphire he'd given me at Christmas.

"I'm proud of you for following up on this. You deserve to know what happened. Miss Sylvie wasn't just a guardian. She was your mother."

I wiped my eyes.

"Are you sure you're ready for answers?"

"Yeah, thanks Sorin."

"I'm going to wait here, kids." Cosmo took his phone out of his jacket pocket.

"Why? Come in with us, Dad."

"Son, you're her man. I'll wait here."

"We won't be long," I said.

"Take all the time you need. I'm fine."

Sorin and I made it halfway up the entrance steps of the estate when the oversized front door opened. Mr. Emil, the elderly man from the funeral, stood in the doorway. He looked stately in his charcoal gray suit, lavender tie, and pocket scarf. His eyes twinkled. "Good morning, Miss Valthea. I'm glad you and your friend came."

"Thank you for inviting me. Mr. Emil, this is my boyfriend, Sorin Dobra."

"Pleasure to meet you, Mr. Dobra."

"Pleasure's mine, Mr. Emil. Sir, my father wants to wait outside, get some air. Is our car okay parked there?"

"Perfectly fine." Mr. Emil turned and called to Cosmo. "Sir, you may come in whenever you'd like."

Cosmo waved. "Thank you."

"Very well, Miss Valthea, Mr. Dobra ... this way please." He welcomed us inside.

"Your home's so beautiful." I scanned the high ceiling and grand marble stairway. Ornate pillars flanked the open living area. Two-story-high arched windows let in the early afternoon light. A large entranceway table showcased a tall cylinder of calla lilies, palm fronds, and bear grass.

"I love fresh cut flowers. Early April always makes me anxious for spring."

"Madam Alicia feels the same way. She maintains fresh flowers all year long and in every room, despite her being bed-ridden."

"Who's Madam Alicia?" I glanced at Sorin. "I thought Mrs. Stanasila lived here."

"She does presently, but this is Madam Alicia Vaslui Adamescu's home."

"Vaslui—as in *Vaslui Mining Corporation*?" Sorin asked.

"Yes, Madam Alicia's family founded the oldest, and currently the most environmentally-considerate, mining operation in Eastern Europe." Mr. Emil's proud expression drooped. "Madam Szusanna is her daughter. She and her husband have stayed here for over three months." He rolled his eyes as if annoyed by the fact. "Madam Szusanna claims concern for her mother."

"Oh." I didn't know what to say.

Mr. Emil led us to the right side of the house.

"Mr. Emil, who do you work for?" Sorin asked.

"I've worked for Madam Alicia for over thirty-five years." The elderly man stopped in front of a pair of French doors. "I've the option to retire this summer. Who knows?" He winked at me. "I may stay on a bit longer."

"That's nice." I wasn't sure why he winked.

He opened the doors, and we followed him inside. The room smelled of *Shalimar* perfume. A mauve velveteen settee sofa faced a coffee table and an ivory and rose brick fireplace. Crystal-cut framed photographs of families with babies and well-groomed dogs lined its mantle. The frames were bookended by goblets of camellias.

"Mr. Dobra, if you'd be kind enough to wait here in the parlor. I'll show Miss Valthea to Madam Szusanna."

Sorin put his arm around me. "I'd like to stay with Valthea."

"I understand sir, but Madam Szusanna was quite specific. Although she agreed to this spontaneous meeting, she insists on seeing Miss Valthea alone. I promise I'll escort her back to you as soon as they finish."

"Thank you, Mr. Emil, but Mrs. Stanasila needs to understand that—"

"It's all right, Sorin. I'll meet her on my own."

"But I thought you wanted—"

"I'm fine."

"Whatever you want, Val. I've my phone. Call me if you need me."

"Thanks. Maybe check on Cosmo in a few minutes."

"Yeah, don't worry. Focus on you and finding out what you need to know."

My champion always knew the right thing to say. I kissed him on the cheek and then turned to Mr. Emil. "I'm ready."

The gentleman guided me past a formal living room. I tried not to walk fast and run him over.

"This way, Miss Ell—I mean, Miss Valthea. Old age." He chuckled. "It muddles your memory."

"It happens at every age. I mix up people's names all the time." The blue rings encircling Mr. Emil's brown eyes reminded me of Aunt Sylvie's.

We veered left. "I'm taking you to Madam Alicia's library. Unfortunately, Madam Szusanna thinks it's her den." He stopped at the last door. "Here we are. Miss Valthea, it's nice to finally see you again. Welcome home."

"Uh, thanks, but I think you're confusing me with someone else. Not that I wouldn't want to live here."

He opened the door.

The sunny room displayed furniture cushioned in striped pink, white, and spring-green chintz fabric. Matching curtains edged the windows. Hardbound books and white Persian cat figurines lined a wall of bookcases. Pink and green paisley-print satin pillows made sitting on the room's chairs look impossible or at least a slippery affair.

Szusanna Stanasila sat behind a long, dark wood desk. "Stop acting timid. Come inside."

Caution isn't timidity. It's smart. I entered the room with my senses alert as a lynx in unfamiliar territory.

The desk she sat at lay void of paper, pens, or a laptop. It held only four items: a crystal-cut bowl of languid peonies, a bubblegum-pink ceramic dish of Jordan almonds, a tall mint-colored candle, and an out-of-place, nicotine-stained bronze ashtray.

"Have a seat," Szusanna said, lighting a cigarette.

I stepped up to the loveseat and chairs, ten-feet from the desk. "No thank you, Mrs. Stanasila. I'll stand."

Szusanna's pinched brow, beady eyes, and algae-green wrap dress contrasted the cheery décor of Madam Alicia's library. Crocodiles don't belong in European Tea Rooms. The reptilian woman's face makeup nearly cracked as she took a drag from her cigarette. She exhaled a stream of smoke. An insight into her past appeared. ...

Szusanna is eighteen. She sat in the passenger seat of a luxury sedan.

"There he is, Dad," Szusanna said to the driver, a man the size of a football linebacker. She pointed to a young man walking on a sidewalk in downtown Bucharest. He carried himself with swagger. "That's him, the future father of your illegitimate grandchild." The young man paused at a street corner, waiting to cross. His profile was distinct and familiar. It was a young Cosmo.

My mind sped backward, in rapid review, to the day I met Cosmo Dobra. Dizzied, I gripped the back of the loveseat nearest me.

"Valthea, why are you here? I didn't think I'd see you until your birthday in June."

"My birthday? I don't under—never mind. I'm here to find out who you are, and why you came to my auntie's funeral."

"Apparently the old woman took a multitude of secrets to her grave. Aunt Sylvie always did try to do the right thing."

"What secrets? And why do *you* call her Aunt Sylvie? And how do you know Cosmo?"

"*Cosmo?*" The lady crocodile sneered. "I haven't heard that name in ages."

"You just saw him at the funeral. He drove me here today."

She tapped her ashes into the ashtray, propped her elbow on the desk, and glared at me.

"Sylvanna Adamescu, or as you know her, by her stage name, *Sylvanna Sarosi,* was my aunt. And *you* ... " She looked me up and down, as if disgusted. "You were a lucky baby. My father had taken you to an orphanage. Of course, first he changed your name from Adamescu to Luca. Even so, Aunt Sylvie found you. But she was too late to save—"

"Wait— I'm confused." My nails pierced the chintz loveseat. "Are you my—"

"Your ancestry, birth mother, and future inheritance were to be kept from you until your eighteenth birthday, this June." Szusanna waved her cigarette as she spoke. "But don't get excited, Valthea. You're not getting one *bani* of that money. Why should you?" She snubbed out her cigarette. "You're not a *real* Adamescu. And believe me, before my mother dies, I'll make sure she changes the parameters of her will. I don't care if she does feel guilty over my sister's death or responsible for not stopping my father from giving my sisters' mistakes away. I'll not be deprived of what should be mine because of her emotions. I'll contest you inheriting anything from this family. You deserve nothing."

"Shut up!" I charged her desk. "I don't care about all that. *Where's* my mom?"

Szusanna sat back in her chair. "My God, you're as naïve as she was."

I leaned forward, planting my hands wide on her desk. "I said, *where's* my mom?"

She pushed out of her chair and lurched over the desk, her snout practically touching my nose. "My stupid, weak sister was your mother. But she's dead now." She straightened. "She died six months after you were born of a broken heart. Boo hoo."

"Dead?" My knees buckled, and I collapsed to the floor. "No ... it can't be. Not now ... " I wept into my hands. "I'm here for her."

"This drama is ridiculous. Your mother died years ago. You need to leave. My accountant will deal with you in June." She slithered past me to the door.

"Wait!" I pushed off the desk to stand. "You're my aunt. I want to know about my mother and my family."

Szusanna whipped around. "Don't you ever call me your aunt. My sister birthed you and then nursed you. That's all. It doesn't make you part of this family."

"*Da o face!* Yes, it does." I walked up to Szusanna, tears blurring my vision. "Aunt Sylvie was my great aunt by blood. Your sister was my mother. That makes me part of this family, and I'll be treated as such."

"Not if I've anything to do with it." She turned to leave.

I grabbed her arm. "Tell me my mother's name?"

Szusanna pulled her arm from my grip, grinning, enjoying my desperation. "We called her *Ellie*." She smoothed down her sleeve. "But her real name was Gisella."

I couldn't breathe. Cosmo's story! *Not a name, but a song—Gisella*. I ran past Szusanna, out of the room, and down the hall to the parlor where Sorin waited. I swung open the doors. "Sorin, my father is—"

"We know." Sorin and Cosmo stood in front of the fireplace. Sorin held up an empty picture frame in one hand, and a worn photo of a young woman and a baby in the other. "We just figured it out."

Cosmo ran up to me and engulfed me in hug. "My baby! My baby girl!"

I cried in his arms.

"I'm sorry, my precious," he cried. "I didn't know. I knew I recognized this house, but had no idea that Gisella's family still—I never even knew she was pregnant, or that you were my—" Cosmo took the photograph from Sorin's hand and gave it to me. "When Sorin saw this picture, he came out to the car and brought me in." Cosmo whispered. "Gisella never told me."

"I know. It's okay." I hugged my father, and then stepped back to study the photograph. It showed Gisella as a teenager holding a baby. Gisella looked exactly as I'd seen her in my readings of Szusanna.

"Read the back, Val."

I flipped it over. It read:

> Cosmo, here's one more photo of me with our daughter in hope that you'll respond to my reaching out. Valthea's nearly six months old. She needs to meet her father, and I need to be with my true love. My heart is breaking. Why do you not respond? Why do you stay away? Please, come see us. Your Gisella.

Tears streamed down my face.

Sorin gently took the photo from my hand, lay it down with the frame, then held my hand. "We're family, Valthea, and I'm in love with you."

"*Da!*" Cosmo took my other hand. "And what a family we have!"

"*Yes*." I beamed. "It's the greatest." The child within me loved holding my father's hand. The woman I'd become loved holding the hand of my champion.

"*Suntem o familie!*" Cosmo raised our arms with his overhead. "Family is forever, whatever kind it is."

"Tea, anyone?" Mr. Emil entered the room carrying a silver tray with teapot and cups.

We lowered our arms.

Sorin and I caught each other's eye and smiled at Mr. Emil's timing.

"Mr. Emil, your graciousness is unparalleled," Cosmo said with a slight head bow. "Thank you. We'd love to stay and celebrate, even with tea, but we don't want to impose."

"Nonsense." Mr. Emil walked around the sofa, set the tray on the table, and then stood poised. "Like you said, family is forever." He faced me. "And Miss Valthea, like I said before ... *welcome home.*"

The Daughters, Book Two

THOMASINA: I STIR PEOPLE

In the middle of Valthea and Sorin's wedding ceremony, they are cursed by Valthea's aunt Szusanna. Despite this, the young lovebirds marry and go on to enjoy their guests, his Gypsy family, her circus family and her newly discovered aristocratic family. Afterward, Valthea, Sorin, and her natural father, Cosmo Dobra, leave their homeland of Romania and move to Sarasota, Florida. Valthea performs as an aerialist for *Cirque du Palm* and Cosmo teaches at it's a circus school, while Sorin interns at a local hospital.

Life gets even better when a young woman shows up at their home claiming to be Valthea's relative. Thomasina Stratham's the same age as Valthea, and the two become fast friends until Thomasina stirs up trouble for, and between, Valthea, Sorin, and Cosmo. Valthea tries to solve matters peacefully until Thomasina's antics threaten her career, her marriage, and her family. Valthea must find a way to protect everything she's worked for. She hopes her gift of sight, and the information she finds in her deceased mother's diaries, provide the answer.

Acknowledgements

Dolly Jacobs-Reis and **Pedro Reis**, founders of *The Circus Arts Conservatory's Circus Sarasota,* inspired me with their intimate, one-ring circus and exceptional, international cast. Dolly Jacobs–Reis's beauty, grace, and charitable character, greatly influenced my protagonist.

Kathy Needham, founder and owner of *Palaestra Gymnastics Academy*, provided enthusiasm and relentless encouragement for *Valthea – I Read People* from the moment I shared the story with her, while sunning one summer at Ogunquit Beach, Maine. From that point forward, she remained a creative confidante. Although Kathy and I live 1,359 miles away from each other, she nudged and advised me by phone, as we read chapters aloud for nine months straight. Her combined knowledge of gymnasts and her compassionate wisdom assisted in growing Valthea's story. Kathy's fierceness provided the fire and coaching I needed to complete my mission of bringing Valthea's story to the world.

Sue Adams Mallick, my mother, and **Carl J. Mallick**, my father, listened to and/or read chapters of my manuscript for years. (They even allowed me to read chapters aloud at the dinner table on Thanksgiving Day!) Thanks Mom for believing in a character who could triumph while doing the right thing. Thanks Dad for believing in the exploration and appreciation of music, food, and people from other countries and cultures. Huge thanks to my sharp and dynamic brothers, **Scott Mallick** and **Blake Mallick**, and my aunt, **Judy Adams** a former physical education teacher. Thank you **Grama Adams** for believing in my imagination and my random intuition. (I miss you!)

Luis Garcia Salobral shared numerous stories of his life in the circus since the day I met him via *Circus Sarasota* in 2009. Born into a circus family, the high-energy, fit man has acted as everything from circus performer to circus electrician. He's presently a tent master for *Circus Sarasota* and many other international shows. A true friend, Luis remained on call for my various questions and curiosities for nearly five years.

Kim Kelley Hackett read a zillion first chapters and query letters, remained calm when I telephoned panicking, and kept me on course. This fellow writer and critique group member never stopped believing in me or Valthea's story.

Anya Terekhova recounted delicious tales and details of her life and times as a professional ice skater in Russia and the U.S. I thank Anya, now a brilliant hair stylist with perfect posture, for tolerating my interviewing her as she painted my hair.

Wendy Dingwall stepped out of her normal bounds and embraced Valthea's story into her publishing castle, *Canterbury House Publishing*.

Tracy Arendt perfected not one but two gorgeous book covers!

Critique Group~ **Kaye Coppersmith**, taught as she lead a *Florida Writer's Association* critique group. Members: **Shelly Akron**, author, **Kim Kelley Hackett**, award-winning author, **Janet Ramsell Rockey**, author, **Laurie Solheim**, award winning writer, Bruce, **Karleen Tauszik**, author. **Eugene Orlando**, author and teacher, led another group with: **Rob Sanders**, author, and **Dan, Bob, Karen, Yemi, Joann**.

Dedicated Readers~ Read and shared notes and thoughts: **Vicki Cole, Daniel Kane, Anna O'Keefe, Angel Shutt, Eleanor Wallace**.

Friends, Co-workers, and Entertainers who shared personal stories and/or lent support~ **Dejana Alijevic, Irina Antipov, Stasia Antipov, Yulia Antipov, Cassie Bale, Olia Chaconas, Veturia Colquett, Valentina Curri, Clark Cutchin, Mirjana Cvijic, Megy Dobreva, Maria DOnofrio, Brittany Fischer, Dyanne Forde, Garrett Fuller, Carlton M. L. Jones, Paval Khabarov, Helen Lee, Andy Lyman, Melissa Pott, Margaret Bozena McQuade, Irfan Mark Radoncic, Slobodan Risivojevic, Freedom Eric Sandgren, Mohsen Sofastaii, Danuta Stykowski, Shannon Tierney, Tyler West, Jessica Wilder, Jeanette Williams, Michelle Brault of Circus Arts Conservatory.** "

ABOUT THE AUTHOR

C.K. MALLICK~ The initial spark of inspiration for *Valthea — I Read People* came from C.K.'s childhood, growing up near Venice, Florida, the former winter home for *Ringling Brothers and Barnum and Bailey Circus*, and of hearing stories of her intuitive great-grandmother. Thirty years later, the idea rekindled after watching a performance by *Circus Sarasota*. Seventeen years in the entertainment industry, including dancing for *Disney's Hollywood Studios* and teaching dance to children and teens, also provid-

Photo credit: Cliff Roles

ed resource. The author lives in Sarasota, Florida. She loves hearing *people's stories*, spending time in nature, and swimming in the Gulf of Mexico.

Short stories by the author:

Skate Walker, *Hooked on Hockey-Chicken Soup for the Soul*

Face Time, *Let's Talk* anthology collection,

Places Everyone! *The Florida Writer* magazine.

CPSIA information can be obtained
at www.ICGtesting.com
Printed in the USA
LVOW12s2129060416

482509LV00003B/168/P